THE VENOM STORM

Also By Brad Mathews

Thousand Branches Series
The Thousand Branches
The Venom Storm
The Satyr of Fulton Manor
Tomb of the Phoenix

Era Sinistra Trilogy
Era Sinistra
Era Sinistra-The Shadow
Era Sinistra-Skyglow

Decay
The Girl from South Track

Revelation Series
Revelation (Book 1)
Reflection (Book 2)
Reincarnation (Book 3)
Transcendence (Book 4)
Enchantment (Book 5)

THE VENOM STORM

A Thousand Branches Novel

BRAD MATHEWS

Unity Star Books

Copyright © 2017 by Brad Mathews

Published by Unity Star Books

All rights reserved.

No part of this book may be reproduced, stored in a data retrieval system or transmitted in any form or by any means without the prior written permission of the author, except by a reviewer who may quote brief passages in a review printed in a magazine, newspaper, journal, or blog.

All characters in this book are fictitious. Any resemblance to real persons, either living or dead, is coincidental.

All opinions quoted in this book belong to the characters speaking and do not reflect the views of the author.

ISBN: 978-1-962577-06-9 (Softcover)

ISBN: 978-1-962577-07-6 (Ebook)

Re-release Second Edition 2026

Virginia Glass

May 16, 2011

21:45

NEON SCUFFED AT A crystal sky where the last rays of sun stretched the clouds with orange. The glitter and sparkle crowded his vision and reflected off the table while splotches of color swam in the martini.

By Ben's estimate, Reno had few of these patio dining experiences and only those on the 'strip' seemed to be equipped with a full bar. He pretended to sip the drink, which he occasionally stirred with a spare toothpick fished from the dispenser. No entrée, just the drink, the way Ben liked it.

For now, his mission required observation only and the drink served to make him look like he fit in. Instead of focusing on the lurid glow of the lights, he shifted his focus far to the northern horizon beyond Virginia Street's excess. There, Washoe County stretched wide beyond Sun Valley and Pyramid Lake. The barren hills seemed to scrape across the sky. A lone bird gracefully swooped overhead and then disappeared into the shadow of the hills.

A pair of drunk pedestrians stumbled down the sidewalk. Their amusement only subtly faded when they noticed the lone drinker staring.

"Nevada," Ben mumbled.

The doors of a nearby casino spread a rectangle of white light onto the sidewalk when they opened. Cheers erupted from inside, only to die into misery moments later. A trio of strangers stepped into the night. A Reno patrol car passed by and seemed to slow when the driver gazed at Ben. He couldn't allow a simple *copper* to bust his cover so easily.

His phone rang. Without hesitation he picked it up and spoke softly. "What's your twenty?"

"More like twenty-to-one, *cavrón*."

"Good odds," Ben said. "Gonna lay down a couple of dimes?"

The line crackled. A black Lincoln rolled by, followed by a parade of white limousines as if either the Pope or the President were in town for a visit. Reno was the last place either of them would visit, so Ben shrugged.

"Sí," Rico said.

"While you're at it," Ben said, still codifying his speech, "put down a couple on Black 43. Something's telling me we've got a ringer."

"A ringer? Damn."

"You're telling me. Looks about five-six with legs ten stories high. The entertainment."

Rico let silence resume before lowering his voice. "You rollin' big time tonight. Ask if she'll go out with me."

Ben hung up the phone and dropped it in his pocket. The leggy woman's heels clicked on the sidewalk as she casually approached without ditching the so-called sex appeal. This would be a good conversation.

"Who are you talking to, stud?"

Ben raised his eyebrow and leaned back, training his gaze on the fading sunlight. Red began to streak through the clouds, reminding him how Rose's hair used to burn silver. Another day, another time.

"You on the job?"

"You tell me," she said. "The name's Amber tonight."

"I'm sure it is."

"Are you feeling lucky?"

Ben sighed and let a smile curl his lip. "Now that you mention it, I think we're going to have some company. I saw your man busting some chops down the block this afternoon, said he'd be expecting delivery of the package in this neck of the woods tonight."

"That's good," she said.

"Now," Ben said, choosing his phrasing carefully. "How much do I owe you for tonight? Two thousand?"

"And change," she said, shrugging. "I think I can manage half."

She reached toward her purse, but Ben shook his head. "Not here. This guy sees you talking to me, he'll paint the sidewalk with your brain matter."

"You know him?" She asked, suddenly more aware of her surroundings. She glanced at the street to her right.

"Well enough to know you don't want trouble with him. You didn't tell me you were sleeping with him."

"Hey, business is business," she said.

Ben suddenly felt dirty. Her line of work remained perfectly legal in Nevada, but then again Ben had never claimed to be squeaky clean either. It was hazard of the job. The more people needed his services, the more they paid, which kept the coffers full, but if his clients weren't as sleazy as the people he investigated for them, Ben grew worried.

Instead of dwelling on it, his mind travelled to Rose's graceful locks. Years had all but bleached the red from her hair, leaving only ghostly strands of silver and white that somehow further perpetuated her grace. If he could make it home tonight, he'd be sure to let her know he liked it. Big 'if.'

"If I were a rich man," the woman sung quietly as a man in a gaudy business suit strolled by.

The reference made Ben cringe. He imagined her employing increasingly scandalous acts on him in some cheap motel room where the neon lights burrowed into the dark. The thought caused Ben to swirl the martini, eyeball it with curious alarm, and then drown whatever sorrows plagued him with it. That would be good enough for a night downtown.

Tanya Allison stood up from the table and did her best Amber impression. She straightened her tight dress and flung her hips before flipping her hair over her shoulder to pursue the 'Fiddler.'

When Ben's phone rang, he set the glass back on the table and tried to ignore the ringing. The longer it persisted, the more tempted he was to drown the phone in his drink.

"What's going on with you?" Ben asked the caller. "How is the weather?"

"What's the weather always like down here?" Jason said.

"I'm on assignment," Ben said. "I'll call you back in an hour and we can talk shop."

"What if it's important?"

Ben acted impatient, switching the phone to his other ear and frowning. "Well, do *you* have an escort who sleeps with her bookie, who consequently wants to whack her?"

"All the time," Jason joked.

Ben hung up the phone, leaned back to stretch his legs, and watched Virginia Street invert itself into some kind of illusory art that seemed altogether wholesome, if not enriching.

Alligator Dan strutted down the sidewalk with his entourage. Showtime.

The man's greasy hair caught the neon and somehow enhanced it, making him look like some sort of impressionistic circus clown bent on collecting dough from dozens of men. Ben had represented men like him more than once. This man crafted a sense of style that would make Ru Paul blush. Alligator Dan should have been in Florida fishing gators out of swimming pools. Instead, he made his bones fishing junkies and deadbeats from the local haunts and shaking every dime loose. Dan's last name, Copperstone, even seemed fraudulent.

You're one to talk, Benjamin Redd Carr. Perhaps it's time to reintroduce Private Trent Cobbs to the world. Oh, the stories you could tell.

Dan's alligator skin boots clunked on concrete as he stared into a casino long enough to catch a glimpse of the bar. It turned out that Dan didn't have to go into the bar after the chump who owed him probably enough to fund the government for about a year. The unlucky sob drifted out of the bar right into Dan's lap.

"Time to pay your bill," Dan said quietly.

The man's eyes darted back and forth. He stepped back and raised his palms. "Honest to God, I'll pay you tomorrow."

"Tomorrow's no good. Tomorrow the interest doubles. What's a hundred percent of twenty five percent, math whiz?"

Alligator Dan stepped away from the man who smelled of vodka and approached Ben.

Ben downed another sip of the martini and shook his head as if drunk.

"Hey you," Dan called. "You seen a good-for-nothing hoe chasing ass for cash?"

Ben rolled his eyes and sat upright but refrained from facing him. "I've been sitting here for a half hour, you'll have to be more specific."

"Five-six, blond wig, too much eye-makeup, legs long enough to kick a sailor's teeth in from here?"

He forced a chuckle. "Yeah. Got in the back of a limo headed up toward the university. I guess the slime preferred the low rent district."

"You're real funny, asshole," Dan said. "Don't you owe me money?"

"I'm here for the spectacle," Ben said. "Nightlife. They say Reno's famous for it. You could say watching makes me take a long, hard look at my life and wonder where I'm not going wrong enough. You ever feel like that?"

"No."

"Wallet's a little tight."

"Not as tight as my fist's gonna be around that broad's neck when I find her. She's on her last meow."

"Well, why don't you just trade services? A little slice of butt goes a long way, at least the way I've heard it."

Alligator Dan stomped toward him, grasped the edge of the table and flipped it. Shards of glass and liquid covered Ben's pants. His stubbly lip trembled beneath his scowl. The man was famous amongst bookies for his fuse. Ben chose to light it without understanding the possible outcomes. The consequence made him queasy. He was too old to get in a fistfight with this goon. After that there would be questions, his cover would be blown, and Tanya's corpse would be buried face down in the hills around Virginia City.

Dan swore and stormed away, back toward his entourage, which consisted of muscular men in tight tee-shirts hired specifically to get physical with people who owed Dan money.

Ben stood up and brushed off his pants while watching Dan stroll southward along the main boulevard. Alligator Dan. Accountant, Bookie, part-time blogger, drug dealer, and the list went on. The man showed impressive swagger, but his bank accounts, not so much. All Tanya wanted to know was where all of the money went. So far, Ben had tracked a number of illicit activities he couldn't report, because client safety was his first priority. For having such a clean history, Ben thought, Tanya chose to consort with some oddities. Sure, investigating her would have been easy and a breach of contract, but her past had its way of laying itself out right in front of him. Easy money was the worst kind.

He'd chosen this profession years ago, after the Montana debacle ruined him and extinguished his career a little too early. He ran his own practice now, which proved a good use of the skills he'd accumulated since Vietnam. Investigation lured him as a good gig. As a 'pseudo-lawyer' he practically ran his own investigations all the time. As his boss at the time had promised, Montana would be easy money. Easy money always accompanied an array of pitfalls and traps, which caused him to devise a strategy to deal with and eliminate such side-effects.

Mario Rico rolled the SUV to a stop next to the shattered glass table. Ben waved at him, stepped inside to tip the waiter, and then got in the vehicle.

"Rough town," Rico said.

Ben didn't speak to him for several minutes, electing to think about the nuance of his last phone call instead. He looked sideways at the interstate traffic while Rico merged onto the freeway toward the company headquarters in Carson City.

"You going to bust that creep?"

"No," Ben said. "I'm going to clean out his bank account. And feed his boots to a shark."

Rico laughed. "Long as I get a cut of the dinero."

Ben frowned while watching the city lights fade away into the countryside. The horizon had gone dark, revealing murky shadows that rose up the crests of the Sierra Nevada Mountains. This case tugged at his suspicion like hissing in a bush. He considered calling Rose and telling her he'd be home soon but decided to call Jason back instead.

The ride to Carson took a good half-hour. Ben said goodnight to Rico and sat alone in his office, admiring the golden ring that stood in the yellow cone of light beneath his desk lamp. He shrugged, picked up the phone, and dialed Jason's number.

"Ready to talk shop?" Jason asked.

"I got a good one," Ben said.

"Sure sounds like it. I got a good one, too, I could use your help on."

"What's the catch?"

"Catch?" Jason Cruz spoke slowly, drawing his words out with deliberation as if he were trying to hide something. "Why's there always have to be a catch with you? Don't you believe in clean business anymore?"

"Not really," Ben said. "You?"

"Hey, I get paid to state the facts, and if the facts are bad enough maybe I make a little bit more money to spend on the wife and kids."

"Except you have neither," Ben said.

"Sure. Hit below the belt. I guess you could say I don't want this getting into the media or law enforcement."

"I thought you were above that nonsense."

"My client is missing. We know this because she's pretty rich, does business multiple times every day for years. Her accounts have shown no activity for six months and as it happens, she's an influential player in the financial market down here. Real estate mogul, really talented."

"And you want me to find her."

"You're the best."

"And the San Diego PD, they've got nothing on her?"

"Hope not."

"Why?"

"If I tell you this, I need to record you vowing complete silence." Jason paused to push a button and waited for Ben to comment.

"Son of a bitch." Ben rolled his eyes and clenched his fist long enough to make his knuckles to ache. "You're in deep shit,"

"No, my client is. I was running some banking records—flow of cash, paperwork, all that kind of jazz—hoping she'd pop up somewhere. She didn't but her shadow did. In Mexico. It seems like a few of her dollars somehow made their way into the hands of a drug cartel."

"Why do you want to protect her?"

"Who said anything about protection?" Jason asked, a little too quickly.

Ben shook his head as if Jason could see it.

"You implied it."

"She does good business. I'm not trying to protect her from the law, I'm trying to find out whether she's safe while taking a few percent off the top."

"Jesus Christ," Ben said. "Skimming now? You're really in over your head. So you're trying to cover your own ass. And here I thought I knew you better than that."

"Well, times change, my friend."

"I can't take it," Ben said.

"It's worth a penny or two. Fly you and Rose off to Europe or something, and maybe flush you into early retirement."

"It doesn't sound like my kind of case." As a matter of fact, most of it sounded illegal. Jason Cruz? Really? Ben didn't need to make his money on shady business deals. In this day and age, easy money seemed dirtier than laundered money, and it sounded as though Jason had enough to open his own dry cleaner.

"Help a friend out. I've made it out to look legit, to the right eyes at least. And no one's going to track it to you, I can promise you that."

"Money changes hands," Ben said. "It always leaves a trail. You know that better than anyone."

"Then don't think of it as a business deal. Think of it as helping out a friend. You can do that. You're a good guy and this is all going to blow over when we find my client. I'll thank you handsomely when it's over."

"Is this a secure phone call?"

"You bet it is," Jason said. "I know how to cover my tracks, like I said. You don't worry about me. You just worry about my client. You can bring Old Rico down with you to enjoy the sun, maybe chase some tail on the beach."

"I've had a strange day," Ben said. "I'll have to think about this a little bit more."

"If you check your drop box, you'll see that all your thinking is already done. What are friends for, anyway?"

Ben hung up the phone with Jason a little prematurely and pondered on the case. How could he let Jason down? He owed him, after all. Earlier in the week the news was mixed, and then good. And now Jason could be involved with drug money. He hated sleazy money almost as much as he hated easy money.

Wedging the key into the drop box next to the door, a strange feeling swept over him. The dark of the office seemed to deepen, almost as if the horrors of Montana were swirling once again. He opened the box and withdrew a package. After checking to see that the box was once again securely locked, he carried the package to his desk and angled the lamp so it illuminated more of the desk.

The box-cutter in his desk drawer proved a useful tool. He unsheathed it and sliced the box open to reveal bubble wrap and packing foam. He dug through the foam and withdrew a bottle of wine. He stared at the bottle for more than ten minutes, mentally attempting to catalogue the value of the drink. This bottle had been produced in a limited production run more than seventy years ago. Gilded writing on the label indicated refined taste and promised romance.

He shrugged, set the bottle aside, ensuring that the cork stayed moist, and then reached into the box to remove a large envelope at the bottom. He sliced open the envelope and pulled out a large photo of a middle-aged male with long, wavy hair. He stared at the face he'd never seen before, the face that now meant so much to him that he could hardly bear to look at it anymore. Jason had promised it would be worth his while. A pang of regret plunged into Ben's stomach like a knife. That face would burn itself into his memory with striking permanence because it belonged to his son.

A smaller envelope inside the big one contained reservations and plane tickets for an expensive Italian resort. Ben gulped when he tried to calculate the cost.

A small, hand-written note was affixed to the plane tickets. He uncoiled it and read it aloud. "Consider this your retainer fee."

Rose for Rose

May 17, 2011

10:08

COLD, UNTRUSTING STEEL BIT into his wrists as Allen Kierstien leaned forward on the stool. White lights overhead flickered, causing reflections to dance off the double pane of glass before his face. He sneered, straightened his back, and faced his visitor.

The chains of bondage succeeded in reducing Allen to something resembling a man. Simple idea, simple uniform, simple stare, all of it reflective of the quintessential image of a hardened felon. He willed himself to shove the ferocity of his attitude on his unsuspecting visitor, but the visitor had a different agenda. He wore a sleek business suit with matching slacks and a too-expensive tie. Allen frowned and sized him up.

He allowed his frown to deepen as he pressed the phone against his ear and twirled the cord on his index finger. Patience or none, he could play the game like a professional.

"You look terrible," the visitor said. "I wouldn't have thought this place could get to a guy like you so quickly. And so fully."

"It hasn't," Allen said, still frowning. "Around here, you don't fit in, you get the child molester treatment. Easy prey. You should have seen what they did to my cellmate last week."

"And I'm supposed to believe you didn't have a hand in that? Word has it you're well known as the guy who pulls strings." The visitor shrugged as if his words had bounced right off Allen and reached toward his briefcase.

Allen didn't wait. "Now that you mention it, you don't look so great yourself. Polished attire, fake expression, perfect hair. You look like a lawyer or something."

The visitor fumbled with a file, which he pulled from the briefcase and thumbed through quickly enough to make Allen believe it was simply an act designed to impress others. "Clever. You want to go over these matters or not?"

Leaning back somewhat and crossing his arms, Allen grunted. "Your good news and bad news. Typical lawyer talk."

In order for good news to be shared, Allen thought, it must be accompanied by bad news. It was sad the way life always turned out, or at least mildly ironic.

Len Carter hesitated and stroked his chin as if trying to construct a trite response. "Mr. Kierstien, they are going to try to get you on the stand to talk about your estranged wife. We need to develop a strategy to deal with that problem, and quickly."

Allen tilted his head and lowered his eyebrows before uttering a subtle *'humph.'* "The real reason I'm in this hole. She pulled a real good one this time, even you gotta give her that."

Carter shot back, "The point is, they already know everything that happened in Montana where she found your men, and they'll push hard to use that against you."

He leaned his head back and laughed without injecting color or humor. It was as if the precursor to this moronic conversation was simply a motion by a lawyer. "You put it so succinctly. *They* found *her*."

"We can't say that in front of the jury."

"It will give them something to laugh at, or at least distract them from the fact that they're all just pawns. Collateral."

A quick frown wiped away the confident look on Carter's face. "They could go to Montana and subpoena her. She tells the truth and you're looking at a prolonged sentence."

"She's not in Montana, I can tell you that." Allen bit his lip. "She ran. To where is anyone's guess right now. But I know her. If anyone I know had her investigative skills, finding her would prove remarkably easy."

"That isn't important. We're here to discuss—"

"Of course it is. You know all about Seventeen Treasures and how she was the first one onto it. It's in your file. She didn't even have to hire a PI, because for all intents and purposes, she *was* a PI."

He paused to think about the bad old days. Seventeen Treasures marketed itself as a fine establishment specializing in intimate apparel and 'unique gifts.' Rose had discovered his shopping experience and used it to track him to the hotel where he tested his gift. Damn it, she was good and it made him feel dirty, which he wasn't used to.

Chaos wasn't his fuel. Instead, money was his game. Sure, the business he'd operated over the years was as legitimate as any. He had to entertain a lot of side projects and unusual beneficiaries, but as they said, business is business.

Carter cleared his throat and leaned closer to the glass. "Now that you understand how serious our situation is, I should apprise you of the good news. Inside sources tell me they're going to grant your appeal hearing this time. If we play our cards right, Montana might not turn out to be your undoing after all."

"If you only knew." Allen pounded his fist on the table, stood up, and shoved the stool under the ledge with enough force to knock it sideways. He left the phone off the hook and stomped out of the room, leaving Carter in shock.

Montana was like a bad dream. This little punk had no right to serve it all up on a silver platter, even if what happened in Montana was the impetus behind his incarceration. Lawyer or none, Allen Kierstien had a lot of work to do.

11:15

THE FRONT PAGE OF the *Washington Post* lay unfolded atop the polished wood desk. Next to it, a cup of coffee emitted steam, filling the room with a fresh aroma conducive to creativity. Rose narrowed her eyes and glanced at the paper before rolling the chair away from the desk. Her eyelids drooped. Another day at the office had come and gone, and hopefully with its passage some extra money would flow.

The office often seemed the coziest room in the loft condo. The large window on the east side of the room allowed pleasant sunlight to fill the room. The floor was constructed with the type of wood that somehow seemed to encourage warmth. The north side window, at which she'd pointed the desk, provided a spectacular view of the lake. Rose could sit in this room for hours. She'd decorated it well and enhanced the feel with a cloth chair on which she could sit with her feet curled beneath her and think.

Tahoe glowed with charm. The crystal sky sparkled on tranquil waters still deemed too cold for recreation. The nearby pines swayed with a subtle breeze. Washington seemed like another world, but all too familiar. This was home.

Something about her main character perplexed her. Some hidden quality not previously explored left curiosity, which if left unchecked could consume her entire day. Rose always let the characters introduce themselves. Contrary to belief, she never constructed them from the ground up.

She leaned back in her writing chair and thought about heading downstairs for some lunch. Maybe she'd even put on socks just to make it seem as though she planned on experiencing life.

Ben had not come home last night and had not called to explain. A guilty feeling of frustration washed over her. She shifted her feet and combed her fingers through her silver hair. That would teach him, even if he couldn't see it.

Her heart skipped when she skimmed the top headline on the *Post* from afar. Synapses whispered in her ear and thought rampaged through her mind. One rule of journalism was that to be effective, headlines had to be short, punchy, and provide a spark that carried readers into the story. This headline had her reading the first few lines before she even realized it. Her heart raced.

Allen Kierstien, convicted of conspiracy and fraud, remained locked up on a strenuous sentence. Lawyers were good at digging up new evidence that hadn't presented itself during the original trial, so this case made the news periodically.

This morning, a federal judge had allowed a new trial. Allen had enough cash stowed away to hire some of the best representation on the East Coast. If a new trial had been awarded, they would twist the jury a million different ways to break them, thereby setting Allen free to finish the job he had failed to do in Montana.

Did he know she lived in California? If he didn't, he could find out. Though she went to great lengths to keep the city and state of her residence a secret, Allen could find her. He had henchmen everywhere. This time, he would kill her.

Or at least, he'd try. Lover or not, Ben had proven useful in a confrontation. He excelled at avoiding contact, but could hold his own if it came to blows.

Ben was just a phone call away. She could call him, tell him about the newspaper article, worry in his ear, and then maybe everything would be all right, at least temporarily. Still, peace in the relationship evaded her of late. Was it all a lie? And if it was, how would she know?

Behind everything Ben did, every action and every inaction, lay heart and desire. Time had fanned the flames of passion, or at least that was the way Ben played it. But she knew him well enough to understand that traces of Private Trent Cobbs still brushed at the corners of his personality. Therein lay the conundrum.

Rose often dismissed these moments as nodes of nature that rarely threatened. The discomfort was another matter.

The thought of Allen caused the corners of her mouth to sag. She yawned as if sleep could save the day if her body were willing.

What was Ben hiding? The last few days, his soul seemed painted with a blemish of darkness that faded the man she knew. Pain and change had marked his journey through life, and at times marred it beyond recognition. Still, Ben usually showed honesty about his past. Not by choice, at any rate, but when circumstances demanded, he broke down and leveled with her. Suddenly, the understanding had gone missing.

It could have been a client, though Ben usually kept those matters well separated from his home life. He didn't have the fortitude to defend real criminals, by his own admission. The last week had provided some perspective. At times, the victims—or at least the people he chose to investigate for—seemed as dirty as the perpetrators. That sort of conflict had its way of eroding his confidence.

She shook her head and leaned back in the chair. She glanced at the newspaper again and then to her bookshelf. Copies of each of her novels stood in chronological order as a testament to her nature. Her personality came with its pitfalls, a tragedy she'd become fond of. Life was never as good as she thought, but nor was it as bad.

Rose caught her gaze falling upon the photo of Allen's face, stained murky with pressures of prison. His stockpile of funds, which had proven far more substantial than Rose had first thought, could get him anywhere. He always had reserved a surprise or two for special occasions. He wielded such an unrelenting power that it made Rose's heart tremble.

As if the lessons from Washington were not enough, the experience gained from the Montana incident wrought life-altering circumstance in every shape and color. She might have been in it for what she perceived as a game at first. Chasing the story was more engaging than chasing a man, but life generated events for the greater good of mankind, and womankind as well. These events channeled much of the turmoil within the pages of *The Thousand Branches,* disguised as the terrors of an investigator named Carrie.

Violence and divorce had chased her from Washington. Montana had felt like home until the violence caught up with her again. At least Allen's famed Michigan Men were behind bars, or Rose would never feel at peace.

Tucked neatly beside her display of novels, the rose delivered to her this morning unfurled toward the sun. Rose stared at it longingly.

Ben never had it in him. The act of giving this sort of beauty seemed oddly gentle. From Ben? True enough, different virtues and talents constructed his personality. His history, however, could never foretell a change in philosophy, much less a change of heart. Just as Rose had learned painful lessons from DC and Montana, Ben had learned from the horrors of Vietnam. He and Rose seemed to be from opposite ends of the earth, but they were perfect for each other.

How had it happened? What change lurked within the darkness that Ben now displayed? She stared at the rose until her mind shifted to something else.

The divorce and Allen's attempts to bring her down with him should have been cause to forsake men entirely, yet love found its way to her heart. She loved Ben. Someday, perhaps, they could exchange it for an eternity. Four-letter word or not, love came in the form of a new journey that promised invigorating turns.

She shifted her shoulders and glided her bare feet across the smooth wood floor. A sigh formed in her lungs, but she didn't let it escape. Instead, she stared at the rose and considered a future without Ben. Was it over?

The lake shimmered in majesty. If ever there was a good day for a walk on the beach, this would be it. She stretched her arms, stood, and tiptoed toward the door, as if to leave her troubles behind.

Flight 5301

May 18, 2011

06:25

HAVING UNCOVERED THE MOST devastating information in years, Ben had become weary and allowed nightmares to pierce an interrupted sleep. He pried his eyes open after one particular nightmare. Pushing aside the bad dreams took longer when the visions were complex and dire. Sometimes a drink would help, but sometimes it would lead to even more lurid thoughts. Instead of trying to push this one aside, Ben took comfort in studying it.

What did it really mean? What was his son's name again? Jason hadn't mentioned it. Or perhaps the revelation had been so sudden and jarring that mere names became meaningless. Then again, it didn't really matter. Ben considered it his duty to track the man down and introduce himself over ice cream or coffee.

The nightmares caused pain to bristle Ben's temple. He placed his palm on his forehead and closed his eyes for what felt like an eternity. Sorrow crept through his muscles. Jason's involvement in whatever scheme was going down presented a firestorm of questions. What did he know, who was he after, who was after him, how deep was he in it, and were the police onto him?

The face of his son reappeared multiple times, growing darker and more harrowing by the instant. Before he knew it, he'd allowed the smile in the photograph to evolve into a stark emptiness and then a fervent terror marked by sweat and scars. He knew nothing about the boy other than his face. What had his childhood been like? Did he still live with his mother? Who was his mother? Ben didn't even know that. He assumed the surname of Cobbs, but then again Ben had already been shipped off to Vietnam before the boy was born. He would likely have taken his mother's last name in that case.

Perhaps aspirin would clear away the headache, and the physical act of moving through the office would sacrifice the nightmares to the churn of history. He tiptoed into the back room where he kept a small kitchen with a microwave, a coffeemaker, a refrigerator, and boxed foods to be eaten off plastic plates with plastic flatware. He flung open the refrigerator door and found a bottle of water, grabbed an aspirin, took it, and then shook his head.

A rustling sound echoed during his last gulp. Ben spun the cap back onto the water and peered into the darkness. His muscles froze and his heart leapt when he saw the figure of a stout man relaxed in shadow.

The cherry smell of cigar smoke wafted into his nostrils. Ben heard a chuckle as he slammed the refrigerator door.

"Not funny," Ben shot.

"Mucho siesta, no?"

Rico had developed a habit of sneaking up on Ben just to humiliate him over his age. This wasn't Vietnam and Ben's reflexes and awareness had gone downhill over the last two decades. A little harmless ribbing never hurt anyone, but Rico had a sickness no one could extinguish.

"Yeah, I couldn't drive back up to Tahoe that tired. What did you do?"

"A señorita," Rico said, smiling.

He was lying, but Ben let it pass. He snarled something under his breath and darted back into his office. Rico followed and took a metal seat next to the wall. He leaned his head back and puffed a heavy ribbon of smoke into the dingy morning light.

He imagined that hearing Rose's voice would fill a void, or at least smooth its rim. Explaining it all to her without divulging important details that could land them both in hot water would take skill.

Rico watched while pretending to pay more attention to his cigar.

The first phone call lasted about ten minutes. The sun was beginning to tinge the eastern horizon over the silhouettes of the mountains to a cool blue. He hung up the phone and immediately dialed Rose's number.

She sounded groggy, but Ben didn't apologize for waking her. "I'm okay, stayed late here in Carson on a case."

"You'll be home today?"

He gulped. "Uh, slight change of plans. I got a different angle to cover on a newer case, and an urgent matter has come up."

"Later tonight, then?"

"Not really," Ben said. "The angle is in San Diego."

"San Diego?" Rose and Rico said in unison. Rico had lowered the cigar and leaned forward while Rose had fallen silent.

"I knew you'd be mad."

"I'm not mad," she said defiantly. "I expect interruptions. I expect you to run off to save somebody's world, just never mine. Because you're good at what you do."

He breathed heavily and rubbed his eyes with his free hand. "Look, it's just a couple of days down there. And then I'll take a few days off and we can go out on the lake, just you and me."

"You know, you used to be a smooth talker," she said.

Rico grinned, signaling that he could hear every word she said.

"I know. Then I met you."

"Ay, ay, ay," Rico muttered, shaking his head.

A sigh from her end pushed static through the line. "Then what's the business in San Diego?"

He thought of telling her but changed his mind. Leaning back in the chair, he chose to relax and let his mouth get him into even more trouble. "You don't want to know."

"Do I ever?"

"Hell, I don't even know. Let's just say I owe Jason Cruz a favor."

"Who is Jason Cruz? Client?"

"Friend."

"I see," she crackled. He could hear the ire forming in her voice. A tremble at the end of a sentence always signaled a train wreck that could not be avoided, no matter what he said to smooth it over. With her, that one little ripple always led to a riptide of agony. She normally excelled at hiding her feelings, but her veneer had cracked, which allowed tiny leaks to turn into major ruptures.

"Well. Jason is... how do I say it? He's got some problems. After this, we can take a trip to Venice and drink seventy-year-old white wine."

It didn't work. Her breathing intensified. "Can't wait."

"Right," Ben said, allowing a defensive stance to creep into his voice.

"Good," Rose said, her voice evening out. "When do you leave? I know you've already bought plane tickets."

Ben placed his hands over the receiver and swore under his breath, which caused Rico to erupt into a muted chuckle.

"Ten," he said.

"Is Rico going with you?"

"Hola, Rose!" He was too cheerful for the situation, and it made Ben want to retch. Instead, he clenched his fist and rose to his feet.

"Sí," Ben answered.

"Keep him out of trouble, Rico," she said. "Make sure he gets back here in one piece so I can take him apart by myself."

"Yeah," Rico said with a grin. "He'll be intact. Can't wait to see his ruins at—"

Ben hung up the phone, dropped it onto the desk, and glared at Rico. He couldn't let a bad day get worse, could he? The good-for-nothing lunatic.

Rico backed off and started puffing on the cigar again while Ben stomped around the office gathering supplies to stuff into his briefcase haphazardly. He'd take notes on the plane if he had the time and Rico allowed him space to work his mind into it. Then again, Rico was always good for a distraction, if not a total sidetrack. Rico sometimes got him lost while finding the way to the destination.

"She's pissed," Rico said, as if hoping to revive the conversation.

"You know her."

"You really going to Venice?"

Ben didn't answer. Visions of his son pocked his mind with dark craters that could swallow his entire personality if he let them. Did his son have something to do with Jason's problem? Though Ben didn't know his son, if Jason had gotten his son involved, Ben would kill him.

Rico stood up and exited the room without saying anything. He paused long enough to peer at the plane tickets and the bottle of wine.

"What about Alligator Dan?" Rico called from the other room. "Did he find his lady?"

"Guy's a slimeball," Ben said. "But I think she's safe for now. We'll get the cops to surveil her just in case. When we get back, we can mop up."

"Then you fly off to Europe."

"Maybe."

Rico returned carrying a duffel bag stuffed with some clothes he kept in his locker just in case. Ben kept a dresser full of clothes for overnight occasions. Lately, he'd been using them more and more.

Ben and Rico dressed in different rooms. Ben pulled out a jacket and a pressed shirt from the closet and flung a tie around his neck while packing a shaving kit and a toothbrush into his bag. This was an impromptu trip, but Ben enjoyed these excursions. They were an excuse to get away from the office for a while. Even though more daunting work awaited at the destination, the trip was always worth it.

Rico didn't know his way around San Diego, and neither did Ben. The GPS system had its flaws, but it minimized Rico's navigational deficiencies.

The drive to Reno-Tahoe airport lasted about forty minutes, but traffic was light. Rico blew through a red light after getting off the freeway and swore in Spanish. Their conversation had been as light as the traffic. Rico offered one-liners at Alligator Dan's expense and then joked about 'female entertainers' collecting fees. Ben didn't find any of it funny. Instead, he allowed Jason's case to fill his mind with shattered thoughts and to mix them until they turned crimson.

"Well, I say Alligator probably just got finished wrestling one. Maybe he even paid her what she's worth by now. Two, three bucks? *Mucho dinero.*"

Ben scoffed.

"Then he puts on his boots and his ugly jacket, lights a cigarette, and pretends she doesn't exist. Then tells her he'll give her a call. Next time he needs an escort. Bet he ends up with an even cheaper one next time, you know?"

"I'm sure."

"And he'll be drunk by two. Prowling outside casinos looking for people to jump. Dude's always around causing shit. And the cops never do anything about him because he's like some dirty informant. He's got the dirt on everyone. They need a tip about a hairdresser skimming, they call Dan. The guy mowing the mayor's lawn leaves a blade uncut, Dan's the man. What do you think they pay him?"

"You're sick," Ben said.

"You know what they say about idle hands."

Ben laughed as Rico found a parking spot in a long-term lot. They'd catch a shuttle to the terminal from there.

Rico's preoccupation with Alligator Dan was predictable. The guy lapped up scandal like the tabloids. He wasn't concerned with the gossip, but it all made for some hilarious jokes. Ben didn't laugh at all of them, but Rico had always loved telling jokes and funny stories. Instead of worrying about the travails of life, Rico chose to laugh it off and to live in the moment. It was an interesting way of living, but something Ben could never pull off. There was always that next thing in the future, that nagging thought eating away at the inside of his mind like a ravenous cancer. The perpetual torture gave way to bliss on some days, but other days made him wish he were alone on an isolated island with nothing to dread. Or maybe taking a gondola in Venice.

This matter had been important enough for Jason to drop significant cash for Ben's retainer fee. And it had to be indirect in the form of valuable gifts for only one reason. Someone had to be snooping into Jason's finances. Police? Nothing about this case sat right with him. The thoughts scattered until they were empty drones placed inside his skull for later consumption.

The wait inside the terminal led to a slew of new jokes and stories about various travelers. Rico was nothing if not keenly observant. Even when he wasn't paying attention, he soaked up information on his surroundings and took in masterful detail. Ben thought Rico could dictate a painting to an artist while he played a game on his phone.

"Brawny guy. In town for the fight," Rico said, eyeing a tall guy with a flat top haircut. "Bookie at home gave him three-to-one odds. I'd say ten-to-one, but who am I?"

"Do you ever stop?"

Rico laughed. "You know me better than that, amigo. Why don't you enjoy yourself a little? You got your head wrapped so tight around this thing a boa constrictor would be jealous."

Rico knew nothing. In order for this to work, he had to keep Rico informed. Rico was no longer just the driver. He was a friend and fit in well with various situations. Ben leaned on him for undercover work often enough, and Rico excelled.

Ben sighed and decided to brief him on the details. When he finished, he placed his face in his hands and rubbed his eyes.

It always took too long to go through security, Ben thought. While appropriate, the measures seemed invasive. The government knew best how to use taxpayer dollars to screw the people. With that nightmare over, the wait only lasted ten minutes. Ben and Rico boarded flight 5301 with their carry-ons. Destination: San Diego.

Ben had one call to make from the plane, after they got settled and ordered drinks. Catching up with Jason for the kick-off meeting would be vital. If he was up to something illegal, the meeting wouldn't take place at his office, and probably not in a public place, either.

Rico made a crude joke about a flight attendant right after the plane took off. "Damn, we a mile high yet?"

Ben pretended not to notice. He leaned back and stared out the window as the hotel skyscrapers of Reno faded to tiny specks and the desert brush landscape expanded and butted up against the green of the Sierra Nevadas.

He waited ten minutes and dialed Jason's number from memory.

"Listen," Jason said. "You're going to need to call me back at my other number. I'm in a meeting."

"Sure," Ben said. He assumed Jason's other number was a cellphone cloned from a discarded device lying mangled in a San Diego alley.

Fifteen minutes later, he tried again. "I'm in the air. You going to send a cab to pick me up or you want me to rent a car?"

"I got transport," Jason said. "Off the books. I don't think it would be that smart for you to rent a car. We'll arrange something when you get here."

"Jesus, how bad is it?"

"Not bad yet," Jason said. "Coop of bad hens keep tabs on whatever they can grab, sometimes just a few morsels, but you have to lighten the load anyway you can."

"Yet? Meaning you expect it to?" Ben shook his head at Jason's language, which seemed like a paranoid version of some sort of garbled military code. The whole affair sounded bad enough, but the possibility of the NSA listening in made Ben's stomach acid bubble.

"Well... Better be safe than dead, as they always say."

"Then what's the itinerary? I assume you want me to get started today."

Jason cleared his throat and pondered for a second. "Gaslamp Quarter. There's a little pub my guys will take you to. I'll be waiting in a cloud of smoke beneath a pendant lamp."

Ben attempted to smile but let the effort pass when he glanced at Rico, who was busy appreciating flight attendants. He half-expected Rico to unbuckle his seat belt and roam about the cabin. Instead, Rico stopped a blond-haired woman every time she passed. First, he needed another drink, then he needed some salt, then a napkin, then a bag of peanuts, then more ice and maybe a kiss on the cheek.

Instead of an icy glare, she returned him a courteous smile.

"Are they going to be holding signs with my name on them, or do I watch for the guys wearing shades and black suits?"

"You think I'm going to be obvious about it? How many spy movies do you think I watch?"

"Too many, I'm sure," Ben said. Spy thrillers were about the stupidest genre of film. Entirely built on cliché and innuendo, they relied on predictable action and stock plot lines.

"They know what you look like. If you see them before they see you, they'll be carrying briefcases."

"Of course they will." Ben didn't bother with the exchange of pleasantries before he hung up the phone and shoved it in his shirt pocket.

Rico turned toward him and smiled. "What do you call a rabbit with one ear?"

"Oh, God," Ben groaned.

Rico's smile dropped. "Ah, you heard that one before."

In fact, Ben had not heard it. If that was the punch line, it didn't make any sense. Then again, Rico often told jokes that accentuated his eccentricity. Ben appreciated it most of the time. But today his sense of humor was as thin as the Monterrey Bay ice in winter.

"What's Jason say?"

Ben turned to look out the window. "He says to stop harassing the flight attendants."

"What's he know?"

Jason had only met Rico once, briefly, at a Sacramento restaurant years ago. For him to remember Rico's personality traits would have been remarkable, but Ben already knew one fact that worried him.

Jason specialized in research. Daily. He'd clearly done his homework before he sent Ben the plane tickets and the wine. He'd have checked deeply, run background checks on all of Ben's associates and ensured security. Ben had no interest in government-related jobs, but this one reeked of federal intervention. The Mexico angle had him most apprehensive. A host of unknowns went into travel abroad, not to mention possible run-ins with the locals.

Instead of speaking, Ben stared into the deep of the valleys and canyons. The mountains below rippled like wrinkles in paper. If he looked hard enough, he could possibly see Lake Tahoe. Rose would be in her office right now overlooking that lake. It was a sunny day. He imagined her fingers dancing on the keyboard as her lips gently moved as if she mouthed every word. She'd stop and run a hand through her hair, ponder a line of dialogue and then stare across the lake to find the inspiration. She moved with both habit and grace. If only he could be with her right now. He'd curl up in her chair and perhaps fall asleep. And she'd watch him between stares at her computer screen. Love always felt so real and serene in such a setting. He'd put her on hold again. Last time he did it, she changed. The prospect of change made him want to bottle his emotions and send them to her one by one, each packaged as if to be consumed only amid moments of longing. Serenity crept up inside of him, and before he knew it, he'd drifted off to sleep.

Sandcastles and Seashells

May 18, 2011

11:45

THE SAN DIEGO SUN peeked from behind banks of low clouds as the typical morning fog started to break up. The teachers had lined up twenty-two students for a walk down the hillside and back. The school was nestled on a lower bluff abutting the ocean in the posh La Jolla district. Along the coast, the trees reached up to grab the sunshine. The ocean breeze swayed the tall palm trees and caused the palm fans to glitter in the sun.

Alejandro had turned five less than a month ago, and the teachers marked the occasion with a trip to the beach. Providing a quality education was the number one priority of Hawthorne Heights, where parents paid good money to place their kids. Alex's parents had divorced two years ago, but both brought home good money. His mother dealt in residential real estate. Middle-class people would consider her fees astronomical, but they say, in that business, you get what you pay for.

His father was a different story. He worked in a high-rise downtown, wore a suit to work, and talked to rich people all day long. He invested their money. He always described his position as a high-risk-high-reward position. The latest economic downturn had merely bruised his earnings, but some of his less-wealthy clients had lost everything.

Alex stood in line behind the wrought-iron fence separating the lawn from the sidewalk. Miss Julie meticulously counted heads and marked each name in her notebook. This walk would take perhaps a half hour. They took this trip often.

After adjusting his hat, he looked up at Miss Julie, expecting her to say something to him. Instead, she marked his name down and moved on. Alex looked down to his feet. His shoe was untied and no one had noticed. This didn't concern him, but teachers always warned him of tripping.

"March," Miss Jennifer said from the front of the line. Her amber hair floated in the wind and frizzy strands stuck to the back of her sweater. Alex followed his classmates down the sloping sidewalk. The estate houses stretched along both sides of the lane. A block away from the school, a break in the lawns appeared. A two-foot high wooden fence separated the sidewalk from an expanse of wild growth. A jacaranda tree blossomed purple in the front yard of the adjacent home and dropped some of its petals into the brush in the wild. Trees of various types scraped against the clouds. An opening in the fence allowed pedestrians to access a trail. Jennifer led the students through the gap onto an earthen trail that gently sloped downward away from the sidewalk.

Alex whispered something to himself, but Milana heard him and cocked her head. "What?"

"Nothing."

Milana played tricks on him all the time. She didn't tease or demean, and she didn't play pranks. Every time Alex assumed she'd react the same way his classmates did to anything, she surprised him. She intimidated him without even trying.

"Something," she said. Her black hair had been scraped into twin knobs on the sides of her head. She smiled just as often as the other kids, but maybe for different reasons. Maybe she did like him, but Alex was simply not worthy of her attention. Then again, maybe he was just a boy oblivious to the way certain girls behaved.

The path reached a slot in the ground where the brush cleared, revealing a rocky cliff about ten feet tall. The slot narrowed and the path turned from dirt to wooden steps that descended along the rock face. The earthen path returned and followed the bluff until the cliff dissolved into a steeper incline. The path meandered through trees and then arrived at another set of wooden steps.

Some of the kids skipped or jumped one step at a time. Alex kept an eye on his shoelace and trod carefully.

"Alex," Milana called without looking back. "Your shoe is untied."

"Yeah."

"Why don't you get Miss Julie to help you? She makes the best bows."

Alex turned pink. The hillsides opened up and the brush thinned, revealing an expanse of placid ocean. They were going to the beach. Alex quickened his step and tried to keep up with Milana.

"I want to make a sandcastle."

Milana turned her head and descended a few steps sideways. "My dad makes the best sandcastles."

She was accustomed to 'the best' of everything, which meant her parents could pay for it. Again, Alex felt out of his league. Neither at home nor at school did people refer to everything as 'the best.'

"My dad never takes me to the beach. He never comes home."

"So?"

"He just goes to work. Maybe sometimes he hugs me goodnight if he sends Angela home before bedtime. He always has papers in his hands."

"Why?" she asked.

"I don't know. He says he has to keep the devil away and pay my mom."

"Oh, no!" Milana expressed dismay, but Alex couldn't tell whether she showed alarm over his plight or a surfer falling face first into the waves.

"I don't get to see my mom anymore. She always came to visit. More than my dad. I wish I lived with her."

"Why did your dad get you?" she asked.

Alex raised his eyebrows and shook his head. What did she mean? "Um."

"My dad says that when people get divorced the mom always gets to watch the kids. Forever, because dads can't do it the same way."

"What?"

She didn't answer him. The steps down the path steepened. Milana shifted her focus to the low-hanging leaves of a eucalyptus tree that seemed to be growing out of the rock below the path. She ran her hand along the low wood railing and a bird flew off the eucalyptus branch and headed toward the sea.

Alex let his eyes wander to the coast. The beach wasn't so far away now. He watched a small family play in the sand, a girl collecting seashells, and some men in wetsuits carrying their surfboards toward the water. Surfing looked like so much fun. Maybe someday, his father would teach him how.

One girl toward the front of the line screeched at a squirrel scurrying up the trunk of a tree. The path descended into the sand after a minute or two and the line stopped.

"Listen up, class," Miss Jennifer said. "Stay in line until we get to the water. You can pick one shell and when you hear the whistle, rejoin the group. Do not wander."

The kids silently agreed. The sand sloped down. Alex looked back up the hillside. Rocky cliffs separated lush, green lawns and houses from the ocean. The houses had big windows through which the residents could watch the surfers attempt to battle big waves.

The roar of the ocean ebbed as one wave crashed ashore and another gathered further out. Alex ran to the water, fell to his knees, and pushed his fingers through the wet sand. Milana dispersed in a different direction, where a few of the girls were pointing out where they swore they saw a seal.

He'd build a castle. It wouldn't be 'the best,' but he'd show her.

After attempting to construct a muddy wall, a larger wave came in and demolished it. The water soaked his pants, which upset him. He didn't wish to call attention, but tears splashed onto his face anyway.

After ten minutes, he looked around for Milana. She had been with Billie and Jessica, but now Billie and Jessica were barefoot, picking shells out of the sand alone.

He looked up and down the beach, and back toward the houses. "Milana?"

Miss Julie heard him call out for her. She called Jennifer to join her and discuss a plan. Jennifer held her fingers to her mouth and widened her eyes. Miss Julie waved her hands in two directions. These gestures continued for a minute or two. Alex went back to dig a trench in the sand, which filled with water from another wave.

Jennifer called out. "Gather up, class. We need to go to the cliff by the trees. Take your shells and follow us."

"We have to wait for Milana," Alex said.

Julie frowned and narrowed her eyes. Alex watched her for a few seconds and finally realized that Julie was upset about something. She raised her arm to shield her face from him, but he watched intently.

"I didn't see where she went. Maybe Billie and Jessica did."

Miss Jennifer stood in the sand facing the two girls, who'd become distraught. She waved her arms in both directions and glanced up to where the sun carved a hole in the clouds. She shielded her eyes and stared along the beach, keeping an eye on the water.

After a few moments, the two girls sat down on the sand clutching their knees and paying attention to their feet. Alex stared at them for what felt like ten minutes. He approached them but didn't say anything.

When Alex looked back to Miss Jennifer, she was on the phone shouting frantically. The teachers seemed more worried than Alex was.

The hole in the clouds grew larger as the fog lifted away. The teacher kept the kids huddled at the base of the rock for ten minutes. Down the beach, a white truck rolled through the sand toward them. A yellow light on top signaled that this would be a lifeguard or a policeman.

Two other teachers from the school appeared at the end of the wooden steps and huddled with Julie and Jennifer. They talked quietly amongst themselves and watched the truck pull to a stop in front of them. Three men got out of the truck and approached the teachers. One of the men was dressed as a lifeguard and the other two were policemen.

One of the policemen talked to his radio, while the other took notes. The lifeguard stared at a picture that one of the teachers had brought down from the school. He nodded silently and climbed back into the truck.

Alex watched it drive toward the water and then turn along the oceanfront, driving slowly and looking for one child who had wandered away.

She'd come back, Alex knew. She always came back. Milana got out of class sometimes for special reasons, sometimes for several hours. But she always returned as if nothing had happened.

The two other teachers gathered all the kids and led them up the steps back to the school. Alex hung his head and watched the sand and the ocean fade further away as he climbed the steps. He didn't know why he felt this way. Milana hardly ever treated him like a friend, but he thought he knew her well enough to consider her a friend. And yet she had wandered away. Maybe she didn't like him that much.

Almost nobody spoke. The silence soaked him with a sour feeling of dread like a water stain creeping up the side of a cliff. Nothing could have prepared him for it. The breeze pushed against the bluff and mangled Alex's hair. He pushed it away and tried to keep his eyes away from the beach until it vanished.

13:10

THE MOUNTAINS BACKED THE lake with grandeur as the sun, set against the cool backdrop of azure sky, glittered on the choppy waters. A breeze whipped Rose's hair in her face, ushering in the rustic scent of pine. She closed her eyes and thought of Ben.

She walked a few paces, training her gaze upon the mountains north of the lake and listening to her heels click on the sun-stained boardwalk. Tourist season hadn't ramped up yet and snow still capped the highest mountains. This was her favorite time of the year, and she wouldn't trade the serenity for anything. It invigorated and inspired her.

A few shops and restaurants overlooked the lake. A young couple dined on Italian food while sitting close together on a patio and gazing at the lake. Rose glanced at them, but tried to focus on the lake. A pair of sailboats about a mile out etched colorful triangles against the mountainsides in the distance.

Ben's refusal to talk about his new client irked her. She'd shut the computer down, rested in the day chair, buried her face in her hands, and let the tears come. Why would he be so secretive, and what would make Jason act so shady? True enough, she didn't really know Jason Cruz. In her mind, the man had a face and the stark underpinnings of a personality, but lacked color and texture.

Maybe when Ben returned, she'd talk to him about it and chide him for his selfishness. Then again, perhaps she could stage an impromptu trip to San Diego herself. She'd be able to find him. With her investigative skills, it wouldn't even be difficult. But would such an action yield anything other than further resentment? It could drive a wedge between them and she could not bear to lose Ben. Her hopes and dreams rested upon him. Without him, it was all meaningless.

She appreciated the lake for one more minute. A couple approached to her left. They talked and giggled as if oblivious to her existence. Rose straightened her back and let them pass. Instead, they lingered. The blonde woman stood about five foot six and sported washboard abs. Her hair was pulled into a pony-tail which had allowed several strands to break free and bracket her face. Rose must have been thirty years older than this girl.

"Are you Rose Kierstien?" she asked.

The man stepped backward and motioned that he was going into one of the shops to look for souvenirs.

Rose had never had an encounter like this. A faint smile pursed her lips, but she kept her eyes steady.

"I read your books. I'm your biggest fan."

A laugh started to escape her, but she let the chuckle die. "Oh, I doubt that. It's nice to meet you."

The girl beamed and glanced over Rose's shoulder at the sailboats. "I don't mean to bother you, of course. I couldn't resist."

This situation made Rose squirm. Making conversation with a random stranger was not her specialty, but being impolite about it repulsed her. "Do you live in Tahoe?"

"Washington," she said with a grin. Her blue eyes flashed like beacons in the sun.

"The apple state," Rose said. "One of my favorite states."

The girl tilted her head. "D.C. They say there it's not what you know, but who you know."

Rose laughed. "It's the truth. I lived there for thirty years."

Seemingly not interested in prying, the woman flipped the loose strands of hair to her shoulder and glanced toward the marina to the west, where the masts of dozens of sailboats and yachts pierced the sky. "Do you miss it?"

Rose relaxed her shoulders and tilted her head back with a grin. "I wouldn't go back if you paid me to."

"It's not that bad anymore," the girl reasoned. "Crime has gone way down, and the heat doesn't really bother me. You just have to deal with the constant B.S. in the news."

"I worked for the *Washington Post*," Rose lied. The lie worked in Montana, and it could work here, but the instant she opened her lips, she regretted it. A lightbulb seemed to click in the girl's mind.

She pressed. "Oh, I... I think I read some of your work. Did you cover the Iraq invasion?"

Rose nodded halfheartedly. "Most difficult story I ever had to cover, maybe apart from Nine-Eleven. Seeing so many families torn apart..."

"They should have given you a Pulitzer for it," she said. "Best reporting I've ever read."

Taking credit for other people's work was sickening, but this woman was force-feeding her. By now, she couldn't admit the truth because she was too deep in the lie. "Well, I was just trying to earn a living. Investigative journalism was my thing, but I gave it up for crime. I don't regret it."

"You're famous."

The praise this woman lathered her with was unprecedented. It would add a bounce to her step and affix a permanent smile to her face if the whole meeting didn't seem so forced. She wanted to talk about Rose, but journalism background or not, Rose knew how to extract a story, even from people who didn't want to talk about themselves. If her tactics had worked on Ben, they'd certainly work on this girl.

"It's such a long way to come for vacation at a lovely time of year in D.C.," Rose struck.

"Anniversary," she said, nodding. It sounded rehearsed, because the reply was so quick it didn't leave time for thought.

"Fourth? Fifth?"

A smile parted her lips and she shifted her weight to her left leg. "First. So I don't really know what to expect."

"You're so young," Rose mused. "Are junior high kids generally that interested in politics?"

She frowned. Another strand of hair fell across her face and fluttered in the breeze. Again, she looked beyond Rose to the glittering lake. "I was on the debate team. And I worked on the school newspaper."

"And sports? You must have started running when you were seven. It sounds like you were really busy."

The girl appeared determined not to concede victory. She shrugged. "You really look great. I loved your hair when it was red."

"I can't go back," Rose reasoned with a smile. "Not without turning it pink and looking like a punk rocker stuck in the wrong decade."

The woman burst into laughter. Rose didn't find it funny and the laughter didn't seem to carry the tone and pitch necessary to admit humor. Rose knew a forced laugh when she heard one, and it always made her want to bust her side with genuine laughter.

"Well..." she stammered and brushed the loose strand of hair behind her shoulder. "I'd better intervene before my husband spends our life savings. It was nice to meet you."

"Likewise," Rose said. The girl had already turned her back and begun to stroll away. "Keep reading."

She stared at the lake for several minutes. The sailboats in the distance had joined together and sailed toward the shore in tandem, invoking a sense of wonder and grandness. The perfect symmetry admitted beauty. Beauty surrounded her.

Running into a fake fan would have been infuriating, but she didn't let it bother her. Rather than let thoughts of the encounter swirl into a storm that could ravage her skull for days, she strolled past the beach and made her way back to the condo. She'd read a book or try to watch a movie, or just sit and think about Ben and San Diego.

First things first, she needed to organize her office. When she opened the door, she climbed the stairs and stood in the doorway to the room. An unkempt stack of notes stood next to the mouse and sticky notes were scattered all over the desk. Cataloguing them would take some time, so she instead swept a copy of *The Thousand Branches* into her hands to place it on the bookshelf.

She scoured the book for missing bits of personality that she could use to further develop Carrie in the new project. She allowed the book to flip over in her hands and she gazed down at the back cover photograph. Her silvery hair flowed past her shoulders allowing a graceful smile to enrapture readers. Not only was it the greatest photograph she'd ever used in her books, it was the only one.

Her heart skipped and she dropped the book and a few sheets of notes on the floor. The smack of the cover against hardwood followed by the flutter of paper shuffling along the floor induced alarm. She seized her chest and collapsed into the chair.

The only official photograph of her depicted her with silver hair. And the woman on the boardwalk mentioned that she loved it when she had red hair. Panic welled in her veins as a tear splashed onto her cheek. She needed Ben. Right now. But he'd be meeting with Jason Cruz in San Diego about now. It couldn't wait.

One Dot

May 18, 2011

13:20

SAN DIEGO'S GASLAMP QUARTER was alight with tourist activity and hordes of shoppers hoping to get their fix. In such a glittery part of the city, Jake's Tavern was as much a hole in the wall as existed. The joint seemed run-down, as dilapidated wood siding and rotting framing barely held in the aluminum windows. On cool mornings, it could get drafty.

Ben had sent Rico out on a tourist errand so he could get a shot at Jason himself. Jason had insisted Ben hand his phone over to Rico just in case.

The tavern had maintained a sort of rustic charm throughout the years. The place seemed more suited to rural Montana than a city of more than a million people on the border with Mexico.

As such, Jake's offered dozens of local brews and Mexican favorites. Ben opted for a Dos Equis, while Jason settled for a local fare called Surfboard Haven.

He leaned back in the padded seat and ran his fingers along the polished edge of a sliced-log table. The décor didn't exactly inspire the imagination. Most of the seats sat empty, although Ben suspected that the place typically came alive by dusk. He stared at the table for so long it made his head throb. Jason watched him intently.

"Funny, I expected the place to be a little more private than this," Ben quipped.

"Doesn't open till three, didn't you see the sign?"

Ben nodded but didn't look up. About a foot from the rough perimeter of the table, near the center between the booth and the wall, a single black dot cratered the wood, as if someone had used the table to put out a cigar. He could imagine the confrontation that had prompted it and the one that must have followed.

"They don't cater to forty-something out-of-work divorcees on welfare. The daytime drinkers."

"Like us," Ben said, prying his eyes from the dot and looking Jason square in the eyes. Jason wasn't going to offer the truth unless Ben reached out and mercilessly dragged it out of him.

"Nothing wrong with enjoying a brew on a warm afternoon. Or in your case, swill."

"Your tastes are so refined," Ben jabbed, "Mr. Hotdog Pool Party."

Jason laughed, then paused to remember the event.

It had never been about the food, but some of the guests had threatened to leave if entrées weren't served. "Then why did I give my phone to Rico? You know he's probably using it to take pictures of women, which will get me in trouble with Rose."

"How is that going?"

Ben considered it and momentarily returned his gaze to the cigar spot. "She's pissed right now because I had to come down here and save your ass. But other than that? Peachy."

"You've got a decent gig nowadays."

"Easy money," Ben said.

Jason titled his head back. "Worst kind. And the tail you're on? Is she easy, too?" He slowly returned his gaze to Ben.

For a moment, their eyes met. His expression suddenly ached of a fury Ben had never imagined yet swam beneath a placid surface. You could tell a lot about a person by their subtlest facial expressions, Ben had learned. Clever people could mask obvious emotions, but never the ones so ingrained as to be forgotten.

Jason bit his lip and reached for his briefcase on the seat next to him. Without speaking, he withdrew a manila folder and pushed it across the table. Ben flipped through the pages as Jason spoke, pausing on a photograph of a middle-aged woman with curled sandy hair and mushroom-colored skin. She carried with her a defining grace and sterling blue eyes that could melt hearts without exerting effort.

The small talk was agonizing. "Tell me about your client."

Jason looked up while sipping his Surfboard Haven. He smacked his lips as he placed the mug on the coaster. "Nina Perez. Real estate agent, and not the cheap kind. We're talking about people looking at dropping two or three mil in La Jolla and North County. She's rich as hell, but keeps all her accounts on shore, on the up-and-up. The fewer foreign entanglements, the better. I'm her banker. Normally, I don't dig this deep on a client, but get this: She hasn't made a single transaction in two months. I was doing account maintenance one morning when I noticed the anomaly. When you're that powerful, transactions come daily, often by the tens of thousands. Transactions that big automatically get flagged by the feds for possible fraudulent activities. It's one of the reasons offshore accounts are so popular with the elite. Not only does it make a good hiding place for dark cash, blood money, things like that, but it keeps it out of the fed's fingers and garners better interest."

"I know how offshore accounts work," Ben said. "You forget I used to be a tax attorney."

"A fake tax attorney," Jason corrected.

"Yeah."

"So when you find things like this, you keep a flag on the account. If it doesn't seem right, you give them a courtesy call to make sure everything is all right, hoping they haven't jumped ship to some competing bank. You look at debit card transactions, anything linked to the client. Sometimes they have multiple accounts. Nina—Ms. Perez—has only one. Checking with a balance so high it will make you dizzy."

"And she hasn't returned your calls, or you wouldn't be talking to me."

"Well, these days, who actually answers their phone when it rings?"

"She probably has to take calls on her cell all the time," Ben reasoned.

Jason clasped his hands and allowed his subtle stare to intensify. "She's independent, obviously. Has assistants keeping track of all her appointments. So I ask around, and they haven't seen her for a month. So many lost clients over missed appointments. The last one was for a Mr. Omar Dominguez. And this is where it gets hairy. Turns out, Dominguez was busted in Tijuana recently for shooting a woman in the hip. He operates out of Tijuana, but I found out a little bit about him. The Mexican government isn't keen to give information on its citizens to American banks, but I know a guy. He's what they call a runner, not officially connected, but does deliveries presumably to the border, where he gets mules to smuggle the stuff in. The ports at Tijuana are too busy, so most of them come in out around El Centro. Just in case they get caught, they hide it in crates of avocados."

"A drug cartel?"

"El Matador, big operation just outside of Mexico City."

Ben uncapped his beer and downed a large gulp. He stared at the cigar burn for several seconds and then met Jason's intensity again.

"You're asking me to go to Mexico? That wasn't part of the deal."

"I know," Jason defended. "But I couldn't say much more because..."

"Jesus Christ," Ben said. "Your whole life you assume a good friend is an upstanding citizen, and then... Look, I don't know what your situation is, and you'll probably never tell me, but your client is where I end and you begin. If I find out anything, I won't hide it."

"Well... It's just that Ms. Perez's employees have assumed they're out of jobs. And she has a son."

"I'm going to cross-check her employees and find out if they have anything shady going on," Ben said. "You can't expect a drug runner to come into America and target a high-priced realtor over nothing. The odds would be astronomical."

"Be careful."

"You too," Ben said.

"I hope you find her. I don't want to lose her business." The fire in his eyes seemed to swell, burning circular holes into his pupils.

It was more than business. Jason always considered himself above reason, which had its way of allowing indifference to creep into him. That was to be expected. But Jason's eyes communicated something deeper. Nina Perez had to be in legal trouble or something far worse.

He stood up, downed a gulp of beer, and placed a five-dollar bill on the table. As he stepped out of the tavern, his muscles tingled, and his legs turned to sand. It was Jason who was in legal trouble. He could hear it in his voice on the phone, and the intensity in his eyes suggested something more complex than a banker-client relationship. He'd seen that sort of fire in Jason only one other time.

Years ago, before the Montana incident, Jason had a run-in with a friend who'd owed him thousands of dollars. Ben had tagged along on a trip to Sacramento, where they'd attempted to coax the money out of the friend. But the friend had double-crossed him and invested the funds into a gambling ring that was attempting to collect from Jason. Jason had seethed at Ben for days when the conflict came to a head, at which time Jason had punched him in the face and threatened to kill him.

Nina Perez must have been taking part in a similar scheme involving hundreds of thousands of dollars or more. If that was the case, what was Jason really up to? And was it really bad enough to attract the federal government?

Then again, Jason had admitted as much when he noted that ten-thousand-dollar transactions drew the attention of the feds. He'd just tacitly admitted he was under federal investigation. Had that been true, Ben's simple presence in the tavern would get the government interested in him, and his entire life would be reduced to ashes.

Benjamin Redd Carr, private investigator, otherwise known as Trent Cobbs, had ostensibly died as a casualty of the Vietnam War. Ben hadn't exactly been living under the radar since the Montana incident, where he'd uncovered a sweeping conspiracy to develop land on the border of the Flathead Indian Reservation. He'd left the 'law' practice and brought Rose back to California with him. His identity as Ben Carr remained intact and had always been secure. However, if the federal government wanted to crack the shell badly enough, they'd find a way. Ben couldn't hide forever.

If they found Private Cobbs, they'd want to talk to him, and even though he had never done anything illegal, he didn't imagine the meeting would be friendly. How would he have slithered out of military contact so easily and so permanently? At the time, it was only convenient. His entire unit had been wiped out. He panicked and ran. The government presumed him dead and forgot about it. If Ben had been interested in visiting Washington, he'd be able to find his former name on the wall.

Ben clenched his fists and hurried down the street to a crowded corner, where hundreds of people were shopping and enjoying lunch. He'd find Rico there, or so he thought.

Instead, Rico staggered out of an alley just as Ben gazed at the crowd. He looked as though he'd had a few too many drinks. His hair was ragged, and a spot of blood tinged his cheek.

"What happened to you?"

"No sé," Rico stammered. "Two guys with hoods. They ran out of here five minutes ago. Stole the phones and my wallet."

"Shit! We can't go to the police." He thought fast and decided to barrage Rico with questions. "Which way did they go? What did they look like? Details, faces, beards, tattoos, weapons. Did they speak to you or each other? Did they have accents?"

Rico pointed toward the west, down a side street toward the ocean. "That way, I think. They had hoods, both had goatees, dark skin, I think, but the alley was kind of dark. No tattoos, but they are Mexican. Didn't speak much."

"How do you know they were Mexican?"

"The green, white, and red flags on their jackets? Plus, one of them shouted at the other. It was in English, but the accent was unmistakably Mexican. From somewhere near Tijuana, I think. Didn't sound Chihuahuan or Jaliscan."

Ben swore. "They took my phone?"

Rico shook his head. "Yeah, um... *una problema poquita.*"

"What?"

He shuffled his feet and stepped toward the street. "Señorita Rose. Tried to call you. I didn't answer it, so she left a voicemail. I accidentally listened to it."

"Well, I'm not going to talk to her now. What did she say?"

"Don't you miss pay phones?"

"What did she say?" The timbre of his voice rose as high as the tops of the buildings and fury brewed in his eyes.

"Something about a lady she met by the lake. Didn't make much sense, but she sounded scared. Then, last thing I heard before she hung up the phone: 'He knows where I am, Ben. He knows.'"

"But he's in prison," Ben said. "I have to talk to her."

"Maybe we'll just have to set up new phone plans," Rico said.

Instead, Ben motioned for Rico to follow him. They sprinted down the block and turned into the lobby of a ritzy hotel. Ben wasted no time in darting to the front desk, where an older couple were checking in.

"How can I help you?" the secretary asked. She brushed a lock of blond hair behind her ear and leaned forward.

"I need to make a call. Can I borrow your phone?"

She picked up the touchtone phone and handed it to him before rolling her chair across the aisle behind the desk to grab the couple's ID cards from the copier.

Ben dialed her number quickly and waited.

It rang six times, but she answered, probably reluctantly, as she wouldn't recognize the number.

"I'm at a hotel, honey. I lost my phone, but you called while I was in a meeting. It sounded urgent."

"He knows." Her voice wavered.

"Rose, he's serving twenty years for a raft of crimes. I think you're safe."

"He's got contacts," she said. "You know it and I know it. And money. You can't count on people who have money and contacts, especially if they have a taste for revenge."

Ben thought about the circular dot on the table inside the tavern, how it seemed to fan tiny lines into all directions like an illustration of a sun. "What tipped you off?"

She allowed herself a moment to gulp. "I met a 'fan' at the lake from Washington. She said she liked my red hair. Only someone connected to him could have known that, Ben. I'm coming to San Diego."

"No, you're not," Ben warned. "A lot of stuff is going on here right now. I'll tell you all about it later."

"Ben."

"Go to my office. Lock the doors and use my office phone to order in. I'll be back in a few days. I'll check in every day, I promise."

Her voice shook and resonated with fear-stained sadness. "I need you, Ben. I need you to hold me."

"I know. I'll get to the bottom of this and then—"

He didn't finish his sentence before Rico tapped him on the shoulder. Ben looked toward him. Rico's expression went blank, which indicated fear. He stared out the lobby window at two men in black jackets. They turned and jogged away just as Ben glanced at them.

"That's them."

"Listen, sweetheart, I've gotta run. Talk to you tonight."

The receptionist had rolled her chair back to Ben and Rico. She took the phone and placed it under the counter and offered further assistance.

"Gotta run. Literally."

Ben hustled toward the door with Rico in tow. He'd track the assailants down and reclaim his phone. The excitement made him bristle with uncertainty and rage. The door whooshed shut as Ben sprinted across the street after the hooded men.

Amber Skulls

May 18, 2011

14:30

RICO'S ASSAILANTS SPRINTED ALONG the broad sidewalk of the side street, swerving between crowds of people and vaulting some of the sidewalk planters. Ben drew in deep breaths as often as he could, but age proved to favor the younger attackers. Rico lagged behind. Ben could hear his heavy footfalls slow and his panting become labored gasps. The men dove into a parked car on the side of the street. After they started the car, tires squealed on pavement. The harbor breeze ruffled his hair. The motor revved and the car sped away.

Ben kicked a nearby planter hard enough to send pain shooting through his right side. He panted and glared. Rico looked worse. His face had turned radish red. He bent down and rested his hands on his knees, gasping for air with sharp, raspy grunts. This might have been the first time in years Rico had encountered any reason to run.

"You... you okay?" Ben asked.

Rico gasped between words as agony sculpted his face into something only resembling the man Ben had known for years. "Never... better... Son of a... You got that... license plate?"

Ben already had it memorized. "AZ45907. Dark blue hatchback Fiesta."

"Afraid not," Rico said. "It was black."

The clouds had thinned out significantly since the morning, which had given way to partly cloudy skies. The clouds painted shadows across the cityscape which made some colors appear darker.

"Are you in pain?"

"Mucho."

Ben attempted a smile, which probably appeared sardonic and callous, but he didn't care. Instead, he pried at Rico. "You must be. Because that was clearly dark blue."

"What are you going to do about it?"

"What I do best. I'm going to run a DMV check, find out the registrar's address, go to that location, and get our phones back. Maybe break a few jaws."

Rico interrupted his gasping long enough to laugh and cough with a concoction of humor and pain. His face was slowly returning to its normal shade. "Sí. While you're at it... you can make yourself ten... ten, maybe fifteen years younger."

That was harsh. "At least I'm not doubled over coughing up my own blood after running a block and a half."

"Uncalled for," Rico panted. "That was two blocks."

Ben gazed back toward the corner entrance of the hotel lobby and narrowed his eyes. Planters housing graceful palms buttressed the entrance and lent an aura of tropical, laid-back luxury. They'd need lodging for the night, and Ben needed to make some phone calls. That hotel would have seemed obvious, but it would do. In the morning, they'd have a rental car delivered for Rico to make fun of.

"So what now?"

Ben stared toward the downtown skyline. "I need to make an appointment with an investment broker."

"Jesús," Rico said, pronouncing it as he always did, "great time to be checking your portfolio, no?"

"Sure." He tapped his fingers on the manila file folder Jason had given him. He'd flipped through the pages quickly and noted that Perez's ex-husband worked as a broker downtown, which meant he was at least as rich as she was. Jason would have tried this avenue already, but it wouldn't hurt to check him out again. Plus, Ben exhibited skill at getting people to talk. He had Rose to thank for that.

"We going to get a room?" Rico stood upright for the first time and took a few waddling steps, which looked both awkward and painful.

"I've got to look over this info more carefully. Jason put this together, so it's likely incomplete and a bit rushed, but it will make a good starting point."

"Tell me what he told you?"

"Well, I have a feeling that this woman we're helping find is trying to pull a double cross on him or something. He definitely has some kind of anger issue with her."

"Maybe they made a few side deals one night," Rico said, "if you know what I mean."

That thought, in fact, had crossed his mind. The fire in Jason's eyes, however, suggested a buried rage rather than raw passion. Clearly Jason had embraced whatever emotion had tugged at him, because he did a poor job of hiding it. Ben didn't bother questioning why. He didn't care and it would be best to let Jason reveal his issues through natural means.

"Nope. Definitely not."

"Let's go to the beach," Rico said, gazing toward the ocean.

"We're here to find a missing woman, not chase tail."

Rico laughed. "Well, you gonna have to give me some info, *amigo*. Either I help out like you're paying me, or I stay out of your way." He panted and lowered his eyes to meet Ben's while bringing his index finger up to point at his bruises. "I took this for you, so staying out of your way isn't really helping."

"We have a lot of work to do. Do me a favor. Don't mention Jason Cruz's name or his business while we are here. Only between us, while no one is watching. You can do that."

Rico squeezed his lips together and spoke in a muffled voice, something that sounded like, "Hey man, my lips are sealed."

"Do me a favor when we check into the hotel room. Call the cleaning lady for our building and have her leave some roses and some food. Alert security, too, but keep it quiet and don't mention her name."

"I'm sure the ex ain't going to bust out of the big house to come get her. Maybe she's paranoid."

"I'd rather take the precautions and be proven wrong than do nothing and be proven right."

"Good idea," Rico said.

They started walking toward the hotel before saying anything. The conversation shifted, but Ben chose to answer Rico's questions with short, clipped replies that divulged no real information. He was starting to not feel like talking at all. A serum of dread spread weariness through his veins. He'd suggest ordering some food once they made it into the hotel room. He'd prefer Chinese, but Rico would probably force him into Mexican food. Southern California was not only home to countless beaches and tourist attractions, but also served legendary Mexican food.

Ten years before he started working for Ben, Rico had emigrated from Mexico on a green card. He moved pipes and picked crops at a large San Joaquin Valley farm outside of Modesto. After the visa expired, he stayed. Ben's firm wouldn't hire him without proper documentation, so Rico went through the process of applying for citizenship. After he passed the test, Ben's firm hired as a transporter, a decent step up from agriculture. The job also offered some benefits and significantly higher wages.

Ben had Rico assigned to him the first time smoothing out legal issues for a cabinet shop in Chico. And then came the long trip to Montana, where their friendship was forged. Ben and Rico both chose to leave the practice after that operation had collapsed into chaos. Ben had been retained to settle a tax dispute for a small contractor near Glasgow, Montana, but that case had spiraled out of control and turned into a wide-arching conspiracy involving the Montana governor and Rose's ex-husband.

The case led to multiple imprisonments and the breaking up of a network of contractors that had teamed up to silence the story of a Native American boy who'd died from toxic chemicals.

When Ben chose to settle with Rose in Lake Tahoe, Rico rented an apartment in Carson City about a mile from the office. From that time, Ben considered him a friend.

But this trip was about business.

"Want some Mandarin?" Ben asked.

Rico stuck out his tongue as if to gag. "I love me some fortune cookies, but when you're in Rome, you eat like the Romans."

Ben planted a dumbfounded look on his face. "I think you said that wrong."

"Whatever. Taco capital of the *Estados Unidos*, tacos. We can have Chinese when we visit Shanghai or San Fran."

Dammit. "I presume you know a place that delivers."

"There are taco trucks on every street corner," Rico said. "I'll just go get some, right after I call the cleaning lady."

"Interested in getting roughed up again?"

"They ain't coming back for me now they think I have a boyfriend to protect me," Rico joked. "Plus, they got our phones. What do you think they wanted them for?"

Ben slowed his pace and gazed at him. "I don't know. Maybe they work for the people who took Perez, or they work for Perez herself."

"I was thinking your banker amigo. The guy's dirty as..." Rico had stopped walking. His mouth hung agape as he stared into the window display of a mom-and-pop tourist shop that sold clothing, apparel, knickknacks, and sundry other items.

"What?"

"Pendejos! Guess they didn't want them after all."

Ben turned his head and stared in the window. Between a black and red-painted skull with gemstones glued to it and a women's tee-shirt stood two cell phones on display. Ben recognized his instantly. "Doesn't make any sense."

"I don't have to use the lobby phone after all," Rico said.

"Yes you do."

"They didn't have time to run them in here," Rico said. "They ran straight to the car."

"How long was it between when you were assaulted—"

Rico looked insulted. He glared at Ben between glances at the ornate skull and the phones. "Fist fight."

"Yeah, how long between you kicking the snot out of some thugs and them running from us at the hotel?"

Rico's angry stare faded. "Twenty, thirty minutes."

"Plenty of time," Ben said.

"What you talking about, *cavrón*?"

"They came by the hotel lobby because they knew you'd still be in the vicinity, and they were trying to bait you. Then they saw me and panicked."

"Like all the women do?"

"They were going to lead you to where they left the phones anyway. It's some kind of threat people are using nowadays. They take something, lead you to it, and leave implicit warnings."

"They think we're going to some *Dia de los Muertos* celebration? In May?"

"Or the subjects of one."

Ben read the white writing on the blue tee-shirt. "Follow me to the beach." He connected the dots faster than he could have anticipated. "And you die."

"Why would they use that as a threat?" Rico said. "They think we know more than we do know? A sign of thugs so smart and creative they make stupid mistakes."

Ben shook his head and frowned. "Nope. It's a threat, but it's also bait."

Rico chuckled. "Are you really going to use fishing metaphors down here? I thought you were the smart one. I think you been spending too much time with a crime novelist."

"They may not be going to the beach at all. This reinforces the notion that they work for either the banker or his subject."

"I didn't go to university or anything, but yeah," Rico said. "Obviously."

"The point is, they want us to follow them. And if we grab the phones like they expect us to, they'll know we're coming and will be able to set up some sort of trap. All they need is a few minutes and they can install apps. There's a new one parents are using to keep tabs on their kids. You enter their phone number and the program pings that phone and gives you an exact location by GPS. Twenty minutes is more than long enough to set that up. It's also long enough to clone them."

"I knew that. So we get the phones?"

Ben stared at the phones for several minutes while he tried to come up with a fail-safe way of keeping the information on his phone safe. He'd be able to back up the data onto a flash drive, and it seemed possible that this shop would sell flash drive keychains as souvenirs. Then he'd have a copy of the data and he could destroy the phone so the thugs couldn't track them.

"Yeah. Let's go in."

A tourist shop this large would also sell convenience store items such as drinks and snack food. Aisle after aisle stretched to the back of the store, where a security camera observed from high on the wall. The shop carried everything from Day of the Dead knickknacks and San Diego tee-shirts to hot sauce, postcards, mini license plates, and keychains. Ben wandered through the store and found a wide selection of keychains.

One such keychain had a flash drive with an orca whale etched on it. The price was steep, but Ben would willingly pay for it. Rico emerged at the register carrying what promised to be a near-death nuclear experiment in a bottle. If you eat more than one drop, your bowels will explode.

Ben paid for both items and told the cashier about the phones left in the display. She had him prove they belonged to them, which proved easy enough.

They hoofed it back to the hotel after at least fifteen minutes of browsing. A nagging feeling began to claw at the back of Ben's mind like a savage, caged beast longing for freedom. He'd taught himself over the years not to indulge these beasts over the torment such indulgence could unleash.

That phone contained everything a criminal would ever need to know about Ben. from credit cards to text messages, voice mail, and even photographs. With that information a crook could sabotage his entire life, and probably worse.

Ben's life included a lot. It included Rose. Ben allowed that thought to roam free in his head until it consumed every ounce of joy and produced a nest of poisonous snakes. Allen knew where she was, and a cloned cell phone could give her away. His office wouldn't be a sanctuary at all. He had to warn her before it was too late.

Ashes of Montana

May 18, 2011

15:10

IF LEN CARTER HAD come here to talk about the politics of criminal justice, Allen would strangle him. Corrections officers had the cafeteria guarded in case Allen posed a flight risk. He frowned at a guard and walked calmly to a table where a steel grid shielded a large window. Allen had always assumed that these windows were made of some kind of indestructible safety glass.

He studied the window for several minutes and watched his faint reflection. From that vantage point, Allen looked like a thinking man, silently discussing the meaning of life and considering the tragedy of his situation. By now, however, the travesty of thought had already led to action. Carter trusted him enough to meet him without the pane of glass separating them like the veil isolating the living from the dead. What a fool.

Carter led a pair of assistants through a door at the end of the room and marched down an aisle adjacent to the windows. He offered a cursory nod to a guard, straightened his back, and lengthened his stride as a vaguely arrogant glare flourished on his face. Allen could have smiled at the image but didn't allow the pleasure to polish his face.

"You look fabulous," Allen sneered. "Like you're about to win a major trial and you know it. Tell me I'm not far off."

Carter's assistants scribbled notes on legal pads without saying anything. Carter ignored him.

"You're really good. Why don't you get one of these guys to order me an espresso? If you put on some shades, you'll have the whole ensemble. You'll own the building."

"Do you want to get down to business, or do you want to obsess over my looks?" Carter looked irritated, which showed another admirable trait.

"You don't want me to compliment your looks, then why do you go out of your way to look the part? You're not here because of your looks, you're here despite them."

Carter frowned and lowered his chin a fraction of an inch, which seemed to indicate that he was ready to play hardball. "Your hearing is coming up, and we need to discuss strategy now."

"Tell me you got your PIs on Rose," Allen said.

"They're looking."

"You'd think a crime novelist would be easier to find. Hell, you go to a local bookstore on a Saturday and they're there right in front of you doing a song and dance in hopes it doesn't look like a PR stunt."

"Do you have a bone to pick with writers?"

"Only one," Allen snapped.

Carter appeared shaken. He shifted his weight and relaxed. "We're off to a great start. I pay these guys by the hour, probably the same way you should be paying me."

Allen grunted.

"We're not going to get the jury to ignore the Montana incident. Your Michigan Men's ties to you were never called into question, possibly because your previous lawyer was an idiot."

That brought an ugly memory. How many meetings had Allen spent directing his people to scour the country looking for her only to come up empty until she popped up involved in a Montana legal dispute? He'd celebrated when they found her. They'd have brought her to him, but they underestimated who she had with her. Allen blamed himself for that failure. It turned out to be the crux of the affair that put him behind bars. He wasn't going to let her get away with it.

After that, Jefferson Marsden could have told the jury that Allen had nothing to do with the Michigan Men, and as long as a better lawyer couldn't find documentation, it would never be proven. But Marsden was worthless. Paying him top dollar proved a foolish mistake that Allen was determined not to repeat. Instead, he tried a different avenue by recruiting a young attorney not experienced enough to engage in politics and make careless mistakes but educated enough to anticipate the most effective tactics.

"You don't know where to look for her now," Carter continued. "She's gone and you don't care. That means we need something else to distract the jury. Some big, perfectly legal financial agreement. Say, five percent of Devon Energy?"

"That's big cash," Allen said. "I can't pay that."

"But the documentation says you already did."

Allen attempted a smile to give Carter the impression that he was interested. "That's never going to fly. Forging those sorts of documents is a federal crime, too. Are you trying to get me to spend the rest of my life in this hellhole?"

"It's a calculated risk," Carter defended. "We don't even have to present the documents to the court because it is a separate affair. All you have to do is not incriminate yourself."

"Even lying about it is obstruction of justice."

"But we're counting on them to not look into it. We just have to mention it once or twice to get the jury on the path to thinking you've made your amends and are reformed. That the criminal justice system in this country really does work."

"Only if you have the money to work it," Allen joked. He stroked his chin. "Let's scale down that investment into a smaller, more obscure company and not claim any kind of percentage. If all we want to do is give the impression that I'm investing, maybe it should be something I can afford."

"It sounds plausible," Carter said. "We'll think about it."

Carter's first assistant, a blond young man, shrugged and scribbled something down while the other assistant whispered to him. Allen gave them a dirty look. The first assistant paused and looked up. Possibly to avoid distraction, he peeled his gaze away and stared out the window.

"See, that's one thing I hate," Allen said, lacing his fingers into a sort of two-handed fist. He didn't look away from the assistant until the last word of his sentence. It was a calculated effort to strike fear into Carter's heart and no matter how effective, the insinuation would not go unnoticed.

Carter scratched his elbow and then rested it on the table. His eyebrows drooped, and he subtly leaned back on the bench. "What's that?"

"Thinking. It's a waste of time. All that work goes into accomplishing nothing. You lose IQ points that way."

Carter leaned forward and cracked his knuckle. That was more like it.

Having achieved the upper hand, Allen allowed a cold silence to drift between them. The assistants scribbled notes onto their pads momentarily, but when they realized no one was talking, they looked up and glanced at one another as if at a loss.

"How close are you to finding her?"

"Rose?"

"No, the blonde from cell block B," Allen jabbed.

He shrugged. "It's going to be easy to find her, especially if she's still using your last name."

"That's the funny thing about celebrities," Allen said. "You know why they don't change their names when they get married? It's because nobody would know who Angelina Pitt is. She'd be some B-movie siren easily tricked into full frontal nudity just to make a buck, at least to the average stupid consumer. Name recognition is number one. Rose gained it after we were married."

"Okay," Carter said. He gulped and then continued. "Then all we have to do is hack into her publisher and figure out where they send her royalties."

"Brilliant," Allen said. He purposely lathered his response in scorn just to watch Carter cringe. His reactions were sweet and addictive, like candy.

"All the footwork is done," Carter said, flexing his wrist. "Some PO box in Lake Tahoe, California. I've already sent someone to investigate."

Allen nodded. "Maybe I'm not paying you too much."

"I suppose you're going to explain why such a risky move makes good strategy," Carter said, perhaps sensing an opening he could exploit. His face suddenly took on a more vibrant color, as if the lure of victory altered his performance.

"I'll know where to find her when I get out of here. Maybe then we'll be able to pick up where we left off. Plus, I'm good enough at what I do to create enough distraction to make several decisions go unnoticed."

"So finding her is a distraction?"

"Maybe I shouldn't tell you this," Allen said. "But you're under investigation. In high-profile cases like this, they dig deep into the defense's history."

"I know that."

Allen shook his head and leaned forward. He squared his jaw and stared for several seconds. "They'll find out you've been snooping."

"You won't be acquitted if the jury thinks you're looking for her," Carter countered. "Nobody is that stupid."

"But the indecision will allow us to launch a detailed plan and all we have to do is convince enough jurors that I'm going to contribute to society instead of being a menace. That brings us to your next task."

Carter allowed his eyes to wander to the window and to the dozens of empty tables in the cafeteria. He shifted in his seat and lowered his eyebrows.

"Once your investigators find her, I want you to send a dozen white roses and a detailed letter. Make it salty and trite, like some of the crap she writes about. Hopefully you make a better actor than a lawyer."

"Is she supposed to buy it?"

Allen bit his lip. "The jury is. I know Rose. It will get her good and spooked and she'll run, like she's always done."

As if allowing himself a moment to gather the absurdity of it all, Carter leaned toward his assistant and started to whisper something. He turned his head and his eyes met Allen's. "And then what?"

Not interested in letting the situation fester, Allen lowered his head, leaned back, and crossed his arms. A sigh escaped his lips. He found it so easy to manipulate Carter that all he wanted to do was cut into him again and again, just to taste the victory.

Then again, Carter knew what he was doing. He considered everything and every strategy. He made thinking work for him, no matter how badly it repulsed Allen.

"Then," Allen said, "I'll find her."

15:30

LOW-VOLUME TELEVISION NOISE FILLED the hotel room as Ben waited for Rose to answer her phone. She may have been in the car, Ben decided. Her Bluetooth often gave her trouble by disconnecting on a whim, which would explain her delay in answering.

Rather than grow impatient, he twirled the spiral cord in his fingers.

Rico pushed the door open with his foot. He tiptoed into the room carrying two Styrofoam plates covered with aluminum foil. A huge grin spanned his face, and he hunched his back as if raw instinct compelled him to protect the food.

"Tacos Ole!" he shouted.

"Can... can you hear me now?" Rose answered.

"Now I can," Ben said. "Where are you?"

A pause drifted between them, during which Rose breathed heavily and then sighed, "Driving down the hill dealing with traffic and crazy tourists."

Ben chuckled dryly and then swallowed. "Sounds about right."

"I thought we'd wait until later to talk when we both have some time. What's up?"

Her question seemed to light his heart like a fuse. His stomach sank and his heart rate intensified, which would have been the perfect ingredient for heartburn even without the spicy food. "I couldn't wait. We have a situation down here."

"Is your client giving you trouble already? I thought Jason was such a *nice* guy."

"Yeah, so did I," Ben said through a labored sigh. Her sarcasm surpassed him. "It isn't him, though. Our phones got stolen and possibly cloned, which means there's a chance they are listening to us right now. They can look at our pictures, view our browsing history, anything they want. They can steal your identity."

She gasped. "Ben. You have pictures of me. Text messages. My phone number."

"And if they're smart enough, they can ping your phone to track you down."

"But why me?"

"I don't know, but I don't want to take that risk. If you really think Allen is coming after you again, he's proven smart enough to track you down once, and he can do it again if he's out of prison."

"Shit. Damn shit." Rose almost never swore, but when she did, the strokes of her voice were delicate, but well-enunciated and straight to the point. You could tell how upset she was by how many curse words she strung together.

"I don't have any reason to think they'd target you but use landlines whenever you can. They are much harder to track these days. And stay away from my office."

"What am I supposed to do, Ben? I don't know anyone in Carson. I barely even speak the language."

For a half-second, Ben thought about her language comment. True enough, the common language in Carson City resembled English, but the dialect confused her ears with unfamiliar sounds, pronunciations, and a special kind of slang not heard anywhere else. She found the environment intimidating, if not downright disrespectful. Even though Lake Tahoe only resided a half an hour away, California infiltrated the language more thoroughly and tourism played a big enough part that strange dialects were usually drowned out if not silenced entirely.

"Maybe go up to Reno. Get a hotel room, something unpretentious, but comfortable. Before you get there, I want you to turn off your phone. Completely shut it down. I'm backing up our data."

"I thought your phones were stolen."

"They were," Ben explained. "Rico got... he beat the hell out of them, but they got away with them anyway. Twenty minutes later, we see the guys running down the street, getting in a car, and driving away. We walked back to the hotel room and found our phones in a window display of a local shop. Needless to say, that's more than suspicious."

"Well, be careful," she said. "Allen's behind bars so he won't come after me in the meantime."

"You be careful, too, sweetheart," Ben said and then swallowed. "I'll call you tonight. I love you."

"I love you, too," she said.

Ben hung up the phone and stared at Rico.

"About time you describe the event in the alley properly," Rico said. He unwrapped his plate and eyed the soft corn tortillas filled with barbecued goat meat, cilantro, onions, and avocado. "*Sí*. Tacos a la mode."

Rico didn't know what that meant, but it sounded fancy to him, so he used it to describe nearly every fancy meal. He loved tacos so much that eating them always marked some kind of special occasion.

Ben stood up from the bed and sat down at the table across from Rico. He stripped the foil off his dish and decided to down a dose of heartburn medication before biting into a taco. Rico watched him spin the cap off the bottle between bites of his taco. Before he swallowed his bite, he said, "No worry, I ordered yours extra bland."

"You could have gone American style."

Rico stared at him as if fury steeled his muscles. "Friends don't let friends eat American tacos."

Ben didn't have time for small talk. As soon as he finished eating, he needed to make several other calls. Rico acted like he hadn't a care in the world, but by now Ben knew that when troubled, Rico offered up a hard exterior shell so as to pretend important events simply rolled off his back. By feigning imperviousness, he gained strength. Ben didn't understand how that could work but accepted and embraced Rico's eccentric personality.

Ben, on the other hand, dealt in logic to describe almost everything. He analyzed everything that happened, which sometimes drove Rose mad. Everything had a rhyme and a reason.

"Suppose you enlist Alligator Dan to cover for her," Rico said after swallowing a bite and wiping his lips with a paper towel. "He has no interest in her, she's not his type anyway, and he can handle barroom brawl like no one's business."

"That's crazy," Ben said. "One little problem, though. He's not supposed to know who I am. If I call and ask him that, he'll kill Amber or whatever her name is."

"Your client? So call the Reno PD. Favors for favors, am I right?"

"The police can't have anything to do with this," Ben said, remembering Jason's warnings.

"Cops have something to do with everything," Rico countered. "It's what they're good at. They won't have any interest in Rose, either unfortunately because no one can prove she's in any danger. Just your infallible instinct."

"I'll have to think about it," Ben said. He wouldn't think about it at all until after he made his phone calls to Perez's ex-husband and her assistants. If Rose would encounter danger at all, it would take many hours for it to reach her, as Reno was a mostly isolated locale.

Rico downed his tacos in a heartbeat and then cracked open a beer and then kicked back on his bed while flipping through channels on the television. He mostly ignored Ben while he made his calls.

Russel Brandt, Perez's ex, didn't answer his phone, so Ben dialed his office number and waited. Brandt answered after several rings and spoke in a hurried voice that indicated stress.

"Mr. Brandt," Ben said. "My name is Howard Luntz, attorney at law. I'm representing Citrus Bank International, and I'm calling in regard to accounts owned by Nina Perez. Citrus has indicated a possible fraud on her account and frozen it, but they cannot contact her."

"I'll pay them the money tomorrow," Brandt hurried.

The sound of him typing on a keyboard echoed through the phone line. It caught Ben off guard, but then again, it was more than likely a canned response he gave to debt collectors all the time. Since Ben framed himself as a debt collector, the response should have been expected.

"You misunderstand," Ben explained. "Ms. Perez is not linked to the fraud. The anomaly was detected because her account has become inactive for months, but a suspicious charge just cropped up in Belarus. Do you know if she's been travelling?"

"Belarus? No, she couldn't locate it on a map."

"Have you heard from her at all?"

Mr. Brandt sounded irritated, but his tone indicated a kind of callousness usually reserved for a jilted lover. "No. Not lately. She sometimes swings by the house to hang out with our son, when I'm not home."

"Your son?" Ben didn't want to sound like an investigator, so he carefully tinged his speech with the acceptance and curiosity of a friendly lawyer working a not-too-important case. "How old?"

"He's five."

"Yeah? I have a five-year-old, but he doesn't stay home by himself after he gets out of preschool. I have a nanny look after him until I get home around seven."

"Same here," Mr. Brandt said. He still sounded callous, but emotion began to leak into his voice.

"Then again, I never see my wife," Ben said. "She's hanging out with some snooty sports car dealer with a big wad of cash and an even bigger... superiority complex."

Brandt didn't laugh.

"I don't mean to pry," Ben said, "but are you alright? You sound a bit agitated."

"Stock market's down two hundred points today," Brandt said. "You should have called three days ago."

Ben hated small talk, but he couldn't come up with any other questions to ask without sounding either deranged or paid off. Instead, he called Mr. Brandt's assistant and set up a face-to-face meeting, where Ben would have to assume another alias. Maybe the stock market would recover tomorrow.

He hung up the phone and quickly contacted Ms. Perez's assistants. One of them answered, but Ben left a message for the other. Eva Crestwell couldn't predict Perez's whereabouts, but she agreed to meet with Ben tomorrow afternoon at her home in Carlsbad. Ben had to find Carlsbad on a map and estimated that it would take a half an hour to forty-five minutes in traffic, but maybe less if he timed the drive right.

Rico laughed at the television just as Ben finished his final call. Weary from the long day, he laid back on the bed, closed his eyes and drifted off to sleep. The image of the fire in Jason's eyes burned holes in his corneas. In Ben's estimation, Brandt was beginning to look innocent. If that were true Ben would have to investigate Jason himself and no good could come of that. The intensity represented something. It always did. The emotion in a person's eyes could give them away and it always proved unavoidable and inescapable. What did Jason Cruz have to hide? And how deadly would his secrets turn out to be?

Spurs of Tomorrow

May 19, 2011

08:00

SUNRISE IN SAN DIEGO was a phenomenon so rarely breathtaking that when it did inspire wonder, people talked about it almost until sunset. Most often, as far as Ben had witnessed, mornings began with a hazy blue light that eventually turned gray until the fog lifted later in the morning.

Ben reveled in the fog. What it concealed allowed the imagination to fill in the details like an artist splashing life onto an empty canvas. Being the night owl type, Rico had not yet risen. Ben considered this mildly annoying, but usually found ways to fill in his itinerary with non-essential work to set up other work. He used the early mornings to prepare himself for the day, to set priorities, and to arrange his thoughts in such a way that he could most easily access them when needed. He'd perfected this tactic so many years ago that it had become ingrained in his lifestyle.

People chided him for being so driven. "How do you do it?" people often asked him. It had never proven easy to answer that question. In truth, dictating the motive behind habit hid more than it revealed. Sometimes he shrugged and sometimes he countered with another question: "How do you not?" Ben could do it because he always had.

Ben stepped out of the hotel room alone, as quietly as he could, and rode the elevator down to the lobby. Several people were waiting to check out, but the receptionist didn't let Ben stroll past him without smiling and wishing him a good morning. Especially for a city this size, the people of San Diego were incredibly friendly. Why didn't Carson City exude the same charm?

The reflection and glimmer from the tall glass buildings infected the void of gray with a certain zeal. From the roofs of many buildings, an observer would not be able to see the street. Living in the upper levels of a condo tower would seem heavenly in that one could wake up and gaze out the windows into nothingness until the sun punctured the clouds.

Plenty of traffic clogged the streets, but few tourists crowded the sidewalks. A horn sounded a few blocks away as brake lights sequentially poked through the fog.

His walk took him several blocks closer to the heart of downtown and then looped him back past Jake's Tavern. Ben glanced through windows as he passed by and met only his reflection in the dark glass. He got the feeling that Jason spent many lunch hours there enjoying some quiet time. The place didn't open until later in the afternoon, but Jason knew the owner and arranged to meet him for beers and hearty conversation at least three times a week. The place somehow fit Jason's style. It was unassuming, but steeped in its own kind of charm, never content to follow the latest local trends.

He turned a corner, walked another block, and then turned again. Gridlock strangled the street with the hotel. A loud motorcycle drowned out all other engine noise until Ben had left it far enough behind that it faded into the hum and drone. Some cars blasted loud music. Others showed the drivers as eerily peaceful as if they hadn't yet awakened for the day.

Rico rolled over when Ben pushed open the door carrying a pair of coffees from the lounge.

"What time is it?"

"Time to get your ass out of bed. I brought something to kick you in the pants."

Rico almost smiled. "For me? Such a gentleman. Did you dream about Rose or something?"

Rose's face always darted in and out of his dreams, and how could it not? More and more in the years since Montana, she'd inserted herself into his sleep as she grew closer in life. He wanted to spend the rest of his life with her, and little did he know that forever would include even the most private of dreams.

"We have a lot to do today," Ben said. "I have a meeting with a broker and we're going up the Five to visit a young woman in Carlsbad and then a guy in Vista."

"What are we going to drive?"

"I was wondering if I should let you pick out the rental car."

Naturally, Rico perked up. "Yeah, I was thinking we could get an Esc—"

"Nothing too flashy."

"You're going to make me drive around in a Fiesta like a single lady in her thirties, aren't you?"

Ben set the coffees on the table and picked up the handset to the phone so he could pass it to Rico should his friend ever get out of the bed.

Eventually, Rico rolled, pushed off the sheets, and set his feet on the floor. He sat on the edge of the bed, rubbed his face with both palms, and then stared through bloodshot eyes. "Gonna need to shower."

"Call the rental place first so we can get accommodated. Less time is wasted that way."

"You're a bastard, you know that?"

Ben and Rico called one another derogatory names occasionally, but true insults only flew when tempers flared. Rico's idea of name-calling often involved curse words '*en Español.*' The more English the insult, the less harm he intended.

"Better than a pungent late bloomer," Ben jabbed. It may have landed below the belt, but it bit with enough ferocity to launch Rico out of the bed and affix a scowl to his face.

Ben sipped his coffee and wrote down some questions to ask during his appointments and, in the case of the broker, how to arrive at asking without sounding either deranged or like a cop.

After at least fifteen minutes, Ben heard the shower turn off and Rico drop something on the floor of the tub. The man never bothered to style his hair. It always fell perfectly into place as though petrified of dryers and combs.

The phone rang while Rico whistled some Mexican folk tune as he dried himself. Ben picked it up and talked to the driver from the rental car place. After he hung up, he knocked on the bathroom door and told Rico he was going down to pick up the car.

Rico had opted for a silver Toyota Camry. San Diego probably had hundreds, if not thousands, of cars that looked just like it. They wouldn't stand out, per Ben's hope. Ben engaged in small talk with the driver and inspected the vehicle from the sidewalk before signing the necessary paperwork and putting down a credit card deposit. The man held Ben's card on his clipboard and copied the card number and the expiration date onto the commitment sheet.

"Enjoy the city," he said. "Make sure you hit up Balboa Park."

The park would never make its way to the itinerary. Ben and Rico were not here as tourists or leisure travelers, no matter how Rico wanted to pass the time. Maybe when the case was closed, they'd bum around on a beach or tour a museum, but for now, work seemed endless.

Ben gave the driver access to the garage in the back of the building and then headed back up to the hotel room. He needed to make one more call before he embarked on the journey. The first stop would be Perez's office, which turned out to be an old house adapted for commercial use about a dozen blocks from the park.

He'd set up the meeting with Russel Brandt for ten. His snooping at her office would take at least thirty minutes and driving time would probably take up much of the rest.

He shoved the door open. Rico stood at the table staring at the phone while sipping on his coffee. His look shifted from intense to something resembling placid concern. "What you going to do about Rose?"

Ben had spent part of his morning worrying about her and had decided that Rico had presented a useful idea for once. Ben strolled to the table and gathered his thoughts. The two of them sat down together and sipped their coffee before Ben dialed the number for the Reno police department. Looking it up would be impossible without alerting Rico's attackers that they were considering it. Just doing that would jeopardize this entire investigation. Luckily, Ben had dealt with Reno cops enough to have memorized the numbers for the main switchboard and some of detectives he trusted. He didn't bother with the main office number. Instead, he dialed Lieutenant Justin Teeger, who had helped him track down a tough Texan with tough luck a little more than a year ago. Lieutenant Teeger knew Dan Schoville, otherwise known as Alligator Dan, but kept their relationship on the QT so as to avoid the image of corruption.

"Good morning, Lieutenant," Ben said. "I don't have a lot of time, but I want to let you know about a case I've been working. There's a Miss Rose Kierstien visiting Reno this week and word has it she may be a target for some bad guys."

"Ben Carr," Teeger said. "Long time. But I'm afraid we don't operate on hunches."

"I believe you are familiar with a bookie-slash-pimp known as Alligator Dan."

"Never heard of him."

Ben wasn't about to deal with the bullshit. "You sure about that? You used him to set up a big drug bust in oh-nine. I'm sure you remember that."

"Say I did know him," Teeger argued. "What would that have to do with... what is she now, your fiancée?"

Ben cleared his throat and pictured her smiling face and her silvery hair. Such unparalleled beauty paired with the lowest of the ugly could be a lesson in disaster, but it turned out that Alligator Dan had several redeeming qualities. Ben never dealt with him personally and Alligator Dan didn't know anything about Ben, even though he'd overturned his table a few days ago.

"Not yet," Ben said, summoning the strength to finish the conversation. "And there is no connection between them. She's worried about her ex coming in to cause trouble, and I think there's some information out there that compromises her security."

"Is her ex an imminent threat?"

"He's in prison. But he knows people. And she thinks she met one of them at the lake the other day. I wouldn't bother you with a project like this because I know this isn't your area of expertise and because you only deal with viable threats. That's why I want you to get Alligator Dan to tail her. Think you can do that?"

"That's illegal."

"But you don't 'know' him. Make it off the books, trade him some dirty money, because he loves it. I can't believe I'm asking for this."

"The man's scum," Teeger said. "I won't be accountable if he assaults her."

"But you know things about him. Be creative. Threaten to blackmail him. Please do this for me. I love her."

"Jesus Christ, enough with the sob story. You'll owe me, big time."

"Yeah," Ben agreed. "I will."

They hung up the phone without saying goodbye. Ben brushed his fingers through his hair and squinted. So far, this day wasn't going as well as he would have hoped. The faster he found Ms. Perez, the faster he could get home to be with Rose, but Ben had a feeling Jason wasn't going to make his investigation easy. He could not shake the certainty that this situation would get far worse before it improved.

In some ways, the events of one day foreshadowed, or even triggered, the events of the next. Over the years, Ben had learned to plan for these unexpected wrinkles and to develop a contingency plan in case things went south. There were many ways to achieve the same ends, he knew, so abandoning well-laid plans had become part of the job.

Rico spent several minutes studying the GPS map on the Camry's console screen. Ben would have typed the address and listened to the directions, but Rico had spent years perfecting his own navigation technique and had whittled it down to a fine art. He knew where he was going and didn't need the "GPS lady" to confuse him into altering his route. The absolute worst thing Ben could do would be to argue with the method or present evidence suggesting it was wrong because that would make Rico angry.

He pulled out of the garage carefully and followed the busy streets to a direct route toward the Balboa Park area. He navigated the crowded streets with ease. If Ben had to drive, he'd be swearing at the GPS within three minutes.

Rows of small houses buffeted the streets in the older neighborhood near the park. Though a freeway cut it off from part of the neighborhood, huge trees shaded the bumpy streets, providing the area with a sort of antiquated charm that could lure a diverse range of buyers. Most houses did not appear to include garages and many residents resorted to on-street parking.

The office of Nina Perez lay nestled between a pair of two-story houses just off the corner where a traffic light dangled from an overhead wire. The house had been converted to an office decades ago. Its design was reminiscent of old Victorian homes but carried over design traits from mission-style architecture. The smaller windows had been cut out and replaced with large windows that would allow ample natural light to flood through its halls. Rico followed a narrow drive to the back of the building, where the yard had been paved into parking for ten cars. No cars sat idle in the lot, which made Ben wonder where Perez lived.

Rico chose a stall facing a small rear window and turned off the car. They scanned the area and made their way to a large wooden door with a 'Closed' sign hanging behind the glass. Ben peered through the windows and tried the door. Locked, of course.

Having used lock-picking skills several times over the course of his career, Ben wielded an array of tools that could open most locks and leave minimal to no damage. He examined the lock and the door frame and decided on a customized hook-device, which he inserted into the lock. He shifted it up and down while pressing against the door, and then turned the device clockwise. The lift and click of a tumbler told him that this tool would do the trick, but it didn't work on the first attempt. He turned the lock back to its original position, flicked the 'key' up and down again, and then twisted more vigorously. The tumbler lifted and clicked again, but a heavy thump allowed the lock to move more freely. Ben spun the handle and pushed the door open.

Rico would have had the nerve to look stunned if he hadn't seen Ben pick locks before. His only reaction was to shrug and peer up to the canopy, where a gap in the thinning fog revealed blue sky and allowed a spear of sunlight to bathe the area in warmth.

The first room had been between a kitchen and a dining room before, but now a small reception desk sat in front of a chamfered wall that concealed what remained of the kitchen. The dining room had been converted into a small conference room with a microphone system and a television screen that allowed wireless connection to a laptop. Another flat screen TV occupied the corner between two windows about ten degrees above eye level. Ben made his way to the reception desk first. Only a small vase of dead flowers and a mason jar containing around a dozen cheap pens rested atop the reception desk. In case this office would be considered a crime scene in the future, Ben took meticulous care not to disturb it. He'd leave behind fingerprints, but parts of hundreds of sets of prints likely cluttered many surfaces.

Rico wandered to a planter holding a fern palm behind the table in the corner of the room adjacent to the television. He exhaled, leaned down, and pulled what appeared to be a toothpick out of the soil.

Ben tiptoed around the end of the desk to the receptionist's chair, which faced an elegantly appointed workspace designed mostly for ergonomic comfort, but also to maximize efficiency. A small scanner/copier rested underneath the overhang within arm's reach of the keyboard. Ben pulled out the chair and sat down. A sticky pad rested about six inches behind the mouse, and a pen lay nearby. A note had been left for him.

Mr. Carr, I knew you'd come. Nina's desk has her most recent work and appointment log laid out.

Never one to accept the word of a note unconditionally, Ben hesitated and turned on the screen for the receptionist's computer. Her background appeared to be a sunset shot of a local beach with a wooden pier.

He navigated to an appointment book, where she had entered the names of callers and visitors so as to keep a running list of phone numbers. Little activity had taken place during the last month, especially in the last two weeks. One call had come in on May 11. The fact that it was listed indicated that someone had been in the office to log it.

The name associated with the number was Ivan Hargraves. Ben noted the name and number, which was prefixed with a Southern California area code. He scanned back weeks to before Nina would have disappeared. In that part of the spreadsheet, the calls and visits had been far more frequent. The last day with multiple contacts had around a dozen listed. Ben picked up the pen, tore off the receptionist's note, and crumpled it. He stuffed the wadded-up paper in his pocket and wrote down the date. Thirteen contacts had been entered, and four of those did not include phone numbers. A total of six had been in-person visits. Of the phone records, four of them had a checkmark under the column 'forwarded.' That meant April 23 had been the last time Nina Perez had occupied her own office.

Rico stood in front of the counter and stared at a smudge on the wall before clearing his throat and speaking. "What do you got, boss?"

"Phone records. Our subject was here on the twenty-third."

"Any surveillance tapes in there?"

Ben looked up. Rico glanced toward the end of the desk and shrugged. "Why would there be? I haven't seen any cameras."

"Me either," Rico said. "But there was one. Up there." He pointed to a spot in the center of the wall where a small square of cleaner, whiter paint occupied the space between four screw holes. It must have been a wireless camera. If it had been removed to cover up a crime, the cover-up would have been clumsy and left behind a set of fingerprints. He doubted whether any criminal would be that stupid.

Ben turned his head back to the screen and scanned up and down the list. One phone number jumped out at him immediately.

He easily identified the number as belonging to Jason Cruz. Jason had called the day *before* Nina disappeared.

"That son of a bitch," he breathed.

He scanned up the list. The number popped up over and over again, sometimes more than once a day. This wasn't the phone activity of a banker obsessed with a client and it didn't indicate they were doing business, either. Only romantic partners shared that many calls.

"Son of a *bitch.*"

Rico stared.

"Remind me to call that miserable, two-faced piece of scum the minute we get out of here."

Ben twisted the chair back and forth and then searched for files from the camera. True enough, he found a folder labeled 'surveillance,' but it was empty. All files, if they had ever been kept, had been deleted. A techno forensic scientist could find the tapes, if they'd ever existed in the first place. Ben didn't have that kind of expertise, but the mere presence of a folder seemed to indicate that the camera's drivers had been installed and set up.

"There was a camera," Ben said, "but no tapes. They've been deleted."

"Now we have that cleared up," Rico said. "Care to visit her office?"

Ben closed the programs on the computer and left the screen on should he need to return. He followed Rico toward the front of the house, where the shades had been drawn in front of the large windows. Two rooms stood behind a battery of closets and stairs. The door on the right belonged to Nina Perez, while the door on the left led to the office of an associate of hers.

The first thing Ben noticed was the portrait of Nina's five-year old son. He searched the desk and found a handwritten note that looked like a woman's penmanship. *Pick up Alex, dry cleaning, pizza & movie.*

Rico stared at the photograph for a long time. "Cute kid."

"His name is Alex," Ben said. Maybe we'll find some info in here on where she'd pick him up from. And where the young man is now."

"Did Jason tell you a kid is missing?"

"No, only his client."

He didn't bother to turn on her computer because more and more evidence turned up on her desk. Not only had Jason called her, but she'd called him. Only one note seemed to have anything to do with Jason and it didn't mention him by name. It referred to him as the "the new guy," and it directed her to pick up some wine.

"Just one outgoing call to him?" Ben said.

Rico laughed. "I got some property in Arizona I can sell you with cactuses and a beach."

"Only one note." Nothing indicated that she'd actually returned his call, but Nina Perez had always been a busy woman. She would have been out as much as or more often than she'd occupied her office, which suggested that, based on the call log, at least a dozen notes should have been left. Ben searched for them, but to no avail.

Instead, he settled on her appointment calendar. It had been booked solid until more than a week after April 23. Ben studied the hand-written names and decided that he wouldn't have to cross-check the call log for names and phone numbers. It seemed to be accurate enough, but one appointment had been erased. The showing was to take place on April 27. Had it been cancelled? He flipped the pages and found that some of the dates were simply crossed out. If she'd indicated cancellations by crossing out the appointment, why would she erase one of them, even if she didn't want the name and number printed?

Ben wasn't the first person to have poked around in this office.

He swallowed and placed the appointment book back on the desk. Checking all the names would have been tedious and time-consuming, and he had a meeting with a broker later.

Her office phone began to ring. The caller ID recognized the caller as Castro. Ben reached to pick it up, but hesitated as Rico shook his head.

Ignoring Rico's warning, Ben picked up the cordless receiver and spoke. "Nina Perez's office, how can I direct your call?"

The caller wasted no time. His voice sounded pragmatic and sterile. "I'd get out of there if I were you."

"What the... Who is this? Castro? What's your business with Ms. Perez?"

"I think we should listen to him," Rico said, pointing to a pair of small colored wires protruding from the file drawer in Nina's desk.

"What the hell?"

Ben didn't bother to cover his tracks. The police would be all over this scene in a matter of minutes, probably, and most of the evidence of his snooping would be wiped out.

He swore as he and Rico sprinted for the exit. Rico started the car, pulled out of the parking spot, and squealed the tires on the pavement. The end of the drive was marked by a large bump, which Rico hit full speed, sending the car thrashing in a briefly turbulent moment of agony. A loud crunch pushed vibrations through the undercarriage of the car. Rico tore away down the street at more than double the speed limit.

"Don't draw attention," Ben warned.

"Too late now."

Ben watched the rearview mirror for smoke and a blossom of flame, but it never materialized. "It was cased," Ben shouted. "They're onto us."

"Who?"

"I don't know, but I'm going to find out. Shit!"

Rico slowed the car to a little over the limit and wound his way through the neighborhood. Downtown was only a few minutes away so he would be on time for his visit to Brandt.

Confusion poured through him, but Ben clung to one fact that fractured every sense of reality his mind had constructed during the last two days. Jason had to have been somehow involved. So why, then, had he called Ben in the first place? Did he think he'd be able to hide his meddling? Or was his romantic entanglement an act meant to divert her from the truth that she was being played? At this point, more questions pushed to the front of his mind than he could answer. Still, only one thing mattered. Jason was a liar.

Secondary Elite

May 19, 2011

10:05

THE LOBBY OF HUTCHINSON Capital Management Services didn't attempt to conceal the fact that the firm primarily dealt with super-wealthy entrepreneurs and agricultural kingpins. Hutchinson occupied floors seventeen through nineteen of an architecturally impressive skyscraper in downtown San Diego. Russel Brandt probably had an ocean view in his office specifically appointed to appeal to the rich.

Ben liked to refer to these people as 'the other rich,' due to the fact that most were self-made millionaires and billionaires, rather than the prime cut of old-money tyrants with East Coast empires. They perhaps didn't seem as important, but they still controlled much more wealth than Ben could imagine.

This would be his most difficult acting job yet. He slicked back his hair and put on an expensive-looking suit in a first-floor public restroom. He didn't bother with the apparel since the optics were the most important part of this meeting. Ben had to look rich, but reasonable and, most importantly, sincere. If he revealed a lack of any of these qualities, Brandt wouldn't take him seriously and the meeting would be fruitless.

Leaning back and pretending to read a copy of Forbes, Ben glanced up at a gentleman who appeared to be in his 60s.

Visual clues may be important, but this man looked relaxed, which helped Ben to settle into his role. The coffee table sat neatly squared between luxurious, leather-clad couches. The table resembled an antique, with dark-colored polished wood carved into an oriental-themed lattice of intersecting arcs and straight lines. A pane of seeded glass served as the tabletop. A stack of magazines for the rich had been flung strategically into the center of the table as if to subconsciously endorse relaxation without looking too disorganized.

The carpet stretched between intermittently spaced squares of marble tile centered between the walls. Each square transitioned back to carpet with thin, brass-toned separators. Hutchinson's logo protruded from the wall behind reception, backlit with a beautiful blue glow. The receptionist was a cute twenty-something with hair pulled into a neat ponytail, black-rimmed glasses, and an expensive business suit. A Bluetooth headset stretched between her ears, but she'd moved the microphone away from her face.

She looked up when she called Ben's fake name. "Mr. Clark? Mr. Brandt will see you now."

Ben stood up, straightened his jacket, grabbed his briefcase, and strolled to the end of the hall. Brandt's office lay at the end of the corridor, punctuated by a heavy, stained-wood door with a mullioned window made of faux glass. Black lettering attached to the glass read *Russel J. Brandt, MBA*. He tapped on the window and entered.

Brandt spun his chair around and faced Ben. He didn't look anything like Ben had pictured from their phone call. A tuft of neatly trimmed charcoal hair topped his scalp and a broad, graying goatee dotted his chin. He had his fingers laced behind his head as he leaned back in the chair. He nodded at a leather business chair across from him and waited for Ben to sit down.

"What can I do for you today, Mr. Clark?"

"I'm interested in opening an account, but I want to review my options first," Ben said.

Mr. Brandt hesitated, unlaced his fingers, and leaned forward. "Well," he started, reaching into his pencil drawer for a white sheet of paper, "you're in luck, because I can tailor-make a plan that will suit your personality. Do you own a business?"

"You could say that," Ben said, attaching a false frown to his face. "Got some acreage outside of town on the other side of the mountains, toward El Centro. Heads of cattle, pretty views. It's called JH Ranch, you ever hear of it?"

He shook his head. "We're tied to JH Feed and Fertilizer Company out of Arizona, headquartered in Tempe."

"What's JH stand for?"

Ben cleared his throat and thought fast. "Jamison Howard. We're sort of still exploring an internet presence at this time. I'm a fourth-generation owner."

Mr. Brandt chuckled and scribbled something on the paper. "Four generations, and you're still not on the web?"

"Old habits die hard," Ben said. Making it up as he went along injected him with an unexpected sense of invigoration. Suppressing the urge to smile became more difficult with every word. "I'm the youngest owner in the company's history. 'Bout time I conceded that everything's going digital. You can either catch up or be left behind."

He swiveled his chair from side to side. "What kind of investments do you hold, and through whom?"

"Mostly small-time commercial stuff, no holdings or shell companies or anything like that. Just an honest-to-god LLC."

The man nodded and glanced up from the paper. "Well, at least you've taken one step up."

"Don't get me wrong," Ben said. "We don't want to get too big for our britches, as the saying goes. And we're not looking at going national, either."

"Where does your capital come from?"

"Small chain of banks in Arizona," Ben said, shrugging and peering out at the harbor seventeen floors down. He'd live for sailing around the harbor and maybe even off the coast a ways, if only this job afforded him the time to do so. If Rose were here, she'd make sure they made time after Ben's investigation wrapped up.

The clock was ticking. He needed to shift this conversation to more personal realms before it got out of hand. Ben scanned the desk and rested his eyes on a small photograph of a boy. Ben recognized the face instantly.

"Pardon, if I may. I don't mean to interrupt, but the way I see it, there's nothing wrong with forming sort of a personal rapport with the man you wish to handle your investment." Ben pinched himself on the leg as a reminder to speak in simpler sentences, so as to not blow his cover.

"Of course," Brandt said. He dropped the pen, leaned back, and laced his fingers behind his head. A smile parted his lips.

"Little tyke at home?"

"Yeah. Great kid. Says he wants to be a surgeon when he grows up. Do you believe that?"

"How old?"

"He's five. He runs around the house hopped up on sugar while my caretaker guards the property."

"Full-time mom?"

"Nah," Brandt said. "His mother is off doing her real estate thing, but she gets to visit three, four times a week. You know, she insisted on the name Alejandro, but we call him Alex for short."

Another idea pushed its way to the front of Ben's mind. "Is she from Mexico?"

"Her grandmother was a Mexican immigrant with her husband, and they had Nina's father after they came to America."

Mr. Brandt looked more and more innocent as the meeting went along, but with one key omission. If Nina visited their son three or four times a week, he had to have known by now that she was missing, yet he hadn't mentioned it. And he didn't show any signs of uneasiness.

"So, Nina," Ben pondered. "You're divorced?"

"A few years ago," Mr. Brandt verified.

"Sucks, especially for the kid," Ben said.

"Yeah. You know, he was just a baby at the time, so he doesn't really know any better," Mr. Brandt explained. "And you try not to teach them that kind of crap when they're so young. Sometimes they ask you why mom doesn't live with you, and you have to come up with some BS."

"I know how that is," Ben lied. "On my second wife now, but I only got one kid."

"How old?"

"Oh, he's grown now, and I haven't seen him in a few years. I think he moved out to Phoenix to be a hotshot lawyer with his girlfriend, or at least that's what my ex tells me. But at least it's lucky your Alex gets to see his mom sometimes. Has she been by this week already?"

"How would I know? She doesn't exactly tell me when she's going to drop by and sometimes my caretaker mentions it. More often Alex tells me before bed."

"I bet he misses her a little more each day she doesn't visit," Ben mused. "Hell, I still miss my son. But it's like that, I guess."

He chuckled. "Isn't that the truth?"

"But I'm guessing Alex talks to you a lot. Does he tell you he misses her?"

Mr. Brandt shrugged. "Maybe sometimes. I think he internalizes it more, which is what kids tend to do, I've been told. They don't always tell you exactly what they're thinking, even when you ask them."

Ben needed to press harder because Brandt wasn't going to admit that Nina was missing. He either had to press him into denying it or assume that he didn't know.

"Yeah, but kids surprise us sometimes. Once my son came to me while his mother was at a funeral in Minnesota for two weeks. He said he missed his mom and hoped she was happy. And he was old enough to realize what it all meant. I mean, you go a week, two weeks, a month, and pretty soon they can't really hide it anymore."

"Not all kids are the same," Mr. Brandt said, "but you know, I'm not too worried about that. Life is good for Alex."

"Does your caretaker watch him all day, or is he in medical school already?" Ben joked.

"No." He shook his head, glanced at the photograph, and then stared down at the paper.

Finally, some body language suggested that he knew something. Ben had to reach out and break it.

"No, I put him in a preschool by the ocean out in La Jolla. They take the kids to the beach sometimes and let them play in the sand. Alex loves it. And he's got some friends."

Ben frowned and glanced out toward the harbor. "Must be tough on Nina."

"It's tough on all three of us," Mr. Brandt yielded. He picked up his pen, clicked it three times, and then spun toward his computer screen as if to completely shut himself off from the conversation.

"And I bet he misses you, too until you get home," Ben pushed.

Mr. Brandt didn't respond. Instead, a frown etched deeper lines into his face and his eyes grew darker. He didn't glance at Ben. Instead, he moved the mouse and punched a few buttons on the keyboard. A cascade of emotion had begun to pour out of him, but Ben didn't need any more. The heavy thumps on the desk were not the keystrokes of rage or aggression, but a grief so deep that his muscles tightened.

"I'm sorry," Ben said. "I don't want to pry. So about that investment—"

"Get out," Mr. Brandt said quietly. Recognizing his abruptness, he shifted in his seat and falsified a plaintive expression. "Yeah, it looks like I have another meeting in five minutes."

"Of course."

"Give me a call next week and we can talk logistics."

"Look, if I offended you..."

Mr. Brandt straightened his chair, forced his face into relaxing, and continued to stare at the screen. "No, you're fine. I look forward to doing business with you, Mr. Clark. Have a good day."

Ben stood up and straightened his tie. He considered offering more than a simple nod, but decided that Mr. Brandt was not in the mood. He'd clearly touched a nerve, and that communicated everything that Ben needed to know. His answers and body language confirmed enough. He knew about it, but he was innocent.

THE DRIVE TO CARLSBAD didn't take as long as expected, as the traffic was relatively light, and Rico managed to keep pace at a comfortable cruise without major slowdowns. Ben relayed what Brandt told him and recounted his body language, which Rico seemed halfway interested in.

"You don't think your *amigo* contacted him beforehand?"

"It's possible," Ben said. "But doubtful."

"Why?"

Ben shrugged and stared at the bumper of the car in front of them, as if momentarily transfixed. Montana. "Well... if it were you... would you talk to your lover's ex-husband?"

Without looking committed, Rico nodded in agreement. Instead of commenting, he let his eyes dart back and forth from the freeway to the dashboard as if he were trying to construct a legitimate argument that could have explained everything.

Ben used the silence to close his eyes. Sometimes Montana felt so distant and surreal, like the remnant of an ancient dream flinging bits of the apparition back at him. Other times, the nightmare seemed so fresh and disturbing that it shook his nerves. The drums... the backhoe... the meetings with crazy business owners, one of whom had tried to shoot Ben... everything wrought agony. The only balance came from Rose, whom he'd also met in Montana.

She was the reason it all took place, Ben told himself. He never believed in destiny, but perhaps all things did transpire for reasons. Rather than longing, he hoped she was safe. Would Alligator Dan be tailing her by now?

"So we got some time," Rico said. "Should we go to the beach?"

"We should get some lunch."

"*Sí.* You paying?"

Ben laughed. "Sure, we'll just put it on my credit card like every other expense this trip. At least we can deduct it."

"And the miles."

Another chuckle escaped his lips. "Only about five million more and I can fly to Sacramento."

"Probably would take longer than driving," Rico assumed.

Ben didn't respond. He flexed his muscles and prepared mentally for the conversation with Ms. Crestwell.

Without suggestion, Rico rolled up to a fast-food establishment and got out of the car. Ben hesitated but followed him. He'd never eaten at this place and hoped the food was good. The meal lasted about thirty minutes, during which Rico told jokes about past acquaintances while chewing. Ben didn't find any of it funny—in fact some of it made him cringe—but attempted to toss in a few labored chuckles to save face.

Rico didn't seem to notice. He launched headlong into story after story without so much as allowing Ben a moment to gasp. Rico excelled at telling stories. What was it Rose had told him after they'd moved to Tahoe? *You can't live without food and water, but stories make you* live.

After lunch, Rico allowed the GPS lady to locate Eva Crestwell's house, memorized the map, and shut her down. The drive took a little less than ten minutes. Rico jumped back on the freeway to advance to the next exit.

Eva's home, located a little over a mile from the beach, consisted of a slanted roof, a set of stairs, a carport, and a tiny patch of grass shaded by junipers and oaks. Tall palms a block away swayed in the breeze and reflected sunlight.

The townhouse was sandwiched between two other units fronting a narrow drive. Rico pulled into the driveway behind a yellow Subaru wagon, which had long ago begun to show signs of wear.

The small strip of lawn between two carports sprung up a thick tuft of grass in dire need of maintenance. Eva either wasn't in charge of the maintenance or had neglected it for weeks. A dog's leash lay abandoned with part of its chain resting on the concrete beneath the neighbor's carport.

Ben attached a solid veneer of business to his face and slipped into the notch housing the front door. He pounded on the door and waited for what felt like thirty seconds. She opened the door a crack and peered out, her expression uncertain.

"I'm Ben Carr. We spoke on the phone. This is my associate, Rico. Can we come in?"

She smiled. "Oh, sure. I almost forgot. I was going to go walk my neighbor's dog by the beach in a few minutes. They're out on vacation."

Eva opened the door and led them through the entryway, past a narrow kitchen, and into a large living room. She kicked a pair of sandals away and closed a closet door on the way. When she turned to face them, Rico eyed her carefully. A colorful shirt highlighted her narrow waist and arms while denim jeans stretched to her ankles. Her face was soft and tan, and blonde curls cascaded to her shoulders and down her back. She pulled out a stool from the breakfast bar and invited Ben and Rico to sit on her couch, which was so comfortable that Ben didn't think he'd be able to get up.

"Forgive the mess," she said, glancing at a stack of books and papers. "I need to get out more."

"You make the commute to San Diego every day from here? Talk about long hours in the car."

"I usually carpool with Davis. He drives in from Vista and picks me up on the way. I think you'll... I mean I assume you're going to talk to him, too... I think you'll like him. I do."

"You're dating?"

"Not really," she said. "He supposedly has some girlfriend hanging on his shoulder all the time. Half the time, he seems annoyed, the other half he dotes on her. It's pretty cute, really."

She shifted and relaxed her shoulders while draping a strand of hair behind her ear. "Of course, I haven't made it into the office recently. I've had to take a part time job just so I don't get kicked out of here."

"But you have made it into the office recently," Ben stated. "Twice."

Her laugh seemed uncomfortable. "Yeah, I guess so."

"You left the note and took a call."

"I was doing some housekeeping, like Nina was paying me for. I guess I've been hoping she'll just come back like nothing ever happened and I can keep on working."

Ben sighed. "Do you like your boss?"

"Nina's wonderful. She treats me like a friend every day and makes me feel great about working for her. I couldn't ask for a better boss."

"So you must talk to her frequently about... things... relationships."

A coy smile creased her lips, but she let it dissipate in an instant. "Maybe sometimes."

"Was she seeing anyone?"

She shifted on the chair, backed toward the countertop, and stared out the sliding glass door, where a small bird was clinging to a low branch on a large tree. "I think so, yes. I think he was a banker or something, which doesn't really surprise me. Nina's attracted to guys like that."

Ben attempted a warm smile, which must have failed miserably. Instead, he pushed and exerted perhaps too much pressure. "She didn't tell you his name, did she?"

Eva swallowed. "No. But I think I overheard her calling him Jason."

"How long had she been seeing him?"

She lowered her eyebrows and shook her head. "Um, maybe two months? I don't really know how they met. I just remember her coming into the office happier than usual and he'd start calling her."

I'd love to hear it, Ben thought. He'd have to get that answer from Jason himself, at such time as he could confront him about it over a beer. The thought of it made Ben's face droop into an ominous stare, which probably freaked Eva out.

She averted eye contact more and more as the encounter wore on.

"She keeps her own books," Ben said. "Doesn't she trust you?"

"I take the calls, sit at the desk, do accounting and other documentation, which keeps me busy. She likes to maintain her own schedule, like she's always done. She feels more connected with her clients that way."

"Any unusual clients the last couple of months? People you don't expect to be buying an expensive house? I noticed she had an appointment on her calendar erased."

"When she cancels an appointment, she does that." Eva folded her hands in her lap and rested one foot on the lower bar of the stool.

"She usually just crosses them out, though," Ben countered.

"I don't know about that. She doesn't usually show me how she keeps her schedule. Maybe she just felt like erasing it instead of crossing it out."

Ben smiled and let his gaze fall to her feet, which she crossed beneath her. "That's not really the point, though. Do you know about any strange appointments?"

"Come to think of it," Eva said, tilting her face toward the ceiling, "there was a guy who came in one time. He spoke perfect English, but he looked Latino. I hate to stereotype, but he seemed interested in a house out in La Jolla."

"Nina's son lives in La Jolla," Ben said. "Did she make that connection?"

"I don't know if it registered at first," she said leveling her eyes once again. She glanced out the window and then at the television on the wall. "But after he'd called a couple of times, she seemed to get pretty suspicious."

"Do you remember a name?"

"Their conversations were mostly in Spanish. Nina is fluent and it makes her clients feel more comfortable if she can communicate to them the way they can best understand."

"Nothing?"

"I do remember something, but I assumed they were talking about Cuba, like he grew up there."

"Castro?"

Her eyes widened and she nodded. Her gaze fell on Ben for one tragic moment where her memory collided with the reality of the present. A tear splashed onto her cheek. "Maybe I should have warned her."

"I think it's too soon to guess that this Castro is the bad guy," Ben said.

"But you know about him, which means you're investigating..."

"I just found out about him while I was at Nina's office. I have to do some digging still to find out who he is."

"I hope you find him," she said.

"Of course I will. But I think I should let you take that dog for a walk. Get out and enjoy the fresh air and the sunshine. In the meantime, try not to worry. I'm an expert."

Rico cleared his throat and slid to the edge of the couch. "One more question: There was a camera above your desk. Did it tape?"

"Yes. I'll show you the files if you want to meet me there." Eva furrowed her eyebrows and looked away.

"Was the camera there the last time you went into the office?"

She looked into his eyes for long enough to ascertain that the question shocked her. "Of course it was. I don't always look at it, but it's one of those things you'd notice if it were gone. Who stole it?"

"That's what we have to find out next," Ben said.

"But the tapes—"

Ben shook his head. "They're missing, too."

"Shit."

"Not your fault," Ben said, all at once warmly. He stood up and paced toward her as if to comfort her, but she recoiled when he neared her. Fear drove spikes into her expression. It gripped her with striking power and so suddenly that it caused an icy chill to shoot up his back.

Without warning, she swore again, this time louder. She covered her face, lowered her chin, and attempted to catch the tears that dripped into her lap. What could have caused this sudden repulsion and reaction? Ben attempted to ponder without looking callous and predatory, but it only made her back further away.

"I think we'll be going," Ben said. "Sorry I upset you. I'm just trying to find your boss."

Rico followed Ben to the door. Together, they stepped out into the sun. Agony poured through Ben's heart. He walked slowly, as if his muscles had suddenly turned to gelatin.

"I don't think that went well," Rico said.

"That *bitch!*" The muffled sound of Eva's screams clawed at Ben's conscience as if to tear the life out of him and coil up his entrails like a ball of twine.

"*Qué?*" Rico said.

"I don't know," Ben said. He could offer no more explanation and he felt as though his voice had been wiped out by a sudden attack of guilt. Eva hid something, but what?

Ben grimaced when he buckled the seatbelt and before he knew it his eyes sealed themselves shut. The color of blood seeped into a spiraling vortex of kaleidoscopic terror the likes of which Ben had never witnessed. The drums from Montana pattered away in his heart. *Ba dump bum, PAT!* The agony creased his soul until there was nothing left inside from which to gather emotion and reason. Ben was a lost vessel without a mooring.

Old Wounds

May 19, 2011

14:30

MILKY CIRRUS CLOUDS RAKED at the sky on the western horizon. Carson City and Reno differed in so many ways that Rose found it difficult at times to believe that they lay only 35 miles apart. Reno offered high stakes gambling in addition to slot machines and all manner of nightlife, while Carson City lacked the same amenities. The city came to life at sunset, when fluorescent ribbons flared up and flashed the night away with glitter.

Rose relaxed on an abandoned bus bench a block away from the city's main drag. Contrary to Ben's advice, she had stopped at his office in Carson. He sounded more and more agitated during every conversation and stress had begun to leak into his voice. Had his investigation, whatever it entailed, grown so serious so quickly? Why?

For answers, she'd resorted to his office. She'd found a bottle of wine, two plane tickets, and a note from Jason. She'd also discovered the photograph of a young man with long, ashen-brown hair and blue eyes. His oval-shaped face seemed to contradict the smile he displayed. His eyes hid so much more than a smile could reveal. Rose had explored this common theme in several of her novels.

She had always used the mystery and intrigue of everyday life to define character flaws, but she also used it as an excuse to get to the center of stories too restricted for average citizens. Claiming to be a reporter from the *Washington Post* came with benefits. It could easily be proven false, but no one had ever bothered to check into her credentials. Freedom of Information Act requests were rarely challenged.

What was it with this young man in particular? She reached down to her bag, withdrew the envelope, and then unsheathed the photograph to study it. Her character development methods were to present faces, explore deeper traits, and let the characters reveal themselves.

The young man's eyes seemed oddly disconnected, as if rife with a certainty that something wasn't going according to plan. Somewhere behind the camera, distraction menaced, but instead of blatantly gazing, his stare had turned blank. The distraction didn't represent fun or excitement or intrigue. Instead, it suggested solitude, deceit, and an abhorrent scent of avowed anguish.

His hair curled and his cheeks flushed. How did he try to fit in with his surroundings? Did he adapt, or did he take on the role of a disruptor? She settled on the latter. At that age, standing out would have been deemed more important than fitting in. The posture of his shoulders communicated a sheepish, but grim fortitude—hesitant, but unyielding.

The note from Jason told a different story. Rose excelled at chipping away the constraints of language to reveal the emotion within the words. Often, notes said one thing and meant something entirely different.

Jason had been transparent in that gifts would have made the best retainer fee. But the meaning behind the photograph of the man was still clouded. She slipped the photograph back into the envelope and considered the letter by remembering Jason's words.

The letter implied that the gentleman in the photograph represented a person of interest. Ben had been investigating him, but why would he turn to Jason for help when he had contacts with Reno and Carson law enforcement officers? He hadn't said much about his situation in Reno, but somehow doubted whether the young man had been involved. Unless he roamed on Jason's turf. If that was the case, Ben had another reason to travel to San Diego.

It was time to use her skills to get to the truth. She had never ditched the DC area code, which had been a calculated decision. When she suggested making the switch to a California number, Ben urged her not to for reasons of strategy. Her fictitious job at the *Post* would come in handy yet again, but she needed to construct an angle of national intrigue that the San Diego police would not see coming. Constructing that story would take some planning, and naming other law enforcement agencies wouldn't work because they would crosscheck her and discredit her as some screwball whistleblower or worse.

Referencing celebrities probably wouldn't work in Southern California, either. That left world leaders and large, organized networks. She could possibly paint him as a source for the NRA crowd pursued for his outrageous opinion on gun rights. But first, she needed a name—a real one, because they would check his social media footprint to determine whether Rose was blowing smoke.

Ben could divulge that information and she knew how to get it out of him. The best way of doing that had always been to paint him into a corner and give him no other alternative. However, it sounded like he had already backed into a corner in San Diego, so this idea would require careful consideration.

Rose leaned back on the bench and stared west, where the hotels on Virginia Street poked at the sky. She placed the folder back in her bag and zipped it shut. Her nerves jolted her with a sudden realization that someone was watching her. She glanced around at her surroundings, across the street, in the windows of the buildings, and even behind her. The few pedestrians that wandered this part of town kept to themselves, but one in particular did not. He leaned against the side wall of a warehouse building and puffed on his cigarette. Though he faced the adjacent street on the opposite corner, he carefully glanced at her from time to time. When he saw that she noticed him, he pretended not to pay attention and to jawbone with someone standing with him. Rose could not see another person but assumed that he or she lurked in the shadows. How had they tracked her to Reno?

Panic swelled within her veins. This would warrant another conversation with Ben, during which he'd attempt to assuage her fears and provide a strict linearity, which she strived for. In that regard, Ben was perfect for her, but he retained many mysteries. His entire life had been a fabrication. She allowed him to shroud himself in secret because it helped provide her comfort.

The man stepped away from the building a few steps, spat on the sidewalk, and then flicked his cigarette into the street. He turned to glance at her one more time and she stared back, intent to take in every detail.

The stranger was a regular Reno scoundrel. He looked like a gangster. Silver chains adorned his neck. He wore a blue silk shirt with the top two buttons opened to reveal part of a hairy chest. A mole dotted his cheek and he had meticulously slicked back his hair. A hint of a tattoo jutted out from beneath the cuff on his shirt. He wore denim jeans and what looked like obnoxious leather boots. Exactly the type of lowlife Allen would associate with.

She could confront him but decided to back off. She stood and walked two blocks south without looking back in case he was tailing her. Without thinking, she darted into an alley and hid behind a trash can. Her peripheral vision didn't reveal anyone when she turned the corner, but she couldn't be certain. She could only wait it out.

After a few moments, she reasoned that this didn't make a good hiding place. This cut-off location offered too few escape routes should the stranger wish to assail her. Thinking quickly, she stared up the blank walls of the two-story buildings. A stack of pallets stood directly below a ladder meant to access the roof of the building against which the dumpster rested. She waited.

The stranger passed by without glancing into the alley. The moment he disappeared from view, she made her decision. At her age, climbing the steel ladder would not prove an easy task. Instead, it presented considerable danger, but the promise of refuge outweighed the threat.

Silently, she slung her bag over her shoulder and climbed. The rooftop offered a rare vantage point from which she could witness the street below. If the stranger looked up, she could simply step away from the edge or duck behind the parapet and retain her cover.

He was a landmine, but she bit her lip and pressed on. They say, "The truth shall set you free," and Rose intended to pursue the truth with such ferocity that she could not be denied. Not only did she have to resort to her old cover as a *Washington Post* reporter, but she had to channel Carrie, the young crime scene investigator from her novels. Carrie was both smooth and tough, graceful in the art being a merciless pursuer of justice. She could use both intimidation and serenity to get to the heart of a mystery. Now, Rose had to adopt the same tactics.

14:45

DAVIS WILSON RENTED AN apartment at the base of a steep hill near the border of Oceanside and Vista. The building rose four stories and stood in a neighborhood of mostly newer construction. Parking on the ground floor extended partially below the building so as to offer better density and covered parking for more upscale tenants. Rico parked the car in the sun about ten feet from the shadow of a tall eucalyptus tree.

"How *loco* is this gonna be?" Rico said.

Ben said nothing and stared at the densely forested hillside before sighing and swinging open the door. He still could not wrap his mind around what happened at Eva's place. Was she referring to Nina when she screamed? Ben stepped toward the end of the car and, shielding his eyes from the bright sun, muttered, "Only one way to find out."

"Guy with two last names in real estate. You couldn't pay to make this stuff up."

The car occupied a stall close to the corner of the parking lot. The hike wouldn't take long, but Davis lived on the third floor, which meant lots of stairs. Rico would begrudgingly climb and complain with every step.

When they stepped into the shadow, the cruel realities of apartment living battered Ben from all sides. A dog in a nearby first-floor unit howled and yapped. The television or stereo in another unit thumped, and a couple on the second floor engaged in a fight about... cookies?

Rico laughed between fits of panting. By the time they reached the third floor, his heavy breathing had mutated into an awful wheezing that sounded like a remote-control toy with old batteries. "Jesús," he gasped.

"The stairs are a real killer," Ben commented.

The apartment jutted off the right side of a long, carpeted corridor illuminated by perfectly spaced wall fixtures that lent a somehow industrial glow. No decorations cluttered the walls. Each door sat inset about two feet from the corridor wall. Ben didn't hesitate before he knocked on Davis's door.

After a few seconds, a skinny girl in a halter top and tight cut-off shorts swung open the door and frowned.

"I'm looking for Davis Wilson," Ben said.

She flung the door open violently and spun around without inviting them in. Davis leaned back on the couch and rested his bald head on the cushioning.

"Can we come in?"

"Yeah, yeah," Davis said, waving his hand in the air. The girl half-danced back to the couch and collapsed partially on the young man's lap. Her curly hair slapped him in the face, which allowed him a moment to look mildly annoyed. He kissed her on the back of the neck and flung his arms around her so as to look halfway interested.

Ben and Rico settled in twin recliners opposite the couch. Still breathing heavily, Rico stared at the girl's tanned legs. A small, heart-shaped tattoo flexed with her skin near her left ankle.

"Who are you guys?" he asked.

"Cops," the girl said.

"Look, I don't know what happened to Nina. I told that to the other guys two, three weeks ago."

Ben and Rico gaped at each other. Ben allowed his jaw to slacken and tilted his head sideways ever so slightly to alter his look of confusion.

"Yeah, didn't they tell you they sent a couple of badges out here?"

"Were they San Diego PD?"

Davis nodded. "Sure were. The one guy had some crazy hairdo I thought only rock stars were allowed to have, but they were pretty polite."

A red sore around what looked like a deep cut healed on his forearm. Ben stared at it as if to question its origin and the story behind it. Judging from the skin coloration, he'd celebrated that mark for up to two years. "Did they show their badges?"

"Of course. Looked legit."

Rico coughed and sat forward. "Easy to fake a badge, *señor*. They sell those at toy stores, or at least they used to back when you could still get slivers playing."

"How would I know? I work a desk job billing clients, pushing paperwork, sweeping the floor, and making coffee."

"Have you been to the office lately?"

"I kept going for a few days after Nina stopped showing up. Eva and I tried to call her on her cellphone two dozen times, probably."

"Did either of you report her missing?" Ben said, prying. He stared at a pair of colorful surfboards pinned to the wall on either side of the television. One of the boards sported the logo of a surfing products manufacturer. He squinted to make out the words. Sex Wax?

"I called, they said they were looking into it. Say, weren't you guys supposed to introduce yourselves, show me your badges?"

Rico laughed. Ben scratched his chin and adjusted in the chair. "I'm Benjamin Carr, private investigator, and this is my driver—assistant, Rico."

"Son of a bitch, that right?" He leaned forward and the girl shifted off his lap but still clutched him with white-knuckled fists.

Rico gazed at her legs as she crossed them, and she tossed her hair behind her head as if doing something made her seem like part of the conversation. Ben assumed her to be the type of woman who clings to her man out of emotional necessity turned habitual embrace. She would interject herself into the conversation at some point to appear as though she had some relevant input. Years ago, the IT guys at the 'law' office were explaining code language to one another over lunch using the same sort of lingo that seemed natural to them. Another lawyer had walked in, heard the conversation, and spouted off some rudimentary computer language to appear impressive. The IT guys had cut off their conversation and stared at him for five seconds.

"Did you know Nina was seeing someone?"

"I guessed at it," Davis said, shifting his eyes up and to the right, "but she never really talked to me about that stuff. She and Eva were closer, always going out to lunch and stuff. You should ask her the same question." He stopped abruptly and exchanged glances with Ben and Rico. "But you already did."

"Did you ever meet him?"

"Nope. He never came in, just called."

"Terrible excuse for a boyfriend," the girl said, clutching Davis even tighter. He darted his eyes toward the surfboard and raised his hand to his chin.

"Eva tells us she had some caller who she spoke to in Spanish. Do you know what she's talking about?"

"Client," Davis said. "I speak okay Spanish, but I think he seemed to have a pretty good attitude about the whole thing. He even had kids."

"But Nina deals almost exclusively in high-dollar properties," Ben explained. "Did he seem like the disposable cash sort of client to you?"

"I don't make generalizations like that," Davis said.

"His name was Castro?"

"Yeah, I kind of suspect that's sort of a nickname. It used to be a pretty common surname I guess, but doesn't it have kind of a bad connotation now?"

Rico halfway nodded but lowered his eyes. "Can you hear dialects?"

"It was Mexican for sure."

Rico pressed. "East coast? West coast? Yucatan, Guadalajara, DF?"

His eyes darted back and forth. The girl loosened her grip on his waist and rested her hand on his thigh. She carefully slid down the couch and rested her head on his shoulder. "No idea."

"Did he ever mention anything about Mexico?"

"Not that I know of."

"Did he ever bring in a friend?"

He shook his head, then widened his eyes and flung his index finger back and forth as if he just remembered an important piece of information. "But he was on the phone with someone once. Nina had gone into her office to look at some listings and he got a call on his cellphone. I kind of overheard the conversation. He looked annoyed and hurried through his speech, I assumed because he didn't want to inconvenience Nina. Talked about a house he was interested in, I think La Jolla. Then he talked about his son, about how he had to pick him up from daycare."

Ben narrowed his eyes. "Did this Castro mention his son's name?"

"I don't remember, bad with names."

"I know that's right," the girl said flatly, as if bored with the conversation. "Remember you didn't memorize my name until I moved in?"

"Of course I did, Sweetcheeks. It's a... it's a game."

"During the few days you stuck around after the last time you saw Nina, did Mr. Castro call again?" Ben shot the question out faster than he could reason. Now he had more questions he'd like to ask Eva.

"Yeah, once, I think. Eva answered the phone."

"How did you know it was him?"

"She called him by name."

Ben recalled the conversation with Eva and mentally went through the catalog of her answers. He hadn't jotted down notes pertaining to the conversation yet, but she never said she talked to Castro on the phone.

"You're sure?"

"Sure as I'm sitting here."

Ben hesitated and considered asking him another question. He doubted the relevance, so he kept it squarely in the back of his mind. The girl patted Davis on the leg, issued a sigh, and closed her eyes.

Gazing at her, Rico leaned back and then pretended interest in the surfboards.

"Like them?" Davis asked.

Rico nodded.

"Won them in a competition at O-side Harbor. They get some great waves there. It's popular with everyone from newbies to pros."

Ben stared at the girl, grunted, and stood up. "I think I have everything I need for now. Can I call you should I have any follow-up questions?"

"Better than driving out here."

"This is a pretty fast-paced case, and I'm very motivated to find Nina. I won't stop until I do."

"I'll be here. You mind leaving your name so I know who's calling?"

Before Ben could nod, he reached to the end table with his right hand and picked up a small notepad and a pen. Ben grabbed them and scribbled the hotel number. "It might be a digit or two off. I'd call from a hotel."

"You really ought to get with the century and get a cellphone," Davis said. "I get the appeal to look old-school, you know. The way I see it, you lose some credibility calling out of hotel rooms."

Ben rolled his eyes while Davis eyed Rico. "Thanks for the tip."

"You drive?"

Ben stared at him and nodded.

"In the garage, cherry-red Camaro Z28. I restored it myself."

Rico smiled and peeled his eyes off the girl's legs. Davis leaned his head down and kissed her on the forehead, then stuck his tongue out, indicating her hair in his mouth.

This time, Ben and Rico didn't have much to talk about on the way back to the car. The mark on Davis's arm burned bright in his memory. How had he gotten it? It had to have been unrelated, so he didn't feel the need to ask. But his mark paralleled Ben's life to such an extent that it caused Ben's heart to beat raw. Old incidents always bore marks, both physical and emotional. The end of the Montana incident crept back into his memory like the closing coda of a chaotic symphony and the last, sharp notes of the violins slicing to a dead stop.

For a moment, Ben tried to add rhyme to the rhythm of memory, but his imagination failed him. Instead, he could only ask himself the question he refused to ask of Davis. *What does Nina Perez do for lunch?*

The Broken One

May 19, 2011

15:25

THE DARK CONFINES OF a universe erased expanded and invaded Ben's mind as Rico sped down the freeway. This time of day, Rico told him, taking "the Five" would be an exercise in disaster. Instead, Rico elected to take Route 78 to Escondido and enter San Diego proper via Interstate 15. This would not provide a direct route to downtown but would avoid many of the afternoon traffic problems on Interstate 5. Ben hoped it wouldn't end up taking longer.

Before they departed the parking lot of Davis Wilson's apartment building, Ben had asked Rico how quickly they could get downtown. When asked that kind of question, Rico always took it as a challenge. He rarely sped, but he maneuvered with the grace of a professional racecar driver. Trucks and lanes of slow, exiting traffic hardly slowed him down.

Ben used the ride to foster an ugly defiance that, if left unchecked, could consume his entire investigation. This negativity triggered a flashback to the simple beginnings of the Montana incident. Rico had driven all day and night to northeastern Montana to settle in the town of Glasgow, where Ben attempted to defend a fraudulent business owner, and where he first met Rose. That businessman had lived in permanent contention. Snippets of the conversations with those two starkly different personalities flashed through Ben's mind.

Later tonight you can tell me about how you escaped the war. Rose's red and silvery hair fluttered in his mind. Mac Walker pulled the gun out of the drawer, aimed it straight at Ben's face and pulled the trigger. The gun didn't go off, but a split-second decision on whether to try again opened enough of a window for Ben to wrestle the gun away. Who had he really tried to defend? Vietnam. Different enemy, same scenario. The gunfire and artillery enveloping the forest had faded. Somehow, the revolver had ended up in the hands of Private Trent Cobbs, the only survivor of that battle. The memory shifted. Trent Cobbs roamed the park at night in search of a friend. A pervasive chill bit at his back. One left shoe dangled from a tree branch.

Ben flung his eyes open and darted his eyes around the eastern portions of San Diego. The rolling hills gently folded into higher peaks to the east and flattened out into a series of elevated flatlands and arroyos that marked much of the city. Tall palms fluttered in the breeze. Off the coast, another bank of fog seemed to be developing, but would not roll in until well after dark.

Rico navigated the network of freeways to downtown San Diego while honking at slow trucks and grunting at inept drivers who apparently did not understand the concept of a turn signal. He swore in Spanish at one driver.

The commute lasted a little more than forty minutes, which Rico claimed would have taken an hour to an hour and a half on Interstate 5. Ben's head spun with the revelations, however muted, that his conversations with Eva and Davis had sprung. Had Eva really spoken with Castro? She had screamed when they left. She loved Nina Perez, but had she colluded with Castro to set her up? If so, for what ends? It didn't make for a very tidy crime, but Ben was determined not to let her get away with it. If he had the time he'd examine her again and hopefully toss out the idea that she could become a suspect. Eva looked innocent, but Davis's statement seemed damning.

The GPS lady helped find the San Diego Police Department Headquarters. Rico parked the car in a nearby public garage and they walked the block or so to the station. Ben hung his head and tried not to focus on the sunshine or the coming fogbank. His strut was measured, but casual. He anticipated the conversation with the detective and planned questions and answers like he had always done. In the old days, while meeting with Mac Walker and his cronies, Ben had learned quickly how to anticipate deceptions and work to neutralize them before they derailed him. Over time, he thought he'd lost his touch. Ben had approached three different interviews with three different methods, and each had delivered surprising results. Ben hated surprises. He'd always worked to crush them, but now he felt he didn't quite know how to handle them.

The lobby of the building stretched from glass doors to glass doors through a concourse paved in marble past the bank of elevators, which they would ride to an upper floor. Ben spoke with the receptionist, an Officer Faulk, who looked displeased with his intrusion. She poked at her black hair and grunted her replies.

Ben took her directions and, with Rico in tow, boarded the elevator. The ride took them three floors before it stopped and a pair of beat cops got on. Rico looked as though he were fighting the urge to joke about their presence.

Ben and Rico departed the elevator on the seventh floor, which housed the Missing Persons Division. The receptionist pointed out Detective Hawks, who heel-toed it to his desk carrying a cup of steaming coffee. He had a pencil wedged behind his ear and his glasses carried the residual film of vapor rising from the coffee. He looked to be in his mid-thirties, which Ben considered a young buck. If the detective's appearance clued Ben in, this session wouldn't last long.

"What can I do you for?" Hawks asked, looking up to Ben and Rico.

"Play it cool," Rico mumbled.

"Detective Hawks," Ben started.

Rico interrupted him. "We were wondering where to find the donuts."

The detective smiled mischievously but allowed it to droop within seconds. "Never heard that one before."

"I'm Ben Carr, private investigator, and this is my associate. As we understand it, you have a missing person case of high value, monetarily."

Hawks shook his head and placed his hands flat on his table. His eyes smoldered with seasoned defiance, the look of a beaten and skeptical cop. "Gonna need to see some creds."

Ben reached into his wallet to show the detective his identification card. Hawks peered at it and nodded slowly before looking up. He reached out his hand and invited Ben and Rico to sit.

An array of knickknacks and items from various trips cluttered the desktop. A photograph of his old partner clung to the edge of the desk behind a stack of paperwork, as if clutching the rubber-stripped edge for dear life. On the other side of the keyboard, a woman Ben presumed to be the detective's wife smiled back at him.

"So you're talking about Nina Perez, I take it? We're pretty light on the details at this point, at least those we can share with PIs."

"Maybe we can trade info," Ben said, straightening his back and grimacing.

"Negotiation? You know cops don't negotiate."

Ben chuckled. Though television shows unfairly painted cops as rigid personalities not willing to explore other avenues and ideas, Ben had worked with numerous cops who had debunked the myth. The cops he dealt with usually acted personable and warm, but with connections that could get them in trouble. They sometimes put on a veneer of ice in dealing with suspects and criminals, but they wore masks of calculated tolerance for the press. Ben knew he had an advantage and worked to exploit it.

"I spoke with Davis Wilson," Ben started.

"Real creep. Can't believe they let him off the hook for petty theft four years ago. Not an impressive rap sheet, considering. But certain people give you different ideas."

Ben didn't get the same vibe from him. The fact that their interpretations of Davis's character clashed so readily gave Ben pause, which was enough for him to understand that Hawks already considered Davis to be a suspect. Was anyone clean? Ben would be careful not to spill all his information before he was ready. Cops didn't always act smart, but they played the same games as Ben did and rarely suffered defeat.

"The thing is, I found out about your investigation through him. Now, I've been on this case for three days and my client never once mentioned police involvement. So, either he doesn't know, or he wants to hide it from me. Probably why he's a client and not a subject."

"Who's your client?"

"I'm not at liberty to discuss that. It's privileged."

This time it was the detective's turn to laugh. "Heard lawyers throwing out verbiage like that but never a PI. Your client isn't in any legal jeopardy, is he?"

Ben frowned. Hawks enjoyed the advantage at the moment, and Ben was beginning to find it difficult to flip it. "Let's just say he wants to maintain his cover for now."

"Well then, what's his relationship? We probably know him by now."

"Possibly."

Hawks slid his hand along the tabletop and glanced at Rico, who purposely remained silent. "Your sidekick knows what he's doing."

A frustrated frown blazed across Ben's face, but he attempted to brush it aside. "It sounds like Mr. Wilson is suspicious of you. What, did you try intimidation or some other bad-cop tactic?"

"All tools of the trade," Hawks said. "You know them as well as I do, I'd presume."

"We're on the same team," Ben said. "So if you could drop the antagonistic charade, I'd appreciate it."

"Also use bigger words than PIs," Hawks said. "Some are dumber than bricks. Did you use to be lawyer?"

"Cops versus lawyers," Rico blurted out. "Classic battle between good and evil."

Hawks pointed at him, but Ben raised his palm as if to defuse the situation. "Maybe I was, but I couldn't keep defending the same crooks over and over again, so I tried my hand at a different trade."

"I can look you up," Hawks said.

"But why would you waste the time?"

The detective leaned back and folded his arms across his chest to indicate an unwillingness to back down. The body language intended one thing but achieved a different effect by signaling that Ben had taken over the upper hand.

"My client wants me to find Ms. Perez, so that's what I'm doing. And you're looking for her too, which is why you've already questioned some of the same people I have."

"The difference is, I'm doing it as a cop, you as a PI. Different methods, different techniques, different questions, and different answers."

"What did he tell you?"

"He told me he didn't know what happened to his boss. That she hadn't shown up for work, that he went into the office for several days before he reported it."

"But you don't believe him."

"You always double-check," Hawks said, citing a rule he'd heard numerous times throughout his career.

"That's why I'm here," Ben countered.

"Turns out Mr. Wilson didn't disclose a couple of phone conversations he had, one with a Carlos Huerra, one with Simon Gutierrez, who was busted eight months ago on a drug charge. No evidence Wilson is dirty at the moment, but that's why you check."

Ben listened carefully for Hawks's tone to shift, which would indicate that he was either about to divulge something he shouldn't or that he wasn't being entirely truthful.

"Wilson wouldn't have told you about that because you're no cop."

"He didn't tell you either."

"Huerra is in the country illegally. Gutierrez is a naturalized citizen. Served a little bit of time after he pled guilty to a lesser charge, and if you ask me, the judge let him off easy. You gotta treat drug trafficking harshly around here."

"Gutierrez must be a mule," Ben said, thinking back to his conversation with Jason over beer. "I bet you checked into whether the two are linked, other than through Mr. Wilson."

"Of course we did."

"And?"

"Nothing came up suggesting Huerra is his handler, if that's what you're suggesting. Not that he isn't, but there's no documentation of Huerra, no criminal record. As far as undocumented aliens go, guy's squeaky clean."

Ben hesitated, clutched his fist in his lap, and swallowed. "I need to question these two. Where can I find them?"

The detective sighed. "You have to give me something in return."

Ben had hoped it wouldn't come to this. He'd skirted around the idea of giving up the name Castro, electing to use it as his ace, but now that Hawks was calling his bluff, he had to lay it out in the interest of getting closer to the truth. If a Mexican cartel used Gutierrez as a mule, then Jason's suspicions had merit.

Clasping his hands together and leaning forward, Ben widened his eyes and glared at the detective. "There's a man called Castro."

"Nickname," Rico interrupted.

"The guy's local, I can assure you that. Ms. Perez had met with him in person and talked with him on the phone and I have reason to believe he may be a person of interest. He may not have been a frequent caller. But I also doubt he's nothing more than a client."

"Tell me about him."

"Nina's assistant Eva tells me Castro met with Nina. She was showing him houses. Eva reports that it didn't seem unusual at first, but he didn't seem like the type of person interested in high-dollar homes. And then Wilson tells me he called on the phone once after Nina disappeared and that Eva talked to him and she knew who he was."

Hawks hesitated. "She didn't tell you that?"

"It's why I'm going to question her again."

"I'll save you the trouble."

Ben clenched his fist and relaxed his muscles as if loosening up for a fight. "No thanks."

The detective raised an eyebrow, glanced at Rico, and then burrowed his expression into Ben's consciousness. "Thanks? Don't misunderstand me, but I'm not out to do you or anyone else any favors. I have my own investigation to run, and I'll take it where it leads."

"You follow your leads, let me follow mine," Ben snapped.

"*Cavrón,*" Rico warned, grasping Ben's shoulder with a sturdy hand. Ben didn't bother look at him. Instead, he intensified his own expression and attempted to plunge it into the deepening lines on Hawks's face.

Hawks frowned and leaned back slightly, enough to be perceptible, but not enough to allow Ben a sense of victory. "Listen to your partner, Mr. Carr. I'm going to question this Castro. And Eva. You get in my way, I put you behind bars."

Hawks, as far as Ben was concerned, just crossed the line from a fanciful newbie cop into a hardened detective. Ben never allowed empty threats to intimidate him. Instead, he took them as challenges and windows through which he could exploit any situation. He'd been threatened by law enforcement officials several times over the years and had prevailed.

"Maybe we should work together," Rico suggested. "Less politics, better chance of finding Ms. Perez."

"What else do you have on Castro? I assume you've done your homework."

"You know, come to think of it, I don't really have anything else. I brought him up with Eva first and then got more in depth on him with Wilson a little while later. And I just left Wilson's apartment a little over an hour ago."

"How did you find out about him, then? You haven't checked phone records."

"I didn't need to. Castro called me."

Hawks seemed amused, but it didn't tug the corners of his mouth into anything resembling a smile. Instead, he seemed to sneer. "You don't say. Sounds to me that your client has been dealing with some unsavory types. He gave you up."

"We have not carried phones today," Ben said, intentionally leaving out that their phones were stolen. "Castro called Ms. Perez's office and I picked up the phone."

"What did he tell you? What did you ask?"

"I didn't ask him anything. He just told me to get out or he was going to blow up the office."

"So a guy calls a phone you're not supposed to answer, introduces himself, and then threatens to bomb you? Sounds like a bad spy movie."

"He didn't introduce himself. Nina's caller ID displayed the name. And he knew I was there at that moment, which I assume means he was across the street or next door." Ben straightened his neck and frowned. "I don't know if the bomb was real, but I suspect Castro has already cased the building and collected all the evidence."

Hawks appeared to sense his frustration and went on the attack once again, as only a hardened detective could do. "I realize you've had a hard day. Castro didn't get all the evidence or you wouldn't have any leads at all. You don't know how to find this guy, do you?"

Ben wouldn't concede that easily. "I'll find him. I've been in this business a long time and I know how to find people who don't want to be found."

"It's going to be easy," the detective said, suddenly mulling it over. He averted his eyes from Ben and stared at a sticky note on his desk next to the stack of papers. His phone started to ring, but he ignored it. "You'll call Mr. Castro and arrange a meeting. We trace the call, follow you to the location, and tape the whole thing."

"You think he's going to make it that easy? I thought you'd been on the job long enough to know better." Ben studied him, but the fact that Hawks exerted as much thought as he did suggested something troubling. Ben recognized it in an instant. Exploiting it could get someone killed. It was what led Mac Walker in Montana to threaten suicide.

"Castro knows something, but if he's culpable, he's already made several mistakes. You don't call the office of your victim days or months after you've taken her, and especially not when you know the place will be treated as a crime scene."

Instead of speaking, Ben let Hawks's words sink in. They offered a sense of finality while asking another string of questions. Without admitting it, the detective was alluding to the fact that he already knew about Castro. The situation sparked with irony. Darkness crowded his mind from all sides, creeping in like oil stains on paper. *Anything you say can be used against you.* Now, both Ben and Detective Hawks possessed weapons with which to assail one another, if the conflict ascended to a battle.

"My next task is to question Gutierrez and Huerra. Can you tell me where to find them?"

"Huerra roams around old town," Hawks said. "After dark, you'll find him on the street. There's a cantina there he frequents. And Simon Gutierrez, he's a little more difficult to track down. Call him on the phone and I think he'll pick up. Give him a reason to meet you and maybe he will."

"How dirty are these guys?" Ben asked.

"Well, I wouldn't go into it unarmed," Hawks said. "Especially if you treat them as suspects."

Ben understood that cops were trained to predict danger. Right or wrong (or even whether the practice was smart), it helped preserve lives and to defuse tension in a logical way. Without knowing what to expect, Ben knew he was walking into a sticky situation. Detective Hawks seemed to relish the idea of Ben making a tragic misstep. Ben wouldn't let it faze him; he'd seen danger before. It made his job worth doing and it some cases, it was the reason he had a job in the first place.

The idea that he'd go this whole trip without so much as laying a finger on a firearm was a farce he'd already confronted more than once from the security of his hotel room. Still, the stakes had already ratcheted up to a severity Ben could not afford to underestimate. Careful planning would be required from here on out.

Getting Eva on the phone and asking her why she didn't mention having spoken with Castro over the phone presented itself as a logical next step.

The situation with Castro struck Ben with a weight he could no longer ignore. Hawks spoke little of what he knew. Instead, he allowed Ben to divulge everything he knew. Castro was the linchpin to getting cooperation out of the San Diego Police Department.

"I think we have everything for now," Ben said. "We'll be in touch."

"Be careful out there," Hawks said, attaching a false sincerity to his expression.

"You too."

Ben and Rico stood up and made their way back to the small reception area. The lady at the reception desk smiled at them, but before Ben could smile back, his eyes fell on the bulletin board next to the wall, which he had managed to miss on the way in.

The board was cluttered with an array of bulletins and memos, but a single photograph caught his eye. His heart sank lower and lower in his chest as he stared at it. The young man's long hair, tangled with sand, fell to his shoulders and highlighted a youthful face so tethered to the spark of life that Ben could not force himself to look away. He clung to a conflicted smile as an invisible man residing in his heart reached out as if to touch the face. He heard the inaudible words before they could form a sentence on his tongue. *Come home, son.*

Shoes on the Back

May 19, 2011

18:10

WHEN RICO PULLED INTO the hotel garage, the streets were still crowded from the commute and tourists hoping to get a taste of the nightlife in the Gaslamp Quarter. Frustration poured through Ben like molten steel, touching every corner of his mind with razor-sharp rage. Seeing this, Rico attempted to massage the anger away by diving headlong into one of his ridiculous stories.

"And I said, '*Cómo está, señor.*' Damn *pendejo* just about shit his pants. It was funny as hell, and we've been amigos ever since that day. Would have never come up again if he didn't start with some woman from Tucson walking around like he owned the place, you know? How do you say, crack the whip?"

Ben tried to ignore him, but Rico's stories found relevance where Ben believed none existed. On some level, it spurred interest, but Rico had always been nuts.

"She puts him on a leash like a *perrito* and acts like a damn ICE agent when he wants to chase cats. Never saw anything like it. One day he's *loco*, uncontrollable, and the next he's a little lady's bitch."

Ben almost choked but didn't manage a smile. His head still spun from how the meeting with Detective Hawks went and its immediate aftermath. True enough, he hadn't invested much into planning for the encounter, but to be that roundly manipulated put a damper on his mood. Seeing the face of his son on the bulletin board under a banner labeled 'missing' shredded what remained of his ego.

Ben had turned around and asked the cop behind the desk about the picture. His name was Tyran Blackmon. Ben had tried to remember his mother's name, Blackmon sounded right, but the encounter had been so brief that he hadn't had much time to learn about her before being shipped off to Vietnam.

Tyran had been missing almost a month and had been reported just days after Nina Perez. Had he somehow been involved with her? The insinuation made his head spin. Other than those details, information proved sparse. Ben got the feeling that whoever had reported the young man missing hadn't really known him at all. Personality exploded and blossomed behind those blue eyes, but it somehow never made it past the exterior.

"So now," Rico continued, "the guy's not a guy anymore. He's got six kids, all girls. Divas, princesses, and dolls, and he gets to play with them while their *madre's* at work. First time they put lipstick and fingernail polish on him, I told him to give it up, turn in his man card."

"Nice," Ben said, attempting to look impressed.

"Course with two girls, you start to go gray. Three, you go bald. Six and you start to lose stuff you didn't know you ever had. One of them probably hid his man card under the sink with the bathroom cleaner and the scrub brush."

Ben laughed. Rico never had children, and as far as Ben understood, had only a few times been in a relationship he could have considered serious. Ben had a son he'd never met. In retrospect, he found it easy to laugh at another's strife. Understanding, however, could only come with the territory and the experience. Ben and Rose were too old to start a family now and Rose didn't have any kids with her ex-husband.

Rico's story ended after he turned off the car. Ben zipped up his briefcase and stepped out of the car into the humid coolness inside the garage. Relaxation beckoned, but the hard reality that he still had work to do pummeled him with an inescapable weight.

"Do you think that *muchacho* has something to do with Ms. Perez?" Rico asked while pressing the elevator button.

Ben glanced at the receptionist and dragged his foot across the smooth tile floor. He hadn't told Rico that the young man in the photograph was his son. How would Rico have reacted? Would he have shoved yet another lame joke into his face?

"Doesn't sound like it fits," Ben said.

"So what are you going to do? Try to find him, too?"

"Can't," Ben said. The elevator door slid open, and they entered. Ben pounded the button for their floor and waited for the door to close before adding to his reply. "It's not like I have time and I'm committed to finding Perez."

Rico pondered on that silently while letting a frown span his face. The expression made him look older and wiser. The lines sank into his face like marks of weariness manifest in a weathered expression.

"You know a funny thing about that detective?" Rico changed the subject again. His new topic made Ben's head throb. "He claims he's got the dirt on these two guys. But one of them he never even talked to."

"How do you know that?"

"You don't mispronounce Simón like a gringo if you've met him. Didn't sound like he was pronouncing it like that in a sarcastic tone, either."

"Are you kidding? Why didn't you bring this up then?"

"Just figured you wanted to be the first to take a crack at him."

Ben considered it, squared his jaw, and closed his eyes. The pieces were beginning to fall into place with such ease that Ben almost didn't feel the need to exert effort. The elevator reached their floor and they walked into the hotel room in silence.

"No," Ben said once the door clicked shut. "Looks like the detective already knows quite a bit about this guy. Only when the timing is right will he reach out and grab him. That, and finding him is maybe turning out to be more difficult than anticipated. He'll use Gutierrez like a chess piece. If there's one thing detectives do well, it's that they don't bluff when they know they've got all the cards. Instead, they use them to raise the stakes."

"Spent too much time in Nevada," Rico said. "I can't believe that all makes sense."

Instead of following the topic to a conclusion, or at least a resting place, Ben allowed Rico to flip on the television while he dialed Eva Crestwell's number.

She sounded morose the way she spoke in a flat tone, with short, terse sentences. Ben didn't want to look at it from her perspective, but sometimes events played out to where they necessitated that personable touch. Ben had never excelled at being warm and friendly during an investigation.

"You want to talk about Nina more," she said. "I don't have anything to add."

"Were you angry with Nina?" Ben asked. He bit his tongue. If he wanted to impart a warm sensibility, his first question would mark the start of a monumental failure.

"Why would you ask that?"

"You called her a bitch after we left."

"I can't take this anymore," she said. More agony leaked into her voice.

Swallowing, Ben reached for whatever tenderness he harbored deep inside and shoved it forth like a basket of fruit after a fight that left tattered threads of bitterness behind. "I know how you feel. And it's perfectly normal to feel angry."

"How do you know? You're not losing your home and convincing yourself more and more that one of your best friends is dead. You don't get to talk like that. Like you know what's going on." Her voice began to tremble. His attempt to douse the flames only seemed to attack them with more fuel.

"You're right."

"Now you're patronizing, so don't."

"Well," Ben said, "in fairness, I think you left something out when you talked to me earlier about this Castro. You didn't tell me you talked to him on the phone."

"You didn't ask."

"Don't you think that would be somewhat relevant?"

She sighed. "It's not like it's something you walk around with, hoping you'll have a chance to share it with someone. Anyone. So you bury it and hope it goes away."

"What did he say?"

"He rambled two sentences in Spanish and then told me how much he liked the house in La Jolla he showed her. That he hoped she'd be back soon so they could talk about a deal."

"What's wrong with that?"

"I knew he wasn't sincere. You know how anger works? It's international and language barriers don't block it. He didn't want her back. He just wanted the house."

"Why that house in particular?" Ben asked. He knew he was reaching but didn't care. Abandoning his attempt to save face seemed to work better. Instead of tired and sad, she was beginning to sound more animated.

"You don't understand how real estate works. Especially for people who can afford more house than what we can even offer. The more money goes into the equation, the less rationality does.

In other words, deals are built on emotion, sort of like buying a car."

"How so?"

"Davis used to work at a car lot," she explained. "When people don't know what they want when they show up to the dealer, it's easier to manipulate them because you know they'll invest more emotion into the experience. The trick is that you show them a really nice car with all the bells and whistles. You talk it up while they drive it and feel how it responds when they press the gas and feel the wheel spin in their hands. You get them attached to that car. Then you show them more cars that don't measure up. They're older, more used, don't have the same features. So they confirm more and more that they want the first one. The salesman knew this from the start because the first one carried the higher price tag. Real estate for these people plays the emotions the same way."

"But you said you didn't think Castro would have been interested in a home like that."

"People grow attached to houses for different reasons," she said. "Sometimes it's the quiet neighborhood or the nearby parks. Sometimes it's the charm. Sometimes it's the convenience, and sometimes it's the schools."

Ben started nodding, but the gravity of what she'd just said dumped gasoline on the fire in his heart. Without saying as much, she insinuated that nearby schools were important to Castro. Nina's son lived in La Jolla and probably went to school there. Only one problem existed with the theory, however. Either Castro didn't know she was missing, or he did. Calling that long after her disappearance didn't admit guilt whether he knew or not.

"You must talk to Davis a lot," Ben said.

"We would go to lunch together two or three times a week and he worked close enough to me that we could have conversations at quiet times from the comfort of our chairs."

The tone of her voice smoothed out. At last, Ben had found an avenue that let her talk rationally, but the conversation was almost over. "Did he ever tell you about a Simón Gutierrez?"

"Never," she said. "Why, who is that?"

"I don't know yet," Ben said. "But the San Diego Police detective seemed to think he was important."

She paused. "I didn't ever call the police. By the time I felt like something was wrong, I figured her ex-husband or her boyfriend would have already reported it."

Ben lowered his voice. "Davis called the police. He didn't tell you that?"

"No. Did the police tell you that?"

"Davis did."

She sighed. "I knew it was him. It was too good to be true."

Confusion towered in Ben's mind. That line skewered him, and he didn't know how to respond except by stammering something that didn't make any sense. "I'm sorry. How is that... what are you talking about?"

"It was him," she repeated, as if almost speechless. "I've gotta go. Call me when you need more."

"Eva." She hung up the phone.

Ben waited until the dial tone droned in his ears before he dropped it onto the receiver. He swore quietly, leaned back, and fidgeted with a pen. Rico had diverted his attention from the television to Ben's face and had begun staring at him as though a large chunk of his soul had broken off and floated into space.

When Ben glanced up at him, Rico spoke. "*Qué pasó?*"

"I need to take some notes."

Rico pointed the remote at the television and lowered the volume. "Need any help with that?"

Ben declined. He reached to his briefcase and pulled out a looseleaf notebook with some old instructions scribbled on the open page. He uncapped the pen and flipped to the next clean sheet. Thinking quickly, he drew a circle in the center of the paper and wrote Nina into the circle. He divided the sheet down the middle with a line bisecting the circle and Nina's name. On the right side of the page he drew three more circles and labeled them *Eva*, *Davis*, and *Jason*. He placed Jason at the top of the page near the line and Davis in the same position at the bottom of the page, while Eva remained near the margin. He connected each of the circles with a line back to Nina before proceeding to the left side of the page. There, he drew circles marked with *Castro*, *Huerra*, *Gutierrez*, and *Detective Hawks*. Quickly, he connected Gutierrez and Huerra back to Davis with straight lines. He also drew one line between Hawks and Castro and one from Castro to Nina. Since Hawks was the primary police investigator, Ben drew a line connecting Hawks to Huerra and Gutierrez.

The resulting diagram indicated that Detective Hawks anchored the investigation aside from Nina Perez. So far, just one little line connected Jason and Nina. What if, he reasoned, Jason had already been in contact with Hawks or Davis? He drew dashed lines indicating suspected contacts from Jason to both of them and then admired his work. Now, only one thing was missing.

After a lump formed at the back of his throat, Ben swallowed, and staring, drew a straight line from Eva to Davis.

He flipped the page and started taking notes. Each paragraph he began with a dash and described incidents with each of the players. The task took at least thirty minutes, but when he finished, it allowed him to paint a clearer picture. When that happened, new ideas sprang forward. Who were the two goons who stole Ben and Rico's phones? How did they fit into the net?

He read over his notes carefully and looked at the embellishments describing the moods and body language of the people he'd spoken to.

This was all a cerebral exercise, Ben reminded himself, but he could not afford to lose sight of the person in the center of the diagram. Finding her remained his only option. He'd go to any length to pursue the evasive tail of justice before chaos started destroying lives. Even with all the intrigue, no one knew where to look for her. What he didn't know bothered him more than what he did, and how could the situation fully unfurl itself while so much information remained hidden? Jason's lack of contacts with the other players grew more and more suspicious the more he stared at the diagram.

Ben formed a fist and pounded it on the table. Since all roads inevitably led to Nina Perez, Ben could only follow the one avenue to her. Whether he liked it or not, that path would at some point pass through Jason Cruz.

"That son of a bitch," he whispered.

Rico turned his head to stare and flipped the channel. His expression drooped to allow an invasive sadness to thrive. He clasped his hands together and leaned forward but didn't dare speak.

Ben didn't expound on his thoughts verbally. Instead, he observed the whole of the web. In comparison to some of the more complex investigations he'd undertaken, this one remained simple in the context of the number of players. Still, so much uncertainly fed the fires that engulfed his mind that he could only succumb to one frame of logic at a time. Ben would have to confront Jason and he had to do it tonight.

Attaching a frown to his face, Ben picked up the phone and dialed Jason's number.

"How's the case going?" Jason asked. His voice leaked with excitement, but Ben could not pin down what it meant.

"I need to meet you. Tonight."

"Can't do it tonight, my friend. I've got a prior engagement."

"We talk tonight or I'm on the first plane back to Reno. Meet me at Jake's Tavern at eight o'clock. Alone."

"That place will be hopping by then," Jason said quickly.

"I don't care," Ben said. He hung up the phone before he let his frustration boil over to a point where he'd spill vital information over the phone.

Instead of talking to Rico, Ben withdrew Nina's folder from his briefcase, spread its contents across the table, and examined them in more detail. He would leave nothing behind.

Seeing this, Rico stood up and paced to the table. He stared down at the chart and sighed as if a deep thread of worry scrambled into a knot in his stomach. Rico's continued silence acted as an antibody to the whole ordeal. Ben had rarely known Rico as measured and calm. It was always the other way around.

Ben stared at the folder, slammed it shut in disgust, and brushed it onto the floor. Jason's touch tainted whatever information it contained. A frown, which had prowled at the corners of his mouth, blossomed into an ugly scowl that could have sent Rico running. Instead, Rico welcomed its darkness the way a lover embraced the flaws of her devotee. Through everything, he stood by as a calm, reasonable force to stem the rising tide and to suppress the fire.

Rico placed a hand on Ben's shoulder.

Ben spoke calmly the one sentence he'd hoped he would not have to utter since Jason first called him. "Jason Cruz, you are now under investigation."

Silver on High

May 19, 2011

20:00

THE GLINT OF THE overhead lights shimmered on the rims of the six mugs the waitress carried to one of the many full tables. Tips would be great tonight, Ben guessed. The rock music hummed and bumbled in deep basses and atmospheric solos. Ben scanned the bar at one of the tables along the back wall, which blue pendant LED lights illuminated from above. The décor suggested something just above a neighborhood saloon where the electricity primarily showered the unsuspecting customer with beer advertisements. It was unassuming and not too haughty, showing the preference for patron comfort.

Jason Cruz relaxed in a booth with a sliced-wood table just as he had done before. This time, he didn't appear to have a file spread out before him. He clasped his hands and, looking up at Ben, glued a false smile to his face.

Rico had been in charge of the pep talk before he left. He advised Ben to not let the meeting get too personal and not to antagonize Jason. By showing a willingness to learn from the mistakes he made during the meeting with Detective Hawks, Ben would avoid painting himself into a proverbial corner, somehow letting himself become the victim.

Though not as old as Ben, Jason had sported gray hair before. Now, he used coloring, which Ben considered pompous. The man tended to bask in his own arrogance, which never seemed assertive enough to weaponize against him. The attitude instead presented a nuisance that would have to be navigated to get to the truth.

"Hey man, have a beer. Maybe you'll branch out and try a local brew this time." Jason grinned, a mocking gesture he'd perfected years ago.

"Maybe I will," Ben said. He pulled a paper menu out of the dispenser near the wall and examined it for more than thirty seconds while Jason waited. Jason started the conversation by imploring Ben to 'branch out,' which would have been a mistake with Ben. Even Jason was not arrogant enough to use that idiom on him. "What did you say?"

"You have to stop treating Mexican corporations like royalty, no pun intended." Jason referred to Corona beer, which translated to 'crown.'

"Branch out? You didn't expect that to work on me, did you?"

"Always does," Jason said.

The joy on Rose's face when she witnessed the cover of her Montana-inspired crime novel for the first time replayed in Ben's mind. The celebratory moment, however, could not hide the events that had led up to it. Conspiracy never allowed for easy, open-and-shut investigations. Jason knew about the situation in Montana before Ben did and assured him it wasn't going to be that difficult. Then again, Jason didn't know that the governor was involved or that huge cash shipments were being sent across the state to one of the subsidiaries of the parent company that owned Burton construction. Ben found the link and then discovered the fact that Burton had been using toxic chemicals near the Flathead Indian Reservation, where a boy had been poisoned.

Ben had taken the case to court in an effort to stop construction of a subdivision near the reservation at the behest on Shawn Lighthand, whom Rose became friends with.

The natives teamed up to stop construction that day by building a human barricade to the sacred ground. Nature had its own idea for how events would transpire that night. Death resulted. Had the backhoe really attacked its operator, or had Ben been imagining that part the whole time?

"I do the same thing with my client," Jason said, changing the subject. "How is your case coming?"

Ben put the menu down and stared at him. "When were you going to tell me you were sleeping with her?"

Jason smiled and rested his fist on the seat. "Don't know what you're talking about. I presumed you'd find my client, not interrogate me."

"The way I see it," Ben started, "you're bringing it on yourself. You had contact with her many times before she disappeared, so that at least makes you a witness. That's what I'm doing. Talking to a witness."

A momentary frown engulfed Jason's face. He glanced up at a waitress and then lowered his eyes and his voice. "All this time I thought you've been a friend. Like I could trust you."

"Did you really think this wouldn't at some point come back to you? Don't forget how good I was before I quit."

"Of course not," Jason said. "But I couldn't just come right out and say it, or you never would have taken the case. And I contacted you because you were the best. I guess that means you poked around at Nina's office."

"You know what's funny?" Ben asked. "When I was counting how many times you called her, Rico noticed the security camera was missing and the files were deleted. Then, we go into her office and what do I find? A sticky note referring to you and an erased appointment presumably for a Castro. You wouldn't know anything about that, would you?"

"She always erased appointments," Jason defended.

Where had Ben head that one before? Why would two different witnesses use key portions of the same excuse, especially when Ben had already determined they were lies?

"Who is Castro?"

Jason raised his eyebrows and shook his head simultaneously. "I have no idea. A rich client?"

"That's a good guess," Ben pressed. "But not unexpected, considering who she deals with."

The waitress interrupted them before Jason could form a retort. She was a tall, leggy woman with curly hair and bright lipstick. Jason allowed his eyes to wander before he ordered. "You know what? Bring us a couple of Silver Cloud Ales. Sometimes you got to start the newbies on house favorites."

Ben didn't plan on drinking but didn't protest. Instead, he waited for the waitress to stalk off, clicking her heels on the floor. Jason stared at her for a moment too long.

"Was it serious?"

"What?"

Ben leaned back and breathed in the heavy air. "Well, you're already here ogling waitresses. Not something I'd expect from you, especially with someone as attractive as Ms. Perez."

"You don't deprive the beast of his nature," Jason said. "What's the harm? Mel and I are good friends."

Shaking his head, Ben retreated and chose a different front on which to do battle. "You've done some legwork on this thing already, otherwise, you wouldn't have mentioned it. Did you link Castro to Mexico?"

"He *is* Mexico," Jason conceded.

"Yeah, I found out about him through her accounts. He'd already paid her a decent sum to show him around. He has one or two connections with the cartel I mentioned, but it's difficult to prove."

Detective Hawks already had it nailed down, which meant that Hawks possibly knew about Jason. Ben wasn't about to spill that information so freely. Instead, he kept that play under wraps in case he would need it for leverage in the future.

"Do you know about a couple of guys called Huerra and Gutierrez?"

"Who?"

"So far, they don't appear to have direct connections to Ms. Perez," Ben admitted. "But I did manage to link them to one of her employees."

"Are you interrogating witnesses?"

"Potential witnesses," Ben corrected. "And no. I intend to find Ms. Perez. I can't know where to look without some suspects. Castro definitely fits the bill."

"So how did you know about Huerra and Gutierrez in the first place?"

"You're not the only one with contacts, my friend," Ben said. "Not that I need them, because Davis Wilson told me about them. He said they're surf buddies."

Jason looked defensive. He leaned back and his eyebrows flinched. "You could be out there looking for her, or at least Castro right now."

"I know how to contact Castro already," Ben said. "These things take some setting up, you know... Hell, you're the one who set up the whole Montana affair. I always blamed it on the boss, but you were instrumental in the decision. But see what happens when you assume? We assumed we were working with a broke cabinet shop in Montana and nothing more. Assuming Castro is a suspect would be ignoring all the other pieces."

"You certainly have been busy," Jason said. "I'll give you that. You don't quit until it's over. I admire that. And you know, I'd be willing to wager that Huerra and Gutierrez know Castro."

"You really think that, Mr. Cruz?"

"Hey, it's common sense."

"What, that all people with Mexican surnames know each other and are involved in some international crime syndicate?"

This comment lit the fire in Jason's eyes. At first, they smoldered with indignation, but they'd become an inferno before long. "You said they know Nina's assistant because he told you about them. And he also knows who Castro is. It doesn't take a genius—or in this case, a racist—to connect the dots."

"Again," Ben countered, "you're assuming. Just because Castro seems dirty doesn't mean Huerra and Gutierrez are."

"You didn't ask her assistant that, because if you had, you wouldn't be asking me," Jason guessed.

"Do you know why we do follow-ups with witnesses?"

"Prodding for more info," Jason said, shrugging.

"No. We do it because certain answers witnesses give seem to contradict each other or lead to more questions. You learn something from one witness, then talk to another, and all of a sudden you need to talk to the first again. You expect inconsistencies with their answers, but rarely blatant contradictions. It's when their stories match perfectly that you start to get suspicious."

"So?"

"Neither of Nina's assistants believe that Castro is a suspect, yet you do. Why is that?"

"I found the money trail," Jason argued.

"Which I'll need to verify. You'll have to give me their banks and account numbers so I can do the digging myself, in case you overlooked something."

"Sure. Expect them at the front desk of your hotel tonight."

Ben stroked his chin and rested his elbow on the serrated edge of the table. A black knot appeared to be falling out a few inches from the rim. The ability to relax came as a surprise, so he didn't quite know what to do with it. So far, it was going smoothly, even if Jason wasn't so interested in cooperating.

"What did I interrupt tonight, anyway?"

"Shindig thing the bank put together. One hundred years in the business, which we celebrate more because there are rumors of a merger coming. You know how the banking industry works. Big fish eats the little fish. Pretty soon, you've got half a dozen conglomerates, and the little guys are flopping on the shore."

"That does sound far more exciting than a beer with a friend."

The waitress returned with the drinks, an interruption Jason used to speak casually. He smiled at her and thanked her by name before reaching for his wallet and scanning for tip money. He'd be insulted if Ben didn't contribute.

Jason tasted his ale and smacked his lips together. Ben pretended to sip his drink and then leaned all the way back against the seat.

"What's old Rico up to these days?"

"Working for me, mostly. Does some side stuff with farmers up in Carson City, helping get work visas for the migrants, which saves the farms some money from having to worry about INS raids. He comes in real handy because he's fluent in Spanish. Then, on his off time, he gets jumped in alleys and gets our phones stolen. Which I have you to thank for."

"How do you figure?"

"You made Rico take my phone, remember?"

Jason scoffed. "I'm not the one on the streets giving people dirty looks."

Ben dug in. "You've gotta ask yourself, what are the odds?"

Instead of conceding the point, Jason shrugged and elected to change the subject. He started recommending iconic San Diego tourist attractions as if Ben and Rico were just vacationers looking for respite from the perils of investigating crooks in gambling country. Ben listened to it all but allowed his mind to drift off. Instead of focusing on what Jason was saying, he allowed his mind give in to images of Rose and her addictive smile. How did she maintain the persona when life had always proven just as hard or more so for her?

For Ben, she made everything easier. He could share the pain with her, and she bore the brunt with such grace that he never looked back. And because his phone got stolen and possibly cloned, she was holed up in some second-rate casino hotel in Reno with a criminal called Alligator Dan tailing her. He silently hoped she wouldn't set him off, because when confronted, the man could get violent. Ben didn't seem to have anything to do with him before and he'd flipped the table on him. But investigating Alligator Dan cued Ben in to some of his more opaque personality traits. If you didn't cross him, he'd leave you alone. And he'd leave Rose alone unless she cornered him.

Rose, however, had her own habits. She liked investigating things. She lived on it because it gave her ideas and a youthful energy for storytelling, of which she poured every ounce into her heroes. If she caught him following her, she might try to investigate him. Her saving grace in this case would turn out to be that she tended to get intimidated when strangers followed her. She sometimes could not escape the horrors of her past marriage to Allen Kierstien, the nationwide millionaire thug. He'd sent the Michigan Men after her, and she suspected that he sent the woman who'd introduced herself as Rose's number one fan. If he could do that, even from within the confines of prison, he could send a bookie goon after her and he'd consider it entertaining, if not retribution for the divorce, which had allegedly cost him mounds of money.

She brought him down herself, because Ben never would have made the connection to him in Montana. Her smarts and efficiency bought her plenty of assets and skills she could use to get anything she wanted. She had been and remained the only person who knew that Benjamin Redd Carr was a pseudonym for Trent Cobbs, who had died along with his entire unit near the end of the Vietnam War.

"...especially for a neighborhood like La Jolla," Jason added to one of his own comments. Ben perked up when he heard it.

"It's a magical place," Ben commented.

"It's also where Nina's son goes to school. They walk down to the beach as a class sometimes. And her ex-husband pays a pretty penny or two for it."

Ben nearly choked on his drink when he pretended to sip it one more time. Jason had guzzled half of his already, which partially resulted in the curious stare he shot.

"Son of a bitch," Ben said. "I think Castro knows about her son."

"Hey, maybe that's why she cancelled the meeting with him."

"I'd say so," Ben said, beginning the wheels churning on how he'd set up a meeting with him. He had to play to the odds but consider all possible outcomes. Castro emerged as a primary suspect because of Nina's son. Jason had told the truth about him, so tonight's quest would lead him into Castro and Nina's finances and any other links between them. A fevered knot of worry provoked him to push the beer away and stand up.

Jason stared at him with one eyebrow raised.

"I've got some digging to do. Have those account numbers ready for me in half an hour or less. I'm afraid we don't have time to spare."

Jason leaned forward and nodded while Ben fished a fresh five-dollar bill from his wallet. Without speaking, he downed at least a quarter of his ale and allowed his eyes to dart around the room. His nerves had spiked. Jason was descending into panic before Ben's eyes.

Splendor in the Stone Room

May 19, 2011

21:45

A SERIES OF NUMBERS were scrawled onto a white sheet of paper neatly folded into quadrants. Jason had quickly sent the numbers to the front desk as Ben had requested. After resisting the temptation to stop for a drink in the lobby, he scanned the numbers and rode the elevator. He nodded to an elegant-looking lady in an evening dress and large brass earrings.

Rico had settled in to watch more television but was beginning to look disgruntled. True enough, Rico could almost always handle himself, but Ben had posited that going out alone would present too much danger. Rico didn't argue, but he was like an animal. Keeping him cooped up would only feed the raw, primal instinct suppressed within him.

"What are you gonna do now?" Rico asked without looking away from the TV. An advertisement for a Mexican beer seemed to promise sun, relaxing beach getaways, and girls in bikinis for those willing to spend the money on the beer.

"*Really* exciting stuff now," Ben said, lathering his voice in sarcasm. "Looking at account transactions."

"Don't think that's a good thing for me to learn," Rico said. "You might find me missing in Belize with some hot waitress and a trunk of money looking for the right bank."

"Right," Ben said, offering a curt smile devoid of humor. Years ago, a colleague Ben had entrusted to run a background check on the person chosen to be his driver had described Rico as a 'man without guile.' The results indicated that he was 'trustworthy as hell' and a fantastic running mate, which had caused Ben to wonder who Rico had to have a drink with to get those kinds of glowing comments. No one in the office disliked Rico except for Ben, at first. But the two became lifelong friends in Montana.

He flipped open his laptop and logged in, deciding not to check his messages. A call to Rose would have to come up sometime tonight, but Ben wanted to take a look at Nina Perez's business dealings first.

At first glance, her finances seemed benign. Nothing unusual jumped out at him until he happened upon a suspicious wire transfer about two weeks before she disappeared. Ben looked into it, but this wasn't the same sort of transaction Jason had described. Ben highlighted the description of the transaction and copied it into his search engine. OGE Holdings/Bookings 92643-1184 brought up thousands of possible matches, but the first seemed most promising. This particular company didn't seem to have a web presence, but message board users noted problems with the company and how they did business. Later, Ben decided he would check whether the company had a Better Business Bureau profile, but scratched the idea when he discovered that OGE Holdings appeared to be an offshore shell company. He managed to track their bank routing number to an account in Cyprus. Rumor had it that Asian firms used Cyprus banks to hide money both legitimate and laundered. Why would Nina Perez wire more than four thousand dollars to them and what were they doing in return?

Ben scanned back and found the transaction Jason had described. She had sent an American company about seven thousand dollars weeks before the OGE transaction. The American company's profile noted that they were building a large resort hotel in Mexico, but when Ben investigated the company, he found large investments from prominent Mexican gangs. One of the gangs existed as a front for the legitimate business of a famous drug cartel. This was the only connection?

He found the other connection rifling through the American firm's other shady business deals. The investments had been earmarked for the construction and occupancy of the new resort.

"So, who in El Canto de los Cantares would be in charge of making the investment?" Ben asked himself.

Rico heard him and sat upright on the bed. "Like the Bible book?"

Ben read it again. "Son of a bitch."

"I've heard about them," Rico said, flinging his legs toward the edge of his bed. "They're supposedly in the heroin business. Using fake investments to turn higher profits on their products is just one of their skills."

"That's highly illegal," Ben said.

"So are drugs, *hombre*."

"What else do they do?"

Rico laughed. "Well, some say they collect the bodies of the people killed in the drug wars and sell them out to some chop shop, but I'm sure that's an urban legend. But it sounds like they do a lot of business in America by pumping dark money into politics. Not proven, of course, but they gotta protect their own interests."

Ben stared at the computer screen. It didn't indicate the location of the cartel headquarters. "Where do they operate out of?"

"All over. I heard about branches in Tijuana and Juárez, but they say most of the cash flows through a hub in Ciudad de México, in the Federal District."

Ben thought about Jason and the fire in his eyes during their first meeting. Jason knew about this link and about Castro. Therefore, Castro was possibly under the employ of El Canto de los Cantares. Ben leaned back in his chair and stroked his chin while looking at the information. Castro still roamed the city. He had to, because he wouldn't have known Ben was poking around Nina's office unless he were in the neighborhood. So then, why the warning?

After jotting down some notes on his coming meeting with Castro, he started hacking Jason's accounts at his own bank. Guessing his password didn't prove to be easy, but Ben managed to eventually type in the right combination of numbers and letters to gain access to his account information. Jason could probably find out if an unauthorized user had accessed his account, but Ben had no intention of stealing any money.

He started scanning through Jason's account history. It didn't take long to discover a common thread of transactions that were linked. Within the last year, Jason had logged a dozen deposits of between $9,875 and $9,999 from what appeared to be an offshore account. When he backtraced the origins of the offshore account, his let his chin droop. Jason himself was doing business with the same Cyprus bank OGE Holdings used. Ben had conditioned himself not to believe in coincidences, but the evidence was damning. Had Jason been involved in the kidnapping of his girlfriend?

The fire in his eyes, the deceit of his emotions, and the tremble of his lip all suggested, in hindsight, that Nina Perez meant a lot to him. Suddenly, Ben surmised that money hadn't been the prime motive. No, he'd been taking payments from the Cyprus bank before he got involved with Nina. Therefore, the entanglement must have resulted from business interactions. How, then, did Nina get swept up in this sort of shady business deal?

That seemed like a question he'd have to ask Castro, but would Castro tell the truth? The only way to ensure honesty, Ben guessed, was to find some piece of information he could use as leverage. He sat back and pondered what kind of threat he could hang over Castro's head but could not come up with anything.

A plot this well-conceived between Jason, Castro and Nina Whatever warned of extreme danger. They would have pulled it off with masterful precision if Ben hadn't decided to investigate Jason's financial history. With Jason, he now had the leverage he could use to get the absolute truth. If he lied, vacant chambers with rock-hard beds awaited him in a federal penitentiary. Still, the confines of his own greed had caught up with him. Ben could not envision a scenario that didn't involve Jason going down in flames.

22:30

THE MAP OF RENO and Sparks lay unfolded and spread across the bed with a black pen resting in one of the creases. A tear formed at the corner of Rose's eye, but she brushed it away. For years, Ben had seemed like a rock, but his stability had begun to crack, allowing change to seep into the void. Why now?

The terror of the day had bled into agony at sunset as the blinding neon of downtown Reno came to life. For more than an hour, she peered out the window at the street below and contemplated the meaning of the latest turn of events. Did they have a meaning at all? She had to talk to him, but only if he called.

Only if he wanted to use the emotion given to him and invest it into her. If the choice were to fall backward thousands of feet or to drag Ben over the precipice with her, she'd opt for the former. There was no shoving Ben. Forcing him to act often resulted in few real results and weak attempts at solace.

Change didn't come upon Ben easily and almost always succeeded such bottomless torment that Rose thought she understood. When they first met, she had erred in not seeing the world from his point of view. She saw a man limited in emotional growth and stunted at best, but had begun to witness something else as she had worked to unravel Ben's history. Even then, the haze of her own eyes obscured the world surrounding his. To begin to understand him had required something deeper and more meaningful than he'd ever experienced. To suggest change was to encourage pain. Rose could not do that to him.

A hopeful pang tore into her heart as her phone rang. She brushed a tear away, allowing herself a moment to note the warm moisture on her fingers. For a half-second, it resembled the texture and the viscosity of blood.

She pressed the phone to her ear. "Hello."

"Rose," Ben said. "Had to talk to you. I made a promise."

His sentences darted through linear space like a serrated edge as if he meant to saw the distance between them into dust. He sounded severely terse, which with Ben, could only mean one thing. He teetered at the edge of himself and an abyss stretched out below him as he clutched at the only remaining strands of reason for a sense of humanity.

Her heart sank. "You sound like..." She didn't know how to finish her sentence, what words to say next, or even what tone to strike. She only knew she had to say something, to get him to open up. Describing his feelings through her own perception almost never worked.

"It's been a long day," Ben rattled. "Meetings, interviews, CSIs. Financials. I've always said it. If I ever find a client I can trust, I'll get out of this business. Now I've got the one who can test the limits of that."

Rose let silence waft between them in a vain attempt to evoke tenderness. "What is Jason up to?"

"I don't think I can tell you that," Ben said.

"But you're calling from your room phone. It's secure." She paused and allowed herself plenty of time to concoct her next sentence. Her voice undulated as she spoke, but she attempted to smooth it out. "But you're not about to breach confidentiality."

"You know the risks," Ben said.

Exhaustion leaked through his words, staining everything he said with the sour aftertaste of defeat. If only he could rinse it all away with a bottle of wine, it would loosen the rigid structure of his words and make them mean something more than a means of communication.

"Are you at a point where you can relax now?"

"It's the end of the day," he said.

"Get Rico to find you a bottle of red. Maybe sit back and watch some TV."

Rose almost never suggested television to cure the ills produced by a ragged day. Television numbed minds and emptied hearts. It split up solid passages of understanding into bite-sized segments to be consumed on a whim and to appease advertisers in pursuit of the almighty dollar. But sometimes she conceded its usefulness.

"Yeah, after what I've gone through," he said, giving the first verbal sign he was opening up. Still, the timbre of his voice didn't change.

"I know," she said softly.

"How are you doing? Have you settled in?"

"I'm downtown surrounded by tourists and people who've had too much to drink. And a little bit... rattled."

Ben waited until she was finished and sighed. His voice sounded muffled, suggesting he'd pulled the phone away from his face like he always did when he emitted a sigh. With him, sighs always suggested one thing—frustration. "What's the matter?"

He raised his voice and then tempered it, making Rose believe the tactic was intentional. "It's this case. There's some really shady stuff going on. As soon as I think I'm getting close to figuring it all out, a new player and a new angle comes in."

"Sounds aggravating," she said, still exuding subtle passion.

"I don't have to tell you the last time I encountered a case like this."

A faint smile appeared on her lips, and for the moment, her heart lightened with the memory. She'd met Ben while running from Allen and considered Glasgow, Montana far enough away from Washington, D.C. "I know."

"And well, there's a lot of pressure. I need to find this woman, but I have to figure out where to look first. I've got one clue, but there's as much a chance this is a false chase as there is it's legit."

"I know how these things go," Rose said. "You gather evidence first. Have you made much headway?"

"Yes, but every question only breeds more of them. Kind of like the first hundred pages of one of your books."

Allowing this vague deception to take root bore an ugly risk, but she let it pass so that she could taste the sweetness of his emotion. She leaned back on the bed to rest her head on the pillow. "Well, now, I guess it sounds like you've got something to write about."

Ben chuckled. "I don't put words together like you do, sweetheart."

"I've got something to write about, too."

"You always do."

A bleakness she could not explain worked itself into her voice. "This time it's personal."

By allowing her thoughts space to grow, he'd briefly settled her mind.

"I caught some guy following me today. I fled, climbed a fire escape, hid on a roof, but he didn't seem to give up. He seemed to know who I am, which can only mean one thing. I'm scared, Ben."

Ben let out a cautious gasp, which sounded nothing like one of his patented sighs. "Can you describe him?"

She shook her head as if he could see her expressions and react to them according to the emotion they displayed. "Greasy, slicked back hair, little goatee, button down shirt, tattoos, and some horrid boots that looked like he'd won them from a cattle drive reenactment at a dude ranch."

He let out a laugh that carried a nervous flutter and paused. Rose pictured him conjuring up the imagery and smiling, but the sound of his voice didn't break. "I don't think you have to worry about this guy."

"Why not?"

"He's been a subject of an investigation or two. I assure you he has nothing to do with your ex."

"Is he dangerous?"

"Only if you give him a reason to be. Just don't get into the vice trade or owe him money on gambling, because he's ruthless."

"Me, of all people. Why me?" A dark emotion burst forth, causing her voice to rise with ire.

Ben's pause lasted a half-second too long. "Well... I sort of... you know, asked him to."

Panic filled her veins. "You? Ben. I thought I knew you better."

"This is why I wasn't going to tell you," Ben whispered. In a heartbeat, his voice changed from agitated and exhausted to emotive and genuine.

"Why?"

"I wanted you to be safe. Alligator Dan is like a pit bull. He can tear your limbs off if you give him a reason to, but he's fiercely loyal."

She allowed her voice to flinch and clutched the pillow beside her with her free hand. "Loyal to whom? Not you, and certainly not me."

"He's got a collar," Ben said. "Reno PD. He makes a wrong move, and they'll snap him up like the last cold beer in a summer brownout."

"I hope you're sure about this," she said.

"Just don't confront him. Don't let him out of your sight."

"I wish I were with you." She lowered her voice and slowly released the pillow before swallowing and pressing on.

"I wish I were out figuring out who was in this photograph I found. It's like it fell out of someone's wallet, so it's only natural I find it on your desk."

"You..."

"I stopped by, mostly to check if I needed something. Who's the man in the picture, Ben?"

He stammered, unsure of his next step. "I shouldn't tell you that right now."

"You can't breach your client privilege, not even once. Or with me. God, it's like you don't trust me or something."

"Rose."

"Just go find him. But be careful, because I get the feeling this is going to get the best of you if you're not careful. I want you back in one piece." Ben had left Montana in two pieces. Each half had made war with the other. Time should have sealed the divide and made him stronger, but instead the schism widened with pressure.

"When I get back, you won't know the difference."

For once, she hoped he was wrong. She yearned for the difference as if their relationship depended on it. Ben was a man of contradictions. Between being whole and fractured—from sturdy to brittle—she ached for the man Ben could become. If he could take his personality one step further and allowed the fire to forge his ego into a cohesive whole, he could emerge better than ever. At fifty-six years old, he was overdue.

"I'll make it all work out," Ben promised.

"I know you will," she said. "You always do. I'm going to bed now, because I'm exhausted. I miss you."

This short, fragmented conversation left a lot of questions unanswered. Without letting fear or pain overcome her, she pondered her next steps. A lone tear dripped down her face and wet the pillow as she brushed the map and the photo of the young man onto the floor and rolled to her side.

By reorganizing and structuring her thoughts, she could keep the pain at bay long enough to see the story through his eyes. *I'll find him, too,* she promised. Ben's subtle deconstruction would not define her.

Searching and digging had always proven cathartic. Investigating always shrouded the pain. Using her brain for deduction rather than destruction healed wounds faster than time itself could. Rose had resources at her disposal, and she'd use them until she no longer questioned the 'who' of the photograph, but the 'why.'

Draconian Force

May 20, 2011

09:30

A STIFF ACHE PRODDED at the back of Rose's head. She stared at the ceiling as if stuck in that morning realm where courage hadn't yet become determination and where terror and confusion hadn't morphed into the sterile reality of a hostile world. After so many hours, Ben's voice still reverberated in her skull, but it sounded even more hollow and insincere. It sharpened the pain.

Sleep had not come easily though the previous day wrought a weariness so deep she felt as though she could sleep for days. The memory of her conversation with him and its aftermath weighed on her consciousness like iron rings. A cacophony of guilt, sadness, and sheer will punished her until nearly one a.m. and had burrowed deep into her heart.

When sleep had finally come, images of the same face flashed in front of her. The soulful blue eyes stared back at her behind the flicker of the evening news, in pixels on newspaper, and in the vapors of noxious gases in the ether.

Rose flung her hand to her forehead and felt the warmth of her skin. She'd perspired at one point during the night. The texture on the ceiling coalesced into thousands of tiny stalactites reaching toward the floor. She hadn't bothered changing into pajamas or washing her face, so she feared what she looked like.

Why would the man in the photograph from Ben's office mean so much to her as to plague her dreams? He was important enough for Ben to have a picture in the first place, but Jason had mailed him the picture. Was he the person Ben was after? She'd never seen him before, and new faces rarely popped up in her dreams.

Thought raced through her with more viscosity when she stood up and tiptoed toward the bathroom. She grabbed a clear plastic cup from the counter, reached into the miniature refrigerator, and filled the cup halfway with fresh, cold water. After swallowing a gulp, she carried the cup toward the small round table next to the entertainment unit. Sitting down in the upholstered chair, she dug into her bag and pulled out a small, yellow legal pad and a blue pen.

She clicked the end of the pen and held its tip to the paper, leaving a dot. Ben poked fun at her for her choice of colors. She used four pens: blue for taking notes, red for proof editing, black for big picture editing, and green for final proofs. The method had served her well over the years, though Ben did not understand. Rose found she could somehow remember notes more clearly when they were jotted down in blue, and so would not have to reference them as often.

She'd left the pad on a fresh, unmarked sheet the last time she'd taken notes. This would have nothing to do with her novel, so she printed in large capital letters on the top of the page: BEN'S PERSON OF INTEREST.

For a few minutes, she sat and conjured how she would get the information on him. Rose Kierstien, reporter for the *Washington Post*, was about to make another appearance. She tested her voice to make sure she sounded young and intuitive, and when she determined she could pass, she looked up the phone number to the San Diego Police Department and dialed it.

"San Diego Police," an older woman answered, "how may I direct your call?"

Rose considered for a second and decided to pose her question straight up. "I'm looking for information, and a name on a man believed to be a person if interest in a homicide investigation in D.C. I don't know if Metro has contacted your office, but my source is reputable."

"Let me direct you to homicide," the lady said.

Rose waited for the phone to ring.

"Detective Ross," a voice answered. It sounded like a man in his forties and his speech pattern suggested he'd been on the job so long that different phrases took new meaning, and he could pass by grunting acronyms and numbers every time he spoke.

Rose went with the same story she'd told the woman at the reception desk.

"Creds?"

"Rose Kierstien, *Washington Post*. I'll fax you the photograph and you can let me know whether you have information on him. You can run him through your facial recognition program, too."

"Who's your source? Cop?"

"Call her an informant," Rose lied. "She works with the FBI, Metro, and Homeland Security once in a while. She prefers to remain anonymous in my story."

"Doesn't matter. Look, I'm heavy on a case, need this to be fast. You have a fax machine nearby?"

Rose stood up, walked to the door, slipped her shoes on, grabbed the key, and strolled through the hallway to the lobby. She didn't engage in small talk, guessing that Detective Ross would become annoyed with her.

She covered the mouthpiece of her cellphone with the butt of her hand and spoke with the desk lady. "Do you have a fax machine? Kind of an emergency."

The lady bobbed her head in half a nod, walked to the end of the counter, and pushed a button on the machine. Rose grabbed a pen from the mesh basket next to a plant and wrote Detective Ross on the top.

"Okay, your fax number?"

She wrote the digits down under his name and then read them back to confirm.

The desk lady held out her palm and only glanced at the picture. She issued Rose a suspicious glance before turning around and dialing the number on the machine. "Confirmation?"

"Yes, please," Rose said.

"Are you at your office?" the detective asked. "Usually reporters send their own faxes."

"I'm travelling for another story," she said. "I decided this one couldn't wait for me to get back."

"It's coming through," Ross said after a few seconds of silence. "Photograph... yep, I've seen this one before."

"You have?"

"You say he's a POI in a homicide? In D.C.?"

She stood her ground. "Yes, my source is sure she saw him."

"Question is, how'd she get the picture?"

"She didn't tell me that," Rose said. "And it would be confidential. I take pride and responsibility in reporting fair and accurate stories, and that can only happen if your sources aren't compromised."

Detective Ross sighed and spoke slowly. "This guy's picture is posted up in Missing Persons and our reception bulletin board downstairs. Let me get you to someone up there."

"Did you say..."

He'd already placed her on hold. She waited while the receptionist handed her back the photograph. She turned around and walked back to her room while keeping the phone clutched at her ear.

The phone started to ring, and a younger woman answered. "Good morning, Ms. Kierstien. Ross is bringing your fax up right now, but it sounds like you're interested in one of our hot cases."

"Yes," Rose said. "My source says she saw this man at the scene of the crime. He'd probably be a witness."

"How long ago?"

"The crime scene investigation was about two months ago. A young woman in her twenties was shot dead, possibly over drugs, my source tells me."

"The man has been on our wall a month. I'm not an investigator, but it seems suspicious, like the cases may be related. Has your source spoken with the D.C. police?"

"I can't say," Rose said quickly. "She is an informant, so she might have."

"Well, I don't know if I should give you specifics without talking to the detective working this case. I'm going to give you to him. Hold on."

Rose rolled her eyes. Bureaucracies could be such a pain in the ass.

"Holcomb here," a voice said.

"Detective Holcomb," Rose said. "I need some information..."

"Yeah, the man on our wall. Officer Rice already briefed me on your request."

"Consider this a FOIA request," Rose said, sitting back down her chair and picking up the blue pen. "You want me to formally fax that request for your records or do you want to stop giving me the run-around?"

Her language and tone suggested an abrasiveness with which she'd never felt comfortable. She preferred talking politely, but impatience began to spurn her into unfamiliar territory.

"Hey, I'm all for it if we can share information with D.C. to locate this guy more quickly..." A pause sounded from Holcomb's end of the line. "Looks like your informant is using the same picture we are."

"Not surprising," Rose said.

"His name is Tyran Blackmon. Last seen on the UC San Diego campus March 14, 2011. Blackmon is majoring in engineering there. Pretty old to be starting a new career, if you ask me, but it seems like he's driven, according to those I've spoken to. Friends, mostly. I haven't gotten hold of the parents yet."

"Who are the parents?" Rose asked. "Not that it's important to my story, but I like to fill in as many details as I can so I can write accurate stories. You know how it is."

"Let's see. Mother's name is Jessica Blackmon, of Long Beach, California. His father is... let me look at my notes, hold on one second."

Rose waited. The ache in her head had worn away with the rigor of the investigation. She allowed herself to smile. The false persona of Rose the reporter was fun to play, even though somewhat unethical.

"Got it," Holcomb said. "His father is deceased. A casualty of war."

Caution flooded through her veins, igniting a new firestorm of dread. "What war?"

"Vietnam," the detective said blankly. "His name is Private Trent Cobbs."

Shit. Those words flung chaos through her heart. She leaned back in the chair, dropped the phone on the table and breathed into her hands. She rolled the pen away from her as agony spread through her joints anew. *Ben. What are you hiding from me?* That question pummeled her mind, brutalizing her soul with repeated salvos fired into the clutter of her imagination.

11:30

UNCERTAINTY RAVAGED BEN'S MIND. He sat on the cold, hard concrete of a bus stop bench with his head huddled and his hands in the pockets of his jacket. Rico posited the idea of Ben posing as a down-on-his-luck hobo until the right moment struck. He claimed that the image of a graying fifty-something with a gun didn't exactly scream 'friendly' to someone as sinister as Castro.

The morning fog had dissipated, leaving in its wake deep blue skies, a pleasant chill, and the aroma of Mexican food and humidity. Ben scooted to the end of the bench when a tall black woman, fidgeting with her cell phone, sat next to him. She acted as though she didn't notice him, but the tiniest sideways glance indicated she did. He was making her uncomfortable.

The bus stop was nestled in a dense part of town just off the Interstate Five corridor, where the old houses transitioned into blocks of apartment, townhouse, and condominium complexes between three and five stories tall. Here, the trees virtually disappeared into the maze of concrete and storefronts, with the exception of sparsely-spaced sidewalk planters that constituted miniature public squares. An empty, vandalized newspaper dispenser stood next to an unused park-style bench covered with dried bird droppings and sunflower seeds. To the left of the bench, a tall fan palm rose to the tops of the buildings, leaning slightly leeward. Its spiny bark rose up about the first six feet of the trunk. Sections of the bark had, over the years, been removed. A cigarette butt had been discarded in the grip of one of the spines. Birdsong echoed overhead. The steel of the gun barrel in his pocket warmed with his touch.

True to his word, Detective Hawks had helped Ben arrange this meeting. Castro had protested at first, but the detective found a way to entice him with the prospect of making money. Castro agreed to meet, ostensibly with the detective. The money-making opportunity, he said, would be seated at a bus stop near Balboa Park.

Ben didn't want to know what would happen should Castro figure he didn't have the money and he didn't trust Castro in the first place. Ben and Rico had both illegally acquired guns earlier in the morning for this occasion. Though Rico had never handled a real firearm, he claimed to be an expert in firing. Ben had left his handgun in a safe in his office. It wouldn't have gotten through airport security, so Ben had decided that, if necessary, he'd simply find a way to get one.

For this meeting, Rico served as his eyes and ears. A block away, stationed himself at the entry of a shop and huddled behind a bicycle-sharing rack. The rack wouldn't fully obscure him, but Rico had adapted skills of blending in. His acting job for today involved maintaining tilework on the exterior of the building near the glass door. A hammer and a handheld scraper rested at his side as he pretended to work.

Detective Hawks had insisted on wiring Ben, but horror stories abounded, which gave Ben caution. If Castro had any sense, he'd ask if he was wired and then sweep for signals just in case. And Castro had already proven smart.

In order to keep the technology to a minimum, Ben and Rico would communicate with simple hand gestures. The signals would have to be basic, so Ben devised a system by which they could indicate threats. An index finger, rather than a thumbs-up, which would have been too obvious, would relay confidence. Two fingers indicated caution, and three suggested that other people nearby took a keen interest in the meeting. A closed fist meant panic and to abort the operation immediately.

Ben nodded subtly toward him as a younger, stocky man approached. Rico flashed his index finger and quickly amended it to two. Ben glanced up at the woman, who had stuffed headphones into her ears. Ben looked sideways at her legs, shifted his feet, and scooted toward her. She could obviously feel her bubble contracting, so she glanced sideways, uncrossed her legs and stood up. She walked away with quick strides and didn't look back. Ben tapped his foot and waited for Castro to arrive.

Castro leaned toward the bench, cast his eyes to the top of a nearby building, and sat down.

"Hear you got some shit," Ben coughed.

"Yes, but you don't look like my normal clientele. Where's the casual business attire and why the jacket, man?"

"Cold. What do you care, anyway?"

"*Sí*, you're an asshole. Got that already. Where's your buddy? Dumpy Mexican with the goatee?"

"The hell you talking about?" Ben asked. His nerves grew thicker, and his index finger inched toward the trigger.

"You got a gun in there? Jesus, and here I thought you were a good PI, not some dopey, inexperienced nutjob with a clumsy streak a mile wide."

Ben didn't bother to look up. He needed Rico to remain under cover.

"Maybe I am packing," Ben said, trying not to look alarmed. "But the guy you are talking about isn't here. He's on assignment downtown in the financial district watching a banker."

"You can take your finger off the trigger," Castro said in perfect, unaccented English. "I'm no danger to you right now."

"You checked up on me. I would have assumed it'd go the other way."

"Wasn't difficult to do. For a small-time guy chasing already-busted gamblers, you don't cover your tracks very well. Then again, it's not like it's dangerous, or even hard work." Castro maintained eye contact, while Ben resorted to glancing across the street between listening to an angry couple tussle over something trivial.

To get anything out of Castro, Ben would need to flip the script. He grunted, pulled his hands from his pockets, and unzipped his jacket.

"More like it," Castro said. "I guess you were going to ask me some questions about Ms. Perez."

He clenched his teeth and met Castro's eyes head-on in defiance. "Why were you calling her? And why in Spanish?"

"I don't remember there being a law against speaking Spanish," Castro countered. "She thought I only spoke Spanish. That's why."

Ben stared at him. "What did you want out of her?"

"Me? I didn't want anything, except to buy a house out in La Jolla."

"That's your whole plan? I might be clumsy today, but I'm not all the time. Let it loose, man. Why was she a target?"

"You keep saying 'was' and it's bugging me. Ms. Perez and I have a good business relationship. Check her books, it's all on the up-and-up. We're both professional about it."

Did Castro really mean to play it so as to assume Perez wasn't missing at all? Or was he admitting that she was still alive? Ben shifted his feet and clenched his muscles. "So, like all good clients, you stake out her place of business like you're about to catch a thief. Then call me to warn me about a bomb you planted."

"I didn't plant it," Castro said. "But turns out, it was a fake anyway. Seems like someone else is interested in her office, too."

"You sure? Because I hear they can match fingerprints really well these days. I'm sure San Diego would be all over that if it were a real bomb."

"So?"

"So you were watching. We've established that."

"Then where is Nina?" Castro said.

Ben chuckled and relaxed his muscles. Castro's brazen attitude had already begun to rub off. If Ben could get him acting defensive, he could trick him into making a mistake and Ben excelled at exploiting mistakes. "Where, indeed?"

"You can't find her? Gritty PI like yourself? Who would have guessed it?" Castro looked pleased with himself. A smirk rose on his face.

"I think you can," Ben said, accentuating the last two words. "Otherwise we wouldn't be here right now and one of us would have shot the other."

"That's true," Castro admitted. "I'd be watching them make a chalk outline right now, and smiling about it, too."

"So you warned me about the fake bomb. Why?"

"Because I'm a decent guy?"

Ben leaned his head back and laughed. Flashing two fingers at Rico, he continued laughing just long enough to throw Castro into confusion. "Good one."

"I'm just not interested in watching PIs bite it. Believe it or not, Mr. Carr, I am an upstanding citizen. I donate to the PTA. I attend public hearings and city council meetings."

"You also take bribes," Ben said. "Why is Nina Perez giving *you* money?"

Castro stroked his chin. "Services rendered. I'm a wealthy man, and wealthy men have businesses. Nina and I get to talking, she mentions a need and I tell her I can help her out with that, because I happen to do that thing."

"And what thing is that?"

"I'm an investor, and I happen to know stock is about to jump with my company. I just gave her a tip."

"That's a federal crime," Ben said.

"Funny, that's what she told me," Castro grated. "But you're both wrong. Because I'm also a broker and I'm about to finalize a big deal in an emerging market. With her on board, she becomes a partner, not an investor."

"So you tricked her into buying a portion of your venture? Why such a small portion?"

"She's comfortable where she's at." Castro shrugged and glanced up toward the bikes. Ben used this instant to glance to Rico in case he was about to gesture.

"She doesn't want more than that, right now. I assume it has something to do with her son."

That comment warranted three fingers. He needed to ensnare Castro in a trap he couldn't sneak out of, and fast.

"What do you know about El Canto de los Cantares?" Ben said.

Castro considered it, darting his eyes to his left. "Rumor has it they sell drugs to Americans and they're also putting dark money into politics. I doubt whether the FBI is investigating it right now, because it's all on the downlow."

"They're laundering money into offshore accounts," Ben said. "Had you heard about that?"

Castro shrugged. "Wouldn't surprise me. Guy named Dominguez told me about it. Omar. Really slimy guy. I warned Nina about him looking at buying a smaller place out away from the coast. He talked to me first, in Spanish, figuring we'd make friends. That's why Nina erased him from her appointment calendar."

"Why wasn't your name in her calendar?"

"It was," Castro argued. "I saw her write my name down, and her receptionist did, too. You must not have looked hard enough.

The security camera had also been taken, Ben thought, but giving up that information at this point seemed to be an opportunity wasted. "You know how to find Dominguez?"

"Of course I do," Castro said. "Want me to arrange a meeting?"

"No," Ben said. "I think I'd like to surprise him. Just tell me where I can find him."

"He's got a yacht in the harbor. *El Corazon del Mar*. He sails every Saturday morning."

"I hope you're right," Ben said. "I wouldn't want to see you end up in prison, too."

"You'll find Nina," Castro assured him. "Tell her I'm still interested in that house."

Ben glanced toward the bike rack. Rico had dropped the hammer. His fist was placed flat on the ground. In unison, Ben and Castro launched out of their seats. Ben's first instinct guided him run toward Rico, but a fraction of a second of hesitation allowed a severed thought to enter his mind. Instead, he sprinted in the other direction, following Castro, who'd advanced a hundred yards in a flash.

In one swift motion, he swung the gun out of his pocket and pointed it at Castro's back. "Stop, you son of a bitch, or I'll shoot!"

Castro darted behind a corner. Ben's heartbeat reached a crescendo and hammered inside his chest. The cityscape around him blurred and twisted further with every step. Peril unleashed the monster within. He increased his pace, flung himself around the corner, and collided with Castro.

Castro landed a single, wild punch, anywhere it could inflict damage. His fist pounded straight into Ben's crotch. He howled in pain and pointed the gun as Castro scrambled to his feet and sprinted down the sidewalk.

Ben managed to unleash one shot, but the bullet missed the mark and embedded itself in the concrete of the building along the sidewalk. Ben breathed heavily, stumbled to his feet, and staggered toward Rico.

Having heard the shot, Rico had ditched the tools and sprinted behind him. They met face to face and hurried to the car four blocks away.

Had any of what Castro had just said been the truth? Jason had mentioned Omar Dominguez. Ben would find him, but if this meeting with Castro could have predicted future events, more violence would ensue. To avoid becoming a casualty, Ben had to take his game to the next level. If that happened, no one would ever find Nina Perez.

Phantom of the Light

May 20, 2011

13:15

PAIN ARCED THROUGH BEN'S midsection like the volts of life punishing his flesh. Life was merciless that way, always brandishing further agony at already painful situations. He rested his palm on his stomach and grimaced as the sun beat through the windows. The low-rise commercial and industrial buildings raced by as Rico roared southward on Interstate 5 toward downtown. On the left, rows of towering palms swaying in the blissful breeze signaled the beach and the carefree. On the right, trees were sparse and the buildings created a mosaic of the cold truth etched like tattoos beneath the shimmering sun.

"Okay, *señor*?"

"God," Ben groaned. "What the hell happened?"

"That was one sneaky *hombre*," Rico said, almost as though he intentionally codified every word. A frown, which he made no effort to change, embellished his face. "I don't think he looked at me, but it was like he suspected I was there somewhere."

"He did," Ben confirmed, still grimacing. "Thinks of you as my sidekick or something. To tell the truth, he may not be that far off because he'd done his homework on me."

"*Pendejo.*"

"Why did that make you panic, though?" Ben hesitated before asking the question, signaling that he wasn't entirely certain how Rico was going to answer it, or even if he wanted to know the truth.

"Castro wasn't there alone, either. When I saw him glance up to the rooftops, I thought something wasn't right. So I kept an eye on him. Never looked up again, but before I put the fist down, I saw the muzzle of a gun. Looked like it was aimed at your head. Semi-automatic."

"He could have mowed me down," Ben said. "Then why didn't he?"

"Too much risk?"

Ben hesitated and tried to remember everything he discussed with Castro. The mutual business deals set up with Nina Perez seemed shady but could be proven legal if either of them had an attorney worth his or her salt. "Insurance."

"*Qué?*"

"You always have to protect your investments. Since Castro had invested quite a bit of time and effort into this meet-up, knowing my reputation gave him some caution. He didn't know he could trust me, plus he knew I was packing."

"Needed to conceal the gun better, amigo." Rico shrugged and glanced toward the beach. An opening in the buildings provided a narrow vantage window through which travelers could view the ocean. The waves were mostly calm, but offshore, a bank of low clouds produced streaks that indicated rain. The clouds filtered the sunshine into a hallucinogenic orange and blue glow that glinted off the calm waters as far as the eye could see.

Ben stared back at the freeway, where a double-lane row of cars slowed in anticipation of the next exit ramp. Rico changed lanes to stay on the Five, showing a readiness to return to the Gaslamp Quarter.

"So, do you think... Castro was reacting to my reaction?"

Rico hesitated. "Too close to call, I think. He might have been on his feet a split second before you. But you're old and rickety, probably took you an extra fraction of a second to stand."

"Thanks," Ben said, frowning.

"Unless, you know, he was being double-crossed or something."

"The guy on the rooftop could have had enough ammo in that clip to drop us both," Ben said. "But he didn't fire a round. We were so busy getting away that neither of us saw who was on the roof. Not that he would have rushed out of there. You don't give up a position that fortified without it being threatened."

"All three of us," Rico corrected him.

"Did he see you?"

"Impossible to tell. Angle didn't work. Castro might have seen me, but he didn't make it obvious."

"He guessed you were there," Ben repeated. "To him, it didn't really matter where you were hiding."

"Castro's crooked as hell," Rico said. "Smart, too. You think he was telling the truth?"

"Everyone has a tell," Ben explained. "When they lie. I'd bank on him having fudged the truth here and there. It's kind of how these goons operate, and some of them are so good at it they make it look effortless."

"Unless he believed in what he was selling you. You don't use the same body language if you don't know you're lying."

Ben considered the comment but shook his head. "Lying is a willful misrepresentation of the truth, not an admission of naivety. If I had substantial video footage of him in an interrogation room, I could pick up on his tells. It's like poker. You study your opponents as much as you study the cards. The more animated a person is, the easier it is to call their bluffs because their tells are equally outrageous. It's where the term 'poker face' comes from."

"Damn," Rico said, his mouth slightly agape. He began to slow down for the exit to the Gaslamp Quarter. "All this time, I thought it meant having too much fun with a *señorita*."

Ben raised his eyebrows, indicating that disgust masked any kind of amusement in his face.

"Or if a fireplace prod came to life."

The first hint of a smile tugged at the corners of Ben's mouth. "Cute."

Rico laughed and lifted both hands off the steering wheel as he pulled to the stoplight behind at least three other cars. "Hey, I don't swing that way, but if you do, more power to you."

Ben chuckled, but the brief period of joking faded away like a hole in the clouds, bringing shadows of gray and shades of misery. Rico fought with the traffic until he reached the hotel garage. Rather than speaking, he tilted his head from side to side as if deep in thought. He showed how perplexed he was the more he thought.

Intending on ignoring him, of course, didn't come without consequences. Rico had always been a conversation starter and often used a ridiculous story to lighten the mood. When the inflections didn't pan out, he grew frustrated. Frustration led to silence and silence had long since morphed into the bitterest of enemies for Ben. Silence begat pain, pain wrought sadness, and sadness shoved hope from the precipice to the inferno. When that happened, the ghosts of his past and his future colluded into a glow that only rendered deeper shadows.

Rico smiled at a mother and her two children as they got off the elevator. The mother looked worn and frazzled but hardly miserable, as though her long day had brought both cheer and weariness. Instead of friendly, Rico wore an expression of deep accord reflected in his smile. How, in the midst of such chaos, did he manage to contain the darkness and mute the damage? Ben chalked it up to one of the many unexpected complexities of Rico's personality and his demeanor didn't always match the surroundings.

Silence reigned inside the elevator. Ben punched the button for their floor, and they rode up without uttering more than a sigh or a grunt. The room had been vacuumed, the beds made, and the trash taken out. Ben immediately felt the heat rush upon him when he entered the room. Without saying anything, he meandered to the air conditioning unit to lower the temperature and then pulled out the chair at the table.

Content to observe, Rico pulled up a chair next to him, but not so close that he could see everything Ben was doing. Should curiosity strike him, Rico would probably ask, but the notion of being uninvited always seemed to bother the man.

Ben opened his laptop, thinking about the yacht owned by Omar Dominguez. What did it look like? Where did Dominguez's money come from and how had he financed the boat? Ben wasn't sure those questions carried much importance initially, but he'd investigate if he needed to. First, he needed to find where it was docked. Since today was Friday, Ben considered the outside possibility that Dominguez had moored the boat in the marina already and wandered off to wherever a drug lord needed to roam.

Rather than trying to figure that out, Ben decided to dig into Nina Perez's accounts once again. This time, he'd focus on how the transaction linked OGE Holdings to Castro and then hopefully check into Castro's own records. Since the holding company deposited much of its earnings into the Cyprus bank, Ben assumed that details would be spotty.

The bank's servers seemed set up similar to American banks. Navigating through the pages would take some getting used to, but Ben could handle it, if he could figure out how to hack into Castro's accounts. That turned out to be a bigger problem than anticipated. Because so much international cash was routinely funneled into the bank, its security systems made the firewalls of American banks look like sheets of construction paper taped together at the edges. Ben's hacking ability would not be sufficient to get him into Castro's records, unless Ben could get lucky attempting passwords. Most banks didn't require account number information to log in, since most users didn't keep that information at hand everywhere they went. To ensure easy access, they used the name on the account with the email address of the user and a complex password.

After dozens of attempts, Ben was ready to give up. Then again, Jason said he'd tracked money payments and was able to see more of a connection with Perez than he had. Jason Cruz had already given Ben the information necessary to get in. He searched for the note and finally found it in a pocket of the bag he stored the computer in.

He flipped the sheet over to find Castro's information and entered it. The Cyprus bank had no accounts that matched, but Ben already knew where to look next. Jason's bank could track the accounts, so he brought up Perez's accounts again, found the tracking number that went with Castro's transaction, and within minutes, he was staring at Castro's account information.

The first item he noticed was a two-hundred-dollar deduction for Marina One Supply & Tackle. Castro also owned a boat? Instead of paying much attention, he searched backward to about the time Nina Perez disappeared. The same tracking numbers shown in Perez' account history showed up multiple times. He'd deposited nearly ten thousand dollars at least half a dozen times. These numbers were not coincidences. They were each within a percentage point of the payments Jason had been receiving.

"Holy shit," Ben said.

Rico leaned closer. "*Una problema?*"

"Looks like money laundering," Ben said. "Julio Castro is in bed with Jason Cruz big time. I'm just a PI so I don't have the ability to press charges, but this raises the suspicion level. It's just too much coincidence."

"Damn."

"I wonder if Jason filed the 8300s. The IRS requires you to file that form to report more than ten thousand dollars' worth of related cash deposits. Then again, it looks as though the funds were wired so they seem to be exempt. And Cyprus probably doesn't have a similar law."

"Why would a Mexican drug cartel be using international banks?" Rico said.

"Why wouldn't they? It makes the money harder to follow and therefore covers their tracks. They'd be stupid to use American banks, and Mexican banks would be too easy."

"Exactly," Rico said. "El Canto de los Cantares probably circulates enough cash from US transactions to power the whole economy of the island."

"All we have to do is prove that..."

Ben stopped mid-sentence, as his scrolling led him past a pair of more curious transactions. Still leaning forward, Rico gaped.

"Castro is linked to El Canto de los Cantares. If we can prove that, we can hit him with money laundering. If the feds start investigating that, they'll stumble on the other crimes. I think I should alert FinCen, except..."

"Except what?"

"That's why Jason doesn't want me using his name. They're already onto him. That makes our jobs much harder. We'll have to get to searching for Perez soon before this whole thing blows up on us."

"Does that transaction right there give you any clue?" Rico pointed to the number Ben held his cursor over.

Under the transaction description, the words United States Customs Service blazed into his skull. Castro was an American citizen and Ben already knew how much money they charged for passports. Nearly two months ago, Castro had paid for the passport, presumably so he could travel to Mexico legally. What if Nina Perez had ended up in Mexico? The possibility seemed tangible to Ben. Due to their business 'partnership,' Castro could have enticed Nina Perez to visit Mexico, where she would have disappeared. In that case, would she have notified her employees she'd be gone? Would Mexican Customs have logged Nina's passport and border crossing? Ben doubted both. Besides, neither Eva nor Davis had suggested they knew she would be travelling. Had Davis Wilson known that, he wouldn't have reported Nina missing.

He considered calling Eva again to get her side of it but decided that not much more could come from conversation with her. Ben had to shift into a higher gear now, because FinCen's involvement in the case would throw it into chaos and violence would erupt, which of course Ben would find himself embroiled in.

The transaction with Marina One Supply & Tackle appeared again. Ben stared at it and decided he'd shut down the banking stuff and start searching for marinas in the San Diego area. Since Castro had specifically mentioned San Diego Harbor, Ben guessed that there would only be a few options available.

The search brought up results for at least a half a dozen in the area with one or two closer to Chula Vista and the Mexican border.

At this point, guessing seemed like the best opportunity. Ben closed the computer and stood up, staring at Rico with baleful eyes. Danger lurked in this arena and Ben would need Rico's services to investigate.

"Where are we going?" Rico asked.

"There are a half-dozen marinas out toward Point Loma. Castro said Dominguez is almost always there on Saturdays, but maybe we'll get lucky, and he'll have docked already."

"I don't know," Rico protested. "If this hombre is even half as dirty as Castro, we'll be in a world of hurt."

"It's the next link," Ben argued. "We have to."

Rico tilted his head slightly and narrowed his eyes. "Then I suggest we wait until sunset. It's Friday night and he'll be out clubbing, if he's rich enough for a yacht."

Ben sighed. Rico didn't often inject truckloads of reason into any conversation, but he was right. "Agreed. And we'll bring the guns, just in case."

"I think we'd better question Huerra and Gutierrez tomorrow as well," Ben added. "Seems important to me."

"Yeah," Rico said. "Maybe we'll catch the thugs who stole our phones, too."

Ben hadn't given that much thought since the events of that day. True enough, looking everywhere for a landline had proven inconvenient. But so far, that piece didn't fit within the equation, and it had to have been connected somehow.

The two of them waited until about fifteen minutes before sunset to set out. Rico elected to take the back streets toward Point Loma. Point Loma appeared to be another rich neighborhood, filled with hundreds of huge houses with ocean views. The horizon soaked with orange as the clouds rolled in. The resultant quality of the setting wrought the quintessential image of San Diego as depicted on all the postcards: sunset on the ocean with towering palms taking in the spectacle.

The drive lasted about as long as anticipated. Ben decided on a marina situated directly across the harbor from the Coronado marine base. The naval ships moored in the distance brought back lucid memories of gunfire and artillery. The smell of humidity and human blood had wafted into his nostrils as huge mosquitoes buzzed through the air. The firefight had lasted no more than ten minutes after the Viet Cong popped out of their tunnels and systematically mowed down the entire unit, leaving only one

American standing. The gunman had moved to execute Trent Cobbs, but the gun had somehow ended up in Cobbs's hands. It had proven easy, but Trent was just 18 years old at the time and fresh out of basic training at the outset of the tour. The girl would have had his child within a month of the battle in which Trent Cobbs had perished and Benjamin Redd Carr had emerged.

He closed his eyes for a moment, replaying the tragedy and hell that poured through his body all those years ago. It was an experience he'd never forget. Among those that returned, Ben considered himself lucky. Violence, hardship, and disease were one thing, but numerous others suffered from post-traumatic stress.

Rico parked the car in the lot facing the marina. Neither of them moved for nearly thirty seconds. The sunset across the waters and the glittering skyline painted abstract splotches on the surface of the harbor. The masts of hundreds of boats, from small skiffs to weekend excursion yachts, occupied nearly every stall. Ben focused on a rather impressive specimen along the outer flank of the dock. The vessel was powered by a large diesel motor and wouldn't need sails to navigate, so it did not have a mast. It stretched about thirty feet long and composed of two decks with large, tinted windows adorning both sides.

The marina grew quiet this time of the evening when it was too late to depart and most of the arriving vessels had already been moored. A pair of men in wetsuits trod by on the sidewalk just above the rows of docked boats.

Neither Ben nor Rico spoke until they started walking on the aisles between the boats. Most of the vessels parked bow forward, which didn't allow reading the names of the boats unless they walked down an adjacent aisle. To get a feel for the layout, Ben proposed starting with the aisle against the hilly portion of the peninsula and then working their way backward toward the front office.

Rico grunted approval. For a moment, Ben considered splitting up, but he'd need Rico at his side should danger arise.

The back row of the marina housed sailboats of various sizes, from small skiffs to twenty-foot cruisers with cabins in the middle. Ben always enjoyed reading boat names, but with tonight's agenda, the spectacle contorted into a sense of dread.

"*Señorita Rosita*," Rico recited, leaning backward to glimpse the tail end of a small sailboat near the furthest inside stall of the previous row.

Ben walked quickly, occasionally approaching a larger vessel in hopes of peering around it at the boat in the next aisle. He passed *Night Wanderer*, *Balkan Breeze*, *The Skiffer*, and *Tell Mona* before he reached the end of the row. Rico had already started to double back when Ben reached the end. Ben glared at him, which Rico took in stride. He pointed to a larger yacht with a large mast three stalls from the end two rows away from them. Rico rounded the corner almost jogging, while Ben simply walked to keep pace.

El Corazon del Mar stood majestic against the backdrop of the remaining orange from the sunset. Ben caught up with him before they turned down the third aisle. The yacht seemed to sway for a moment, but with the subtle current in the marina Ben couldn't decipher whether the boat had actually moved.

They moved closer and approached from the front. Faint voices sounded from somewhere. With each step Ben took, the sound grew closer. He put his index finger to his lips, drew his gun, and tiptoed toward a ramp that had been lowered from the deck of the vessel to the walkway.

The men spoke in Spanish, which Rico didn't bother to translate. Instead, he followed Ben's example and withdrew his gun. Ben stepped sideways to the ramp and looked up. A closed door with a small window revealed a pale-yellow light that would obscure the men's vision if they tried to look out the windows. Ben assumed that he'd caught Dominguez in the act. He clenched the gun tighter and quietly stepped up the ramp, which emitted a dull creak. Looking up to investigate the source of the noise, he caught the staring eyeballs of a dark-skinned man. He seemed to sneer, but laid eyes on the gun. In a flash, he screamed in Spanish at his helper. Ben slipped on a small puddle next to a rope, which had been used to tether the boat to the dock.

Dominguez was already about to depart, but to sail in the dead of night?

His knees hit the deck and he winced. Rico pointed the gun at the onlookers, who scrambled out a door on the starboard side of the boat and leaped onto the walkway behind them.

Ben's heart flung into overdrive. He scrambled to his feet, slipped again, and pointed the gun and the runners.

He recognized one of them from a portrait Detective Hawks had shown him. "Simón Gutierrez! Stop, or I'll shoot."

Gutierrez buried his hand in his pocket as he bounded toward the office. A glint of moonlight on polished steel caught Ben's eye. He pulled the trigger but knew within a split second he'd missed. The man Ben assumed to be Huerra didn't hesitate to pelt the craft with bullets two at a time. He wielded the pistol sidearm the way thugs did in the movies. Gutierrez unleashed a couple rounds of his own, while Rico returned fire with three quick blasts, all of which missed.

"Conserve your ammo," Ben directed between shots. He tripped down the ramp and sprinted toward the end of the dock. His heart hammered out of his chest as he pushed his feet to keep up with the intruders, but he already knew they were out of reach. Still, he pursued, with Rico thundering along the concrete yelling directions in Spanish at the two men.

Ben swore when his ankle twisted as he rounded the corner. Huerra and Gutierrez reached the parking lot and scrambled toward a black Honda. Ben climbed up the steps and ceased his run just as the Honda tore out of its parking spot, squealing its tires on the pavement. "Son of a bitch, stop!"

He sent two bullets into the vehicle's rear window, which shattered into thousands of pieces. Rico answered with one shot and tapered to a halt when it was clear they'd never catch the two conspirators.

Another round of curse words broke the silence. Ben's ears rang from the gunfire as a shroud of failure blanketed his mind. The men had escaped, but they left the boat. Quietly, he jogged toward the craft and trod carefully up the ramp. Rico followed.

He pushed open the door and gasped at what he saw. An entire crate of bags stuffed with a white powdery substance had been forced into a corner behind the wheel that controlled the rudders. Ben stared at the heroin and then turned his attention to the dashboard of communications controls near the wheel. A stack of papers clung to a clipboard with a pen tethered to it, which had rolled toward the tinted windows and halfway down a vent. Ben didn't bother with attempting to limit his fingerprints. The cops would be here within a few minutes anyway, because the men in wetsuits would have called after witnessing the gunfire.

He picked up the clipboard, flipped a page, and read two lines to Rico. Rico grunted in understanding and then put his fist to his heart.

"Shipping manifest. One crate, six hundred thirty-three pounds, delivered 20 May, 2011." The ledger had a slot for signatures. The signature of Simón Gutierrez polluted the empty white space with a series of chaotic swoops and slashes. The darkness outside seemed to loom and gather as if to force its way into the lighted chamber. Ben's heart slowed its frenzy as he concentrated.

"Churro," Rico said, staring at the floor.

Ben's eyes followed his gaze. A half-eaten churro lay abandoned near the foot of the chair behind the wheel. Gutierrez and Huerra would not return, because the police would confiscate their entire shipment.

His eyes followed the line to the departure description. "Left the port south of Tijuana yesterday," Ben said. "More than 600 pounds. That would collect quite a stash."

"Who knows who they were distributing it to?" Rico asked.

"No idea," Ben said. "They might be local dealers."

"Mules," Rico corrected. Dominguez might own this thing, but Simón's footprints were all over. He stared at dark treads to the opposite door and toward a small seating area through an opening toward the stern end.

"I thought Dominguez was the mule," Ben stammered.

"Mules don't own forty grande yachts, *amigo*."

"Shit, you're probably right, again," Ben said. "Dominguez is in Mexico. And so is Nina Perez."

Simian Drones

May 20, 2011

21:40

THE NIGHT DROOPED LIKE a heavy mist as if to shroud the entire city with a veil that could separate the people on earth from the ones in heaven. The warmth had succumbed to humidity off the ocean, leaving pockets of cool enhanced by breeze. Alejandro dodged a fern palm shrub and paused next to the ragged bark of one of the giant windmill palms.

She said she would be here. And he had to ask her where she went and why she didn't tell anyone. Of course, Milana had disappeared before, sometimes for days. But she always came back. It caught him off guard when she called. Milana was slightly older than Alex and showed wisdom beyond her years. She hardly ever talked to him in school. Rosita handed him the phone and muttered something in Spanish before reminding him it was bedtime.

"I want to go to the park," Milana had said.

"It's night," Alex had protested, uncertain that he'd want to waste this opportunity.

Alex didn't enjoy much friendship. He played with kids in school like any child naturally did, but no one had ever called him.

With that short conversation, Alex had already developed a place in his heart where friendship could blossom. They'd talk and go down the slides and have fun and the dark couldn't dim the spirit.

Rosita had told him no when he asked. Of course she would, because grownups sometimes didn't understand the little things. He could go a lifetime, he thought, before something similar happened again. He clumsily walked toward the stairs and asked Rosita if he could have a glass of milk. "A small one," she agreed before making her way to the kitchen.

The cool humidity greeted his skin when he silently unlocked the door and stepped out. Rosita would carry the milk up to his bedroom and leave it on the dresser for him and then go back downstairs and watch some television before his dad got home. Him working this late had become more routine than normal in the last six months. He got to spend meaningful time with Alex a few times a week and for most of the day on Sunday, but other than that, he made himself scarce because he had to work. Why did that man make his father work so much? Why wouldn't he at least understand?

The dark spread its wings as he stepped off the paved path that wound into a mostly wooded portion of the park where the birds would sing. It would be too dark in there, so he veered away from the path and used the eucalyptus trunks as his guide. This park wasn't that big, maybe enough space to fit five or six houses like the one he lived in if the yards were small enough. At the other side of the park, a bench offered ocean vistas. A small figure hunched forward on the bench. Alex passed a volleyball pitch and a playground before the setting began to change.

One of the swings caught a concentrated stream of wind and gently creaked back and forth. Alex and Milana weren't the only ones here. A whisper turned his veins to ice. Instinct charged him to run toward Milana, but he stayed frozen in place. Within seconds, a cloaked face poked from behind one of the huge oaks and stared at him. Alex peered back as shivers raced across his skin.

He began walking again, but altered his course when another face appeared. Hair clung to his chin and gathered in a point. His arms stretched past his waist as he carefully stepped toward him.

The eeriness confounded him and he abandoned his plan to see Milana, but it was no matter. She'd disappeared again, maybe into the woods to escape the people who spied on her.

The two men moved slowly to flank him without saying a word. The hairs on the back of Alex's neck stood on end and his heart raced. Breathing in a draft of humid air, he ran as fast as his legs could carry him, to the only place that made sense. In the woods he could evade them and get home in safety. But they pressed after him, picking up their pace and flinging themselves through the undergrowth.

"Ouch!" A jagged thorn caught Alex's leg. It would be bleeding, and if the cut were bad enough to notice, Rosita and his father would scold him for wandering out after dark alone.

Neither of the men spoke as they slowed. Alex glanced back while attempting to sidestep a low-hanging branch of an oak tree. A warm, dark hand gripped his arm and he let out a yelp. Terror pulsed through him.

"No. Milana!" Tears streamed down his face and cooled on his cheek. "Daddy."

"Señor Alejandro," the strange man whispered. His face remained clad in shadows that concealed his humanity and morphed his image into that of a monster. His voice trailed away into the night.

Another swallow allowed him time to think.

"We need to talk."

His voice stounded stern but wrought a sense of security. He relaxed his muscles and let more tears spill onto his cheeks.

"I know you're scared. You're supposed to be."

"Milana. Milana!"

She didn't answer. A pocket of warmer air erased another chill that gathered under his spine. He stayed still as the other two people approached. They loomed darker and somehow realer than the prowler that gripped his forearm. They formed a triangle around him.

"It isn't about her," the man gripping him said, admitting that he knew who Alex was talking about.

An idea formed the structure of trust in his brain and he instinctually lowered his guard and his tears slowly abated. "Are you a policeman?"

"Of course I am. And I'm your friend. We need to get you back home safe. Where do you live? We'll get you there after we talk."

Alex relented and stood like a statue. The stranger's grip loosened. Shadow engulfed him as he stood upright and relaxed his shoulders.

"It's about your mom. We've been trying to find her. Do you know where to look?"

"My mom's at home. By the college, but she always comes to visit me after she's done selling houses."

"But you haven't seen her in a while," the policeman said. "It's all right. There are lots of people looking, but understand something, not all of them are good guys like me."

"Have you tried to call? She always has her phone with her for emergency. It's easy."

"Of course we did. Did your mom tell you she was going to go on a trip? Or that she'd be busy with clients for a while?"

Alex remained defiant and wiggled within the officer's grasp. His hand dug into him like a warm prod plunged into a bucket of cold water. He shifted and knelt next to him. The other two man gathered a little closer and revealed their faces by the light of phones. They didn't look like policemen.

"Milana! Help me!"

"Milana is not here, Alex," the stranger said.
"I saw her, there on the bench. Milana!"
"It's okay. She's safe."

That statement froze Alex's heart in a flash, before it even dawned upon him what the man actually meant by admitting she was here in the park. He struggled to break free and kicked at the man, but he tightened his grip.

"Let me go!"
"Alejandro, think clearly. Milana is okay."

For the moment, Alex wasn't worried about her safety. He called for her to help him. But she couldn't hear him, or she couldn't come because strange men had her, too.

"Has your mom ever been to Mexico?"
"No... um, I guess?"
"But she speaks good Spanish, I hear. Did she ever tell you about a trip to Mexico?" The man moved his hand closer to Alex's shoulder and momentarily loosened his grip. Alex squeezed his eyes shut, letting the pain relent, but the fear ratcheted up inside like the hopelessness of being perpetually lost.

"Milana."
"Please, answer me."
"No. Just a trip to San Bernardino. To sell a house."
"San Bernardino?" The stranger seemed perplexed, and his moment of hesitation showed it. Alex stepped away, flung his shoulders in a sweeping semicircle and staggered backward. The other two men reached out for him, one of them grabbing his shirt. Terror ripped through him, rending the fabric of his nerves with a torrent of adrenaline. The policeman lost his grip.

"Milana, where are you?"

The three men pursued him deeper into the woods as Alex could only think to dart in the direction he'd assumed Milana had gone. He stumbled on a root and slammed shoulder-first into another tree before regaining his step. His progress slowed as his shirt caught on something. One of the dark-faced assailants had a hold of his clothes. He struggled in the underbrush and grass as his shirt tore. A scream escaped his lips. One bigger step, he thought, would separate him from the men. A screech interrupted the night. He vaulted in that direction like a gazelle evading its predator and warm sweat covered his forehead. He breathed in the misty air, which carried the scent of saltwater being pushed ashore by the strong winds preceding a storm. The air grew damp and chillier as the wind swept through the canopy, its roar fashioning a sense of doom.

He didn't see the protruding root in time to adjust his trajectory but attempted to raise his foot just the same. The resultant tumble caught him off guard. He flew face-first toward the earth and in the split second he was airborne, he heard the cry that confirmed his worst fears. The tide of adrenaline ebbed as his hands dug into the rocky earth. Pain shattered his wrists and tears flooded his face.

The policeman reached down and grabbed his ankle as if with a vice. Alex kicked at the man's arms with his free foot and attempted to wrestle himself loose. The other two pursuers no longer observed them. Frantically, Alex shifted his eyes randomly through the darkness, but the two men, who had seemed so lifeless, had fled.

"Milana! No!"

"She's going home," the stranger said calmly. His voice seemed to soothe even as the force of agony shredded him. The tears blinded him and left blurry streaks through his vision.

"We're all going home."

Terror punctured his skin as the pain in his hands spread to his wrists as if yearning to consume every part of his body.

The man squatted next to him, grabbed his shoulders with both arms and lifted him up. Alex kicked his legs in all directions, hoping his foot would collide with the stranger's face. He peered through the forest as the moonlight faded into utter blackness. The tears dripped off his face as the man slung Alex over his shoulders and began his careful trek through the woods.

He exited the park via the path on which Alex had entered and trod down the sidewalk to Alex's house a block away. He knocked on the door, and quietly stood Alex on his feet. His breath seemed heavy as Rosita marched to the door.

With more force than he could imagine Rosita wielding, the door swung open, revealing Alex's father. A look of relief pushed across his face as Rosita appeared at his shoulder.

He stooped to his knees as Alex buried himself in his dad's arms. Rosita wept.

Picking him up and holding him with one arm, his dad rose to his feet and stared at the officer. Relief turned to anger as if dad had argued with the policeman before.

"You. Get off my property before I shoot you."

"Daddy."

"It's okay, son."

The stranger turned his back and stalked away, as if pleased with himself. Alex could not fathom the encounter turning out this way. Why would his father be mad? And after so much work finding him in the park, why did he give up that easily? The only valid explanation that could enter his imagination brought a cataclysmic change of mind that destroyed the foundation of Alex's perception of life. The man was not a policeman. He was a bad guy.

22:50

ANOTHER DAY WOUND ITS way to a close as Rose stared at the glimmering computer screen and decided to give it a rest for the night. Writing did not go smoothly, she thought, and she'd scribed only about a thousand words. She never forced herself into evening work, as the flow usually reached its peak viscosity in the morning. Still, there was only one way to keep the ghosts of agony at bay. She leaned forward and, squinting under the glare of the lamp, angled the screen toward the window so that the computer screen's reflection danced behind her. The last paragraph was choppy but ended with a forceful calamity that she'd have to resolve later.

Entrenched as though he seemed in his own dreams, the steady sound of his breath sent warmth through her body. A smile parted her lips as she closed her eyes. It had never been like this with him. But how and why did he love her like this? Every day brought another tragedy and every night delivered her into the arms of a man she felt she hardly knew. His hand rested upon her shoulder as she at last drifted off to sleep, but the sleep lasted only minutes before horror crept up through her bones as if to grab her skull and fling it across the room. He'd been here for years, and she had the evidence. She gently kissed his lips and slid away from him under the satin sheets. The only thing Carrie could do now was to call, because she had the perpetrator in her grasp at last.

"The words are dead," she whispered. "No emotion."

She wanted to cry at her failure but knew that she could edit more passion and fire into the scene tomorrow or a week from now. It wasn't the end of the world, but the reason she'd failed lay face-up before her on the table next to her computer. The photograph of Ben's son stared back at her.

She'd glanced to that picture intermittently throughout the day and began to get the feeling she knew him more intimately than Ben did. His eyes communicated both satisfaction and disarray, displaying the kind of raw emotion a younger man would embody. He must have been in his late thirties by now, if he'd been born before Ben had been shipped off to war.

How long had Ben hid him from her? That was a question only he could answer, but she got the feeling that he didn't know the man at all. But it was his son. Either he knew that, or the man was a key figure in his San Diego investigation.

She never let Ben use her computer, but one night about two weeks ago, his battery had died while he worked. He'd saved his work onto a flash drive and promised he'd be done in a few minutes. That day he'd worked on her computer for almost a half hour. There was probably some record of something, or at least a ghost's whisper of something important.

She'd dig into that tomorrow after the clumsiness of sleep wore off.

Rose closed the computer and slithered into bed. Her last thought was of the face of Ben's son, looking forlorn and distant. Some fragment of her soul reached out for him in the darkness, its fingers twitching with the hope for gratification. Yet the nearer it seemed to get, the further his eyes faded until he was nothing more than a vapor in the darkness. The weathered face of a different man appeared with a deceptive smirk and a manipulative flicker prodding at his eyebrows. Allen.

His image smoldered in her perception, undulating like a reflection on deep, sparkling water. He reached out for her, climbing the blankness toward the center of her soul where he threatened to reside for the rest of the night.

Images of Ben resounded somewhere beyond the veil separating imagination and reality. His hand spread warmth to her shoulder as his lips danced near her chin. His ashen complexion and the tenderness of his voice could suspend the chaos in her heart, but she could only enjoy the memory for now.

But Allen returned. He followed her down a dark street lined with empty buildings as the neon danced and flickered in the distance. She quickened her pace, but hope flitted away inside of her, leaving nothing but a pit of sallow anguish that could engulf her heart.

His steps thundered along the pavement. "Rosie, sweet Rosie," he said. His voice echoed as though trapped in a vast, underground chamber with stone walls. "Reunited at last. I hope that little thing in Montana won't keep us apart."

Desperation clawed at her. "No," she whispered. "I love Ben."

"You think you do. But he's wrong for you, sweetheart. I know the truth. Come back with me, to Washington and be loved by a real man."

"Ben is twice the man you are."

"And still so angry."

"I love him."

His breathing seemed to take his voice asunder, lowering it to a blunt whisper that could only inflict more damage than his otherwise piercing timbre. "Rosie, Rosie. Is he really so honest? How much more can you be expected to take? I'm not blind, Rose. Don't let your feelings blind you."

"I love him."

A grimace played on his face but vanished in the darkness. Rose backed against the cold plaster of the nearest building, its gray membrane piercing her back like a thousand needles. Allen moved closer and closed his eyes. "You. Me. Together again."

He grasped her hand and gently pressed it against the wall. Violence flooded through her veins as she turned her face away. His lips connected with her neck but pulled back. She glanced sideways as his tongue emerged, growing longer and longer until he appeared like a demon with charred flesh.

Her back scraped against the wall, emitting a dulcet groan. The scent of blood trickled into her nostrils. She twisted her hand in his, allowing his body to push against hers. With a swift lunge, she shifted her knee into his groin. He gulped in pain and released her wrist. Instinct flushed her through the neighborhood. Looking back, she understood that now two people pursued her. The man in the alligator boots sprinted along the sidewalk behind Allen. She'd run forever, and Allen would never stop.

A scream, distant at first, screeched into her eardrums. The cold street was gone, and she lay on her side panting, in a sweat. Her hands twitched at her waist just as she recognized the scream as her own. What did it mean? The dreams had stopped years ago while Allen wasted away in prison. But he still had contacts, and she knew him well enough to understand that no cell could contain him forever. A vicious hate spread through her muscles, but instead of pushing it away with images of Ben, she allowed it to fester inside her, where it could thrive on the flesh of her own emotion.

Ben roamed Southern California for now. All she had was the fear. And it dug in.

The Blood Storm

May 21, 2021

TIJUANA BRIMMED WITH LIFE as Rico navigated an intense maze of teeming roads and avenues that weaved through the city like spaghetti. He'd been south of the border many times and claimed he knew Tijuana better than the back of his hand. More importantly, he knew the parts of the city to avoid due to the violent crime and drug wars that plagued much of the city.

The highways should have been the more efficient means of travelling, but Rico claimed they could be dangerous for citizens of the United States.

One avenue on the south side of the city, a few miles inland, served as one of the central commerce corridors in the area, and as such bustled. Thousands of shoppers and residents scampered along the sidewalks and in the gutters. Lines formed at the several taquerias, which were a staple of urban life in Mexico. The wide avenue was jammed with cars. Horns sounded in the distance above the hum of chatter on the sidewalks.

"This was the best route you could have taken?" Ben said.

"I had an amigo who used to live here," Rico reminisced. "You know how many tapas and tacos we shared in this neighborhood?"

Ben shrugged and stared out the window, where a dense throng had gathered to watch some kind of spectacle unfold behind the windows of a shop. The crowds added a layer of intensity that would have doubled again if he needed to step out of the car.

"One time we got into a bar, which down here can be a little rough. Loose laws about underage drinking, but Paco said we were there for the *señoritas*, said if you bought them a cerveza, they'd go home with you."

"Jesus."

"Of course he was full of shit, so he tried it. Picked some mild-mannered señora, flabby around the pecs, and came on to her like a drunk mariachi. She was married to the owner of the establishment, Señor Marco de la Esposa, who was thick in the neck and in the skull. If she didn't squeak like an old hinge, the old man never would have found out and Paco would be married to her.

"Marco punched him in the arm and Paco hit the deck while the old man—honest to God—pissed on him. And Paco said it was better to be pissed off than pissed on. He at least knew the difference."

"Does he still live around here?"

"De la Esposa? Probably retired on a beach right now."

Ben rolled his eyes. "Paco."

"Paco had a fight with some quicksand, or so his *hermana* says." Rico slowly rounded a corner and cut toward the coast on a narrower, less crowded avenue. "He met his destiny in Yucatán, when he stayed a week near Mérida in search of Mayan ruins, which if you can get in, legend has it that you dine on golden china. He was a fool, but a student of history."

"What happened?" A truck making a delivery rolled to a stop in front of Rico. Rico honked, glanced every direction, and whipped around the truck while passersby gawked.

"I don't know all of it. Some kind of run-in at a tourist attraction with the wrong American, and it escalated. That night, back in his hotel room, arsenic got into his beer."

Ben stared. "That's kind of shitty."

"Not a good tip to leave the bellman, either," Rico surmised. "That son of bitch had too many years left."

"Did they ever catch the guy?"

"Well, seeing as how he was an American," Rico explained, "you can bet they tried. But even when they are motivated, Mexican law enforcement can be notoriously slow. I wager that the guy had already crossed back into the EU before they'd caught him. And I'd guess he killed a few men in Texas or wherever he was from. If they ever picked him up for another crime, they'd rough him up, put him in jail and then extradite him back to Mérida for round two. *Mi papá* always said, you can be *un jodón*, but justice always wins."

"Always," Ben said plaintively.

Rico visibly shrugged, but Ben understood the expression to be deliberative rather than a display of a compulsive, careless attitude.

Silence lasted the next few minutes, while Rico continued to navigate the maze, working his way farther south into the suburbs and closer to the ocean. He let the car coast down a hill and then eased onto the accelerator when the road began to grade upward.

"We're going to find Ms. Perez." Rico said. "Today's a good day, I can feel it."

The buildings gradually began to thin out, leaving expanses of open space littered by oak, eucalyptus trees, and the green ground cover that coated the hills. He rounded a corner and crested a hill, which revealed the endless blue of the Pacific Ocean. Rico spent a second gazing to the horizon, where a pair of distant ships emerged. The sun seemed to dance off the sparkling waves like moonlight on the rim of glass of chardonnay. The typical morning fog had not formed as densely and, as a result, fizzled by oh-nine hundred, leaving behind a crystal sky.

Rico had narrowed down the port from which *El Corazon del Mar* had sailed the previous day. The vessel would not arrive back today, which could result in murder. Ben impatiently tapped his feet as Rico waited for traffic to clear on a cross street that paralleled a virtually abandoned beach.

The remainder of the drive took a good five more minutes, which allowed Ben time to process the wealth of information he'd uncovered in the last forty-eight hours. Pursuing leads on Castro would waste more time than Ben had, but more intelligence on Huerra and Gutierrez would go a long way. More importantly, Dominguez prowled this area.

The port described in the shipping manifest consisted of two parallel piers and a single berm that reduced the tide and stifled the waves. A small marina occupied the harbor. Half of its two dozen stalls were unoccupied, while the other half housed small yachts, fishing vessels and day sailors. Rico pulled into an empty stall next to a pair of newer SUVs and patted his pocket to check for his gun.

Ben kept his eyes fixed on the horizon. The ships gradually slunk toward the shore angled northward, probably aimed for San Diego harbor. A light breeze swayed the tall grass and caused a trio of palms to lean back like the kick of a salsa dance.

Two men, one wearing shades and the other a straw cowboy hat, glanced at the open waters and discussed something that didn't seem to be about drugs.

Rico flung his door open, stood up, and stepped toward the man with the cowboy hat. The man nodded and removed the cap, revealing a thick tuft of matted black hair. The lines in his cheeks showed his age and exuded a simple air of trustworthiness that Ben always admired.

"*Hola, señor,*" Rico said. He spoke in a hurried Baja Spanish, slightly embellishing the trilling 'R's and double 'L's that gave so many novices trouble. Ben perked up when he heard the name Omar Dominguez.

The aged man placed the straw hat gently on the top of his head while keeping his face in the sun, stroked his chin, and considered the question. "*Sí.*" He dashed through a quick sentence and pointed toward the dock on the left, where eleven vessels were moored.

"*Dos?*" Rico said.

The old man nodded and rattled off another sentence, while Rico listened with a curiosity he rarely showed Ben.

"*Bueno, gracias,*" Rico said.

Ben leaned against the door and folded his arms across his chest while Rico turned toward him. The smile vanished, leaving in its wake the same Rico Ben had known for years.

"Did you catch that?"

Ben laughed, unwilling to crease his lips into a smile. Instead, he showed the tinder of a lifeless face ready to explode in sparks and flames if the right conditions were met. Somehow, the expression always made him teeter on the brink of fragile and insincere, which Rose hated. It always led to the patented 'what's wrong?' or the more painful sigh of frustration. "I speak such great Español."

Rico flashed a smile, but then glanced toward the marina. A man and a woman in a bikini boarded a sailboat carefully, as if they'd never ridden the winds before. "Maybe you should tell me what you heard, and I'll fill in the details."

"*Hola, sí, dos, bueno, gracias,*" Ben snapped. "I may speak in choppy sentences sometimes, but even I'm not smart enough to figure that out."

"Señor Omar Dominguez owns two boats," Rico explained. "He comes here three times a week and probably lives a mile or two away, considering that he often rides his bike here. He lets friends take his yacht from time to time, which to you and me means that he contracts out the drug-running activities to Simón Gutierrez and company. You know, the expendable resources. Meanwhile, he takes a daysailer called *Ave Maria* out pretty often to enjoy the sunshine and the quiet. Guess the guy likes opera."

Ben stared at the masts of the dozen vessels remaining in the marina. "It's not opera," Ben said. "I thought you'd know that, being from a Catholic background."

"*No importante*," Rico snapped. "Maybe we should do a stakeout."

"We're too obvious sitting here," Ben countered. "He'll pick us out from a mile away and bail and we'll never know the difference. Let's go see the *Ave Maria*."

"Sure," Rico deadpanned. "Two strangers admiring your boat like they want to buy it is *mucho* less suspicious than waiting in a parked car sipping margaritas with our sunglasses on."

Ben smiled at the imagery but let the expression fizzle as he stared to the waters. The couple on the sailboat navigated the craft to the mouth of the marina and shared a quick kiss before exploring the vastness of the wind-whipped waters. The waves began to crest higher before subsiding into mere ripples along the beach. In search of surfers, Ben stared at the empty beach and yearned for Rose's hand. If this were a vacation, she'd be here instead of Rico, and they'd be investigating the beauty of the land and the sea rather than the darkest reaches of human depravity.

The longing always wrought a pit of agony that started as hunger groaning at the bottom of his stomach but began to consume him as his attitude soured. For more than a year, the pain grew deeper, and the yearning more fervent. Now, he'd have given anything to share the beach with her and to forget about the rigors of life, if only for a few hours.

"Well, what are we waiting for?" Rico stepped toward a concrete path, which a film of sand partially covered, and then casually led Ben toward the water. A wave crested with a long, white line and died with a sparse roar that almost sounded more like the cold waters of a mountain creek.

The paths of the marina allowed just enough width to moor the larger of the vessels and to dismount safely. The concrete spanned four feet at its widest point but tapered slightly toward the end of the row. Rico eyed a daysailer at the end of the row and deliberately marched toward it while Ben positioned his hand over his weapon just in case chaos sparked yet again.

As narrow as a midsize car, the *Ave Maria* stretched between sixteen and twenty feet long. Its hull was painted a milky cream color, while broad, uneven red stripes extended along both sides and tapered into pinstripes at the bow. A stainless-steel handrail guarded the perimeter of the deck, which consisted of cast plastic form with molded cutouts for seats that could accommodate eight adults. Built-in thermal coolers with hinged lids occupied both port and starboard sides and could be accessed from either end of the vessel. The single mast rose at least fifteen feet and would host a broad sail while at sea.

"*No mucho*," Rico said. "A huge yacht and a little sailboat."

"Business and pleasure," Ben confirmed, staring at a small green, white, and red Mexican flag tied to the railing on the port side.

Ben approached the craft, lifted his leg to straddle the rail, and then slid into one of the seats and leaned back. He scooted sideways and flung open the lid to one of the coolers. It contained an empty beer can, a broken and discarded wine cork, and a few unfolded napkins. Near the mast, Ben spotted another hinged lid, where the sailor could access a large storage trunk in the center of the hull. The door had a small, sleek handle just beneath the rim of the opening, which included a lock no bigger than that of a mailbox. He tugged on the handle, but it was useless. What secrets lay within the storage box?

Dominguez would not be foolish enough to store the key to the box on the vessel, would he? He searched inside both coolers, along the deck of the boat, and around the base of the mast, but found no key. He shrugged and stared at Rico. Rico cautiously climbed aboard and exhaled when he settled into one of the seats. "Comfortable," he said.

"Where's the key?"

"Just a minute, let me call Dominguez," Rico joked.

Ben marched along the starboard side and around the stern, before dismounting. He ran his hands along the smooth railing until he reached the butted end. The rail was a hollow, bent length of stainless-steel tubing with a plug on the end. Most of the rails' endcaps were welded, but this one was fitted with a metal disk that fit snugly inside the tubing. H pushed at it with his index finger, but it would not budge. The disc was not welded into place, but it fit tightly enough that it would not come loose.

"Got a knife?" He asked.

Rico dug into his pants pocket and produced a small utility knife that a Boy Scout would find useless. At least it served as a backup weapon, should he ever find himself face to face with someone who wished to kill him with his bare hands. He tossed it to Ben and leaned back again. "What do you know?" He exhaled and stared out at the open ocean. "I could see how a guy could find sanctuary in this. Get me a Corona and a *señorita* or two and it would make a fine day. I could go swimming."

Ben flipped the knife open and wedged it between the rim of the disk and the butt end of the tubing. The blade was so broad that only a corner of the point would insert. "You'd be shark food," he joked. "And those *señoritas* would have to sail back alone."

"And snorkeling. Fishing. I could find a shipwreck."

A laugh escaped Ben's mouth while he shoved the knife into the slot as far as it would go. With a few more wriggles of his wrists, the plug popped out. Inside the tube a small plastic bag was taped to the metal. Ben inserted his hand and yanked at it with his fingers. The bag came loose, and Ben pulled it out. The brass key to the storage box glittered in the sun.

"That's some booty," Rico said, attempting to imitate a pirate.

The key spun in the lock effortlessly. Ben left the key in the lock and flipped the lid open. A square of light illuminated a blue tarp, vinyl rain gear, and a half dozen life jackets. A rope net was affixed to the fiberglass sides of the vault, and inside of a plastic sleeve, a pair of papers yellowed and wrinkled with the stains of seawater at the corners caught his eye. Ben lay down and reached for the sleeve. He grasped it with his fingers and held out his hand for Rico to pull him up.

The front paper appeared to be a hand-written receipt of some kind, but Ben could not make out the writing. The back page had been bifolded for an envelope at one time. Ben scanned the letter, which contained language referring to the manufacturer's warranty. "Please keep this warranty information in a safe place. We do not recommend storing it in or on the craft."

"Only an idiot would do that," Rico said.

Ben gulped and returned his eyes to the addressee line at the top of the page beneath the manufacturer's header. It had been sent to Dominguez himself. Ben showed the address to Rico. "Think you can get us there?"

"No," Rico said. "Don't know this area, but I think the GPS lady can help."

"Let's move," Ben said without hesitating.

Rico rose to his feet and stretched while Ben again dismounted the craft and stared at the script writing on the back of the boat. *Ave Maria, Tijuana, Mexico.*

"You know what would be funny?" Rico said. "Say we untie this thing and push it out to sea. Bet that would make Omar go on a rampage."

"We'd be liable to get shot," Ben scoffed. True, he didn't know how deep this ring went, and Dominguez garnered enough suspicion for American cops to investigate for numerous crimes at any time. But all this evidence was circumstantial, he reminded himself. If enough accumulated, it would push a jury to consider a specific ruling, if the judge permitted such evidence to enter the case. Then again, Ben had financial information on Castro, which would prove far more convincing.

Nina Perez had done business with a few shady people in the last few months. Had she known about any of it, or was she just naïve and in search of the almighty dollar? Nina had enough money to last her a lifetime, if she were fiscally responsible and a wise investor. In fact, she probably owned a portfolio at her ex-husband's firm that could rake in huge dividends.

The shady businesspeople had to have been party to her disappearance. The more he investigated, the less likely he assumed it to be that she'd simply wandered off without telling anyone where she was going. A knot of displeasure rose up in his stomach as he followed Rico back to the car. Something about this whole affair touched a sensation of foreboding in his veins, as if darkness approached ahead of a storm.

The blackness of the clouds spawned waves and swells that could swallow *Ave Maria* whole, yet if he could just make it to the other side, the distant patch of sunshine could offer refuge from the winds. Until that time, the violence of the storm would thrash at him, tossing the vessel about the raging seas with tumultuous motion that could burst Ben's stomach. The howling winds would rend the sails and the rain would pelt his face with a remorseful agony that could shroud his perception with a translucent veil of red and the torrent would spatter him with scarlet.

Rico mentioned something about Gutierrez, but Ben considered it nothing but a side comment that could really mean nothing. Still, the notion played at him like the faint undertones of a timid violin beneath a crescendo of brass and bass. "Simón Gutierrez was selling drugs to Eva's friend... Davis? You think so?"

Ben sighed but allowed the thought to develop beyond Davis Wilson or Eva Crestwell. Something more sinister lurked in these waters, and if Ben considered his luck a precursor for events to come, the waves would crash upon him so soon that he'd have little time to react. If Davis were not buying from Gutierrez, then he was doing business with him, unless Detective Hawks was wrong.

So far, Hawks had not been wrong about anything, yet he didn't tell Ben everything. His version left gaping holes that only solid investigation could fill. Ben and Rico were searching Mexico because the evidence led them to Mexico. Hawks, however, had not confirmed Mexico to have even played into the whole scenario. That suggested a different side to the tale and told Ben that he'd need to explore that side as well. If Mexico didn't yield answers, then he'd have to either bait the San Diego Police Department into helping or steal the information from them. Neither option presented a desirable outcome as far as Ben was concerned.

Rico remained on the avenue that paralleled the sea and sped up when the hills caused the road to twist and the slopes would not accommodate homes. The trip lasted only a few minutes. A large hacienda-style mansion with a sprawling footprint and a mission-style roof rested amidst a gently sloped lawn overlooking the ocean. Large date palms, tall fan palms, and bush-like fern palms decorated the exterior of the home. A small sports car and a large, black SUV occupied a wide, arcing driveway. Rico passed the house and slowed in front of a more modest dwelling that would still cost a fortune.

The lawn of the second house was separated from the first by a twenty-foot-wide berm of wild grass that swayed with the breeze. Along the north side of the property, a row of bushes and rough-barked palm trees provided privacy. This house was constructed of beige stucco and a veneer of red brick along the bottom half of the walls. The large, arched windows offered a pleasant vista of the ocean and the rocky coast below. No cars sat in the driveway, but smaller windows on a flank of the home indicated a spacious garage, where the vehicles were likely parked. The property came with more open space than the adjacent parcel, with a patchwork of smaller oak and locust trees that could harbor plenty of sunshine during the afternoon hours.

Rico cautiously pulled the car into the driveway and parked it near the road. He reached down to his pocket and gripped the gun as Ben slowly pushed the door open, keeping his eyes on the front windows, which seemed to be dark.

If gunfire rang out and a fight ensued, Ben and Rico would be poorly positioned and would likely be the first to be hit. A car rolled down the avenue and accelerated as they tiptoed toward the house. Ben drew his firearm, gulped, and darted into shelter next to one of the windows. Rico followed.

A breeze shifted the air around them. Ben turned his head and glanced sideways into the large front room where a large sectional sofa provided comfort for only a black cat. The television wasn't on, which brought a relaxed sigh between them. Rico lowered his gun as Ben did the same. An overwhelming sense of doom poured into Ben's veins as he darted past the window and up the steps to ring the doorbell.

They waited and the ocean breeze ushered in the cool scent of tropical summer.

Dregs of Mortality

May 21, 2011

11:45

A SERIES OF HIGH clouds floated on the horizon, casting dark blue and gray shadows over the ocean. The sun beat down on the shores, which would send temperatures into the eighties. Ben thought about Rose and how the streaks of red had flowed through her silvery hair while he faced the door with his gun raised. Rico followed suit. The door was locked, but Ben had already charted a possible course into the house if all other options failed. He lifted the porch mat, and to his dismay, found no key. Together, they walked around the perimeter of the house, carefully checking whether anyone lurked inside before they tried the windows.

None of the windows could be opened from the outside, making Ben's previous thought the only alternative. The attached garage sported nested plastic windows in the overhead door, and due to maintenance issues, one of the windows rattled loose. The windows stood more than five feet high, so getting through them would not be an easy prospect. Ben surveyed the land around the house, stowed the gun, and pulled the knife Rico had given him out of his pocket. The entire blade could fit through the gap between the window frame and the metal of the door. Carefully, he wedged the window open further and pulled the loose part outward.

Rico offered to give him a boost by lacing his fingers together just above his knee to hoist Ben high enough to scoot through the window. Ben ran the knife carefully along the perimeter of the window to loosen it further, and with one strong push, the window frame popped out of the door and clattered to the concrete inside.

Without hesitation, Ben stepped into Rico's hands and grasped the blunt metal edges of the window opening. Pain scraped through his midsection as he scooted through the opening. Darkness crept over his perception as he felt for something else to grasp. By reaching just under two feet toward the center of the door, he managed to grip the wire mechanism that lifted the door. He indicated he was ready by pulling himself through at an angle while Rico pushed. A motor revved from somewhere down the road.

Flipping his heels over the metal edge, Ben gripped the wire with all the strength he could muster. His own weight forced him to flip backward, but he could not swing his legs far enough in time to land on his feet. Instead, he knees collided painfully with the window frame while his torso slapped the concrete.

"Shit, that hurts."

"*Cuidado, cavrón.*" The thin metal of the door managed to muffle Rico's voice, causing him to sound distant.

Ben pushed himself off the fallen window frame and dragged himself up by the door control mechanism. A small, glowing button had been affixed to the sheetrock wall next to the door above the stoop. Ben breathed in the musty air that carried the scent of sawdust laced with the dismal vapor of turpentine.

The door rose slowly, allowing the sun to reveal more and more of the interior of the garage. What had been bathed in a sea of gray and dusk stood out in stark detail. Neatly tucked into a corner of the cavernous, three-car garage stood a work bench with slider saw and a router. A film of sawdust covered the surface of the table, while straight mounds of dust piled up where lumber had rested until recently. Sometime within the last two days, Ben guessed, the floor had been swept, but the cleaner hadn't bothered to reach into nooks, and around other equipment. The dust was swept into a large pile below the table.

"No wood," Rico said. "Must be a hobby and he's finished cutting."

Ben snorted. The door into the house wasn't locked. Ben pushed it open effortlessly and stepped onto a sweeping tile floor that somehow made the spacious living room look huge. The sectional where the cat slept faced the television, while two remote controls occupied an oval glass tabletop that reflected the track lights on the high, arched ceiling. Rico stomped on the floor to verify that the tile was real stone and nodded with a grin.

"Best real estate in Baja California right here."

Ben nodded slowly and marched through the room to the kitchen. The kitchen looked as though it hadn't been used in more than a week. No dishes rested in the sink and no crumbs littered the marble countertops. Beyond the kitchen, hallways darted in both directions at a tee junction, where a sideboard and hutch combination displayed relics of the wild. A small, glass case guarded what looked like an exceptionally well-preserved Spanish doubloon. Next to the case rested the obligatory bleached-white cow skull, and a wide tray displaying a variety of seashells.

The next shelf boasted prized Spanish china and sterling silverware, which had become tarnished through oxidization and skin oils. Ben glanced left and opted for the right corridor, which led past several closed doors. A messy office room awaited behind the last door on the end. A square of sunlight illuminated stacks of papers on the floor as the sun cascaded through the giant window. The center of the room featured a hand-made desk that housed a computer and many stacks of papers. Ben scanned the room and found just what he was looking for standing in plain sight atop a dusty stack of boxes next to a filing cabinet and a copier machine.

The papers were from an American law firm based in San Diego, California. The top page had been addressed to Dominguez personally. Ben scanned it and then read the first two paragraphs aloud. "Dear Mr. Dominguez, thank you for your inquiry regarding representation in opposition to the Bayfront project. At this time, I'd like to introduce you to your expert legal counsel team. My name is Hans Rummington, PhD and I boast thirty years of experience litigating cases just like yours. My staff consists of Jennifer Huston, Sabine Cater, and Davis Wilson. This is a dream team tailor-made for your case. Should you file a retainer fee, we'd like to meet you right away. We would be happy to meet you at the time and place of your choosing. Please give us a call and set up a date."

"Wilson?" Rico perked up when he heard the name.

Ben nodded but kept a mostly rigid face. The next page consisted of a lot of legalese that Ben didn't care to read. It didn't mention names of any other players. Ben turned to the next page and immediately dropped the whole package to the floor.

"We've gotta get out of here," Ben said. "This is a trap. They've led us right where they wanted us to be."

"Who?" Rico shrugged.

Ben sprinted down the hall and back into the kitchen as hot adrenaline poured through his veins. The tangled mass of what remained of life collapsed into a heap of semi-molten steel and shattered glass, the refuse of a life constructed for only one purpose.

No answer escaped Ben's lips. He flung open the door to the garage with enough force to jam the door handle into the adjacent wall. He suspected that he broke the sheetrock, but didn't care. He didn't bother closing any doors or lifting the window frame back into place. With guns drawn, Ben and Rico darted down the long driveway, frantically glancing up and down the road. Rico started the car, shoved it into reverse, and pulled out of the driveway backward. He turned the vehicle north, flipped the clutch into drive, and floored the accelerator.

Scattered breath and arcing adrenaline pushed his system to the brink. He clutched his heart. Rico coaxed the car toward sixty miles per hour. Ben groaned when he looked in the rearview mirror. A full-sized black SUV with darkly tinted windows sped toward them at an impressive speed.

"Son of a bitch, no," Rico growled.

He tore through a tight bend on the road, punched the gas once again and glanced into the rearview mirror. The vehicle pulled closer. A loud revving sound and the smell of burning rubber flooded Ben's perception. The SUV lurched forward and slammed into Rico's tail end. Pushing through another series of curves, Rico swore in Spanish and swerved into the left lane to pass a slow farming truck. The pursuers didn't even bother to look before again pushing toward the rear bumper of the car.

Rico flung the vehicle into the right lane and fishtailed through a patch of standing irrigation water that trickled toward the sea. The SUV cut off the farming truck and backed off momentarily, before exploding in flurry of acceleration aimed directly at Rico's rear bumper. A narrow side road jutted off the main road, curving down a slope that led to a beach. The SUV eased closer to Rico's bumper. The front end of the other vehicle pushed Rico forward, while Ben spun backward and attempted to aim the gun at the truck's windshield.

Another curse word shot from Rico's mouth. He spun the steering wheel hard to the right. The crunching sound of metal on metal tore into Ben's eardrums as the truck's momentum spun the car sideways. Rico slacked off the gas as the car slid sideways on the gravel road for up to twenty feet. Again, he floored it, sending a blinding cascade of dust and gravel at the SUV's windshield.

The other driver attempted to alter his course to chase Rico down the dirt road but miscalculated a critical bump at the side of the road. The mistake flipped the truck sideways. Its roof gave in as all of the windows shattered. The driver's head flung in all directions as the truck tumbled to a dusty stop in a field of swaying grass.

Echoes of squealing tires punctured Ben's eardrums, as if the harrowing end of a dark nightmare sent spasms through his limbs. He faced forward, and his eyes widened. Rico laid on the horn as a troupe of young boys loaded into a minivan parked in the center of the road.

Rico slammed the brake pedal to the floor and eased the car into a sideways skid. When the sliding stopped, the nose of the car pushed into the field of dry grass.

Rico spun the wheel to the left, gripped the shifter and pushed uphill in the grass. He sped toward the mangled SUV, where the pursuers climbed out of the wreckage. Ben clutched the gun tightly and aimed straight ahead while Rico coaxed the vehicle to angle right. The going was bumpy and would severely damage the chassis, especially if Rico ran over a boulder.

The gang of pursuers jumped to stand and pulled out automatic weapons.

Rico swore again and allowed the field to pulverize him. Ben's perception vibrated up and down, leaving streaks of yellow and green, as if the image sped across a screen faster the speed of sound.

With one click, Ben pulled the hammer back, aimed toward the assailants, and fired.

They returned fire with gusto, spraying the vehicle with hundreds of bullets. The rear tires gave out and Rico continued on his rims. Following the slope of the field to a more level path,

Rico allowed the front tires to pull the vehicle through the dirt and grass.

Having unloaded their clips in a heartbeat, the attackers reloaded and continued to fire. The back window shattered as Ben's heart raced. If they could not make it to a road soon, the car's transmission would give out and the other people would kill them.

Another dirt road, this one narrower than the first, cut a slot through the grass. Just down the hill, a small shack sat on the beach while near the end of the road a fern palm bush marked the avenue.

Rico spun the car sideways and punched it as the car rumbled back up the slope toward the main road. Rapid-fire bullets plunged into the sheet metal and shattered the side windows. Ben and Rico both lowered their heads. When the vehicle at last got back to the main road, Rico floored the accelerator once again. The screech of steel on pavement scoured Ben's eardrums with splitting zeal. With no rear tires, Rico could not control the back end of the car. He spun the wheel and pointed the car south on the main road, but the steel rims slid across the pavement, sending the car into a mailbox.

The box flipped off its post and Rico corrected. More bullets flew toward them, but most of them missed. Instead of wasting a second, Rico made the front tires squeal on the pavement. The rear end fishtailed, leaving trails of sparks and smoke as the steel heated.

At last, the wreckage of the SUV faded out of sight. Rico pulled the car down a series of side roads, and then found another main road heading north back into the city of Tijuana. They could only ride the rims for so long before the car was completely disabled. They wouldn't ever make it back to the city. Rico pulled the car to the side of the road and parked it to let the wheels cool.

"Gonna need tires or another car," Rico said. "And you can tell me what tipped you off."

Ben swallowed a knot of throat-scratching agony and stared toward a canopy of oaks, eucalyptus, and palms. He only wanted to call Rose and to tell her what had just happened. Rose would of course panic and leave Reno for the only city Ben didn't want her to be in, for her own safety. Neither he nor Rico had brought their phones, but the bad guys didn't even need their phone signals to track them. They predicted Ben's every step and followed him there, into the heart of wasted pain awash in torture.

Pastel Horizons

May 21, 2011

13:25

NO ONE COULD DESCRIBE Mexican architecture as bland, devoid of color, or lacking character, as far as Ben was concerned. Few buildings, it turned out, matched the image he'd planted in his mind since a young age. The beige and yellow stucco patterns with mission tile roofs and dry lawns didn't appear to be a trendy style. Instead, the décor suggested that only the elite could afford such luxury.

  The car rested in the shade of a towering eucalyptus tree, which leaned over the two-lane road and joined in an arching canopy that covered a sweeping hillside. From the top of the hill, residents could possibly see the ocean, but the trees and the housing in this area was clustered densely enough to qualify as a suburb of Tijuana. The single-family homes and townhouses in this neighborhood formed neat rows between narrow streets. Few of the structures sat on sites that could accommodate lawns, and those that did showed preference for green, tropical shrubbery and gravel.

  As opposed to California developments, this neighborhood blossomed with a rainbow of colors, from cool greens to friendly yellows, burnt reds, and even sea blues. The roofs were mostly low-slope gravel or asphalt shingles, rather than the heavier, more expensive mission tiling Ben had long imagined.

King fan palms poked through the canopy in multiple locations, while broad date palms and even a few sleek palmettos transformed the semi-arid locale into a tropical landscape. Ben rubbed his temple and attempted to collect reason. His midsection ached from scraping against the metal of the overhead door and chaos still littered his mind. As his heart rate slowed, more order began to reign, and Ben was once again able to categorize his thoughts.

Rico glanced back and forth between hillsides. To the northeast, rocky mountains with steppe vegetation created a jagged horizon painted with a spectrum of colors that Ben could better appreciate in a simpler time fraught with less agony. He shrugged and stared at the gravel while hoping Rico would strike up some kind of conversation that related to neither what had just happened, nor stories from a long-past glory era.

"Are you going to tell me what just happened?" Rico asked. "Or am I going to tell you?"

Ben looked up and took in his expression, which was tainted with an underwhelming sense of frustration. Before he could open his mouth, a pair of cars sped by. He waited for the rush of wind and road noise to subside before he burst into conversation. "Actually, I'd rather hear your version of it."

"Don't know what you saw in that paperwork," Rico said. "More to do with Davis Wilson? I figure that Wilson working for the law firm is not a coincidence. They recruited him to look into the Bayfront project, which, by the way, is legit. Supposed to be a high-rise resort style hotel overlooking the ocean south of Tijuana. It would accompany less dense, upscale residential development and a row of commercial with a boardwalk along the ocean. Only shows reason that Dominguez would oppose it, you know?"

"No," Ben said. "But continue."

"It can't be coincidence, but it's *loco*. We hear from the cops that Wilson was in bed with Gutierrez, who just the other day attacked us while unloading dope from the yacht, and then he turns up working for a law firm representing a drug runner? That's a conflict of interest, if I've ever seen one. And both sides revolve around Nina Perez. I'm hearing conspiracy, *amigo*."

Pain buckled in Ben's midsection. The last time he'd encountered a conspiracy, a team of developers and contractors had partnered with the Governor of Montana to build a housing development on sacred Salish and Flathead land. The dispute culminated in a headline-grabbing RICO case that had sent multiple parties to prison. And who else had turned out to be involved than Rose's ex-husband Allen, a real sleazeball with a despicable agenda. As a result, the Michigan Men and Allen Kierstein went to jail. Parson ended up in a maximum-security penitentiary, while Mac Walker had pled down to a lesser charge in exchange for a lighter sentence.

"You know what I saw on that last page?" Ben asked.

"Nothing *bueno*."

"Our names. Mine *and* yours. And you wonder how it could be a coincidence? They were talking about a meeting between Dominguez and the law firm, and our names pop up. They set up the meeting in that house at that time because they knew we'd be there. They set us up. Not only that, but they have clones of our phones."

"Shit," Rico said.

"It sounds like they know more about us than we know about them, yet we're the ones who have been investigating all this time. Something just doesn't add up. I've run across Jason Cruz's name so many times it's making my head spin, and every time he feeds me some story proving he has nothing to do with this case, like I'm supposed to believe him. My friend. Not only is he sleeping with the victim, but he's got money riding on her. I need to call the son of a bitch right now."

"It's not like we're connected to the outside world right now," Rico said, biting his lip. The frustration seemed to bloom within his face, causing deeper lines to dig into his cheeks and chisel a weathered look into his expression.

"We're going to need burner phones," Ben said.

"Makes us look guilty."

"So does breaking and entering, trespassing, and shooting," Ben countered. "We need to get new tires on this car and keep driving it. We leave it and the police will link us with the shootout and the wrecked SUV. It would be really easy to track it to us, since this is a rental car. The last thing we need is the cops on our tail."

"When you took this case," Rico said, biting at his lip, "did you think it would get this dangerous? Can't we just give it up right now? Tell the *pendejo* we don't have enough invested in the case to get shot up, head back to Carson City and live a normal life."

"We can't," Ben said. "Too much riding on it."

"So you're going to get us killed? Make the call. Or I'm walking."

Ben sighed, wishing that Rico could see the scenario unfold from a perspective tangential to his own. Whatever direction this case would ultimately lead, only more danger would follow. From now on, he'd have to operate incognito, even more so than he had. A burner phone would be a good start. Carefully following the evidence and double checking for setups and traps would be necessary as well. Ben needed Rico.

"Just sit there planning our next near-death experience," Rico shot. "You know what? Drive it yourself."

"No," Ben said. "You're not going anywhere; we both know that. Besides, even if you leave, Dominguez and company know who you are. I'd say your odds of making it back to Carson in one piece are about ten-to-one. You know what odds mean. I'm not playing this game with you."

"Maybe the odds of us getting shot dead in Mexico are five-to-one," Rico argued. "I'll take ten-to-one any day and twice on Sunday."

"Fine," Ben said. He swallowed hard and pressed his hand against his stomach as a fresh headache pounded within his skull. "Let's get burner phones and I'll call Jason. Threaten to leave. I don't want either of us to die down here."

Still fuming, Rico rested his head on the headrest as an armada of cars flooded down the road. Dozens of them passed. The wind in their wake shook the car like a moderate earthquake, sending cold shivers through Ben's spine. The noise faded away and Rico's expression slackened. Behind them, one of the cars pulled out and made a U-turn. Rico started the engine and casually rolled away. The crunching, grinding sound of steel on pavement followed them. The other car followed, also casually. Ben and Rico peered into the mirrors in unison.

It was not a cop and the driver wasn't trying to kill them. Rico gently pulled the car back onto the shoulder and waited for the following car to stop. He pressed the power window button, almost as if hoping something would happen before resting his elbow in the window opening and gesturing for the driver to speak with him.

A short conversation in Spanish followed. The act of speaking seemed to still Rico's nerves. Ben watched his expression dance between coarse anger and gentle friendliness. The woman was as fair as white sand on a tropical beach. Her long, black hair fluttered in the breeze as she posed her hand above her brow to shield the sun.

Rico had probably only stopped because she was a woman, but she didn't seem to speak seductively, or even mildly flirtatious.

"*Habla Inglés?*" Rico asked her.

"Yes," she said. Her accent was thick with a Baja zeal that seemed to blossom in the breeze as though pushed through her windpipes via a spring breeze. "I do business with lots of Californians. You are?"

"A Californian," Ben said. He wasn't willing to allow trust to endanger another encounter, so he kept his sentences short and rested his hand near the seam of his pants so that he could grab the gun should it become necessary.

"*Norte*," Rico expounded.

"Why is your car so damaged?"

"Little run-in with the wrong people," Rico said.

"I do know a rental place until you can get this fixed," she said.

Rico shook his head. He opened his mouth to speak but allowed himself to gaze at the mountains and the canopy once more. In the meantime, he attached a quixotic smile to his face and let reason slide.

"You know, I think I am a little attached to this car," he said. "We've been through a lot together. Driving a rental would feel like betrayal."

Ben scoffed but attempted to stifle the sound.

"We're just going to get new tires." He shifted in his seat and studied her face. "Not that we're bad people, he and I, just forgive us for being a little untrusting. You know how phone signals can get crossed this close to the border. Do you know where we can get a couple of burner phones?"

She laughed. "Yes, I actually hear that a lot. With the drug wars going on, I think Americans are starting to get cautious. You're going to want to talk to a man called Jorge Villanueva. He owns his own tire shop near the arch."

"He sells phones, too?"

She nodded. "*Sí*, and no one ever gets tracked. They are the cleanest phones you can get, guaranteed."

"*Gracias*," Rico said. He uttered a short sentence in Spanish and nodded just before she casually walked away. Rico gazed into the side mirror and watched her until she climbed behind the wheel of her car, probably focusing on her rear end.

"What's life without a Good Samaritan?" Rico said.

"That's one *muy* Good Samaritan," Ben said with a mocking smile.

"I should ask for her number. Think she'd like to tango with this *hombre*? We could travel North America together. I always wanted to see the Washington Monument and the giant cheese wheel. Never pass up a good *queso*."

"I think she's a little out of your league," Ben said.

"What's that supposed to mean?" Rico's expression shimmered with the glow of a newfound charisma and energy he hadn't encountered since they left Reno. "I mean, *you* got *Rose*."

Ben tried to laugh, but the thought of her could only shoot fragments of worry to every corner of his brain until thoughts of her consumed him. She waited in Reno within the eyesight of a creep who just happened to be an unsuspecting ally, and she didn't really know what the man was capable of. Instead, Ben allowed a grimace to crisscross his face and his eyes to narrow into weary slits that darkened the landscape into a dreary world with fuzzy lines and edges. Nothing good could come of her visiting San Diego at this point, and if her suspicion that Allen was after her again proved correct, she'd be in danger soon, if not already.

With that, Ben surrendered to the pain. He pictured her walking along Virginia Street below the dancing neon as her world brimmed with the sort of excitement she'd left behind in Washington D.C. Rose was smart. Smarter than Ben and Rico put together, and she used her intellect to good results whether they served her well or not. She would stroll down the street like she owned it, her silver hair floating behind her while sly Alligator Dan lurked in the shadows, watching and waiting for the moment to strike, if he had a reason to.

After a moment of hesitation that Ben hardly noticed, Rico waited for traffic to clear and pulled out slowly onto the busy road. Keeping the gas steady, he travelled along the edge of the road so that faster cars could pass him while pointing and laughing. The trip was excruciating and the steady rip of metal rolling on asphalt ground Ben's perception to nothingness. Halfway through the drive, he closed his eyes and allowed Rose's sweet smile to fill his void with something that resembled hope. He'd tell a joke and she'd laugh. He'd give her a little kiss on the cheek, and she'd push him against a wall. The way she played with him wrought a youthful energy between them and for a few hours, Ben didn't remember being a nearly fifty-eight-year-old private investigator. She saw in him something different, the smoldering remnant of humanity restored after decades of deconstruction.

The suburbs had faded, and the canopy of trees had fizzled out. Tijuana was a mass of buildings and apartments pressed against streets jammed with life. Here, the houses took on a more industrial feel, cloaked in light pink, brown, and cream white. They stacked on top of each other, clustering on hillsides and interspersed with a few high-rises. Having spent lots of time in Tijuana when he was younger, Rico knew how to find the arch.

Sticking to the side roads, Rico passed the arch and searched the storefronts for the tire shop the woman had described. Before long, he found it and pulled in behind an aging black Buick.

Rico sat still with his hands on the steering wheel and waited for a man with slicked hair and a moustache to greet him. Their conversation burst forth in blazing-fast Spanish, none of which Ben could understand.

The man nodded and walked away before Rico silently pulled through one of the open bay doors and positioned the car so that the shop men could install new rear tires.

"Jorge is inside," Rico said.

They walked through the double doors and found themselves in a small waiting room. Four other customers waited. One of them perused a catalogue at a coffee table while the television displayed some strange Spanish-language nonsense. Another customer gazed at a set of rims and flipped through a brochure.

A muscular man in his forties stepped out from a double-hinged swinging door that led to a back room, where the real business was done, or so Ben imagined. He held out his huge, meaty hand and extended it to Rico first, followed by Ben. "Jorge Villanueva," he said. "Allison said you need tires and something else I can help with."

"Allison?" Ben asked.

"The woman on the road," Jorge confirmed. "I can hook you up, just come on back to my office."

Ben and Rico followed him beyond a single rack of tires and through the swinging door. The small, smoky room beyond the doors contained a pair of vending machines, a small round table, and three plastic chairs. Jorge turned right and entered another room through a regular door. He pressed the door closed behind them and offered Ben and Rico seats.

The atmosphere caused a certain flair of delirium. The office was cluttered with paperwork and stacked car maintenance manuals, while an overflowing trash bin sat next to the desk, which Jorge sat behind. He pushed his chair back and stretched out his legs.

"Burner phones. Popular tourist item, believe it or not. Lots of San Diego people complain that they get wrong number texts in Spanish because of the overlapping cell networks. And they think it makes them targets. Lots of them are phishing. Just ignore them and go on your way."

"I heard about that," Rico said.

"So why you need them, eh?"

"Let's say we need to be off the radar," Ben said, perhaps oversimplifying it. "Need communication without being tracked, and we don't have any phones at all."

"Prepaid? Network coverages are great if you need them, but most people just use them as temporary until they get home."

Ben nodded. "International calling, too, mostly to talk with contacts in San Diego."

"*Sí*," Jorge said. He shrugged and flexed his biceps with his hands laced behind his head. "And tires. I hear your car got shot up by some drug people. If you need a body shop I can recommend one."

"That won't be necessary," Ben said.

"It's not as uncommon as it sounds. Cartels have been at war down here for decades, but the police start to get suspicious when they see a car with California plates and a hundred bullet holes. Grab some Mexico license plates and they'll leave you alone."

Rico rested his shoulders and pressed back against the back of the chair, keeping his eyes on a maintenance manual.

"I suppose you know where we can get fake ones," Ben said.

"Sure. But probably better not try to cross the border with your car like that. American customs isn't about to let Americans with gun holes to enter, even if you are a citizen and your passport checks out. They'll assume you've been involved in a drug war. Which honestly, I can't blame them for it. This city has problems, you know."

"Where do we get license plates?" Rico asked.

"Got them here, for a little extra. I just need you to sign a waiver saying you won't try to hold me legally responsible if you get in a dispute with police. Also, obey the laws."

"Of course," Rico said, attempting to smooth out his accent.

Jorge stood up, opened a cabinet, pulled out a pair of phones and a laptop computer and placed them on the desk. He returned to the cabinet and withdrew two license plates.

The man worked his magic quickly, making sure that the phones were properly connected and clean, he punched buttons on the laptop furiously until he was finished. He pressed the phones and the plates across the table and smiled.

Rico returned the smile. "*Señorita* Allison," he started. "What's with her?"

"Don't think she meets many Americans for pleasure," Jorge said. "Americans call it dating."

Rico uttered something in Spanish that, for some reason, Ben assumed to mean, "Look at me, I'm Mexican."

"You can call her," Jorge said, raising his palms. "You might have a better chance if you speak Spanish."

"What does she do?" Rico said.

"Tourism. Americans still come here, so she meets with them and tells them which hotels to stay at, which attractions to visit, and where in the city not to go. She always tells them not to get dental work done. But you're not here for that, otherwise your car wouldn't have more bullet holes than parts."

"Good guess," Ben said.

"Curious, what does bring you down to our fair city?"

"Not at liberty to discuss that," Ben said.

"No trust?"

"Hardly," Ben confirmed. "You work at a job long enough, you start to learn that you can't really trust anyone, not even your friends."

Jorge nodded and stood up. "Fair enough. But be careful, my friends. Tijuana can be dangerous for Americans, too."

Without saying anything more, Ben and Rico stood up and followed Jorge back into the small lobby. Through the large windows into the shop, Ben glanced at the car, which had been hoisted onto a platform. One of the tires had already been installed, while two men spun the other on a balancing machine.

Ben offered Jorge a wad of cash for his help. Given the currency exchange rate, the money he paid was likely worth more than the tires, phones, and license plates combined. Jorge nodded at them as they waited and disappeared behind the doors once more.

An uneasy feeling crept over Ben, like shards of history brimming with memory that could reduce him to dust. Jorge Villanueva had been friendly enough, which set Ben on edge. Why the mask? he wondered. He didn't imagine that someone in another country dealing in illicit business would act friendly. Either he had a reason to act that way, or he was playing them.

Ben swallowed hard and waited for the car. Haunting melodies colluded with droning engines and drums somewhere in his imagination, burning the tune into his fragile memory like the venom of a thousand snakes. Mexico could not offer relief, only Nina Perez. And finding her only led to more danger.

Entropy Seven

May 21, 2011

15:00

BEN PUNCHED HIS LEFT knee as he waited outside a shopping center near the border for Rico to emerge with a simple list of supplies. Impatience had already worn him thin, but expecting a call from Jason Cruz redefined the experience. Every few seconds, he glanced in the mirror by accident, and upon promising himself he wouldn't look again, observed the lines running ever deeper into his face and his gray hair growing more unkempt.

At some point, the torture of waiting had invoked the opening salvos of a war that could not be won. He was pissed, but knowing that yelling at Jason wouldn't help, the prospect of devising a new plan would prove just as dizzying as opening up.

Years ago, Ben had mastered manipulating his own emotions to reveal the right face for the right situation, but time had gently ground that skill into powder. Ben still practiced it but enjoyed favorable benefits more and more rarely.

His phone rang and he bit his tongue. The landscape around him grayed with dreaded blight. The shopping areas in this part of the city merged with less-dense housing that had sprung up less than a decade ago. Steadily, more and more homes were abandoned, becoming havens for drug activity and squatters. The steeper hillsides grew over with dry grass and sparse vegetation, making the area seem derelict.

"You finally decided to call," Ben said. "And don't bother asking, because I wouldn't have dialed your number if it weren't safe."

"Where are you?" This time, Jason pressed the attack. "I tried your hotel room this morning and the phone just rang. We've got problems."

A frown engulfed his face, and he pulled back his incendiary speech and relied on a cooler tone. "I'd say that's expected. You want my news first?"

"If you haven't found Nina, why would you even make this call?" Agitation flooded Jason's voice, making him sound foreign and bitter. "But you'd never let up, because you are Benjamin R. Carr."

Ben considered the scathing commentary and momentarily made the mistake of wondering what he'd done to elicit such a charge. Jason, however, displayed more traits of an animal when backed into a corner. As such, he played his hand early, leaving him less with which to bargain.

"We're close. That might be why it's getting so dangerous."

"You want to talk about dangerous? Find Nina. Walk a mile in her shoes. Because you don't know who you're fucking with."

"I'm beginning to," Ben said. If he kept his cool and practiced this level of indifference, he'd succeed in getting Jason to explode. Fury was what he needed and he knew how to push Jason's buttons. Jason, however, understood the game. When pressed he sometimes forgot the rules, which only benefitted the opposition. "But perhaps you could have saved us all of the trouble and disclosed this information ahead of time."

"Maybe I should have."

"I should explain myself," Ben lamented, letting out an exhale slowly so as to not allow Jason to hear. "I'd say we were ambushed. Evidence pointed to a house south of Tijuana, the home of one Omar Dominguez. I think you know about him. Omar had two boats. One of them he used to send his goons to San Diego with product and the other he used as a leisure toy. Warranty information on the second boat led us to the house. But they already knew we were going to be there and they explicitly wrote it out. It sounds convenient, wouldn't you agree?"

"Jesus." Jason's voice lowered and his tone suggested a sly ambivalence that Ben could not embrace. Instead, he'd let it play out, but it vanished like fog on a hot day. "How did it work?"

"You know, I wonder if they stacked the evidence to make it appear as though Omar lived in that house specifically because they already had a meeting set up to oppose some project called Bayfront. You'll never guess who is on the legal team."

"I wouldn't know that."

"You would. You know him."

Jason sighed. "Are we done playing games yet? Just tell me who it is."

"I'm not ready to," Ben sniped. "But you'll probably figure it out if you put your mind to it."

"I didn't hire you to ask me how to figure out your case, you son of a bitch. You know why you're here. Do your own job."

"And who was it that got me on this tangent in Tijuana in the first place? Your good friend Castro."

"I don't know Castro."

"Of course you don't. Castro has proven to be a slippery shit, and I think San Diego PD should collar him. He told me about Dominguez's boat and knew I'd use that information to eventually find his house. And the letter from the law firm hadn't been there for very long. By the time I pieced the information together, it was already too late."

"Tell me you didn't break into the house," Jason said.

"Should I have just called and asked him how to get in?"

"Maybe."

Ben gritted his teeth and gathered his strength for one more push. "Tijuana is a lovely city. Where do you stay when you come here? How do the locals treat you? I'd wager you've been here a half dozen times in the last six months."

"I... have never been... to Tijuana," Jason growled.

"Doesn't matter if you have or haven't," Ben admitted. "You just gave me all the ammo I need. Now you have to go along, because there's enough there for money laundering charges... against you."

"I don't know what you're talking about," Jason said.

The strands of ironic humor in his voice were easy to grasp. Confronting him with it was one thing but getting him to admit it over the phone would be like asking him to sign his own death warrant.

"Now it's your turn," Ben said. "What could you possibly have that warranted calling me in my hotel room so early this morning?"

"I heard about your little gunfight," Jason jabbed. "The department is nice and amused over it. They are on to Nina's son, Ben. They lured him to a park late last night, got him to talk, and delivered him back to his home. Then his father called the cops. The boy is in danger."

"They brought him back? Great kidnapper."

"You know what I'm talking about," Jason blasted. "Don't even try to spin it like that. Alex is a special kid and I've been trying to protect him. You know he's going to work for NASA after he gets out of college. That kind of ambition can't be taught in public school, let alone some Catholic preschool for the children of the rich."

"So you're trying to use him as a ploy to get me to find his mother when you haven't been able to do the same thing yourself?"

"Shut up," Jason spat.

"Oh, but you're just a banker. It's beyond the scope of your interest. Just looking after the bottom line. When does your company fire you for going too far?"

"You know what, Ben? It must be fun and games for you. Anyone can see that. But this boy's life is at stake and so is his mother's. I was wrong to hire you, but you're here and we can't give up now. I'll give you Dominguez. But you've got to save the kid's life."

"*You'll* give me Dominguez? Like you've been sitting on his information the whole time?"

"I mentioned him at the outset." Jason's defense was simple and justified but could not have come at a greater cost.

Ben had made a big mistake in ignoring Dominguez until this point, but to admit that error would be to call into question his career and thus, his entire life.

"I thought you would have been able to find him easier. If I give you this information, you stop looking at me and you stop looking at Castro. Am I clear?"

Ben's jaw dropped. He stared at the skyline of the mountains in the distance to the east and noticed Rico strutting out of the store carrying two bags. That big of a mistake should have doomed Jason Cruz, but how untouchable was he?

"I don't need to look at you anymore," Ben said. "But I'm still not defending you in court if they call me as a witness."

"There's no evidence suggesting I ever did anything wrong," Jason said. "You don't try someone if you have no evidence. And you don't call witnesses if there is no trial. It's bullshit. And it's getting in the way of you finding Nina. I need her."

"Yes, you do," Ben said. "I have no doubt about that. I'm not going to make that pact on Castro, because I have enough on him to put him in jail for twenty years. And that's even if he had nothing to do with Ms. Perez's disappearance, which I'm not so certain about. I'll look at Castro for as long as it takes."

"Shit. If this goes down, I'm going to kill you. You know that, right?"

"Yeah," Ben said. "I know. So tell me about Dominguez."

"Omar Dominguez has an apartment in Tijuana, but he's only there for a few weeks in April and from June through August. He spends the rest of his time in Mexico City, where he contracts with a drug cartel. He ships the merchandise to the port in Tijuana, where it gets loaded onto a boat bound for certain harbors on the California coast. In the case of really important shipments, he goes with the merchandise to Baja California and sends it off himself by some hired hands. Taking it in by boat bypasses the stuff you hear about on the news, where mules die of exhaustion or gunshots while trying to cross in the desert. It avoids the scrutiny of Border Patrol and Homeland Security. After that, all you have to do is get by the Coast Guard, but that's easy when you're using a boat registered in San Diego."

"You're sure about Mexico City?"

"Absolutely," Jason said. "When have I ever lied to you?"

Ben laughed as Rico slammed the door and settled into the driver's seat. He was halfway finished unwrapping a candy bar, when he glared up at Ben as though a lightbulb had just gone off inside his skull.

"Are we talking just the last few minutes?"

"Another thing," Jason said. "You know that man whose photograph I sent you? There's been some activity on that. A reporter from D.C. inquired about him, but now they understand she's not really a reporter. For everyone's benefit, I'd suggest you get Rose off it."

Ben hesitated. "I will, but she's probably got everything she needs already."

"San Diego PD is going to find him, I'm sure of it," Jason said, lowering his voice to something resembling thoughtful discourse not bent to destroy Ben.

Ben's heart leapt from the precipice into a furnace that fueled discord and concocted a potion that rend his senses with waves of burning agony. This knowledge tore his heart with thorns as he pushed toward an all-too-tangible truth. Only one person could save him from the brink and cool the flames. And her hair once blossomed with those same dances of fire.

16:30

THE TELEVISION DRONED ON at low volume while a news commentator explained the phenomenon of a large protest in Taiwan over concern that the local or Chinese governments were not seeking any resolution to a growing human-trafficking crisis. Rose had turned the volume down an hour ago while some idiotic daytime soap opera was running. Sometimes, background noise seemed essential to quiet the din of the screaming inside her head.

With one pillow wedged vertically behind her back and the other, more flattened pillow stacked on top of it, Rose propped up the laptop on her knees and steadied it. She had positioned her body in such a way that she'd have to physically move her head and her computer to look at the TV. This method of avoiding distraction usually worked, but more often she worked in silence, when the thoughts could organize themselves into cogent ideas and logic could erect the structure behind her words.

The police detective she had spoken with had mentioned that Tyran Blackmon was last seen on the campus of the University of California, San Diego. If Tyran had been on campus, especially such a large campus so far away from his home, Rose considered it likely that he was attending classes.

She'd shaken her head once at the possibility that a 38-year-old would be exploring a new career but decided that at no age could one be disqualified from furthering his or her education.

Her assertion had proven correct. Tyran was seeking an engineering degree, according to deep searches on the school website. With minimal hacking, she had managed to find a list of emails associated with one major-related class. She had hurriedly typed out an email to which she had sent to every address on the list.

Hi, I am Detective Rosalyn Kierstein, San Diego Police Department. We are looking for information on Tyran Blackmon. I understand you shared Applied Materials classes with Tyran. Would you be able to call me this afternoon so I can take your statement? It is imperative that we find Tyran as soon as possible for his own safety.

She'd left her number after the message and continued searching. Tyran's last-known address was in a neighborhood on the inner side of National City. The house was a narrow two-story structure with a yellowed stucco and brick exterior with windows framed in whitewashed wood. Tyran's address indicated that his unit occupied the second floor of the International Arms apartments. Three small units on each floor composed the complex, and surprisingly, rent ran far below averages for both the neighborhood and the San Diego area. Photographs of the building did not show Tyran, but she tried to imagine his home life.

In her scenario, Tyran would return home from school, exhausted from the traffic, and spread his books across the small, circular dining table with a crosshatch lattice wood imprint surface and steel banding at its rim. He'd flick on the lights, kick his shoes off, lean back on the couch and surf channels until he found something to distract him from the chore of homework. While his girlfriend waited tables at a nearby restaurant, he'd pretend to care about the assignments until less than an hour before she was scheduled to return home. She'd want to snuggle and watch a movie, so he'd agree to take his books to the couch and use her shoulder as note-taking surface while she gradually drifted off to sleep.

He'd wake up with a headache in the morning, scan the newspaper for interesting headlines, shower, and then jam the necessary belongings into his bag to start the whole process over again while he dreamed of the beach.

She glanced at the clock on the bottom of the screen and decided to check her email again. Seven classmates had replied to her email, but none had called. She read their messages one by one. Angie Duston said she studied with Tyran and promised to call her when her class let out.

Two others denied knowing Tyran, while a fourth seemed apathetic to the entire affair. Two of the classmates acted as though Rose were just another authority figure not worth their time. While both knew Tyran, neither cared enough to cooperate with a law enforcement officer so readily.

Rose's phone vibrated at her side. She stretched her fingers, picked it up, and continued to stare at the screen while she spoke.

"This is Detective Rose Kierstien,"

"Hi, Detective Kierstien." Her voice resonated with the weak echo of apprehension, dulled by wisps of exhaustion. "This is Angie Duston. You wanted me to call?"

Rose hit the 'enter' key and pressed her head against the pillow more forcefully while pushing her legs down far enough to reveal the top half of the television screen. "Yes, thank you for your call. You know Tyran Blackmon?"

"I do."

"How well do you know him?"

"I guess you could say he's a friend. I mean, we've never hung out or anything, but he seems pretty cool. Likes surfing a lot." Her voice remained mostly flat, but she spoke naturally without unnecessary pauses or stressing odd syllables.

"What was your first impression of him?" Rose let her imagination ask the question, hoping to build a more concrete profile in her mind, and every detail Angie injected further fleshed out the portrait.

"Oh, I don't know. When you're just starting your major and you look around and see someone his age, you kind of get a little culture shock. A couple of girls were annoyed that someone so old would be starting a degree. They were worried that he'd slow the class down. But he seemed pretty smart, I guess. When he started giving thoughtful, detailed answers to the professor's questions, people started taking him more seriously."

Without speaking for a moment, Rose readjusted her legs and leaned her head forward slightly. "Did he attend class every day?"

"Just about. He mostly kept to himself, but I guess you kind of have to when you're... I don't know, mid-thirties... compared to everyone else. But then he stopped coming altogether about a month ago. Most of the girls I talk to assumed he'd dropped out, but I'm not so sure."

Rose's ears perked up when she said it. The sentence didn't change in tone, but one accentuated syllable caught her attention immediately, inflecting the statement with just enough passion to elicit concern. The accent indicated a flicker of sadness and the understanding of a cruelty so grave that any possible resolution caused her heart to leap. Rose latched onto the impression and followed up.

"You're not sure? Why is that?"

She hesitated. "Well. He had a career mapped out. He wanted to design high-rise buildings and he knew people in the construction industry who he thought could help him get the perfect job."

The answer seemed stock and labored, but Rose allowed her to continue.

"And then there was the part where he confided in me. It was about two days before the last time I saw him. I think he liked me, but I'm way too young. He said his girlfriend was going to leave him, but he already had a plan to deal with it. I told him… I said not to do anything, you know, stupid because girls tend to panic when guys do crazy things to win them over. And he didn't seem to know any of the sweet gestures, or care about them."

"And then he just vanished?"

"He said something about Mexico. He was going to get it, but I don't recall him telling me what it was."

"But it must have been important."

A coy silence slipped between them. Rose allowed it to wrap itself around the conversation, enveloping it with a dour scent of evening fog and wine.

"Important enough to go to the end of the world? He didn't tell me anything about her, so I thought maybe she sought after a family heirloom or something, because he seriously seemed to lack the emotional quotient to make a long-lasting gesture of love, which probably would have worked. But it was the thought that counted."

"Mexico?"

"There was a picture of one of the pyramids down there in his binder, the ruins of an ancient city."

Rose leaned her head backward and absorbed another moment of silence. "Did he mention anyone going with him, or going to see anyone?"

"No, not really. But from the way he stated things, it sounded like he had some relatives down there. I think so, anyway, but..."

"But?"

"I don't think he has a Mexican bone in his body, and he's never been before. He flashed a copy of a passport application at one point a few days earlier."

"Is there anything else you can remember that might be important?"

"Um, can you hold on a second?"

Rose agreed and waited in silence. The television droned, but only every other word was audible, even during the commercials, which often drove her mad with increasing regularity. Rose rubbed her shoulder with her free hand and stared down at the screen in dismay. Tyran Blackmon was not in Mexico. He'd appeared on a surveillance camera on campus yesterday.

"Hi, I'm back," Angie said. "Just a friend from a study group. She just mentioned that she saw Tyran walking across campus toward the library this morning, like he was in a hurry."

"Can I talk to her?"

"Sorry, she's gone," Angie said. "I've got to run too. So maybe it's a false alarm and no one has to worry about anything."

"I hope he found what he was looking for," Rose commented.

She hesitated but stayed on the line. "You're not really a cop, are you?"

Rose sighed. "Why would you ask that?"

Her voice strengthened immediately, pressing her into a territory Rose had not fully explored where surprises could abound.

"You don't talk like one. It's just so simple."

Rose thought she knew how to ask questions like a cop. After all, her main character Carrie was a cop, and Rose had studied videotapes of police conversations and had even sat down with a homicide detective once. It wasn't in the lingo, she'd taught herself. The tone and delivery of every sentence and every syllable was packed with an explosive compound of sterile and rigid emotion. In this conversation, Rose had given too much, but she'd gotten Angie to speak, which had been the motive all along.

"Don't get me wrong, whatever you're doing is cool. Like genealogy stuff? I hope it works out. I've got to get going."

"Thanks for the conversation," Rose said.

She hung up the phone as a brief flash of victory floated through her veins, leaving behind a void of shallow hope. Something didn't seem right. In crime cases, the victim never just turned up during the investigation like nothing had happened. Something deeper always lurked beneath the surface like a serpent ready to strike.

The flicker of hope vanished, and a roaring fire took its place, reaching for the stars like the invisible Native American spirits on a cold summer evening. The embers flashed and burned. For now, only one logical outcome existed. Rose swallowed hard and closed her laptop. Tyran Blackmon turning up alive and well could only be a curse disguised as a blessing. She had to tell Ben.

Silhouette of Justice

May 22, 2011

09:00

RIBBONS OF STEAM EMANATED from Styrofoam cups situated on a long table in front of those privileged enough to drink coffee. For others, water would have to suffice. Water had its uses, Allen thought, but drinking was hardly one of them. When thirst struck, more appropriate means existed to combat it.

A half-dozen people dressed in business attire occupied one side of the table, which had been arranged along one of the large cafeteria windows. The light spilled in spectacular rays, illuminating the table, but leaving much of the remainder of the cafeteria bathed in shadow. Allen took one look at the set up and decided a different arrangement would offer more advantages.

By placing the parole commissioners and the examiner in the light, the warden had ensured that all attention would fall on those people. It also commanded authority. The warden was a prick, but Allen couldn't deny that he was gruesomely intelligent.

Allen eyed the coffee and then glanced to Carter, who had taken a seat next to him behind another table facing the commissioners. That sleazeball had taken it upon himself to dig up dirt on every member of the parole board in order to form a strategy. His first order of advice made Allen frown.

"No coffee. Remember, it's less about the evidence than the image at this point. It's really stupid, but coffee evokes a seedier image."

Allen rolled his eyes and frowned while making a fist under the table because Carter was right.

"Let's get started," the examiner, a gray-haired man in a black suit said. A hush fell over the room. "This is the parole hearing for Allen Kierstein on the twenty-second of May 2011. Be advised that this hearing will be recorded and all of your statements will be considered when the board makes its decision on whether to grant you parole. If any answer you give purposefully omits facts or misstates events, your parole will be denied. Do you understand?"

And Carter was crazy enough to implore Allen to tell the truth? Truth existed as a construct only in the mind of the one who told his story. Whether or not his record coincided with the actual events was irrelevant, as long as one relayed that story with absolute honesty.

Allen could only muster a sheepish nod. Acting submissive drove him insane, but as big a pain in the ass as Carter could be, he could read situations with striking clarity.

The silence only afforded him time for a single gulp. He turned his head and surveyed the team of board members. Russ Cohen had a career of legal service behind him and wielded it to achieve many special perks. He rose up the ranks in the Maryland system, where he'd amassed enough influence to lobby for out-of-state interests. Carter had unearthed a juicy pay-for-play scheme involving Cohen and the governor of West Virginia, but as always, no charges were ever explored. Another attorney, a woman named Rebecca Hargreaves, donned a navy blue dress and shiny earrings. A sheath of black hair draped the sides of her face and gathered into a loose ponytail. She made her earliest strides as a public defender for an accused murderer, which had always been described as a thankless, but necessary job. As such, she won few cases. Her strut indicated a strict formality and her face remained expressionless. The façade of emptiness, Allen always thought, was one of the easiest to break, because keeping the image required more work than allowing nature to dictate the path of questioning. While she busied herself constructing the framework of her outward appearance, Allen could combat by deconstructing. Then again, he had to be careful. Attitude and arrogance could be the only thing keeping him locked up. He could play the innocence card like none other. It was all in the tone.

"Mr. Kierstien," the Examiner Rosenfelt started, his voice flat and his head level, "You were convicted of conspiracy, extortion, and attempted murder in the aftermath of events in Montana. Can you speak to those events?"

Allen cleared his throat and gazed at him. Contempt filled his veins, but he controlled his body language with the kind of precise command that politicians employed when telling their adoring fans how they would work for them instead of moneyed interests.

"Of course, I was not in Montana when the incident took place—"

"But you directed it."

Allen nodded and swallowed without diverting his attention. It was important to play for the board in this case, not the examiner, so his body language needed to incite emotional response in them foremost.

Allen offered a curt glance to Carter and leaned forward in his chair. "That's correct. I had some contacts, guys I called the Michigan Men, due to their home state. They attended to matters in a way that wasn't always lawful."

"And is it true that you did it all just to get back at your wife, who had left you?"

"That she'd left me was unimportant," Allen intimated. "I understand how she perceived it, but the incident didn't have much to do with her."

"She made off pretty well," Rosenfelt said. "Not to mention, fear had become part of life for her."

The examiner could manipulate emotions like world-class attorneys who represented high-dollar foreign agents and mob bosses. Allen didn't let his comment bite him where it mattered, responding at first with a dull look of aged animosity that would only look like the after-effects of years in prison.

"The details of my divorce are irrelevant," Allen said with a flick of his eyebrows. "She left me because I made a mistake. Too many bad deals and an affair."

"Mr. Kierstien," the examiner said, shuffling his feet and squaring his shoulders, "could you describe how your wife leaving you was unimportant?"

"They are two separate events. I sent the Michigan Men because a conglomerate I'd invested in had some legal issues over a development that borders an Indian Reservation. The Michigan Men were there to report back to me."

"Did you know that Rose Kierstien was in Montana at the time?"

Allen glanced at Carter and then subtly nodded. "Yes."

"So it would seem that her leaving you was not as unimportant as you claim."

Allen flashed a smile while studying the expressions of the board members. They stared at him as if with rapt interest, but Allen hadn't yet stolen their compassion. They were, after all, seasoned lawyers. Hargreaves bit her lip and offered a funny expression that communicated first, that she believed him, but also that she wasn't ready to invest trust in his story.

"After all of that, she has chosen to continue her life elsewhere. Do you know where that is? And would she still have reason to live in fear?"

The examiner worked Rose's angle so hard that it made Allen want to strangle him. Instead, he let the comment pass and rested his gaze on him. "I can't see how it matters."

"Answer the question," he grated.

"Even if I did know, I wouldn't do anything about it. I recognize that I screwed up and I wouldn't dream about going after her. I think Rose knows that."

"You have financial entanglements all over the country and outside of it," the examiner explained. "Can you tell me how your portfolio has changed since the incident in Montana?"

"Most of the investments have been liquidated," Allen said. "I sold shares of everything local and international. My only remaining assets are in banking."

"Do you have any remaining 'Michigan Men' or similar agents working for you at this time?"

"I've cut ties. The Michigan Men have disbanded, and I have not been in contact with them personally." Telling the truth made his stomach turn. To hide the agony, Allen frowned and sipped from the glass of water in front of him.

Rosenfelt continued to grill him, resorting to an aggressive tactic that Allen didn't expect. Instead of letting this cause alarm, he met it with a simplistic glance and a concealed air of defiance.

"Are there any other business ties that do similar work?"

"No," Allen said. "It's over."

The examiner squared his jaw and lowered his eyebrows. "This may be compelling evidence, Mr. Kierstien, but we haven't discussed your emotional state in the aftermath of all this. And that's what really matters."

"It doesn't matter at all," Allen countered, trying not to sneer at him. He caught Carter extolling a virtuous thumb of his nose, and then made up for his blunder by slumping his shoulders as if in shame.

"It *doesn't matter?* Mr. Kierstien, do I have to remind you that you attempted to obstruct justice and that you had threatened to have Mrs. Kierstien killed? You were found guilty in a court of your peers."

Allen looked down and offered a short, contemplative sigh. "Yes. It's true. I don't deny it."

To stir up the demons of a troubling past was an interesting and regrettably efficient tactic, but Allen had expected it and had conditioned himself to wait out the storm until the fury of his accusations subsided. Allen added nothing more.

"Mr. Kierstien."

Allen frowned and let his eyebrows slacken while remaining motionless in the chair. His speech carried a firm and direct message that could not be understated. The examiner would use it against him, but the power with which he spoke could elicit some compassion amongst the parole board.

"I did not attempt to have her killed and I did not try to obstruct justice. The Michigan Men were there to report back to me. Once there, they encountered an opposition they did not expect and fought back, but they acted of their own accord. I had no influence whatsoever."

The examiner lowered his eyebrows and glanced down to a sheet of paper perched in front of him as though he'd worked himself into a hard spot and wished to consult notes to free himself. Before he continued, he curled his lip and aimed a contemptuous stare at Allen meant to ignite ire. Allen shrugged and relaxed his shoulders, a tactic he'd learned in prison that almost always caused prosecutors to retreat.

Instead, the examiner escalated the salvo. "Remarkable constraint. Either prison didn't have much effect on you, or you think you're innocent."

Carter sighed. "Entrapment is not allowable!"

Rosenfelt glanced at Carter and subtly leaned toward the table, as if to offer an explosive retort. Instead, he held his opinion. Allen caught the notion immediately and moved to attack the second of aggression with another powerful statement.

"I was not innocent of most accusations, and if being locked up has taught me anything, it's that the value of human life is too great to overcome with money or influence."

The examiner moved to tear apart his statement, but before he retorted, he bit his lip. "Influence is the kicker here. Influence. You've managed to corrupt too many people in this world. Your Michigan Men sought to influence a court case. I'm afraid to say that your influence is all over the map and perhaps four years is not sufficient to change that. Do you disagree?"

"I can't deny that I made mistakes, but it's over. To a man dedicated to self-improvement, change doesn't take a lifetime. I think I've proven that."

"How can you demonstrate that you have reformed? Are we supposed to take you for your word?"

"I've divested all my holdings," Allen said, leaning forward and ignoring Carter, who seemed to nonverbally warn him not to explore this avenue. "I've started from the ground up. All my old contacts are gone, and I have started to invest into companies I believe in that are doing a lot of good in the world. I've given to charity, and I've forgiven my past."

Rosenfelt stared at him, awaiting more.

Allen didn't immediately respond, which caused the examiner to change the subject. "What is your relation to Rose Kierstien now?"

"She's my ex-wife and I have not spoken to her in more than four years."

"Do you know where she is living now?"

"I don't care where she's living now," Allen said. "She's free to make her own decisions and I am not a part of them. I don't know where she lives."

The examiner backtracked and offered a quick glare. "You say you've liquidated almost all your investments from before you were incarcerated, and in the last year, you say have entered new deals. Can you speak to that?"

Allen flexed his hand and at last discovered a passion within him that could burst forth with enough ferocity to scald everyone in the room. He allowed his speech to carry in waves what shouldn't have conveyed so much emotion. "The offshore accounts I once held are closed. The one foreign deal I had, I sold my shares for bottom dollar, even considering the recession. All my money is handled up front and documented fairly, ensuring proper taxes are paid and obligations are met. Almost all domestic investments are gone, from New Jersey to Michigan to Florida vacation properties. I own one apartment building in D.C. and the title to acreage in Virginia. I've since purchased shares of GE and have invested in commodities."

"That sounds like a diverse portfolio. Why is that?"

"You can't have too much diversity in an economy like this. Some types of investments will perform better than others at certain times. A financial adviser I used to hire routinely pounded that into my head, and it seems he was right."

"Are you making lots of money on that?"

"They're investments," Allen said. "Dividends don't accumulate rapidly in the first year, usually. The rental property is currently my biggest source of income."

"You have been in prison for four years," Rosenfelt said. "How good has your record been?"

Rosenfelt enjoyed the authority to look up the answer to that, which made it a softball, which caught Allen off guard. Instead of appearing stumped, he leaned into it and injected his response with a fickle emotion that wouldn't go far in earning compassion from the board. "I'd say better than good."

Ms. Hargreaves visibly rolled her eyes. She'd heard that defense before, and even to her, it sounded pathetic.

"How so?" the examiner prodded.

"I've helped the guards without being asked. I've never had any incidents with other inmates, and I refused to complain about the conditions."

"Do you feel there is anybody that would attest to your unworthiness for parole?" Allen recognized the question as a trick before Rosenfelt had finished speaking.

Maybe Rose, he thought. He deflected the attempt to trip him up by burrowing a strong expression into his face. He wanted to recoil at what he was about to say. "It seems that at the end of the day, only God can judge me. I've made peace with my past and made good on my contributions to society."

Rosenfelt launched into a disgustingly accurate portrayal of Allen's finer personality traits as a naked attempt to spark caution in the board. "You appear calm today, but your reputation is manipulation and deceit. You know how to game casual onlookers, and you have played people your whole life. Business deals constantly break your way because you know what buttons to push. Furthermore, something still seems to be amiss in your relationship to your ex-wife. She fled you in fear for her life. In the divorce, she made off with a large share of the estate, which brought you financial ruin. All those investments and business deals you described selling were either transferred into her name or crashed with the economy. You have always played the system. You will not play the parole commission.

Allen carefully made eye contact with each of the commissioners before returning his gaze to Rosenfelt. He leaned back slightly for dramatic effect.

"I have shown a willingness to cooperate with authority and clearly demonstrated that the offenses that landed me in prison are behind me. I no longer have contact with my ex-wife despite the very real possibility, that with her fame, she'd be relatively easy to find. Financial investments are not games to be won or lost, they are savings for retirement. Even if certain investments underperformed over the years, my restructuring is concrete proof that I've managed my money. I have had no incidents with guards or other inmates. I served my time and have demonstrated with my actions how I have changed. Please consider that in your deliberations. Thank you."

Allen turned to face Carter and offered a grin and Carter allowed himself to nod slowly.

"Mr. Kierstein, please allow up to two weeks while the parole commission reviews your testimony. Your actions in the meantime will be considered during the commission's deliberations. Unless you have anything to add, this meeting is adjourned."

Allen had mastered himself with precision throughout the hearing. Almost any other convicted felon would have cracked. Rosenfelt's closing argument, though severe, rang with more truth than his own. Denying that fact would be admitting that Allen was no longer suited to play the games of life. No one in the room managed to throw a situation at him where his best defense was to lie. Telling the truth, in hindsight seemed weak, like the fragile embers of childhood waning in the light. He didn't need to exert power because the examiner was too efficient. Such a boring person. While others despised attorneys due to arrogance, Allen confronted them with spite because they were too predictable. Predictability, however often proved virtuous. Unpredictable attorneys were losing attorneys.

With any luck, he wouldn't have to deal with lawyers again for a long time. Still, luck wouldn't have anything to do with it.

He'd made his presentation. The parole board would rule in his favor, and somehow, Rose would regret it.

Hallowed Obsolete

May 22, 2011

15:30

THE SCARS OF HUMANITY burned discolored splotches into the mountainsides as the sun highlighted the towering edges of cumulonimbus clouds. Ben stared at a black section of mountain where an outcropping of granite conjured a spire near the peak. The suburbs of Mexico City stretched far and wide, while the valley was as densely populated as nearly any region on earth. Rico had pulled the car off the highway so they could discuss strategy. The address Jason had given them lay in a central neighborhood of the city, which would present numerous points of potential conflict. If not fully prepared they could find themselves in a disaster from which no escape would be possible.

"You can get us there, right?" Ben said. "You know the streets?"

"GPS lady can," Rico said. "I've never been to the D.F. You know Washington well, right?"

Ben frowned. "Well, they have maps."

Rico pointed at the GPS screen and countered Ben's expression with a glowing smile that oozed with sarcasm. "Look, *señor*, a map."

"I'd say we case the area a little bit, on foot and in disguise. I don't know if there is a 'they' down here, but if they see a car with bullet holes and a gringo in the passenger seat, they're going to know who we are."

"You say 'gringo' like you're the only one, *amigo*," Rico said. "Lots of European-looking people."

Ben shrugged. "Do they all drive shot-up cars?"

Rico grunted.

"Do they have mass transit? Maybe we take a taxicab to within a block or two of the address and poke around. Learn about the neighborhood, grab something to eat, look in the windows. The more we know, the better prepared we'll be."

"Also need to watch our sixes," Rico said. "You got mine, I've got yours?"

A slow nod displayed thoughtful agreement. Ben allowed silence to stretch as he gazed out the window, where dense neighborhoods resided on the gently rolling hills and cut into the base of the mountains. "We'll need to maintain line of sight and have our weapons ready to fire. In a location like that, you'll have a little more than a second to respond, so practice sharpening your reflexes."

"You're one to talk," Rico said. "They dropped you into 'Nam today, you wouldn't make it to sunset."

"Neither would you," Ben said. "But we're not going to have time to train. Just be ready. We know our exits well enough, maybe we don't get shot down."

Rico stared out the window, perhaps thinking about what he would say next, but no words formed. Instead, he paid attention to a group of children crossing a street adjacent to the multiple lanes of traffic rushing by. A young teacher led the group, and the humid wind made her long, black hair flutter behind her. Ben watched his lips for a smile, but none came.

Rather than break the silence, Ben found something to study. A quiet side street cut a jagged slot through a tight cluster of two- and three-story buildings. Idle cars sat along the street, parked within a few feet of the buildings and allowed enough distance between them for one car to pass through slowly. If the whole city sported a similar layout, Ben decided, any escape would present unparalleled danger.

He raised his eyes and gazed at the horizon. The thunderstorms brewing over the mountains convalesced into a giant cloud that would cause torrential rains and a risk of flash flooding. After a minute, he spoke. "This city is insane."

Rico nodded. "You're looking at the biggest city in North America. Eight or nine million in the Distrito Federal alone."

Ben stared at the side street while Rico entered something into the GPS. The neighborhood looked sterile, somehow taking on an artistic feel that lacked emotional intensity, instead choosing to convey an austere product of humanity long since derelict and forgotten. Still, vibes of character leaked through. A cross on a shorter structure jutted out between a pair of ten-story apartment buildings. It evoked a sense of wonder, though it pressed a shadow that seemed to reveal emptiness.

When he focused on the dashboard again, Rico pushed the car into gear and plunged the car into the maze. The traffic whizzed by as he pushed the accelerator and negotiated with the driver of a pickup truck who seemed apathetic that Rico was trying to merge. Horns sounded as the traffic slowed to a crawl. Brake lights formed rows so long Ben could not see the end.

"You didn't think there would be much traffic, no?" Rico smiled, as if amused, but when traffic stacked up, Rico grew impatient as quickly as most other drivers. Instead of focusing on the anger, he often resorted to stories.

"*Mi papá* travelled all over Mexico when I was a *niño*. He used to bring me souvenirs. Los Cabos, Mazatlán, Puerto Vallarta, you name it. Made me want to go. He came back with a bottle of tequila from the ciudad and told me about how it would gather dust on a shelf and maybe be worth money, too. I never forget the tequila. It's the bottle that caused the family to split up. Padre spent a lot of time in cantinas, watching the dishwashers and the waitresses, maybe looking for an opportunity, but he drank. Lots.

"It took years to come to a head, I think. But the bottle of tequila stayed on the shelf. I remember the dancing *señorita* on the label, wearing a grass skirt and fire behind her. All the time, I thought of a party on the beach, but it wasn't a party. It was a crisis. *Mamacita* knew about the drinking problem all along but didn't complain about it. Until one night he came home so smashed that he couldn't tell which way was up.

"You know what she said to him? Seemed kind of heartless and I could only understand two words: Cavrón loco. And then he hit her. And again. She screamed, reached for a bat, which he put through the window, and she took the tequila off the shelf and waved it at him by the neck. He swung at her again, and she smashed the bottle over his head and ran. He didn't follow her. Tried to apologize years later after he'd come to his senses and told her all was not lost. She promised him a new bottle of tequila.

"I must have been too young to understand everything, because holes come up in my memory, like I blocked it out. They say like father, like son, but I told myself I never do that shit. People call me a *malparido*, I tell them why."

"Jesus," Ben said. "Did you ever talk to him again?"

"Of course I did," Rico said. "When I got to twenty-one, he threw me a fiesta, he called it '*años*.' Basically 'of age' with women and cervezas and *mariachis*."

"You became good friends."

"You didn't with your dad?"

Ben frowned and reminded him just as the traffic jam loosened and Rico brought the vehicle up to speed. "I didn't see my dad after my eighteenth birthday. He's gone now, and maybe I should have gotten to know him, but you know sometimes things don't always work out."

"You had many years to revive Cobbs," Rico said, understanding the point of the story. Ben revealed that deep information to Rico two months after they returned from Montana, when the secret was already in the open. If Ben didn't tell him about it, perhaps Rose would, and Ben didn't want him to hear it from her, because she'd inadvertently paint him as some kind of double agent. She didn't understand the agony that wound through him, the nights of post-traumatic stress symptoms, the echo of the gunfire and artillery, the smell of blood in the boiling, humid air. Ben never brought it up, because forgetting that hell kept the demons at bay.

"I think you know why I didn't," Ben said quietly. "Of course he didn't know about my son, either. And now Rose is investigating him."

Rico glanced at him while he turned a corner onto a busy boulevard paralleled by rows of tall buildings. "*Qué?*"

"Rose likes to investigate, because it gets her more detail for her books. She found the picture and is using that to find him."

"She probably will," Rico said. "If she found out about you, that would be *muy fácil*."

Ben swallowed, wishing he'd change the subject.

Rico glanced at a street sign as they proceeded down the broad avenue shaded by numerous trees and skyscrapers. "Paseo de la Reforma. We're almost there."

Many people filled the sidewalks, darted in and out of buildings, and crossed the street carrying bags or wearing business suits. So many people and each had his or her own unique story. Ben watched them until his head began to throb. Rico turned from the avenue after passing a construction site where the structural steel columns were rising toward the sky. He proceeded two blocks before pulling into a congested parking lot. From here, they'd take a one-mile taxi ride to within a block of their destination.

Rico took the ticket and parked the car, hurrying faster when a taxi approached the curb. A pair of younger girls staggered out of the backseat and danced toward their car.

Ben fished out his wallet and simply stared out the window at the sidewalk during the trip while Rico conversed in Spanish with the driver.

"*Dinero Americano*?" Rico asked when they reached the house.

"*Sí*," the driver replied. He squeezed his cigarette between his fingers and turned around to regard the passengers with a friendly smile that revealed decaying, yellowed teeth. He counted the bills and wished them good luck in Spanish before Ben and Rico stumbled to the sidewalk.

They stood shoulder-to-shoulder looking up at a handsome three-story house with a small balcony facing the street that would afford views of the skyscrapers on a clear day. A long, curved-metal railing guarded the edge of the balcony, braced to the stucco exterior wall via metal nuts that glimmered in the sun. Hanging plants flanked the ends of the railing, making the dwelling reminiscent of a classical European villa.

The windows sat deep in the walls, leaving wide sills. A set of concrete steps led to the first floor of the unit, on top of which stood a single potted plant. Ben glanced up and down the street before he stepped toward the building. In the sun, the windows did not reveal much detail and dark shades mostly restricted the view.

"Gonna need to get out of plain sight," Rico said.

Ben nodded and stepped into a narrow alleyway just wide enough for a fully-grown man to walk through unencumbered. Only two windows faced the next building, and they were simple egress windows. Above the windows, a wire hung loosely between the two buildings.

The back side of the unit faced a wider alley that would allow passage of a pickup truck or a garbage truck. Two cars sat idle a few units down and trash cans bookended them, sitting in neat rows between narrow concrete stairs. The backside of the building would offer them an advantage should they need to escape quickly. Ben surmised that people approaching the house would access the front of the building by foot and the rear by car, though Rico always warned him not to make assumptions.

The windows punched holes in the back wall of the house like a confused, disorganized jumble of openings designed with no real aesthetics in mind. One first-story window led into what appeared to be a small kitchen, while second- and third-story windows offered views of the alley and the houses on the opposite street.

An uneasy feeling crept over Ben as he studied the building. A narrow metal ladder bolted to the side of the building allowed access to the roof. That wouldn't be a safe climb, especially if in peril.

The adjacent building, attached to this house through a common wall, stood several feet shorter and the house on the end stretched across the block which resulted in a dead-end to the alley. The end house stood a single story tall with a gently graded roof atop which stood efficient white gravel and tar. The drop from one roof to the next in this case would result in pain, but no broken bones. The parapets on the adjacent buildings would allow scant shelter from people below, and once on the roof of the end house, no shelter would be available. In that case, Ben would advise running to either side of the taller building to use its walls as cover and then dart over the gable of the shorter house and simply drop to the sidewalk, which would bring excruciating pain, but probably no broken bones.

"Need you to cover the roof," Ben said.

Rico sighed. He understood what Ben's scanning meant and indicated that he didn't want any part of it.

"Stay beneath the parapet when people pass by on the street or the alley. You'll have a good vantagepoint up there, so you'll be able to alert me via speaker phone if something is not right. We'll wait until we know we'll have some time to poke around. Don't mess with the ladder down if someone comes, unless you feel safe doing so."

"I'm supposed to jump to my death if someone does come?" Rico said, staring at the end house. The eave hung more than eight feet above the concrete.

"You land right, and I'd be surprised if you break any bones." Ben regarded Rico with a curious smile and then glanced back up to the parapets.

"Damn."

"Don't shoot unless you are fired on and only if you can get off a clean shot. We don't want a firefight, because those guys that rammed us in Tijuana showed us what kind of weaponry these guys wield."

"Can we drive out of here?" Rico said. "I don't want to guess whether a taxi will be available a block away."

"They'd probably enter the neighborhood the same way we did, but at any rate, we'd need to obscure the car. It would be a dead giveaway."

"What if we rent another car?" Rico said.

Having expected that question, Ben quickly shook his head. "Won't have time for that, and the nearest rental car place is probably too far from here. We're going to need to analyze the local map and plan on an escape route should all hell break loose. I think the near entryway to the neighborhood would be too easy, so we'll check for a back route."

Rico cut him off and, with a curt smirk, spoke in a low voice. "Basically, we need a good spot to hide the car. We'll look around and find one. Maybe even the alley on the next block will do."

"What if they follow us there and cut us off?"

"Run them down," Rico said. "We're all on foot, then you and I will be the only ones with a car. You just duck and mow them down."

Ben raised his eyebrows. "You've seen too many action movies."

"Just enough," Rico said. "You know the hero always lives."

"That's the spirit," Ben admitted. "Treat this just like we're in a movie and maybe we live. Or we could get shot and bleed..."

"Let's get out of here," Rico interrupted. "I smell something wrong."

Ben sniffed the air.

"No, *señor*. This don't feel right. I think we might have company soon."

They shuffled through the narrow drainage alley and to the frontage street. Across the street, a pedestrian walked a dog and waved at them while a woman peered out the second-story window with a glum expression on her face. Ben pressed Rico to retreat down the adjacent street, which doglegged right after two blocks. They hurried along that route until Ben discovered a notch in the buildings. He pushed Rico into the notch, where a tiny stream of water trickled down a concrete gutter toward the street. They peered around the corner and waited for about ten minutes. A car rolled down the street and disappeared around the bend.

Glancing in that direction, Ben decided to sprint to the corner.

Nearly out of breath from the block run, Ben peered around the corner. Two men got out of the car and approached the front door of Dominguez's house. They glanced up and down the streets, and with hands concealed in leather jackets, they knocked once on the door and entered. Ben waited for about four minutes while Rico crept up behind him. When the door opened again, Ben glanced at the older green Toyota and back to the door. Three men emerged, each carrying a small one-foot-square box.

Ben and Rico dashed back to the notch for cover before the men had a chance to turn around. The car drove along the street slowly the way it came and stopped at the intersection. They seemed to wait a half-second too long before proceeding again, carefully. The car vanished from the street and turned on the main boulevard that cut to and from the dense financial district of the city.

"What do you think?" Ben asked.

"We go get the car now?"

"*Sí*. We'll park it in the next alley and hoof it."

Rico hesitated. "We don't know how long they'll be gone. A little risky."

"They're distributing," Ben said. "My guess is somewhere in the downtown area. We'll have a little bit of time. A short taxi ride to the car, then we drive back here. We know what they're driving now."

"Sure," Rico said. "But we don't know they'll come back in the same car."

"My guess is they will," Ben said.

"Assuming again?"

Ben shook his head and simply waited for Rico to give in. After waiting and discussing strategy for a few minutes, they moved down the block to the nearest boulevard. A taxi rolled past, followed by another. Within a minute, a third taxi pulled to the curb. Ben and Rico rode back to the parking lot to retrieve the car in silence.

After paying the driver, Ben scooted closer to the window and surveyed the area. The central district of the city, which housed most of the skyscrapers, occupied a broad, mostly flat portion of the valley. The area stretched on for a long time. A glass, triangular-shaped building slanted up toward the walls of an adjacent building that shaded the area with a dominating presence.

The city was beautiful and not at all what Ben had expected. He had envisioned a bigger version of Tijuana, both more dense and more spread out. Where few skyscrapers dotted Tijuana, the tall buildings peppered the center of Mexico City and popped up in the surrounding areas as well. The mountainous terrain offered seasonal vistas, but frequent rains visited the high plateau, particularly later in the summer, when the monsoon season in the southwest would join forces with the tropical systems that approached mostly from the east.

The area seemed odd and foreign, which caused Ben more than just confusion. Nothing felt comfortable, and every activity came with the unescapable sense that Ben was an outsider intruding on a home that millions of souls clung to. Rico would help him blend in, but neither of them had set foot in this city.

Distractions and surprises loomed around every corner. When life gifted the unexpected, Ben grew cold, weary, and distant, as if reality spread its wings and slid away from him as he clung to the familiarity he treasured. Life went on just the same, but Ben could not be a part of it. Instead, he could simply watch from the outside as a spectator in a brutal, never-ending blood sport.

Hearts with Faces

May 22, 2011

17:05

RATHER THAN RISK STANDING out on the boulevard, Rico navigated a complex network of back streets to the house, which doubled the trip. It took little effort to convince Rico that using the main roads incorporated unnecessary risk and Rico responded by programming the GPS to take them to the house and making intentionally wrong turns. This would prompt the GPS to recalculate the route. The route would have taken them back to the main arterial four times, but a series of wrong turns through dense neighborhoods confused it. After the fifth such turn, the GPS lady seemed annoyed with the process and her tone of voice seemed to change from accommodating to antagonistic.

"*Recalculating,*"

"You son of a bitch." Rico finished her statement for her.

Ben attempted to smile, but found that his lips only curled downward, slightly revealing his bottom teeth. "She's just a computer," Ben said.

"That's what I said about an ex-girlfriend," Rico said. "Then she pushed me in a dumpster, made off with my credit card, and smashed my mailbox."

Ben raised his eyebrows and stared at the narrow streets, where pedestrians walked dogs and stumbled into houses at the end of a long day. "Hard life."

"*Sí*," Rico said, rounding a corner and peering down a straight avenue that led to the main boulevard.

Ben recognized the street instantly. Double and triple story houses and apartments occupied both sides of the street, standing end-to-end with a few drainage alleys cut between them. A couple of homes one block down shared similar qualities, structured with orange, clay-like bricks half way up. Pairs of arched windows cut uniform holes in the brick to a few feet above the second floor, where beige stucco reigned. The parapet had been structured and sculpted to angle upward like a storefront, and mission tiles painted rigid stripes. Rico rounded a corner and advanced a block, before finding a mostly-abandoned alley, where trash cans and refuse piled against the exterior walls of the houses. He slowly backed the car into the alley until his rear bumper came to rest a few feet from the end house. This left three houses' worth of alley to make up, but the further back they parked, he reasoned, the less likely someone would notice the car and take appropriate action.

The walk to the back door of the house seemed to take half as long as Ben anticipated. He half-expected Rico to finish his story about the ex-girlfriend, but instead, he remained silent. Ben had already determined how he would get into the house. A flimsy wooden sill framed most of the door, which would allow Ben to wedge Rico's pocket knife into the gap all the way to the lock. This tactic would work, he guessed, because the door had been trimmed smaller than the opening by a matter of a centimeter or two, which would provide ample operating room for the blade to do the trick.

They advanced down the alley and up the concrete stairs, stepping gently. Ben approached the door, flexed the sill near the lock, and worked the knife into the gap. This action necessitated loosening the finish nail fasteners on the sill above and below the notch. Once the opening was wide and long enough, Ben angled the blade downward while thrusting forward. A loud click echoed through the alley, indicating that the door had unlocked. The door pushed open effortlessly.

As expected, Ben found himself in the entry to a small kitchen. He turned to Rico and pointed at the fire escape before dialing the number for Rico's burner phone. Rico answered on the first ring and said nothing. Instead, he inserted the phone into his jeans pocket and climbed down the stoop with a harrowing frown attached to his face.

Ben groaned at the mood but made little of it. He about-faced into the kitchen, where dishes and pans clung to yellowed-tile backsplashes and congregated in the sink. He reached for the gun in his pocket on instinct and withdrew it. The cold metal slid across his fingers with ease as Ben observed the kitchen. Some of the cabinet doors stood ajar. Ben pulled the remainder of the doors open one by one, revealing only stacks of dishes, boxes of unused food, and an impressive collection of spices and hot sauces.

Once he decided that the kitchen did not hold any secrets, he made his way through the living room, stopping at a lamp table, where a Mexican magazine promised unparalleled beach fun. He ignored it and sidestepped a pair of bookcases with DVDs and CDs. At the end of a short, narrow corridor, a staircase with burnt-red carpeting ascended to the second level. Ben climbed carefully and listened to Rico's panting grow increasingly louder.

"What's up in there?" Rico asked.

Ben spoke in a low voice. "Seems to be empty. Climbing to the second floor now. What do you see?"

A brief pause highlighted the low groan of the stairs beneath Ben's feet. He stepped lighter while rounding a corner and sticking with the far outside edge of the stair treads.

"Neighbor smoking a cigarette. Woman walking a dog. Car coming from the boulevard… not our guys… turning now."

Rico's panting subsided. Ben eased his grip on the revolver and proceeded up the second flight to the corridor above. The red carpeting gave way to a deep brown like stained wood grain with a sharp seam atop the stairs. Ben renewed his grip on the pistol and pressed his back against the wall. He pointed the gun in both directions, but saw no one. The stairs continued to the third floor to his left. Ben pushed through an open door after passing a bathroom. An unmade bed indicated that Dominguez had guests overnight at one point recently. He flipped the closet door open and examined a shoe box overstuffed with what appeared to be stolen jewelry. The box had dropped to the floor and cracked open and gold chains and pearls spouted out through the cracks.

The bedroom at the other end of the hall also seemed in disarray, but held no secrets, other than a standup lamp leaned against the corner between two windows. Ben shrugged and made his way back to the stairs.

Rico breathed heavily and spoke quietly.

"Another car is coming now."

"Stay down," Ben said.

"*Sí*. Car turned on the next street, but another car is turning. Also not our guys. Everything is quiet."

Ben's stomach churned as a knot of agony rose up toward his throat. He swallowed and continued up the stairs. The master suite occupied the entire third floor. The queen-size bed had been made and the closet was well-organized. A pair of shoes sat idle in front of a bench facing a full-length mirror. Ben dropped to one knee when the corner of what appeared to be a black box poked out into the open. He reached under the bed and withdrew a thin black binder stuffed with pages.

Without thinking, he flung the binder onto the bench and knelt before it. The blood in his veins curdled when he opened the first page. A horrified face stared back, revealing harrowing blue eyes pleading for mercy. The boy wore a teal shirt and his mouth hung agape. The remnant of tears crusted near his eye and his ragged hair tossed in all directions. The back of the sleeved photograph listed detailed information on the boy.

Chills raced through Ben's body as he read the information that included his height, weight, estimated body mass, expected description of health, and hometown. The boy had travelled from Bogotá. He was nine years old and… Ben's heart sunk lower when he read the last line on the page.

BT: O positive.

Ben cursed. "Blood type? Why?"

"*Qué?*" Rico asked.

"I found a photo album loaded with pictures and personal information about the people in them," Ben explained.

Rico remained silent.

Ben swallowed hard and, giving in to the idea of thirst, flipped a blank page that acted like a divider between the boy and the next photograph. A man in his late thirties stared back icily, his gaze fixed on a point somewhere behind the camera. His jaw formed a tight square below his face and his thin hair had been combed back.

"Pedro Bulesco, from Chile," Ben breathed. Pedro was thirty-seven years old, married with one child, in good health and decent assets. His blood-type was AB negative.

The next page revealed a woman smiling. Her shining, pale face illuminated the room with a gravitating levity that suggested good intentions. The photo had not been taken in the same room as the previous two, but one thing in the background caught Ben's attention quickly.

A corner of a stained-wood hutch was visible beneath her left shoulder. On a plate stood a tiny piece of bleached white with the apparent texture of bone. He mentally categorized it as the cow skull in the mansion south of Tijuana.

The back of her page told a detailed story of intense desire. Mariah Munchen had made her living as a call girl in Germany before taking the trip to London, where she had entered the financial sector. Over two years, she accumulated more wealth than Ben would have deemed imaginable. Her portfolio purportedly consisted of accounts in the Caymans and a property in the exclusive Canary Islands. Her business had taken her to the United States. She sported B-positive blood and a clean health history, with the advisory of her history as a call girl.

Chu Yunxian had travelled from Taiwan to Disneyland on vacation. Her health was fantastic and her dark skin highlighted hypnotizing brown eyes. She stared back with pallid candor, the type of expression one normally exhibited after a long, dreamless sleep. Her hair curled at the ends and her lips revealed starkly white teeth.

Ben furiously flipped through the pages one by one. Each page wrought more agony and torture than the last.

Tamarick Odessa, Joaquin Sabatos, Daisy Garland, Marlette Pointin, Tyanna Colvin, Archie Black.

Near the back of the book, Ben stopped on a photograph of a young girl with dark skin and tightly braided hair. Her eyes whispered solemnity, like the remainder of ache left over from a funeral two days prior. He flipped the page as his heart raced.

She was from San Diego, but a question mark had been haphazardly scrawled at the end of the line. The name burned into his skull like the rapid fuse of dynamite. Milana Devreaux sounded like a French name to Ben. He examined her particulars, which were spotty at best. She stood four feet, two inches, which Ben considered to be tall for a seven-year-old girl. She had green eyes that would sparkle in the sunlight as the shade of fan palms flitted across her skin. Her blood type was unknown, which gave Ben an idea.

All these dozens of people had one thing in common, Ben reasoned. They were part of a scheme, and it didn't seem like it would have much to do with drugs. Would they all have been entrants in some kind of medical study? Ben stroked his chin and thought about it. The faces didn't seem to fit either scenario. The idea made his head spin.

Turning the next blank page, Ben emitted a hollow gasp as horror dripped through his veins like venom. Nina Perez stared back at him. The warm smile had vanished, leaving empty traces of a parasitic frown, as if worry had pushed her to the brink and nothing remained. Her hair no longer flowed in sandy waves, and her eyes were now glazed with an eerie sensation of dread. Ben's heart sank and he swore.

"*Qué?*" Rico heard him.

"There's a photograph of Nina in here," Ben said, flipping the page.

The information on the back of the page was accurate, as far as Ben could tell. They knew she had a son. At the bottom of the page, her blood type caught his attention. As he read it to himself, the sound shredded his soul. Nina Perez had a heart, but according to this page, she was nothing but data.

Ben slammed the book shut with a fury he could not fully comprehend. A slip of dog-eared paper detached itself from the back of the binder and fluttered to the floor. Still on his knees, Ben picked it up and read it to himself. The binder belonged to El Canto de los Cantares, the cartel operated by Omar Dominguez. At the bottom of the sheet, tiny print directed him to the website of OGE Holdings company, based in Cyprus. Ben crumpled the paper and stuffed it in his pocket, issuing a sigh that doused the room in cold water.

Outside, a loud pop scattered through the neighborhood. Within less than a second, Rico swore.

"What the hell is up?" Ben shouted.

"Get out of there. *Chinga!*"

Ben launched himself to his feet as a cascade of bullets tore through the side of the house. Adrenaline pumped through his veins as bottles of whisky and tequila shattered. The bullets reduced the bedspread to fluttering bits of cotton and wool, and fragments of splintered wood filled the room. A pause afforded Ben time to escape the room untouched.

"I'm climbing down the fire escape," Rico said.

"Rico! What happened?"

Rico grunted as the gunfire resumed, echoing through the neighborhood with fury as distant sirens joined the din. Ben tripped on a subtle ridge in the carpet before falling face first down the stairs. His hands managed to shield his head and face from the damage of the fall, but his legs bucked, spreading excruciating pain through him. He issued an agonized, gravelly grunt, before pressing his arms against the bottom step and springing himself onto his butt.

Bullets continued to penetrate the house. Glass shattered and furniture tore. He sprinted down the next flight of stairs without fear of injury. Rico breathed heavily as he climbed down the ladder. Within seconds, the bullets ceased. Ben vaulted down the last section of stairs, tore through the living room, and flung the back door against the wall hard enough to punch a hole in the sheetrock. Ben gasped. Rico leaped down from the ladder and, succumbing to a throat-rending roar, issued an impressive string of both Spanish and English obscenities.

With one huge leap, Ben skipped the concrete stairs and sprinted toward the end of the alley. The pain in his legs increased as he rounded the corner. Rico came along slower, as his bones would not allow him to keep pace.

"Faster," Ben screamed. A trio of voices sounded from around the corner. The hurried to the end of the block as the sirens drew closer. A man in a house on the corner, having heard the commotion, yelled at Ben and Rico in Spanish. They ignored him, but the man's biting tone suggested that he blamed them for the violence.

Rico shouted back to him a half-second later. "*En la casa! Ahora!*"

The heavy sprint led them to the alley as a weary thread of pain worked its way through Ben's legs. The scent of sweat in the humid air wafted into his nostrils as the adrenaline found a new crescendo. Another round of gunfire, this time closer, tore through the street as Ben and Rico ducked into the alley. Ben carried the gun in his right hand while he clutched the binder in his left. When they reached the car, Rico slammed the door, started the car, and pushed the accelerator to the floor. The pursuers could run much faster than Ben and Rico. They reached the mouth of the alley by the time Rico made it halfway to the street.

Three men pointed automatic weapons at the face of the car. "Down!" Ben screamed.

Rico ducked as the men sprayed the car with violent waves of leaden aggression interspersed with spat obscenities. He punched the accelerator and ground his teeth. The car veered right and collided with a trash can, sending garbage fluttering through the alley. "*Chinga tú madre!*"

He corrected the car as the bullets punched hundreds of new holes in the body and destroyed the windshield. When the gunfire paused, Ben poked his head above the dashboard and pointed the gun at one of the shooters. Terror shot through the man's face as Ben unloaded three rounds of ammunition into his chest. He dropped the rifle, clutched his chest, and fell to the ground. Ben knew he only had three shots left, so he used them wisely.

The ferocity of the gunfire dropped as Rico sped out of the alley. The two remaining men retreated and one of them managed to dive out of the way just as Rico slammed the nose of the vehicle into the third man's legs. He flipped backward and landed on the hood of the car as Rico spun the wheel hard to the right. The shooter tumbled off the hood and reached for his gun in agony, while his companion flipped to his feet and unleashed a steady stream of ammunition their way. All the bullets punctured the car, but one of them grazed Ben's shoulder. He howled in pain as he spun sideways and emptied the chamber on the man firing. Each of Ben's bullets missed.

The shooter loaded a new magazine and emptied it rapidly. The tires squealed on the pavement as Rico turned his head sideways and coerced the car into a tight turn that caused the back end to fishtail. Onlookers gathered on the streets and sets of eyeballs appeared behind the windows as the neighbors investigated the commotion. When the firing ceased, Ben reached for the ammunition box and in the center console and loaded six new bullets into the chamber. As outgunned as Ben and Rico were, a sense of passionate dread shared between them leveled the playing field.

Ben swore as Rico pushed the car toward seventy miles per hour approaching the busy thoroughfare. At the intersection, he slowed and banked into traffic, sideswiping another vehicle. The scraping sound of metal on metal and breaking glass didn't deter him. Again, he pushed the gas and wove through traffic.

In the rearview mirror, a police car made its way through the traffic, but it didn't get closer. Rico spun the car into the far inside lane, laid on the horn to warn a foursome of pedestrians, and then launched the car into the median to avoid a line of cars stopped at a traffic light. He swore and punched the gas again, blitzing them through the intersection at a terrifying speed.

Ben shrieked as another car sped into the intersection. Neither had time to react. The impact cased the car to spin 270 degrees. Instead of facing straight ahead, the car now pointed directly down the side street that had lain to their left. Rico spun the tires on the pavement before barreling in that direction. The other vehicle, a black Chevrolet pickup truck, regained its stance and pursued them.

"Motherfucker!" Rico screamed. The truck inched closer to them as the passengers rolled the windows down and brandished guns. A trio of police cars began to assemble in the road ahead. Rico poured every ounce of energy the car could muster into the straightaway, sending the speedometer past ninety. The people in the truck sprayed at least two dozen shots at the back of the car, but not one of them hit.

Before Ben knew what was going on, the driver of the truck slammed on the brakes and decided on a different route. Still having the cops to deal with, Rico ducked as bullets began to embed themselves in the sheet metal and *tink* off the frame.

The officers left a gap between their cars and Rico continued to accelerate. Sparks flew with the screeching sound of metal scraping against metal. Shocked, the officers returned to their vehicles. Rico sped away, turned down a less-busy street toward the skyscrapers, and then slowed down.

More sirens echoed in the distance, but Ben and Rico were not finished with the bad guys yet. Rico honked and swerved when a pair of girls pranced into the street ahead of him. He left the blocks behind quickly as he made his way toward Paseo de la Reforma. Ahead, the green car the runners had loaded with drugs waited behind a stop sign.

Ben groaned. "Turn around."

"Not gonna happen," Rico said. He floored the accelerator and blew past the car, before spinning the wheel so hard that the car spun in nearly a complete circle. Momentarily, they faced the men in the car. Ben recognized one of them as Omar Dominguez. The green Toyota lurched into gear and turned toward them. Rico slammed the car in reverse and backed into a blue truck. Ben's neck began to ache with the impact, but Rico spun the wheel and buried the accelerator.

Pointing the gun at Dominguez, Ben swore and sent two shots his way. Both missed and the Toyota bumped off two idle vehicles near the median and tailed Rico too close for comfort. Seconds later, another round of gunfire sounded. The shooters were not very accurate and didn't aim for Rico's tires. Ben turned around, slithered to the floor, and twisted his body so that he knelt in front of the seat facing the shooters. He waited until both Rico and the driver of the other car stopped swerving and emptied the chamber into the other car. Ben's fourth shot hit Dominguez squarely between the eyes.

"Jesús," Rico shouted, looking in the mirror. "Hell of a shot."

The Toyota pushed into their bumper and nudged them forward. To avoid two lanes of stopped traffic, Rico laid on the horn and leaped the curb onto the sidewalk slaloming between trees and pedestrians. The driver of the Toyota didn't act with as much caution. Rico swerved past a throng of people waiting to cross the street and bumped into a car waiting at the light. Instead of making such a correction, the Toyota thrust itself into the throng, likely injuring a dozen innocent people.

Ben swore loudly and struggled to reload the gun. Without much coaxing, Rico banked the vehicle against the median and swerved between stopped cars. Ahead, the light turned red and Rico again punched it. The Toyota followed suit. A heavy truck carrying what appeared to be a concrete beam approached the light as Rico tore through the intersection. The truck plowed into the side of the Toyota and flung it sideways into a pair of pedestrians and two cars. Steam emanated from the grill of the truck.

"We aren't out of the dark yet," Rico said. "It's time to abandon the car and take a taxi."

As Rico slammed on the brakes, Ben grabbed the binder and clutched his gun. Rico flung his door open and Ben decided to drop the gun. He had everything he needed from

Mexico. Dominguez didn't have Nina Perez, only her photograph. Wherever that led them, Ben knew for certain that he would find her. He knew exactly where to start because he had links between El Canto de los Cantares and the Cyprus holding company in his pocket.

"What are you doing?" Rico asked.

"Leave the gun," Ben said. "Let's get to the airport and fast, before they have our pictures all over the big screens and the security is alerted."

"They won't be able to organize that fast," Rico said. We'll be airborne before airport security knows about us."

"Will they ground the flight?"

"Possible," Rico said. "But it will take more investigation. They'd be better off alerting customs in San Diego."

"Let's do it," Ben said, clutching his right leg as they walked away on the sidewalk. The sirens neared, filling the air with the aftermath of violence and tragedy. Ben didn't want to think about how many people had died, but one seemed to matter more than any other. He'd gotten Omar Dominguez. It was time to set his sights on Castro, who would lead him to Nina Perez. Ben swallowed a painful lump in his throat and jumped into the back of the taxi Rico had summoned.

"What's the next move, *señor*?"

Ben could only say one word and he bit his lip as he spoke. "Castro."

Never the Flame

May 22, 2011

19:30

THE COMPUTER SCREEN FLICKERED in her peripheral vision as Rose glared at the television, which was showing an advertisement for a new drug promising to cure dementia without all the dangerous side effects. When the voice-over guy began to list the possible side effects, Rose turned the volume down. Suicidal thoughts or actions, and they didn't consider that dangerous? *That's how it works,* Rose thought. *If you kill yourself, you're cured!*

She glanced back to the computer screen and clicked on a link as someone knocked at the door. That would be room service. Sure, ordering room service indicated a simple and uncreative solution to a problem, but it beat going out tonight. The crowds, the people, and the creep Ben hired to follow her made the laziness more tolerable. For her, trust was a commodity earned rather than given, and the threat of danger from any angle set Rose on edge.

She pushed the computer aside and hurried to the door as her slippers clicked beneath her feet.

A young man stood behind the door with a tray full of stainless steel, two glasses, and a bottle of wine. He shook his head when she asked for salt and pepper, before reaching into his apron to produce two packets. A frown engulfed his face as she brandished a clean five-dollar bill for his tip, which he snatched out of her hand. A man sauntered down the hallway behind him, halfway glancing at Rose without turning his head. She'd seen the man before. His alligator-skin boots clashed with the hues and tone of the carpet. She peeled her eyes off the server and glared at him as he stalked away.

"Who is that guy?" she asked, half nodding at the man.

"One of our valued hotel guests," he said. That he'd use an obviously canned response on her almost didn't register, but his tone didn't manage to ease her mind.

"I don't think so," she said. "I saw him bothering a housekeeper the other night asking for access to his girlfriend's room. He seems suspicious to me."

"Thank you for your concern," he said. "Alert the manager, I'm just a server."

"Can I have half of that tip back?" She lowered her eyebrows, knowing she'd crossed a line and that she'd done so on purpose just to elicit a more emotional response.

He shook his head and started to push the cart away.

"Maybe I will call the manager," she said quietly.

He stopped and turned around slowly. "Do you have a problem with your service this evening, ma'am?" His tone leaked with the typical niceties, but his frown told a different story.

She chose not to push the subject, but the server had already reached into his money pouch for change before she could close the door.

"No, you keep it," she said.

"I'll... I'll tell the manager. Should I have her call you?"

"No," Rose said. "I'm a little busy right now. Just for the sake of safety, get that jerk out of here before he hurts someone."

"I'll do it," he said. "Still want your change?"

"No thanks," Rose said. She closed the door and grinned, then shook her head. She always acknowledged the presence of an evil side of her but kept it as a joke in her head just to keep the real danger at bay. She'd used similar tactics several times on Ben, and each time, it received an icy response. The server didn't deserve it, but she had a little bit too much fun toying with him.

She rested the plates on the bed next to her computer and set the glasses on the nightstand before reaching to turn off the TV. The page she'd loaded displayed the names and phone numbers of each member of an engineering class at the University of California at San Diego.

The piquant scent of hot food wafted through the room. She took it in before uncovering her plate and digging in. With her mouth still full, she popped open the wine and poured a small glass, which she sipped for taste before loading her mouth with another bite.

Half the glass of wine was gone as well as most of the food when Rose reached for her phone next to the wine glasses. She dialed the number for Tyran Blackmon as her heart raced. As the phone rang, she thought of a good cover story.

"Hello, what's up?" Tyran asked hurriedly. His voice churned with a sparkling energy Rose didn't expect. The sound resonated in her ears until it reached a pitch she could use to grasp his emotion. Talking to a man whose voice displayed the hallmarks of stress wouldn't work very well for her. She needed to find a way to tell him what she knew without coming off as crazy or obsessed, and she needed him to open up.

"Is this Tyran?"

"Yeah."

"Hi. My name is Rosalie Connor, I'm with the San Diego Marine Aquarium Society. We're teaming up with Scripps Institute of Oceanography to run a new feature in our newsletter on the dangers of climate change and its effect on marine wildlife and recreation. I understand you are an avid surfer, and I'd like to get your opinion on some things if you have the time."

"Maybe call me back?"

She shrugged and considered his uncertainty a sign that she should slow it down further. "I'm sorry if I have called at an inopportune time. Do you have training or classes, or have to get to work?"

A pause resounded, suggesting that Tyran could make time. "Is surfing your favorite pastime?"

"I guess you could say that," he said.

She paused as if she were scribbling his responses on her notepad. "Yes, I've been a time or two. As I understand it, the better you are the more fun it is. Are you good?"

"I guess so."

"How often do you get out?"

"Once, maybe twice a week," he said. "My girlfriend is kinda nuts about watching me from the beach, but I'm trying to juggle classes at UCSD with her and work. It's a little hectic right now."

She paused again and let a thread of concern trickle into her voice. "Oh, I understand. Modern life and all that. How long have you been with your girlfriend?"

He sighed. "Two, going on three years. Hopefully three soon."

She'd managed to get him to mention the point of her call without even asking about it. A grin crossed her face, but she erased it for fear that she'd let slip that her emotion had changed. Instead, she feigned a deeper concern, which would successfully lighten his mood.

"Hopefully? I hope there isn't something bad going on. With me, I'd be worried too if I were a little younger and hadn't already chosen my partner."

"Yeah," he said. "She's cool. Just a little confused right now, that's all. Were you going to ask me about global warming?"

She used a quick nod to set the timing of her response correctly, so as not to seem impatient or overly curious. "I know of a beach in Cancún I used to visit with my husband," she lied.

"Have you ever been to Mexico? I hear the surfing is better than California in some places."

"I'm sure it is. I did just get back from a trip." He paused, but Rose allowed him to continue. "Are you really who you say you are?"

"Of course I am," she said.

"No more personal questions, then, please."

She sighed. "Right. Sorry about that, my head just gets a little bit wrapped up sometimes. My first question is this: Do you believe that global climate change is an issue we as a society need to tackle now?"

"I don't know," Tyran said. "I don't follow politics. I guess I've heard both sides, but I don't really care that much, to be honest."

"Do you enjoy marine life?"

"Yeah, I guess. Just from the zoo and the occasional Sea World trip with my girlfriend. She loves the whales, I love the rides."

"The reason I ask this," Rose said, stalling, "is that our wildlife faces an unprecedented threat. By running this story, we are hoping that our members will become more engaged and willing to help protect our wildlife."

"Look, I don't have the money to donate to your cause right now. Maybe you should call my girlfriend."

Rose took another sip of the wine and smacked her lips. "I'm sorry, I'm not soliciting donations, just gathering facts for my story. As I understand it, a warming ocean produces stronger, more frequent storm systems on the west coast. Recreationally, that's got to be a boon for surfing."

"Sure. If it's true. But I hear that lots of people say it's just a stupid scheme for scientists to get more money from the taxpayers."

"I wish it were that simple," she said. "Our society depends on marine wildlife for a number of things, and I think we should protect the habitat whether or not the science is accurate. Wouldn't you agree?"

"Maybe. Yeah, I guess so."

"What do you do, as a surfer, to help protect the wildlife?"

"Well, I don't throw plastic into the ocean, if that's what you're asking. Look, I don't really have much time for this. I've got to go."

"Tyran, please try to listen to me," Rose said, straightening her voice and her back. "I know you recently travelled to Mexico to get something for your girlfriend, to win her back. If you won't talk to me about her just listen. I'm…"

"Who the *hell* do you think you are?"

"I'm here to tell you to be careful. If you don't want to tell me what's going on with your girlfriend, all I can do is…"

The dial tone signaled the end of the conversation. She pushed the computer away and slid to her knees in front of the bed. A sense of dread tore through her like the remains of a nightmare so realistic that it shook her to the core. The fire flickered in her heart, begging for life-sustaining fuel. She stoked it with the brittle emotions she knew all too well how to produce. If she could feed it, she reasoned, it could last an eternity, but once extinguished, it could seldom be relit.

She meditated for more than five minutes before her phone started to ring. The number was unlisted, but she gulped and picked it up anyway, hoping against the dread that Allen would not be on the other end of the line.

20:30

A STRAND OF DESPERATE sadness crept into Rose's voice as if to remove the vitality and energy from her and transform her into a shell Ben didn't know. He rubbed his forehead as he spoke. Boarding would take place in a few minutes.

Above all, he needed to hear Rose's voice. Familiarity or not, her voice would soothe the pain and make everything acceptable or even worthwhile.

"Why weren't you in your hotel?" Her tone was biting, almost callous and accusatory, but the thread of sadness remained. "Were you busy?"

"Travelling," Ben said. "We had to go to Mexico to search for this woman. And we didn't find her."

"Oh my God."

"We had to find this guy who we linked to her disappearance. A drug cartel attacked us."

A cool silence suggested not all was well. She spoke softly, but her words were ice. "I don't know what's going on, Ben, but this has got to stop. Come home. Let the police find this woman."

"I can't do that," Ben said with no sense of subtlety. Those four little words would sterilize her heart in a block of panic and cause her to creep further into her shell. Sometimes, however, only the truth presented an acceptable alternative to making her feel good. That was something Ben had never been good at. He'd tried and failed so many times that misery occasionally took hold.

"Of course," she simmered. "I wouldn't expect you to."

"Rose, you know..."

"What do I know? I thought I knew a lot. I thought I knew everything, but the deeper I go, I realize more and more that it's only a lie I know."

"What are you talking about?"

"Your guy in the stupid boots is still following me. You say he's safe, but I feel this constant paranoia. You don't know what that's like."

"No?" Ben bit back with a padded ferocity that he didn't quite understand. The animal inside him was getting loose and he could only respond by loosening its chains. "I wouldn't call tripping through the rainforest knowing the Viet Cong could pop up any second 'paranoia.' Or expecting someone to find me someday and bring Cobbs back."

"Ben."

"But what do I know? I almost got killed."

She sighed, but her breath quivered in her throat, making her sound both sick and terrified. "Today or in 1971?"

"Today."

A bitter pause worked its way between them. Every second of profound silence punished Ben's senses until his emotion would be nothing more than powder. The animal clawed at the emptiness, baring its teeth.

"I found your son."

"I told you to leave it alone," Ben grated.

"When have I ever listened to you? I did it for you. Funny thing is, *he* also went to Mexico to search for something to give his girlfriend. He's back now and the police are no longer looking for him. He'll be back in class tomorrow."

"Well, thanks." Insincerity licked at his tone, but he could no longer hold back the tide of pain.

"Don't mention it." Her sentence was over before it had a chance to take on life. The hard stop punctured Ben's soul with guilt.

"Uh..."

She paused for long enough to think about her next sour statement, but Ben didn't want to hear it.

"The thing is, he turned up voluntarily. I don't have to tell you that never happens. It suggests that there's another player and the missing person could still be in danger."

"Jesus Christ."

"He's a lot like you. He covers with a shell to protect himself when times are tough, just like you do. He bottles it all up instead of letting it out. Some kind of stress is eating him alive."

"Did you tell him about me?"

She paused again. "I thought that would be better coming from your mouth, assuming you can force yourself to face him after all these years."

Ben bit his lip. "I want to meet him. Where is he?"

"He attends UCSD and he'll be in classes tomorrow. Look for him around the engineering building at around four to five."

"I love you, Rose," he said. "Give me a couple more days to figure this situation out. You'll be safe, I can promise you that."

"Ben."

"I'm sorry."

"Stay alive for me." Her voice cut out at the end of the sentence, leaving a slice of finality that somehow only worked to further poison his heart. The animal inside him curled up in a dark recess of his heart for long enough to talk to Rico.

His phone buzzed, indicating he'd received a text message. The message was from Rico.

> *Text me.*

"Are you serious right now?"

"Better for us not to talk about this out loud in the airport or getting on an airplane. People get crazy." His voice dipped lower as he spoke.

> *What the hell happened?*

He typed with such a fervor that a knot worked its way through his hand.

> Maybe you tell me first.

"Shit." Ben tilted his head to the side and affixed a dumb expression on his face that was meant to infuriate Rico. In response, Rico could only offer a contemptuous nod.

> I found the photo album, flipped through it and all of a sudden, you're swearing and there are shots. How did you not see them coming?

> They weren't coming.

Ben only stared at him. The automated intercom voice in in the airport suggested that their flight was ready to board. The attendants in the waiting area pulled the doors open and began collecting boarding passes.

Hesitating, Ben and Rico stood up, grasping what little they'd brought and filed down the corridor into the plane. They took their seats before either of them could concoct a response.

> They were already there.

Ben leaned back in the seat and softly pounded his head against the headrest. "I didn't think about that."

> The neighbors were on the same team. I had no warning. They came so close to hitting me that I could hear the bullet.

> Were they across the street?

Rico nodded.

> *Inside the house. What about Castro? You're sure he's involved?*

Ben sat the binder on his lap and pulled out the crumpled sheet of paper from his pocket. Smoothing it out, he relished a pang of relief that altered his chaotic perception. Rico stared at the paper for longer than Ben wanted. He pulled it back and stuffed it back in his pocket before issuing a cold grunt.

> *Don't know what that means.*

Ben sighed and gritted his teeth while watching an older couple stalk the aisle hand in hand to their seats. "Castro was making money from OGE Holdings. They are a shell company for the cartel. Which means everything he told me is a lie. He was involved and I think he knows where to find Nina Perez."

"How do you know that?" Rico said while staring past Ben into the window. The darkness outside caused a hollow, dark reflection to play out on the glass like a mirror, showing the scene in an alternate light so stark that it could wield further meaning if Ben let it.

"He and Dominguez know each other," Ben said. "It's obvious, and Castro knows quite a bit about his operation, considering how secret that trade is supposed to be. He talked like that to get us to Mexico and out of the picture."

"What does he plan to do with her?"

Biting his lip, Ben focused on Rico's reflection. "I have a suspicion. I just hope I'm wrong."

Rico stared at him for so long that Ben lost interest in discussing the optics of what had happened. Instead of saying anything, he pushed his legs out beneath the seat in front of him and rested his head. He stared at a flight attendant for almost a full minute before his eyes sealed themselves, leaving Ben mired in the depths of his own thoughts.

Misery coiled up inside him and colluded with a virulent strain of pain and weariness. The plane was speeding down the runway for takeoff before Ben could give himself a final thought, but its structure lingered on his mind like the fog on a cold winter morning.

Rose's words from years ago repeated back to him like echoes in a glass room. *Tell me about how you escaped the war.* Ben never had escaped the war. He only fought it on a different front. The war would never cease because the demons owned his mind paraded torture through its center so often that Ben simply ceased paying attention.

The plane lifted off the ground and the last thing Ben saw before he gave in to sleep was his own reflection, pallid and bruised, bleeding and cold. This was the man Rose said she didn't know. Ben would beat it out of himself if only he could muster the strength.

Dissonant Songs

May 23, 2011

14:40

SLEEP HAD BEEN ERRATIC throughout the night as the echoes of shrieks, screams, and tires on pavement filled his consciousness. For two broken hours on the plane, Ben's weariness could not quiet the demons in his head. When they reached the hotel room and collapsed onto their beds, Ben allowed the monsters to invade his mind and to prowl in darkness where greater danger lurked.

In the night, he only battled himself. There was no Castro or Dominguez or Gutierrez or Huerra. During the dreams, Rose showed her face several times, but only as a silhouette, dancing like a flickering hologram hundreds of miles away. It made her feel lifeless, yet serene, like a photograph of a tranquil sea at sunset.

Rico sawed much of the night away with an impressive slumber, but Ben caught him with his eyes open a time or two. Instead of staring or speaking, he grunted and rolled over.

By five in the morning, Ben's mind had been so drained and his veins so numb that sleep had become possible. That sleep had lasted until almost eight, when he heard Rico stirring. He'd sat up in the bed, removed the covers, and rubbed his eyes before slipping on his socks and setting up his laptop on the circular table. He'd laid out his notes in front of him and dug in. The first task had involved searching the web for Nina Perez's realty and looking for any official connections to El Canto de los Cantares.

Officially, at least, no such connection existed. Instead of diving deeper, Ben researched El Canto de los Cantares. His search came up empty as website after website listed numerous Bible verses. The morning disappeared as he examined bank accounts and researched payments. All the large transactions made directly to Castro had originated from Cyprus, which would have indicated the involvement of El Canto de los Cantares, but nothing was official. Did the company have its own account? Proving it would be nearly impossible because Cyprus housed one of the most notorious money laundering banks in the entire world. As such, their security would likely be much more stringent than that of American banks.

There was a reason so many American corporations and businessmen hid funds in offshore tax havens, and taxes were only part of the solution. Even for a skilled hacker, defeating systems that strong would prove costly, time-consuming, and dangerous.

Into the afternoon, Ben searched another avenue. Digging into the property tax rolls in San Diego County proved easy. Most of them were public records. The system allowed him to search through listings, but only provided names and addresses for businesses. El Canto de los Cantares resulted in a single hit.

The website directed him to a warehouse near the Old Town district beneath the junction of Interstates 8 and 5. With that address in his memory banks, he summoned Rico for another round of searching.

"You think Castro would be stupid enough to keep her locked up at his own business?"

"No," Ben said. "I'm surprised it's even on the tax rolls. OGE Holdings is laundering money from all over the world and this guy doesn't even want to hide his property from a county?"

"Gotta be abandoned," Rico guessed. "Maybe they use it to traffic heroin."

"Possibly," Ben said.

"We're going to just go knock on the door, or will we have to break in?"

Since they'd abandoned their guns before entering the Mexico City Airport, Ben laid out the next task as finding new weapons. Ben wouldn't have even thought about another operation without a gun, given their recent propensity for getting shot at.

Instead of going through the usual channels, Ben charged Rico to set up a sale through a local militia that was known to have bent the rules in firearms trafficking a time or two. They were smart enough to evade the arm of the law over the years, but several lawsuits had been brought against them. Since Ben didn't look the part, Rico would do the dealing. Ben laid it all out for him, including the details of the conversation.

He'd walk Rico through it step by step over the phone, if they allowed it. If not, he detailed every question and every answer with such precision that it made Rico look stunned.

The meeting place was at a ranch just off Interstate 8 on the east slopes of the mountains, beyond where the desert brush and cactus replaced the suburbs.

"Remember," Ben said as Rico parked the car. "These are burner phones, so they are secure. If they make you ditch it, remember to mention the drug cartels. This is a patriotic group and vigilante justice for them is just as good as real law enforcement."

"They'll expect a sting," Rico warned. "Not going to work."

"That's the spirit."

"Then maybe you should come with me. They'll probably check our creds, and your ID is as good as mine. Don't say it's only because I'm Mexican."

"Of course not," Ben said. "But do you really think they're going to trust a white guy that could be their father?"

"Then maybe you play the personal relationship card and link it to the drug cartel. They'll probably give you a discount."

After debating on it for a few minutes, Ben agreed to go along. They waded through the weeds, the tall grass, and the cactus plants and found the ranch. A pair of white gentlemen carrying hunting rifles with scopes greeted them and led them into a barn, where they displayed their merchandise. Ben and Rico each stuck to the script. One of the men used a laptop to check their credentials.

Within twenty minutes, Ben and Rico left the ranch armed. Their next stop was a sporting goods store to pick up ammunition. The guns each had higher-capacity magazines. They opted for 9mm handguns that could hold fifteen rounds. They had shelled out a small fortune for the guns, an expense that would be tax deductible, but which Ben could not hide from Rose even if he wanted to. She'd probably call him tonight to grill him about it.

A line of thicker clouds marched ashore, threatening rain, which would more than likely be a light, hour-long drizzle, knowing San Diego's climate. Rico used the back streets through the city to arrive at the large warehouse district. On one boulevard, a newer multi-story building housed retail on the lower levels and apartments above. In every other direction, warehouses, repair garages, and storage facilities occupied many blocks of real estate.

Rico turned off a side street and slowly rolled past the address. Tiny lawns with juniper trees lay interspersed with one- and two-story joints. Where signs allowed parallel parking, each stall was filled with a compact car. Shipping vans and trucks came and went all day. The sidewalks had been so long forgotten that concrete began to crumble in spots and weeds shot up through the cracks. Most of the buildings fronted the sidewalk with no setback. Rico turned down another side street and parked the car a block away. They each loaded their guns, slipped them in their pockets, and made their way to the building in question.

The building was at least forty years old, constructed of concrete masonry blocks with steel stiffeners, which were covered with a faux-cement finish that cracked and crumbled at the sidewalk and around the overhead door. Taking up no more than three thousand square feet in a neat rectangle, the building covered a smaller footprint than those of its closest neighbors. A mezzanine level with office windows overlooked the street, but they emitted no visible light. The man doors were locked, and the overhead door looked sturdy enough that breaching it would not be easy. Immediately to both sides stood other businesses.

Ben stared at the door and decided that Rico's pocketknife would be of no use and attempting to pick the lock through other means would prove time-consuming and suspicious, especially in a neighborhood where so much activity took place. The police would arrive within minutes.

To look like a prospective customer, Ben reached for his cellphone and dialed Rico's number. For a few minutes, they talked on the phone to discuss a way in.

"What, do you think there is an alley or a back door?"

"Maybe."

They strode to the end of the block and slipped into a narrow, gravel alley shaded by buildings on both sides. Dumpsters rested against the walls of most of the buildings. The home of El Canto de los Cantares, which was advertised as Morton Interiors and Fixtures, appeared to be in disarray. The backside of the business had not been caked with the faux cement as texture, and instead opted for the industrial look with stained gray concrete blocks that stacked up to a parapet. A hole cut in the parapet allowed a downspout where a small storm drain line emptied into the alley. Beside the dumpster, a steel ladder was bolted into place with what appeared to be industrial-strength steel fasteners embedded into the concrete. The oxidized steel of the ladder had bled into streaks of iron red on the wall making the building look even more foreign.

He reached the rungs of the ladder and hoisted himself up. Rico followed, panting heavily as they reached somewhere near where the mezzanine level started.

A white layer of poly film over metal decking covered the roof. Between the parapets, the roof sloped from front to back toward the drains. Air conditioning units and exhaust fans were scattered on the rooftop. Near an exhaust port, a neat rectangle cut in into the surface. A handle with a large lock kept the hatch secure. Ben searched the roof for a possible storage container for a key, but found none. He worked at the lock for a few minutes and offered a frustrated sigh.

"You could shoot it open," Rico suggested.

Ben laughed. "That only works in the movies. Plus, we'd have the cops here in a minute and a half."

Rico pondered for several minutes, stroking his chin and looking at a dark blue patch in the clouds. "Well, I heard about one method. Do you know where we can find bolt-cutters?"

"Construction sites..." It clicked instantly. Ben hurried back to the ladder and started to descend it. He glanced up at Rico and offered a sincere expression of flattery. "I'll be right back. There's a small project a half a block from where we parked. They'll probably have a pair handy."

Rico ducked behind an exhaust fan and lay down on the poly coating to hide himself should intruders arrive.

With a hurried gusto, Ben darted out of the alley and jogged back to the car, which they had rented from a small rental office on the outskirts of downtown San Diego. Getting onto the construction site didn't prove difficult. The chain-link fencing had been so poorly constructed that Ben managed to find a slot just wide enough to wiggle through. A large, orange tool chest cowered under a makeshift cover that extended from the cantilever of an existing building's roof. The chest appeared to be unlocked, as the buckle of a yellow work belt with black grease stains dangled from a narrow gap where the chest opened. A box of fasteners labeled with a brand name rested next to the tool chest. According to the smaller print on the box, the fasteners were designed to embed steel female threads into concrete. He kicked the box aside and lifted the chest's lid.

A wide array of power and hand tools lay jumbled on shelves. Drawers holding screws and other fasteners jutted out from their openings. A bundle of shiny steel threaded rods rested vertically in an open bin.

On the center shelf, two pairs of bolt cutters rested. He grabbed one set and slithered out through the opening in the fence.

The neighborhood stood mostly silent, but for the running motor of a shipping van idling outside of a business across the street from the car. Ben jogged back to the ladder and lugged the bolt cutters up. When he reached the top, he handed them off to Rico.

"Convenient," Rico said.

"Good idea," Ben said with a simple hand gesture. He rose to his feet and clamped the jaws of the bolt cutter around the body of the lock. Slicing it open wasn't as difficult as Ben feared. With little effort, he flung open the hatch and peered down into the dark. The sun illuminated a square of light on a catwalk constructed of rigid metal framing and grating. A ladder extended down from the opening about seven feet. The catwalk crossed the upper part of an expansive room and joined another catwalk in a T-junction at roughly the halfway point. They carefully stepped down the ladder. The walkway didn't sway or move when they stepped onto it. At the end of the catwalk, the rails surrounding a second floor set of offices parted and three steps descended from the walkway to the second floor.

Beneath them sat a moving van. Ben surveyed the scene from above. Stacks of boxes occupied a corner of the interior, along with a work bench and some sundry tools. A small lighting display under construction lay on the bench, and several fixtures sat nearby with insulated extension cables coiled beneath the tabletop. Ben hid at a spot next to a window into an office cluttered with mounds of paperwork, partially dismantled light fixtures and locks, and open boxes of door handles. The room's previous occupant had left the light on. Peeking around the corner, Ben observed the room quickly. No one was in it. For some reason, he doubted Castro would leave the lights on in one of his offices before leaving for the day. Either he was somewhere in this building or had stepped out.

Every room on the second floor stood empty, and no offices occupied the first floor. With a flick of his wrist, he opened the door and searched the office. Castro was drowning in paperwork and busy work. Ben shuffled a stack of papers on the desk and then slid open some of the drawers.

In the pencil drawer above the kneehole rested a .45 caliber handgun and a box of ammunition. Ben quietly slid the door shut and shuffled papers in a plastic tray holding mail items and a box cutter. A cup of pens, one of them uncapped, sat nearby. Nothing seemed to have anything to do with OGE Holdings or Castro's drug cartel, El Canto de los Cantares.

Frustration built as Ben unloaded drawers and scanned page after page of legal mumbo-jumbo, shipping manifests, cargo invoices, and numerous batches of paperwork. He overturned the trash bin and began to smooth out partially crumpled memos and invoices before something caught his eye.

The paper in question didn't mention OGE Holdings or El Canto de los Cantares, but in small print near the center of the page, he noticed the name Nina Perez.

He read the letter aloud in a hushed voice. "Dear Mr. Filando Castro, As we understand, you are involved in an investment business in San Diego, California, revolving around futures and construction bonds. We represent a company building a resort hotel on the Mexican west coast near Tijuana. They are seeking approval to license a bond using your services.

"We understand that you have a small array of clients. We are working with Ms. Nina Perez on the property. This is her first international venture, and she is investing in a retail slot. Ms. Perez, we learned, mostly deals in residential estates, but is willing to sell condo units at the development in question.

"She is looking forward to getting involved with this project, but a strong opposition has formed, and she has received threats. I believe that your firm specializes in protection services. If you are so inclined to take this job, please contact us at your earliest convenience. Ms. Perez also wishes to keep her son Alejandro out of harm's way.

"Thank you for your interest in representation. We look forward to hearing from you. Sincerely, Eduardo Castille, Operations Manager."

Ben stroked his chin.

"He's protecting Nina?" Rico shuffled a look of alarm across his face. Downstairs, a bang erupted. Ben dropped the letter in the trash, tiptoed toward the door and peered into the darkness below. A man had entered through the door and Ben reasoned that it could only have been one person. Rather than fight Castro, he slid out of the office into the darkness with Rico in tow.

Together, they climbed the short set of stairs and crept along the railing at the edge of the catwalk back toward the ladder. Ben looked down as the man emerged from behind a reception desk beneath the stairs.

Castro.

He gulped hard and stalled as Castro peered up into the dark. His gaze seemed to be aimed at the light coming from the open hatch. Castro shifted his hips sideways, pulled back the flap on his jacket pocket, and produced a handgun. He pushed a pair of boxes aside and began to climb the stairs with the gun at his side. When he ducked into the first room on the second floor, Ben and Rico bolted the remaining forty feet to the ladder and stalled again when Castro emerged.

Castro invaded his office and a cold gasp emanated from the room. Ben and Rico climbed the stepladder quickly. Rico ascended to the roof first, followed by Ben.

A loud, Spanish curse word came from the office and Castro slammed the door in rage. Just as Ben lifted his feet through the hatch, the door opened. A shot rang out. The bullet collided with a stretch of angle iron between ceiling joists. Ben scurried through the opening. Rather than risk descending the ladder, Ben reached the side parapet, flung his legs over the edge, and jumped down to the adjacent roof.

"Son of a bitch," Ben breathed. "I think he saw me."

They darted to the other end of the roof and Ben peered over the parapet, where a rigid metal awning had been attached over the door of the building. Ben flung his legs over the parapet, fell to the awning and waited. From here, he could see neither the entrance to the building or the hatch through which they'd climbed.

The wait lasted almost ten minutes, after which the front door of the adjacent building slammed shut. Ben peered over the top of the awning and watched carefully as Castro stalked toward a black car parked near the street corner.

Castro started the engine and tore away, squealing his tires on the pavement.

"That was close," Rico said.

"He's coming back," Ben cautioned. "We've got five minutes to get the hell out of here. Let's run."

Climbing down from the awning safely required exertion of strength and a willingness to sprain an ankle or a wrist. Ben gripped a chain and grasped Rico's hands as he climbed down to his knees and dangled his feet over the edge. Having estimated the fall to be around eight feet, Ben guessed that landing on the sidewalk would not prove to be pain-free.

Carefully, Rico grasped Ben's hands and reached for a rope hanging a makeshift sign from the bottom of the awning. He let go as he grasped the rope with one hand, resting his foot on the top of the plastic sign. Sliding down the rope, he let go and tumbled onto his knees. He rolled over and gasped in pain.

Ben followed his example and waited for Rico to rise to his feet before resting his foot on top of the sign and sliding down the rope. He fell the remaining six feet and landed on his feet, though his momentum carried him forward. He flung out both hands to brace his fall, but Rico grabbed him as his knee crashed into the sidewalk.

"Thanks, *amigo*," Ben said.

Tires squealed on pavement as traffic roared by on the interchange. The commotion feathered out into the distance and filtered into the various sounds of the city as Ben and Rico jogged back to the car. Rico started the car and pulled away carefully. He took a back route to the main boulevard, which passed under Interstate 8 and doglegged toward the bay. Signs pointed out Sea World, and Rico followed them. They turned onto Sea World Drive and returned to Interstate 5 before joining into the traffic jam headed for the downtown area.

Little conversation took place between them. Ben allowed the distant harmony of indigenous drums to fill his conscience as the specter of Montana loomed inside his skull. The drums faded and the backhoe began to jolt and rock wildly from side to side. Ben flung open his eyes and allowed himself to consider Castro's business name. El Canto de los Cantares played a tune built on disharmony and discord. It ratcheted its way through Ben's brain like an industrial buzz saw, consuming everything in his mind. El Canto de los Cantares, while allegedly protecting Nina Perez, was laundering money through Cyprus. Ben shook head at the irony. Taking money from one person targeting Nina Perez while Castro protected that target seemed a glaring conflict of interest.

Nina Perez had always been exposed, but perhaps Castro had not taken the job? Ben shuddered at the idea. Of course he had taken the job, or he would never have contacted Nina and attempted to get close to her son in the first place. This connected Castro and Jason Cruz at many points. Jason and Castro didn't merely interact with one another. They were friends. And if Filando Castro had ties to OGE Holdings, so did Jason Cruz.

The Return of Talamantez

May 23, 2011

16:30

BEN AND RICO SAT down on their beds to brainstorm, but when the conversation struggled to get started, Rico leaned against the headboard and flicked on the TV. He reduced the volume so that Ben could barely hear it. Although the visit to Castro's office had yielded a significant piece of information, Ben couldn't banish the guilty feeling that the break-in had accomplished little.

Was Castro really innocent? Something about the letter seemed off. Rather than genuine, the text sounded contrived, but that could have been due to the fact that it was a business letter. Ben had received multiple business letters and each one carried the distinctive hallmark that defined the genre: a lack of personality.

Instead of assuming the letter to be authentic, Ben set off to verify its claims. His first start would be to find the law firm that had sent Castro the letter. In that case, finding the person who wrote it would prove to be easy.

Ben made it to the company's main page before the room phone began to ring. He set his laptop aside and rose to answer it. Expecting another torrid exchange with Jason, Ben steeled his nerves and flexed his jaw.

"What's up?"

"Ben Carr," the voice said. "Or would you prefer Cobbs?"

Ben didn't answer. Shock flowed through his veins and a shard of weakness clawed its way through his muscles. He sank into the chair and listened.

"Yeah, I did a little checking on you. Okay, a lot. It's kind of crazy what you've been up to. And all this time, Cobbs was supposed to be dead. Who knew?"

"I don't know what you're talking about."

Detective Hawks shot back. "You're wondering about now how we pulled that off. Simple facial recognition software. When you and Gutierrez got into the shoot-up at the marina the other night, I tried to track you down with old-fashioned police work. As luck would have it, the software returned two results. I'm thinking that there is no Benjamin Redd Carr. Just Trent Cobbs."

"There is no Trent Cobbs," Ben said, clenching his teeth. "He died in Vietnam."

"So after I got everything set up, my phone rings, three hours earlier, you and your pal Mario Rico entered Mexico. What were you doing in Mexico?"

The anger in him burst forth like golden flames fed with alcohol. "Searching for Nina Perez. We had a lead."

"Feel free to share such leads next time," Hawks said. His voice dripped with arrogance, which lit Ben's fuse. "If your lead were believable, we'd have found Nina Perez by now. I chose to not let the Tijuana police know about you, believing in the trade-off. Now I assume you've returned empty-handed."

"She's in San Diego," Ben growled. "I'm sure of that."

"Well, you were sure enough she was in Mexico to go there."

"I don't know what you're doing, detective, but I am an experienced private investigator. I know how to find leads and I know how to track them down."

"Maybe it's time to accept the obvious," Hawks said.

"The only obvious thing is that she is in San Diego. And Castro knows where. Arrest him."

"On what grounds? 'Well, Mr. Castro, this is because some PI I know said you've got Nina Perez.'"

"It fits."

"I've labelled her file as 'presumed dead.' Maybe we'll prove otherwise, but we still have recovered no evidence she's alive."

"Go to hell."

Hawks sighed. "But that's not even what I called to talk about. We apprehended Simón Gutierrez and Huerra on drug trafficking charges. We recovered their cellphones. Gutierrez texted a Randy Paige, telling him to meet at Balboa Park on Eighth Avenue. Paige is a regular client of an investor named Brandt, who just happens to be Nina Perez' ex-husband. We're going to use this as a sting to bring in Paige, get him to incriminate Brandt."

A hammering in Ben's head wrought another round of pain. He scooted the chair back and rubbed his temple. "I think Brandt is innocent. Charge him all you want, but I talked to him, and everything about him told me loud and clear that he had nothing to do with it."

"I also know that Brandt and Perez have a child together and that this Castro lured him to the park near his home the other night."

"Castro brought him back."

"Yeah," Hawks said. "I don't believe Castro is involved."

"He is," Ben said. "I've sensed it all along, and I'm close to finding info to prove it."

"You're barking up the wrong tree."

"He's going to lead me to Ms. Perez." Ben allowed the timbre of his voice to crest with a crown of anguish and ire. Detective Hawks wasn't going to buy it, but by now that would work to Ben's advantage.

"So Gutierrez won't be attending tonight's meeting," Hawks explained. "You will. And about thirty police officers. We'll set up around the meeting site like a noose. You get what we need from him on tape, and we arrest Paige."

"You know, last time you had a plan," Ben grated, "you almost got me killed. Maybe you should outfit me with a vest."

"Not gonna happen," Hawks said. "You'll be wearing a wire. If anything goes south, my men will be in a position to shoot Paige before he even pulls the trigger."

"I'm not playing this game. If you want to arrest Paige, go do it alone."

"Fine," Hawks said. Ben suspected that Hawks was giving up the argument prematurely, but he didn't let the suspicion swallow him. Instead, he decided to let Hawks do whatever he wanted while Ben explored the Castro angle.

"Good."

"Mr. Carr," Hawks said before Ben could hang up the phone. "I know your son also returned from Mexico, the day before you did. I'm glad you found him. Now if you could get Ms. Rose Kierstien, the author, to quit bothering him, everyone would appreciate that."

Ben slammed the phone down on the receiver, picked up a pen, and flung it across the room as the anger reached a boiling point in his veins. Agony worked its way into his muscles, and before long, it would reduce Ben to nothing but a pile of smoldering refuse. The concoction was as potent as a snake's venom, but this time it would not bring him down.

Ben now had direction and a way to beat the ruins. Determined anger brewed in him, bubbling like storm clouds over the desert.

Instead of watching TV, Rico affixed his stare to Ben. After almost a full minute, he spoke. "Don't let the stress get to you, *amigo*."

Ben ignored him. Instead, he picked up the phone and dialed Brandt's number. This wouldn't go over well with Detective Hawks and might even land him in hot water, but he didn't care. Was Brandt as innocent as Ben had assumed?

"Mr. Brandt," Ben said when he answered. "This is Ben Carr. I met with you a while back."

His voice resonated with a dismal fury, the agonizing pulse of a man on the brink. His sentences choppy and his tone erratic, terror must have clung to his bones. "I remember you. How's the ranch? And your son?"

"Both good," Ben said. He hurried through the conversation without bothering to let pauses inflect greater meaning and mood. Instead, he hurled questions rapid-fire, knowing they'd catch Brandt off-guard and cause him to reflect with his responses. "I have a few questions for you. The other night, when your son went to the park, did Castro bring him back?"

"What the hell? Who are you?"

"Please answer."

Brandt cleared his throat and allowed his voice to waver. "Yeah. That guy is a son of a bitch."

"Do you know a man called Randy Paige?"

"Are you a cop? What is the deal here?" Mr. Brandt could hardly contain his anguish. His voice trembled as if he were about to break down into angry, petrified tears.

"Please."

The trembling continued. "Paige? I do business with him. He's one of my regular clients."

"Don't trust him," Ben said. "I know he's been in contact with a Simón Gutierrez, who deals drugs in the San Diego area. San Diego PD thinks Gutierrez was involved in your ex-wife's disappearance. That's all I have to share right now."

"You're a cop."

"Has Paige ever mentioned your son?"

"Not really. But I have a picture on my desk. Our first meeting, he grins and tells me what a cute kid I've got. But he's not a bad guy. He has a family of his own, three kids, a beautiful, devoted wife, nice boat, you name it. He's not a criminal."

"Any questionable account activity?"

"Clients voluntarily give up information on their spending habits so I can match them with the best investment opportunities," Brandt explained. "It's almost always straightforward and honest. They guy is clean, I promise you."

"Listen, I can't tell you any more right now," Ben said. "But San Diego PD might be working on pinning you as a suspect. They always suspect the spouse. They're going to get aggressive on you. But remember that I believe you. We'll find Nina."

Brandt lingered on the line for long enough that Ben assumed he was ready to field another question, but Ben didn't have one. He said goodbye abruptly and hung up the phone. Rico stared at him for a few more seconds before raising his eyes and refocusing on the TV.

Ben worked away in silence, without stopping to allow anything to sink in. Desperation clawed at him and worked its way up to the base of his brain. He pounded the keys on his keyboard with increasing intensity until at one point he slammed the enter key so hard that the table tilted. The information he found confirmed that Gutierrez had been in contact with Nina's ex-employee Davis Wilson, but that didn't prove anything. Since Gutierrez worked for Omar Dominguez (he visualized the circle of blood on his forehead after Ben's shot nailed him), any contact with Wilson was coincidental, unless Wilson knew Castro. Ben doubted that.

After an evening of digging, Ben told Rico what was up. He explained his plan in detail and Rico agreed to it. They left the hotel in haste and made their way to Balboa Park.

The trees on Eighth Avenue provided a thick canopy of eucalyptus, oak, and palm. Rico stopped the car about five hundred feet away from a lonely park bench with a garbage can. The shadows loomed thick after the sun set. Ben reasoned that Gutierrez had chosen this corner of the park due to the cover of darkness. Ben tapped on the glass when he closed the door and wandered to the sidewalk. He watched as Rico drove away.

The rushing sound of traffic on the nearby 163 Freeway drifted into his ears. A car horn honked and faded away. The sidewalk meandered along the street and wound into a notch between countless trees. The humidity pressed down on him with an unexpected weight, which caused Ben to shudder. He positioned his hand near his pocket so that he could grasp the gun if he needed it, but something about this setting didn't feel right.

The park was too quiet. This situation had set-up written all over it, Ben thought. Still, he pressed on toward the park bench. A lone car appeared beneath overhanging oak branches, but passed out of view as Ben quietly stepped into the thicket of trees.

The trimmed grass sparkled with the first droplets of dew or the remaining moisture from the sprinklers. Along the perimeter of trees, the lawn faded into a manicured field of taller, dryer grass that bordered the wooded area. Ben's heart fluttered as the darkness overtook him. The tree trunks allowed scant light to enter the grove. Ben drew his gun and brushed away a low twig of eucalyptus, which caused his heart to leap in his chest.

Nothing happened. Somehow invigorated with the passing cars on the freeway, the quiet pressed on him like waves as they undulated, waned, and then dominated. The waiting car, Ben guessed, would be Paige. Ben staggered after he tripped on a ledge of cracked concrete, where roots had pushed up a sidewalk panel. After regaining his balance, he carefully stepped toward the perimeter of trees.

The dark sedan still waited. Ben clung to the shadows with his gun drawn, keeping his eyes fixed on the car until something else drew his attention. A reflection of white on the ground beneath a huge tree could have been a discarded coffee cup, but when Ben laid eyes on it, terror struck his heart. He gripped the handle of the gun, lifted it up and pointed it in all directions.

What lay on the ground at his feet was a shoe, belonging to a young boy. Ben didn't want to shout, to gather the attention of whatever criminal lay in wait. He glanced down as sweat broke out on his brow. The Nike swoosh painted a dash of black against the canvas of white, and the serpentine shoelaces formed a neat bow above the tongue. The shoe was a right shoe.

Ben's heart sunk even lower when, almost on instinct, he peered up into the tree. The left shoe dangled from an out-of-reach branch, as if taunting him. Ben's mouth grew dry. This all seemed too familiar. His heart pounded in his chest as he continued to point the gun in every direction. He called for Rico over the radio.

"Keep your head up and be ready to get back here on my command," Ben whispered.

The freeway answered with the wind-whipped rush of tires on asphalt. Ben staggered again and left the shoes. He quickened his pace as he made his way to the car.

The left shoe, tied around a low limb, swayed in space with the light breeze. Trent called for his friend, yearning, hoping, and praying. "Tom? Where are you?"

No one answered. The shoes told Trent all he needed to know. He already knew the shoes belonged to Tom, but his heart would not admit it. As if pretending not to know the truth could somehow delay the inevitable, Trent searched for him still.

Something like this had been in the news recently. A teen had disappeared, never to turn up again. And then another had.

The park offered a dreary solitude so fortifying that Trent could hardly contain the panic. He struggled from side to side, zig-zagging between the tree trunks. "Tom!"

What was it they called him? Talamantez?

The river bank loomed ahead. Trent reached it and stared at a metal grate guarding the end of a corrugated metal culvert that drained into the river. A face appeared behind the grate. "Tom!"

Tom could not respond. His eyes were soaked with the tears of terror. Trent stepped to the edge of the river without looking. Something lashed out of the darkness, grasping his shoulders with an invisible force.

He struggled to get away, but could not break loose.

Talamantez. His breath was cold and filled with a tempest that undulated like a deep hallucination. Ice filled Trent's veins.

"No. Let them go."

In the distance, the sound of a motor hummed. It accelerated and drew nearer as the headlights appeared. Talamantez relinquished his grip on Trent and raced away.

Trent recognized the glare of the headlights before the car jumped the curb and stopped in front of him. His heart raced with panic. Talamantez had gotten away. His name never graced the newspapers in connection with a kidnapping again. Trent could feel heroic, but instead cowered in defeat.

The face that had stared back at him, his best friend, glared with empty eyes and a soul a million miles away. Less than a month later, he was dead.

The car waited in silence. Ben stepped toward it and raised the gun. "Rudy, come out with your hands up."

The car remained motionless. Someone slumped down in the passenger seat. Ben shifted his stance, ducking below the weather seal on the window and then peered in. He popped open the door. The driver didn't move. Ben prodded him with the gun, but he remained motionless. No smell of alcohol wafted into his senses, only the odor of blood.

Paige lay dead inside his own car. Ben pointed his gun in every direction and called for Rico to return. Waiting could only mean further trauma. Ben abandoned all emotion and sprinted up the street toward the traffic and the safety of light. Every so often, he glanced behind him. The left shoe danced on the tree as a bush shuffled. Ben swallowed hard, blinked, and fired a wild shot.

The terror caused him to hallucinate.

Talamantez.

The name burned into his memory like a metal prod rife with imagination. Nothing could replace the emptiness but more of the vacuum. Ben sprinted harder and attempted to listen for any sign of movement. None came. Rico breathed into the radio. "I'm here, pal."

Ben responded with fury as his pace slowed. Rico's headlights appeared in front of him. Ben swallowed and screamed into the night a raspy threat that would only fall on careless ears. "I'm going to kill you, Castro!"

Ben flung the door open and violently slammed it as the sweat on his forehead beaded.

"Shit, you look like you saw a ghost, *señor*."

Ben wheezed and folded at the waist to huddle his head between his knees. The torture drifted through him as the smoke of his worst memory faded to oblivion. The hallucination had shredded him, but what if all of it (or none) had been true? "I did," he whispered. The vapor of his breath pulverized his throat as with a thousand fangs. "Mine."

A Statue of Cinder

May 24, 2011

08:30

THE SUN BURNED LOW over the eastern horizon, looming above the mountains with a warm, yellow glow. The trees on campus filtered and absorbed the sun's rays, allowing patches of yellow to penetrate the long shadows. A young woman lay on a bench in the shade, face up, cramming for a test by reading a book.

Two young men passed by her and smiled, glanced at one another, and then broke into laughter as they staggered away. Birds chirped overhead. Offshore, the fog lingered and drifted as it began to dissipate for the day.

Moments later, a face appeared behind a tree, studying the young woman and watching her read for more than a minute. Startled, she looked up, placed the pages of the book face down, and glared into the shadow.

The man she knew stepped out and approached her with a look of serene anticipation spanning his face. His lips curled as she pulled herself to a sitting position. A frown stole a piece of her expression and lingered until he spoke. Her eyes flitted off to the entrance to one of the dormitories, which had mostly been abandoned, but for a few stragglers bolting off to class late.

"Fancy seeing you here," he said.

She stared at him sympathetically but averted her eyes within moments. "I don't think so. You knew I'd be here."

He shrugged and let his brows drop into a morose line on his forehead before he attempted a half smile. Shifting his feet and bending his knee, he reached to pull back a strand of his hair to rest it behind his shoulder. The zeal in his face could not be missed. It shone like the sun on a cold winter's morning, blasting the gauze of fog into oblivion.

"Maybe," he said, as if unsure of where to go next.

"Where have you been? Avoiding me? I thought you'd rather have stayed with friends instead of sneaking around and making my friends nervous."

"I brought you something," he said, pulling his bag from his shoulder and letting it fall to his elbow.

A grim scowl bristled her face, but she suppressed it and waited for him to show it to her.

Instead of opening his bag, he stood motionless and stared into the shadow before combing his fingers through his hair with his left hand.

"Tyran." She paused. "Whatever you're doing, it isn't going to work. You've gotten weird. And I thought you'd dropped out or something to go work. You don't call or text. And now you show up with a—"

He raised his index finger, which caused a frown of frustration to slither across her lips as her eyebrows lurched downward, creating wrinkles at the crest of her nose. After several seconds, he unzipped his bag.

A gold chain sparkled in the sunlight, dancing like a glimmer from a dream, whose remnant caressed the mind in poignant, warm hues. When he reached in and lowered the flap, the crest of the emerald shot daggers of green into her eyes. Its ornate backing of mosaic, glittering bronze captured the beauty of the piece. He grasped it by the chain and dangled it in front of her face, allowing a sly grin to gather the ashes of her expression into energy.

She inhaled and placed her hand over her mouth as her eyes widened. She reached for the chain and peered up into his eyes, her gaze warming by the second. "You've…"

"You have no idea what I had to go through."

"I can't believe it." She pulled the gemstone closer to her heart as a light breeze caught a strand of her hair and floated like a lingering wisp of incense. After moments of joy, she pulled the jewel away from her breast and again lowered her eyebrows to reintroduce the cold. "I can't take this."

"It's what you've always wanted," he said. "It belongs to you. If you don't have it, then it's better off at the bottom of the gulf of Mexico, or Chichén Itzá."

"You don't understand, Tyran."

"You don't steal stuff from the Mayans," Tyran said. "If security doesn't catch you, the curse will. Even if it belongs with you."

"I can't believe you found it. All these years. Centuries. Thank you."

He shuffled toward her and held out his hands to grasp hers in warm, subtle embraces that leaked with empathy. He lowered his voice and let the sun warm its tones. "Can I take you to dinner tonight?"

She pushed backward and settled the chain of the jewel on her lap. She tucked a strand of her hair behind her ear and glanced toward her feet. "I sort of have a date tonight. We've been going out for a couple of weeks. I'm sorry."

He looked hurt. "You…"

"Tyran."

"Whatever." His voice cowered behind a web of darkness that blurred his vision with streaks of clouds and sweat. "I don't know what I was planning to change. God, you're so…"

"I'm sorry." He released her hands and backed away as his face flushed with the color of the sun.

"All of this time we've spent together, and I've risked my life, and you... don't care."

"You know I'll always remember what we had. But sometimes it's over and you have to move on. It sucks."

He shook his head, shuffled his feet, and turned his back as he tossed his hair behind him and flung his bag over his shoulder. Grasping the golden chain in her fingers, she gazed after him, alarm and sadness erasing whatever elation the jewel had caused. At this point, changing her mind would be impossible.

On the stairs leading to the engineering building, a man in a gray coat waited, his expression stony.

Tyran saw him and adjusted his course. Another man appeared at his left, and then one on his right. Tyran stepped backward and stumbled over a loose rock. The men approached him, reached into their jackets and brandished automatic guns. They took aim at Tyran.

As the first man squeezed the trigger, a girl screamed. Somewhere near the end of a winding path, a man emerged, carrying a black handgun. He screamed something that sounded like Spanish, pulled to a stop, and opened fire.

The blasts of the gun bounded through campus, leaving a ringing sensation in the ears of nearby people. Another round of screaming preceded more shots. One by one, the attackers dropped, but the assailant did not give up.

In panic, Tyran staggered backward. The man raised the gun, pointed it at Tyran's chest, and plunged three shots into his heart. The bag dropped to the ground. Horror spread across his expression and blood and life oozed from his open wounds.

The attacker wielded the gun, froze in place, and placed the barrel of the gun in his mouth. Screams scattered through the campus as sirens wailed in the distance. The sunshine had turned sour and scurrying feet pounded pavement and grass in every direction.

His four victims bled from mortal wounds. A spark appeared in his eye and flashed as orange flame burst across his face. The last shot boomed through the campus, rattling windows and nerves. The shooter fell to his knees as yet more chaos churned between the buildings.

Tears obscured Tyran's ex-girlfriend's vision. She had frozen in place as the scene unfolded like lightning. Disbelief roared through her eyes as her nerves vibrated with unceasing torture.

The girl fell to her knees and allowed tears to streak her vision with a warm liquid stained with blood.

"I'm sorry," she sobbed, lurching her shoulders in misery. "I love you. Forever."

The Naked Abyss

May 24, 2011

09:15

SLEEP HAD PEPPERED THE night with a sparse coating of haze through which Ben could barely see. When he at last surrendered to the unavoidable fact that he could not fall asleep again, he tiptoed to the table in the dark, grabbed his computer, and brought it back to the bed.

He worked away in the dark for more than an hour before Rico stirred. After dawn, Rico, laying on his side, peeled open his eyes and stared at Ben in the semi-dark. Seeing this, Ben simply shrugged and then rubbed his eye with his fist, causing blurriness to wash away the solid edges of reality.

Rico retreated to the shower, and upon his return, Ben allowed a dark smile to envelop his lips. Believing he'd have to track down Castro again at his business, Ben had doubled down in planning the trip, but a different idea occurred to him. Rico glanced at Ben and nodded.

"*Qué pasa?*"

"I'm going to find Castro today," Ben said.

"And kill him?"

Ben shrugged, letting the darkness span his face for a second too long, which caused Rico to recoil. A look of mistrust spread across his face, and he leaned his back on the headboard and reached for the television remote on the nightstand between them.

"I think I know where he's going to be this morning," Ben said. "He visits the same diner at around the same time every Wednesday for breakfast. Going back months. You can break your habits, but what do you do when your habits break you?"

"You're thinking of confronting him in broad daylight in a public place? *Cavrón*. You are not thinking clearly. I think last night put a..."

Rico froze when he turned his head to the TV, where the news displayed a grisly scene. Ben didn't care to look, but the way Rico's eyes laid transfixed caused Ben a moment of hesitation. He focused on the screen. Across the bottom a ticker rolled with a caption. *Five Dead in UC San Diego Shooting, Suspect Committed Suicide.* Beneath that, a sub-caption read: *Police Chief: Worst campus tragedy in San Diego County's history.*

The words the reporters spoke hammered away in his skull like slow pellets of lead. Ben turned his head and stared at the computer screen. Before he could type anything, his phone began to ring. Not bothering to read the caller identification, Ben flipped open the phone and answered it.

Silence crept through the line like a serpent on the cusp of attack. Ben almost hung up before the caller responded.

"Ben Carr, this is Detective Hawks, San Diego PD. Are you sitting down?"

Why did it always start with that question? Ben pondered on this shortly before answering. "Yeah."

"Are you watching the news?"

"Now I am." Ben stared at the screen and frowned. How could it all culminate in this? He wondered. Was Nina Perez one of the victims? Ben knew the answer to that question before the last words formed in his mind. His heart leapt.

"We have IDed the body of Tyran Blackmon on the scene. Details are still sketchy, but it doesn't look random." Hawks continued to speak, but his words blurred and floated into a haze as Ben's heart dug deeper into his chest as if to burrow to a place of absolute safety and solitude. His hands began to shake as torture spread through his veins.

"Four of the victims were armed, but all of the casings we found appear to be from the same gun. We're running ballistics in the lab to determine what happened. I'm terribly sorry. Do I need to put you in contact with his mother?"

Understanding that Hawks had just asked him a question, Ben allowed his lips to quiver as he stared at the television. His eyes narrowed and a single tear splashed onto his cheek.

After a few moments, Rico had peeled his eyes away from scenes of frightened students and tears as a young woman, huddled with several friends, wailed.

"Shit," Ben said quietly.

Rico stared as Ben bit his lip, swallowed, and made a fist. He slapped the computer shut and refused to speak. The pause bound him in a tight vortex where the darkness coiled around his limbs and clawed away at his emotions.

"Is there something I can help you with? Ben?"

"I'm still... I'm still here,' Ben said.

"I'm going to need to ask you some questions later," Hawks continued. "Will you stop by my office around three this afternoon?"

"We'll talk then," Ben confirmed. He hung up the phone and cocked his arm to toss it across the room, but before he hurled it, the phone on the table rang.

His bones ached as he strode toward it and picked it up. The beast inside cowered behind a cloak of tarnished rage, the kind of veil that could smooth turmoil into placidity.

"This is Ben." His voice trembled with the rise and fall of confusion.

"Ben?" Rose breathed heavily. "When I started my writing this morning, I saw something. There was a shooting at UC San Diego. Are you alright?"

Ben allowed his eyes to glaze over. For a moment, he didn't know what to say, but his voice carried him into a soulless reply anyway, somehow further encapsulating the torment that blazed through his veins like wildfire.

"I'm fine, Rose." Faking his way through a conversation with her had, over the years, worked out to be impossible. Always the attentive one, Rose could sense the tiniest shard of emotion and enlarge it into something she could sculpt with her hands and her words. "There's just a lot going on down here. I'm tired."

"I know that," Rose said. "You know why I'm calling, Ben. Your son attends that school. Has your friend Jason said anything?"

"Not a word," Ben said.

"Ben."

"I'm sorry, I don't have much time to talk." Ben trembled more at the sound of his own voice, which shook with suppressed fury. He put the phone down and sat back down on the bed.

Rico glanced between him and the TV. His look of curiosity had transformed into one of understanding. He slid off the side of his bed and reached across to rest his hand on Ben's shoulder. Ben buried his face in his hands. If he'd only known Tyran, if only he'd had the nerve to call him, perhaps the outcome would be different. He'd never met his son, but the news battered his brain into sand.

"What are you going to do?" Rico said.

Ben shook. "I'm going to find Filando Castro. And I'm going to shoot him."

"*No está* justice, *amigo*," Rico said. "I know how you feel."

Rico couldn't possibly understand it. Rather than let Rico's words wash over his skin with the cool touch of comfort, he slowly gathered his energy into a finite storm deep in his heart. This was going to end today. Too much blood had been spilled and Castro had stepped too far into the madness.

"You need company," Rico said.

That Rico assumed he'd be able to talk Ben down seemed crazy, but Rico was always good for a shoulder to lean on. More and more, Ben had come to admit that he'd gained a friend in Montana's aftermath. He could not shut him out that easily, but plowing forward with Rico's eyes suffering everything he did would hardly erase the sorrow or the anger.

Isolation would be a tricky endeavor worthy of its many pitfalls, but Ben wouldn't last a minute with that arm holding him back. Instead, he had to rely on the emotion to propel him forward. Without it, Ben was nothing and this situation would drag on for weeks and the bodies would begin to pile up.

There was only one path.

"Drop me off and then go to the beach," Ben said.

"No way in hell," Rico said.

"Do it, or you're fired," Ben shot, the anger suddenly caressing his voice with a coarseness that caused Rico to recoil.

"*Chinga*," Rico growled.

Ben stood up and paced between the table and the bed as thoughts filled the cracks in his mind like rivers of fire.

After staring for five minutes, during which Rico's face had slid from pallid to grim, Rico stood up and grasped the keys. They reached for their guns and filed out of the room in silence. Neither of them said a word during the drive.

Castro's breakfast diner occupied a narrow stretch of commerce along a mostly industrial section of the city immediately north of downtown between the harbor and Balboa Park. Rico stopped the car a block away and wished Ben well. He didn't pull away immediately, but Ben didn't care.

Patiently, Ben stalked the perimeter of a rectangular planter adjacent to an upscale shopping destination and stroked his chin, The building's doors were set back from the sidewalk in a deep, trapezoidal recess that wrought the building's upper floors a class and angularity that suggested modern style. Ben waited with his shoulder resting on the glass of the inset for almost two minutes. When he poked his head out, he watched the diner's doors open.

Wearing a loose white sport jacket and denim jeans, Castro stepped out, gestured to someone inside, and pushed his wallet into his pocket. Ben allowed Castro to wander a block before he began his pursuit. He prowled along the bases of the buildings, bowing his trajectory into alleys and parking lots as he went.

After another block, Castro turned north on a street that skirted the base of a gentle hill. Two more blocks later, Ben allowed suspicion to break over him. Castro knew Ben was following him. His pace had quickened, and his steps grew longer.

Ben responded by erupting in a jog. A pair of trucks waiting at a traffic light turned up ahead, blocking Ben's view. Ben jogged faster until they passed. Castro had disappeared. Ben slowed down to taste the fury flowing through his veins. He withdrew the gun and aimed it around a corner. Buildings of varying heights skirted both sides of the avenue, which ascended the broad side of the hill. This portion of the neighborhood was packed with mostly warehouses and run-down shops. A few shoppers staggered out of a store and Castro reappeared. Ben sprinted toward him, but Castro acted first.

Chasing a younger man up a hill at his age would be futile. Castro far outran him and disappeared into an alley between two aging brick buildings. Ben aimed his gun into the alley. From behind a dumpster, Castro lunged at him. In the confusion, Ben loosened his grip on the firearm, which allowed Castro to kick it away effortlessly.

With a lunging grunt, Castro pummeled Ben's stomach with a pair of jabs and then kicked Ben's legs out from under him. Collapsing to the asphalt, Ben roared, "You son of a bitch!"

Aiming a kick at Ben's side, Castro pushed a bolt of anger at Ben. Ben defended himself by rolling away. Castro lunged again, but Ben twisted his foot away and slammed it into Castro's knee.

Rather than dropping in pain, Castro merely reached for his knee and turned away. Ben leapt to his feet and staggered toward Castro. Both fists collided with Castro's shoulder, and he jabbed his knee into Castro's abdomen. Castro grunted in pain, but backed away. Again, Ben pursued him with packets of fresh anguish bruising his face with a lucidity that bordered on insanity.

Ben threw a kick at Castro's stomach, pressed him against the wall, and slammed his fists into his stomach with repeated blows of defeated rage. "No more," Ben said.

"Fuck you," Castro yelled. He gripped Ben's hand as Ben landed another blow and then twisted. Ben staggered backward before spinning into the brick wall.

Instead of pushing his advantage, Castro slipped into a stance of defense. Ben's lips curled as he regained his balance.

"Stop, you crazy bastard!"

Ben lunged again. Castro's fist clocked him in the face. Staggering backward and instinctively reaching for his face, Ben stood, off-balance and vulnerable. Again, Castro refused to strike. Understanding flooded him and his attacks grew weaker until Castro no longer defended himself. He stood firm as Ben rested his palms on his knees.

"I know what happened this morning," Castro said. "You know I had nothing to do with it. But you've been pushing me a little bit too much lately. It's time to show you what I know."

"Why did you kill Paige?" Ben growled.

"Who the hell is Paige? You've lost your mind."

"You wanted me dead all along," Ben said. "Why didn't you do it the first time we met instead of sending me into a hornet's nest in Mexico? Instead of letting drug dealers spray me with bullets?"

"I gave you the lead," Castro said plainly. "Now I'll give you one more." He grasped Ben's hand and shoved him toward the street. One block up, a row of empty buildings painted the side of the street with dingy gray and white. He stared for a few seconds before pointing at the building on the end of the block, across the street from where they stood.

"Who's in there?"

"I don't know," Castro grated. "But I'll help you find out. Pick up your gun. Go."

Ben didn't allow himself the mistake of suddenly putting trust in Castro. He stood sideways to pick up the gun, gripped it tightly, and waited. Castro moved back toward the street quickly as Ben pursued. A feeling of discord shattered his spine as they ascended the block and crossed the street. His heart pumped his veins full of adrenaline that dulled the pain as his breathing became heavier. Sweat poured from his brow.

The front of the building was covered with plywood. The door had been shuttered and padlocked. Ben kicked at the framework, but nothing happened. Instead, he positioned his gun in front of his face, and blew three holes through the plywood. With one monstrous kick, the door slammed open. A cascade of light swept into the darkness, falling on a gray partition where a narrow reception desk once stood.

He kept the gun ready as he and Castro invaded the darkness. A corridor ran along the banks of the front windows and banked hard left at the corner of the building. Ben paused at the end of the wall, inhaled deeply and peeked his head around.

Yards of plastic sheeting fluttered in the darkness, making walls and covering what appeared to be glass display cases. He swallowed deeply, nodded at Castro, and flung himself around the corner. The room was unoccupied, but Ben noticed something that caused the storm to stir once again.

A flesh-colored haze appeared in one of the display cases, illuminated by a crack of light that leaked in from the edges of the plywood. Ben glanced down and nearly swallowed his heart. A hand reached for him in the dark, pushing toward him with enraptured frailty. The arm was severed at the wrist, the wound cauterized and gauzed to a white stump. Little blood appeared to have tarnished the edge of the slice, suggesting it had been cleaned.

Suspended in agony, Ben breathed hard, glanced up at Castro and stared through the room. The display cases each oozed with a scent of cooled decay. Castro flipped a switch, and light filled the room with a musty, dingy atmosphere of light, shrouded by thick plastic coverings. The coverings filtered the light down to gray that dislodged Ben's pain and allowed hopelessness to creep through his bones.

The gray glow illuminated miles of bare flesh, mounds of it piled on top of one another in the cooling chambers. Arms, legs, hands, and feet lay parallel and rested in the cold. The hands clasped together, the legs entangled like lovers' limbs, they lay in a still haze and nightmarish gray. The dark prodded him. Bones and limbs filled each case. Handmade tags were tied to fingers and toes. Rage scoured Ben's heart.

With one fluid motion, he flung Castro into one of the cases. The glass cracked with his weight and Ben pressed down with his own weight, aided by his gun. Ben grasped Castro's collar and ground out a merciless sentence.

"What do you know about this?"

"Nothing, I swear,"

"Don't lie to me, you piece of shit." He lifted Castro up and slammed his head into the glass. It shattered, raining shards of glimmering, flaked glass on the severed limbs.

"I did some investigating of my own," Castro said. "I'm in this neighborhood often. One day, I saw some guys unloading crates from a truck into this building. So I found out who owns the building. That led me right back to some law firm that was looking to renovate and turn it into offices."

"What law firm?" Ben shouted.

"One representing opposition to a hotel development project."

"In Tijuana," Ben finished for him. His head throbbed with the revelation. He lifted Castro to his feet, raised his gun again, and pressed forward through the warehouse, glancing into every refrigerated case to see more flesh.

The limbs of hundreds of bodies, preserved in cold storage, probably drained of blood, wielded a power with which Ben could scarcely grapple. His heart fluttered in his chest until he came to a freezer door. He pulled it open. Dozens of empty faces stared back at him, their eyes wedged open and their mouths loosely agape. Icy, dead faces blurred, faded, and coalesced into an unearthly haze that tore through Ben's heart. His eyes settled on one face in particular. Her curls fell flat against her scalp and her eyebrows danced firmly on her forehead. Her lips were the color of plums, and her eyelashes sallow and muted. Ben could not mistake the face as that of anyone but Nina Perez.

Ben held his hand over his face and looked away. A flash of anger soaked Castro's face, only to have solid determination replace it. Neither said anything. Like a page torn from his nightmares, the scene would not allow Ben to look away, where thoughtful reflection could resume. Staring meant descending into a frigid, dark chamber, where empty thoughts ravaged the lifeless. Castro retrained his gaze on Nina's head, surgically removed from her neck with one precise slice.

Ben got the feeling that disassembling the bodies had become a practiced art. An ugly thought came to him. He analyzed it before allowing it to play out. If dismantling the victims required such precision, where was the cutting room floor? These bodies were shipped to this location already cut up.

"Shit," Castro said, at last glancing away from Nina's cold face. Instead, he focused on Ben. Ben channeled his emotion into the one thing that mattered.

To Jason Cruz, Nina Perez represented a lifetime of choices gone awry. She was all that mattered to him—she and her son, Alejandro. This would not be over until Ben could ensure the boy's safety.

With the same resolve that pushed his every move, he glared back at Castro. "Alejandro. Where is he?"

"He's at school," Castro said. "It's the safest place for him."

"You're sure about this? Because I'll kill you if we recover his body next."

A look of defeat crossed Castro's face. "You'd try, old man."

Ben stared, pulled away from the cold storage, and retreated through a maze of glass storage containers holding bones. Steps away, the contents of the cases changed. Instead of bones or limbs, the vaults held several frozen plastic bags. Ben leaned down to examine one bag through the side of its container.

The plastic and ice partially concealed a human liver. Another bag stored a kidney. Four bags, four organs. Most of the vaults doubled up on the number of bags. A lurch of disgust rose up his stomach and his head spun. Ben placed his hands on his knees, hoping the knot in his abdomen would resolve itself. Instead, one spasm sent the energy of the day up his trachea as a dense sweat condensed on his brow. He deposited the vomit at the base of the container near his feet.

Castro could only stare as if in shock.

There had to be hundreds of people stored in this building. Hundreds of limbs, organs, and bones. That the bodies had to be shipped here from remote chop shops indicated a massive human trafficking scheme. The organs, bones, skin, and hair would be stripped and sold for profit. More money existed in the blood market than in the sex trade, Ben presumed. How much money did they rake in? How much did they redistribute through offshore tax havens, namely in Cyprus?

Ben wandered through the last few chilled storage containers and pushed open a door. A computer rested on clean desk. Ben paused at a stack of papers and rifled through them before sitting at the desk and examining the computer. He opened some files and an elementary tracking program meant to keep track of the victims. Each victim was assigned an alpha-numeric number starting with what looked like a blood type. He passed easily a hundred records until he paused on the photograph of Nina Perez, the same picture from the binder. Like the others, she had a number. Hers started with 'B-.'

The record was built into a spreadsheet. Columns labeled skin, hair, marrow, kidney, spleen, gallbladder, white blood, and liver spanned the top of the record. Most of the cells below the columns featured the letter 'M,' while one, her kidneys, were marked with the letter 'S.'

"Sold," Ben guessed.

"This is a black market for human organs?" Castro doubled over and pressed his hand against his stomach.

"Your people are on the school?" Ben said.

"They are my people," Castro corrected. "Alex's teachers. I placed them in their positions. I know Alex's father, too. He paid me good money. My job was always to protect him, even before the developer's lawyers asked me to protect Nina. Alex is safe."

"Why did you lie?" Ben shouted.

"Trust," Castro explained. "In this business, that's as valuable a commodity as there is. You don't take it for granted for the same reason you don't shell it out to people you don't know deserve it."

"You made a mistake just like that," Ben guessed. "That got Nina Perez killed."

He nodded slowly and paced toward the door. "Even if you are totally careful, it can happen."

"Who was the recipient?" Ben asked.

Castro pondered on the name and laid it out so plainly that it caught Ben off guard. "Wilson."

"Davis Wilson? He's the one who reported her missing in the first place. You think Wilson was running the operation?"

Again, Castro shook his head. "I thought he deserved my trust, that he would keep an eye on her while I checked on houses for sale near the school. He left her alone."

Ben's lip quivered. He flipped through the records until he neared the end. Four records were not marked with blood types, and the boxes under the organs contained nothing. Four people were still alive. He immediately dialed Hawks's number on his phone and waited.

"Yeah, make it quick," Hawks said.

"I found the remains of Nina Perez," Ben struggled. "There are four living victims remaining. Get your people to find them, now."

"Carr…"

Ben cut him off and slipped the phone into his pocket. His bones vibrated from adrenaline as his heart careened out of control and his brow leaked with sweat.

The last record on the list belonged to Milana Devreaux, a beautiful young girl with olive skin and a mystifying smile. Milana resided in La Jolla and attended the same school as Alejandro Brandt-Perez.

Ben pounded his fist on the keyboard and the screen went dark. Ben moved the mouse back and forth until a different program popped up. He stared at the name on the screen asking for his password for almost a full minute. *SexWax1975?* owned the domain.

Castro stepped toward the door and cut him off. "I've got to get out of here," he said. "Good luck with this one."

"Castro!" Ben pulled out his gun and followed him through the carnage. Castro spun around the corner of the wall heading for the entrance. Ben followed with torture burning a hole in his emotion. He yelled something incomprehensible as Castro exited the building at a sprint. From around the corner, a car appeared.

The car paused at an intersection long enough for the passenger to roll down the windows. Ben witnessed the barrel of a gun and dove for cover as the passenger opened fire. Three bullets ricocheted, followed by two more. Ben pointed his head around the corner and unloaded his clip as the car squealed its tires on the pavement. Sirens split the silence in the distance. Four more gunshots went off as the car disappeared behind a bank of buildings. The only option Ben had was to run. He sprinted down the block the same way they'd come without pausing to reload the magazine.

Nothing would stand between Ben and Milana Devreaux, but at last Ben came to one disturbing conclusion. Filandro Castro was innocent.

Candy in the Shadow

May 24, 2011

12:40

WITH A NEWFOUND ENERGY, the sun beamed down, warming the coastline temperature into the eighties. Sweat dripped on Ben's brow as he leaned forward on the bus stop bench where he'd first met Castro. There had to be something he was missing, but his heart managed to cloud his mind, rendering rational thought impossible.

His subconscious began to fill in the gaps that the TV coverage of the campus shooting didn't cover. Every angle, every facial expression, and every emotion of the day ravaged his mind with demons. He put his face in his hands and bled himself dry, not bothering to look up at passersby, and not caring what they thought. The pain was like an aged wine, sparkling with mystifying character, but always leaving some thought unexplored. Focusing on it wrought speculation and torture, the kind of frustrations with which Ben had never familiarized himself.

After ten minutes of pondering, Rico rolled up in the car. After scanning the neighborhood, he tapped the horn just enough to grab Ben's attention, but not enough to distract others in the area.

Ben stood up, opened the car door, and leaned back in the seat. Instead of talking to Rico or even looking at him, Ben lowered his eyes and watched his reflection blur with the glare of the afternoon sun. The image built a ghost in front of his eyes, youthful and charming. His eyes leaked with a pang of yearning and adventure. In his mind flashed the photograph from the police station of Tyran Blackmon. His eyes cooled the setting like a sea breeze and faded into Ben's reflection. Their faces were constructed on the same structure. As he stared, pain spread through every extremity.

"What happened with Castro?" Rico's voice sounded blank, as if the mere act of talking could somehow ease the pain so deeply entrenched in Ben's heart. "*Muerto?*"

"Didn't do it," Ben mumbled.

"You didn't?"

"*He* didn't. He's got suspicion a mile long, but he didn't do it."

Rico stared straight ahead and accelerated. "How do you know that?"

Rather than give a refreshing answer, Ben allowed the cancer to eat at his bones, gnawing them into a lumpy powder. By now, the only thing that mattered was making sure the police found each of the remaining live victims.

Ben already had a lead. The little olive-skinned girl, Milana Devreaux, attended the same school as Nina Perez's son, which likely meant that she knew him. And Castro had been involved in selecting the teachers, so someone had to know something.

Ben encountered more difficulty in making decisions and connections, but he knew one thing. Castro and Jason Cruz were entangled financially with the same kind of questionable transactions. Whatever Castro was involved in, so was Jason. If Castro represented one aspect of the connection, Jason occupied the other. Ben's heart sank into his chest. Jason Cruz likely knew where Milana was.

"Where to now?" Rico asked.

Ben looked at the clock on the dashboard. About this time of day, Jason frequented the same tavern where they'd met before.

"The hole in the wall," Ben said. "I need to talk to a friend."

"Gonna tell him everything now?"

Ben shook his head and glanced out the window as Rico navigated the surface streets toward the hotel. "That son of a bitch is going to tell me."

Rico offered a frown, turned a corner, and then let a flicker of restful indulgence pass over his face. "It's over?"

"Not yet," Ben said. "But soon."

Ben's words had imparted a vein of finality that explained enough to prevent more questions from Rico. Ben could escape into silence; it offered a realm surprisingly uncluttered and sparse where his thoughts could flourish.

Within five minutes, Rico pulled to the side of the building with the tavern. Ben nodded at Rico and then crossed the sidewalk. He pushed the door open and stared at the dozens of empty tables. In a dark corner, five feet past the last window, where a dusty, hazy trapezoid of sunlight crowded into the room, Jason lurked. In front of him, his laptop flickered. A stack of files stood next to his fist. He didn't look up, even as Ben lowered himself into the seat opposite him.

"Not looking too good today," Jason said.

"You heard about it."

Jason shrugged, still without looking up. "How could I not? Probably everyone from here to Sacramento has heard about it. Newspapers and websites nationwide are covering it. It's a blockbuster."

Ben's lip quivered. He sat silent. Every second that Jason failed to look him in the eyes, another layer piled on to Ben's ire. He bounced his knees up and down and waited.

"I'm sorry about that. You know I am."

Instead of ignoring him, Ben allowed the words to inject energy into his emotion. He sparked with suppressed rage.

"What do you want?"

"Just one thing," Ben growled. He reached out his hand and forcefully pushed Jason's computer shut. The frown rumbled across his face like a shadow of lightning evicting the electricity and sparking thunder.

"Where is Milana Devreaux?"

"Who is Milana..."

"Tell me," Ben said. "Or I'll kill you."

Jason exhaled a distressed "Jesus Christ" and leaned forward. "Maybe you need to step back a little bit. Your emotions are too volatile."

"What do you know?" Ben shouted.

"I know that you're in pain and..."

Ben narrowed his eyes, grasped a bundle of silverware, and filled his voice with rage. "Tell me where she is!"

"Go to hell."

The energy burst out of him the instant Jason finished his sentence. Jason's tone rocked him with a sense of purposeful torture. He arced with the voltage of agony and rage. He could barely control his muscles, he discovered, as he flung the silverware at Jason's face. Trembling, he stood up, approached Jason's side of the table, and wiped his files and his computer to the floor.

"You're going to pay."

Without knowing his fingers had curled into a fist, Ben launched his right hand at Jason's face. Jason doubled back with the impact and allowed his head to wobble as a spot of blood appeared at the corner of his eye.

"Son of a bitch," Jason said.

"You know!" Ben pummeled him again. "You tell me, or I'll beat the fuck out of you."

Jason raised his palms and cowered in Ben's shadow. His eyes had transformed from careless to giving.

"Okay. Jesus." He breathed deeply. "I don't know what Castro told you about our deal, but he didn't tell you everything. The guy's a total snake. He didn't do anything illegal, so if you're holding him, you've got to let him go. Milana has been his bargaining chip since day one, because she and Alex are friends. He's been holding onto her, but a couple of days ago, the day after Castro used her to lure Alex to the park, she got away. They took her."

"Who?"

"Castro said they looked like lawyers."

Ben raised his eyebrows and straightened his back. Lawyers. The only time any lawyers had been involved or mentioned in this scheme, it had to do with one fight. The resort development project in Mexico.

Everything crowded into his mind in a heartbeat. Every emotion and pang of regret punctured his skull. He leaned back, and with a wisp of a fervent frown, he stormed out of the tavern, stepping over the wreckage of Jason's computer and his paperwork. He'd get back to Jason later, he promised himself.

"Hey," a waiter called out after him. "Never come in here again."

Ben ignored him and prowled the sidewalk. Rico had elected to circle the neighborhood to wait for him. Their next place of business would be the home office of Clarke and Moreland, Attorneys at Law.

Ben stared at the clock on the dashboard and swallowed. This time of day, the office was probably buzzing with life.

Rico parked the car in a narrow pay lot a block away. In the distance, the high-rises of downtown sparkled in the sun. In the median of the street, date palms stood silent and still, as if awaiting an uncertain outcome.

Ben left Rico and pushed the gun deeper into his pocket. The double glass doors led into a finely furnished foyer with an ornate glass coffee table and comfortable-looking upholstered chairs gathered around it. A half-dozen magazines were neatly stacked in the center of the table. Aides clamored in the office. Ben entered the office area without so much as looking at the receptionist, who glowered at his approach.

"Sir?" she called after him.

Ben ignored her. A young man in glasses carried a cup of hot coffee down an aisle with a stack of files tucked under his arm. He nearly collided with Ben, said he was sorry, and asked how he could help as Ben passed him by.

At one unmarked cubicle, Ben noticed a picture of the hotel development. He spun the chair toward him, sat down, and brought the computer to life. By pressing a few buttons, he forced the current user to log out. Ben stared at the login screen for longer than he could have anticipated. Behind him, a small group of legal assistants conferred behind him, exchanging hushed small talk.

The new login box flashed in front of his eyes. Ben stared at the name in dismay. He typed several passwords before he remembered something. The cursor flicked across the screen as he typed, *SexWax1975?*

The login box disappeared, and the image of the Mexico development popped up in front of his face.

"Who are you?" Ben whispered to himself.

"Sir?" The group of people behind him had expanded. Ben spun the chair and faced a security guard. Ben glared at him and then glanced at a calendar pinned to the wall. Miss May sported a blue and red bikini and stylish blond curls. Behind her stood a light blue surfboard. It was the last piece of the puzzle.

The owner of the calendar was in the building already. Ben stood, gazed at the security guard, and attempted to push past him.

"I'm going to have to ask you to leave," the guard said, attempting to block Ben.

"What do you think I'm doing?"

"I'll escort you," he said, gripping Ben by the arm.

The rage boiled within him once again. He willingly walked toward the exit with the security guard guiding him. A fern palm in a planter swayed as they passed, and the can lights offered a grim shade beneath their feet.

Ben didn't know where to look, but a single idea brushed at the center of his mind. He walked to the end of the block, where a multilevel garage stood. The dark from the entrance beckoned him, and with hollow footsteps he approached.

A muffled shriek split the air around him as he entered, emanating from the caverns of the basement level. To his left, a trio of parked cars glowed with reflections of the afternoon sun. Beyond that point, the lot was barricaded with a retractable metal accordion fence topped with reflectors. The ramp descended into darkness as if by layer, beginning with shades of eerie gray and deepening to absolute black. Without a flashlight, Ben thought, he would not be able to see well enough to confront whoever lurked in this underground cave.

A stepladder lay sideways next to an equipment bin to his right. Temporary floodlights were pointed toward the deck above, resting on the floor and on a drivable scissor lift, where a lone hardhat lay top-down. Ben stepped carefully past the equipment and tucked his trajectory to the inside faces of the square, concrete columns.

As the descent seemed to steepen, he allowed his pace to quicken while stepping lightly to avoid echoing footsteps. The fear and pain in his heart propelled him like an invisible, magnetic force pulsing with energy. If the light could illuminate his face, it would reveal a frown bathed in murky distress, fragmented by the shattered remnants of ire. Nothing could stop him now.

The descent leveled off at the turn. At this level, a heavy structural wall separated one drive aisle from the next. Still lurking in the shadows of the columns, Ben turned the corner and stepped downward. Helpless gasps, issued from a woman, fluttered in the dark. Ahead, a patch of refracted sunlight leaked through an exhaust fan toward the bottom of the ramp. The light scattered, rendering everything in a gray so thick that only silhouettes and shapes could be visible.

Ben drew his gun the second he witnessed the source of the noise. A man stood tall, embracing the figure of a woman. Ben crept through the shadow of the column and listened to the desperate sounds of gasped breathing.

"They're going to sell you for parts," the man said. His voice echoed gravelly yet smooth and calm. Understanding flashed over Ben so quickly that it corroded his veins with sparking energy. His heart rattled out of his chest as she gasped her response.

"I trusted you. You were her friend. Son of a bitch!"

Ben recognized her voice the moment the sound burrowed into his ears. She'd sat across from him in her home as stress ate away at her persona. He'd heard her scream after she closed the door. It clawed at his eardrums to reduce him to shreds. Eva.

"Always too smart," he said, pressing his arm against her throat.

"I know what you did," she gasped.

At that instant, Ben raised his firearm and stepped out of the shadow of the column, inching closer to them as he spoke. "So do I."

"Carr," Wilson croaked. "I'm surprised you still have both shoes."

Dread gripped him. "Let her go."

"You and that pudgy Mexican guy, Rico... you were smart enough to ditch your phones. And I thought I got rid of you finally when you went to Mexico and got involved with the drug war."

"I know about your connection to Simón Gutierrez," Ben said. "And Dominguez. You hatched this plan while you still worked for Nina and moonlighted on a legal team representing Dominguez for the hotel development. Give it up, Davis. And maybe you'll live."

"And Eva?" His voice rose with enthusiastic amusement. "If you don't think your shot will rip through her heart down here, I've got some beachfront property to sell you."

"Please," Eva whispered, flashing terrified eyes up at Wilson's face.

"You tell me where Milana is," Ben said. "Right now."

"Tell me," Davis rasped. "Did Nina look happy? Like the satisfaction of a long nap took hold?"

"Let Eva go."

Eva emitted a throat-rending shriek just as Davis attempted to twist his arm around her neck. She raised her foot and stomped down on Davis's left foot with enough force to cause him to stagger momentarily. In that moment, his grip on her throat seemed to loosen. She doubled over as if to vomit. Ben didn't think before he pulled the trigger.

The flash coalesced with a boom that rolled through the emptiness of the garage, bouncing off distant walls as Davis Wilson fell backward onto his side.

Wilson lay motionless. For more than thirty seconds, Ben stared at him, keeping the muzzle of his gun aimed squarely at Wilson's head. The threads of animosity churned into defeat. Eva scooted away on her butt, and placing her palm on her throat, lowered her head and sobbed.

Ben stepped away to comfort her. He wrapped his arms around her as the tears streamed down her face. The only thing that mattered to her now was safety. Ben offered what little he could. The dark enveloped them.

"I need to find the little girl," Ben said dryly after two minutes of listening to her sniffle.

"I know where he took her," she said quietly.

Ben recounted the number of places that would have meant anything. Only one seemed to make any sense. He breathed his answer with a defeated sigh. "*El Corazón del Mar.*"

She nodded.

The police had seized the drugs, but details on ownership of the yacht were still being worked out. They'd tow the vessel away in due time, but for now, Dominguez's cronies could access it. With Gutierrez and Huerra behind bars, chances seemed slim that the boat would set sail anytime soon.

Ben glanced sideways at the lifeless body of Davis Wilson, grunted, and let his heart chew him up. He withdrew from Eva, folded his arms in front of himself and allowed his head to sink to his chest.

Eva watched with a sense of empathy shining through her tears, which began to glisten like sugar in the dark.

Agony worked its way through his bones. She inched nearer and rested her face in her palms. "He left me a note. Davis was going to quit because of his other job. So he told me he was taking her out to lunch. I left for lunch that day and didn't come back. We both showed up for several more days, hoping she'd show up, but we were wrong. I realized it when you visited me at home."

"Davis stole the cameras," Ben guessed.

"And deleted all of the files."

"We got him," he breathed.

She could only nod, but the sadness sank lower into her face as her hair tangled with sweat, grimy dust, and the moisture of tears.

"I loved Nina. She was my best friend." The tears flowed more readily, but she attempted to hold them back. Ben watched as they wet the concrete between them.

After several moments of silence, Ben rose to his feet and reached out his hand. She gripped it with her narrow, dainty fingers and lifted herself off the floor. Ben dug the burner phone out of his pocket and dialed Detective Hawks' cell phone number. Together, they strode for the exit, toward the light, and toward the promise of freedom.

Viper's Kiss

May 24, 2011

21:30

TWILIGHT SCARRED THE SKY with the long shadows of the Sierra Nevada Mountains, tinging the dirty cobalt blue with luminescent burnt orange at the skyline. Rose scanned the area as she sipped her drink and pretended not to care what was happening.

On Virginia Street, the city was coming to life. A couple fled a nearby casino, laughing hysterically as they staggered to the street, arms interlocked. A man with slicked black hair lurked in a shadow, surveilling the street with a surreptitious stare. The couple darted out of sight while a taxicab stopped across the street. A woman in a yellow dress stepped out, carrying a horrible matching purse. She slipped inside the casino.

The slicked-hair man briefly stepped out of the shadow. Rose glanced at him while shifting her shoulders and bringing her elbows in closer to her sides. Her eyes narrowed focused on what remained of her meal.

Out of the corner of her eye, the man's alligator skin boots caught a glint of the dancing neon. There he lingered for up to five seconds. Rose scooted closer to the table as an older couple took seats at a nearby table. Instead of staring at her food, she casually observed the couple. The woman's floral dress shifted in the breeze. Dirty blonde hair, skimmed with tinges of gray, slid into a curled ponytail at the back of her head. Her smile reflected in the man's narrow, black-rimmed glasses with squared lenses. Somehow, he looked much older, as if whatever had sculpted him had simply lost track of time.

His eyes leaked with a genuine, youthful wonder, the kind of stare that invoked memories of childhood summers, splashing in the puddles, and running on the lawns as if time would never cease. Some people, she thought, decided not to grow old while aging. His partner's eyelids fluttered as his gravelly voice scraped through the night. He told her an inside joke while pretending to grimace. Her laugh, only halfway genuine, carried with it enough gravity to hush the monsters in Rose's head. Alligator Boots had slinked back into the shadow, but there he remained, smoking a cigar while keeping his eyes on her.

Rose allowed a frown to overcome her face while again glancing at her food as the torment built up inside. She watched the man tell his partner another funny story. His lips wrinkled with traces of wry satisfaction. He didn't take himself too seriously and surely believed his partner knew where he was going with the story. She didn't assume; she only listened while letting her silver earrings dangle from her lobes.

The woman glanced at Rose as she retrained her gaze on the last few bites of her pasta. A certain warmth seemed trapped in her eyes. She nodded slowly and continued to listen to the man's tale.

Rose looked up and, stuffing a bite of twirled noodles into her mouth, leaned back and let affinity grace her brows. Rose could communicate worlds nonverbally. She considered it a rare gift, but oftentimes a curse. Reactions always ranged from unpleasant surprise to rapt admiration, even occasionally meddling in coy emotion.

She stood, sipped the remainder of her wine, and strode south along Virginia Street. A respite from Alligator Boots would feel nice at this point. She blended into a crowd and stepped inside a casino surrounded by men in matching suits. They eyed her suspiciously as they separated and attacked the slot machines. The lights inside flashed with just as much obnoxious candor as those outside. The spectacle made Rose consider the words of a book she'd once read.

Resort owners, the book had claimed, carefully engineered the experience to make money. Everything from the lighting to the floor arrangement to the music grasps the patrons' emotions. Make the atmosphere feel fun and rewarding and you make them stay longer. Likewise, slot machines offered decent winnings early in the playing session to grow the gambler's confidence white winnings became sparser the longer the person played, guaranteeing even more profit. Food and drink offerings were comparable to other casinos, and usually within a couple of bucks of the nearby restaurants for the sake of competitiveness.

Rose jaunted down a narrow corridor to the bathroom, closed the door, and stared in the mirror for more than five minutes. She combed a hand through her hair and peered out to the end of the hallway. Alligator Boots stalked past while carefully observing the rows of slots. Rose quietly kept to the wall as she made her way past a token booth where an impatient line of people looked to cash in winnings.

The man in the alligator boots ran a hand through his hair and approached a craps table, where a small circle had assembled. While the man turned his back, Rose quickly strode toward the exit. She shifted her shoulders as the breeze outside warmed her.

The walk back to the hotel would be peaceful, she guessed. The horizon had darkened, leaving streaks of luminescent cirrus clouds tailing above the mountains. Rose flung her hair over her shoulder and turned north. Sadness crept over her. Ben's son, just like that, was dead. It would be a blindside to him, and the effects would be devastating, she guessed. He had not called her. since he'd found out. She hoped he wasn't in peril, but Ben had accumulated skills in getting out of sticky situations. Rose, on the other hand, experienced no such gifts. She watched a flock of people enter a casino across the street, while out of the corner of her eye, a man lurked in the darkness of an alley.

Bleakness patrolled his aura like the halo of shadow caressing the dark side of the moon. He watched and waited.

Rose stepped backward, attempting to smile while the agony flourished in her heart. She tripped right into the hands of the stranger. With a familiar strength, his shoulders propped her up.

"Excuse me," she said.

The man reasoned with a simple response that spun a web of torture in Rose's mind. "No need."

Her eyes widened as she turned her neck to gaze at him. As she struggled to break loose, his hands closed around her arms. The fading sunset ignited a flicker in his eyes. Emotion spread its wings and then vanished in a flash. Darkness resumed. Rose had only seen this echo of controlled aggression once, and it had been a moment she'd spent years trying to erase.

The neon reflected in his eyes. Rose squirmed, but he held her tighter.

"Rosie."

"No," she said.

"I knew we'd meet again. You know, you hear stories about prison, and you think, *oh my God, what a horrible place.* That doesn't really prepare you, of course. Everyone makes it on their own. It's like living in a controlled city alone when you can't leave. You still get to make deals, work, form alliances. But the police are a little more brutal and a little less trusting."

She struggled but relented. Sensing this, his grasp loosened. A brilliant flash of green tore through his expression and turned into a somber yellow. Grief brandished itself at her emotion, which stained blacker with every second.

"You understand that, of course," he said. "Let me see those eyes, Rosie. Just one more time. I like the way the light catches them when it's low. When there's fear and mistrust. You always looked so beautiful."

"Go to hell," she said quietly, her lip quivering and her voice wavering.

"Such a nice evening, don't you say? You know, they say this is the 'Biggest Little City in the World.' More like biggest shithole in the world. I assume Tahoe is more your speed."

"How did you..."

Her voice trailed away, and he let the moment linger. "Have you forgotten? I always said we were a match made in heaven. You're good at being sneaky, and so am I, just in a more... transparent way."

"You're a sleaze and you always were."

"I don't suppose this Ben Carr taught you that phrase and a choice few others," he said. "No, that's the perfect man. Just a little bit less than me and little more than nothing. Easy to manipulate."

"Ben is ten times the man you are," Rose said, grinding her teeth.

"You put me in that hellhole. I'll never forget that."

She said nothing and let the vacuum of thought play into her emotions. She narrowed her eyes, raised her brows, and let the tears come. The memory of her dream flooded back into her mind as he caressed her cheek with the back of his hand.

"At least we're alone together now." He shot a serpentine smile into the dark, while the neon from the street cast reflections on his lips. His expression was poison, the kind of potent concoction that, at the right purity, could burn holes in concrete. As the smile widened, his lips peeled back. Rose sealed her eyes shut and imagined his tongue from her dream.

His hand gripped the back of her head. Rose flung herself away from him with a violent twist of her hips. She didn't get far before his hands closed around her wrist. With a strength that at one point had defined him, he pulled her toward him, reeling her in.

Just one kiss.

The tongue lashed at her cheek like flame. Her eyes grew wider as his lips connected with hers. For a moment, she let it happen. The shock folded into the agony in her veins. Within a second, he pulled away so quickly that it seemed he was being forced to retreat.

"What are you doing?" Allen asked, glaring at her.

"I'll tell you something, scum," a voice in the darkness said. A glint of red light illuminated greasy streaks of black hair. "I'm going to beat you bloody. She's mine."

"You're this Ben Carr? God, you look like shit."

"Carr. Where do I know that name? That's right, it's the name of that bastard PI costing me money. And you," he said glancing at Rose, "they didn't tell me you were his little woman. What's a sweetheart like you doing with a man like that?"

"Asked myself the same question," Allen said.

Alligator Boots punched him square in the face. Allen swatted back but didn't inflict damage. In response, the man with the slicked hair reared his fist, flexed his shoulders, and pummeled him with repeated blows to the face. Attempting to retaliate, Allen grasped at Rose's arms.

Rose retched, spun, and sprinted into the night. Allen would never bother her again, and the man in the boots would disappear into the city.

From behind her came the grunting voice of the man in the alligator boots. "There's no mercy here."

Instead of relief, the understanding wrought a sense of icy despair. Her heart sank as she remembered the face of

Ben's son and imagined it lifeless, staring up at a sterile reality that brandished truth like a piercing sword. Cold, hard, and unrelenting, the bitterness clung to the insides of her skull and would not let go.

22:05

BEN RUBBED HIS EYES as the lights in the skyscrapers loomed high overhead. An abandoned park stretched along Harbor Boulevard, spanning a block between an exclusive hotel with balconies overlooking the harbor and a San Diego public building. The play equipment sat silent. Beneath the park rested an underground garage. Stairs descended into the dark between two planters. Across a narrow path, Ben and Jason occupied a park bench facing each other. A line of fountains splashed on concrete behind the bench.

"So it's over?" Jason asked.

Ben nodded. He raised his eyes to a balcony on the hotel and lowered them at last. "Mostly. I just want to know one thing."

"What's that?"

Speaking slowly, Ben dismissed the question and placed his fists on his knees. "We'll get to that later."

"So? You found Nina? She's safe?"

Ben burrowed his stare into Jason's expectant eyes. Light reflected on the calm surface of the water behind what looked like an old pirate ship. "She's dead."

Jason looked down, burst into a frown and began to shake as with a low fever. Nothing could have prepared him for the news,

Ben thought, so it was best to give it to him cold and to see how he handled it. The reaction would take time for Ben to process.

"See, she *was* doing business with Castro," Ben explained. "Lots of financial stuff, brokerage, things like that. But he was protecting Nina. And her son Alejandro."

"Alex."

"A law firm representing a hotel developer sent him the letter asking him to protect her, because she was looking at investing in the property upon completion. But it seems Castro misplaced his trust. He sent me on the trail of the drug runners in Mexico, but they were expecting me. Castro told me that the headman was Dominguez. He owned two boats and a house near Tijuana and a house near central Mexico City, which served as the headquarters.

"El Canto de los Cantares didn't just deal in drugs. They found a much more profitable business. Human trafficking and what's known as the red market. Think of it is a black market for human organs and tissue. People will pay hundreds of thousands for a liver if they can't be matched at a hospital."

"Jesus," Jason said. "Don't tell me this shit. Nina?"

Ben could only exert a nod. Jason's face fluttered as his lips trembled. Ben leaned closer, allowing his fists to slacken.

"She was... sold... piece by piece?"

"Yeah. It looks like it."

"Fuck."

"But, here's where it gets interesting." Ben stared without altering his expression. "Dominguez was using his yacht to ship victims and drugs into the US, completely under the radar of the Coast Guard. They didn't look into it because the yacht was registered in San Diego and because someone from a local legal firm represented Dominguez. Two guys called Huerra and Gutierrez were the ship men. They unloaded and distributed. You follow?"

Jason nodded.

"If it looks bad, that's because it is," Ben continued. "The law firm representing Dominguez had some info on the resort development near Dominguez's property near Tijuana. Call it research on the opposition. It's pretty much a cut-and-dried legal case, usually fairly straightforward. These things rarely go to trial, but this law firm was gearing up because they must have believed they had a leg to stand on."

"The development is illegal," Jason said. "Because the financial structure was weak."

"But being that the project is in Mexico, they figured everyone will just look the other way. Face it, lots of developers go international, and it's nothing new. But you can't finance a hotel on laundered blood money if you are a United States contractor."

"True."

"Usually, foreign investments are looked at with more scrutiny. But Nina was also looking at investing in the property because Castro was. Castro was taking money out of a Cyprus bank, presumably to pay you. Castro ran his own business, which sometimes included drugs, but mostly legal stuff. That doesn't clear you of money laundering."

Jason sat still and allowed his face to sink closer to his chest. "It won't turn into anything."

"Because you work at the bank, and you are stacking the paperwork. You don't have to report to the IRS because are you going to report yourself for failure to file the 8300s?"

"You could call it that," Jason said. "But I'd do it again and again to protect Nina and her son. I loved her."

His lips trembled and anger filled his eyes.

Ben responded by leaning against the backrest and listening to the splattering water on concrete for just long enough to wedge deeper emotion between them. The catastrophe of this morning struck Ben's heart with a heavy load of guilt. What if he'd been there? What if he'd known about Tyran and gotten to know him instead of hiding in the open as Benjamin Redd Carr? Would it have made any difference?

"Did you get Dominguez?" Jason asked.

"I shot him. He's still got people in Mexico. You know what they say about organizations like this. You cut off the head, it grows a different head. But at least now our law enforcement is onto it. That effectively shuts down their preferred shipping method, so the trail of bodies should stop."

"Tell me Alex is safe."

Ben nodded. "It seems Castro was effective at one thing. But I'd assume his father won't want you around."

"He knew about it," Jason said. "He's smart as hell, but really protective of his son."

"Agreed," Ben said.

"So Dominguez was the end of the road?"

"He was the head. But like I said, he was employing several people at a law firm here in San Diego. Do you want to guess who worked at said law firm? You've met him before."

"Son of a..."

"Davis Wilson. Castro trusted him. You trusted him, but you were both played. Castro had a task to undertake looking at new house listings near Alex's school and charged Wilson with looking after Nina. Davis decides to take Nina out to lunch and instead he just takes her. Right into the arms of Gutierrez, who sends her to Mexico for some testing."

"I'll kill him." Jason's muscles trembled and his jaw tightened.

"Already done," Ben said. "He was holding Eva Crestwell hostage, but I caught him just in time. Shot him as he attempted to kill her. But Davis Wilson knew when he had his opening and he acted on it. He also knew a lot more about me than I bargained for."

"He did a lot of research."

"Funny thing is, my friend," Ben said, narrowing his eyes. "That information had to have come from somewhere. I can think of just one person on this planet who could possibly know anything about Trent Cobbs. That would be you."

"Bullshit."

"You know who I was. You looked it up, and you had access because we worked together with Mortenson. Remember that? My file had my old identity. They burned it when I left."

"I didn't do anything wrong," Jason said.

"Don't feed me that shit," Ben said lurching to his feet.

Jason bounded to his feet as well. In the light from the streets and the buildings, they eyed each other. Ben's baleful stare prowled at the edge of insanity, while Jason's sank into despair.

"There's no crime," Jason said. "You of all people should know that."

"I do," Ben said. "It just makes you an asshole."

"I did what I had to do. You don't know what kind of resources these sons of bitches have. They knew about me, and they would have killed me."

"Fine," Ben jabbed. "Then I just need to do one more thing. Something I should have done from the start."

Stepping forward, Ben flashed sorrow on his eyes while gathering his fist as his side. At the last second, Jason attempted to dodge, but Ben tightened the trajectory of his fist and landed his punch with enough ferocity to knock Jason off his feet.

Ben stalked away toward the street, swinging his arms as he went.

"I deserved that," Jason said.

"Damn right," Ben said softly without turning to look back.

The cars on Harbor Boulevard cruised by. Ben took in the sights of the Naval ships in the distance at Coronado, the lights on the boardwalk, and the towers of the U.S.S. *Midway* Museum.

The fragility of life took hold in his brain as he made his way along the docks. Man always stalked at the edge of death, a void of uncertainty and darkness that consumed all knowledge. There was always a way to hold on in the dark, Ben reasoned, but all roads had to terminate. Tyran was no different. That truth spilled into his heart with a flood of pain that boiled over. He clutched his chest and waited for Rico to arrive. The lights above faded into glowing orbs in the night sky, reminding Ben that all experiences came through the filter of mortality and human perception. Without knowing what existed on the other side or what motives propelled the madness, he had no choice but to press on.

There was one escape. And he loved her with all his heart. Would she forgive him for the trap he'd stumbled into? There was only one way to find out.

Time and Gondola

May 25, 2011

08:15

THE PUZZLE DEPICTED A princess in white, her dress flowing and trailing on the stone courtyard. Her crown shimmered in the evening glow, as if the sun cut a hole through thunderclouds. Two little girls searched for side pieces, speaking simply the only way they knew how. To them, Alex barely existed and that he attempted to put the puzzle together with them must have played like a nuisance.

Was it girls or was it Alex? Or both? Not as if he cared. Friends were fun, but only boys cared to play with him, and only a few. More or less, Alex preferred to watch and listen rather than talk, and because of that he had encountered few true friends.

He pushed a corner piece to the girls face up and attempted to smile. Without even looking at him, Allison snatched the piece out of his fingers and attempted to place it where it obviously didn't fit. She spun it, tried again, and then tossed the piece aside with the others that didn't fit.

They had such a narrow view of puzzle-building, Alex thought. Instead of focusing on one area and finding one particular piece, his own practice was to go by colors. He would assign different color combinations to separate piles and then attempt to place the pieces one combination at a time until he found one that fit. When he'd assembled enough combinations, they would grow, and he'd be able to attach more pieces. This puzzle came with fifty pieces, and the girls would hardly let him help.

A mom appeared at the door as Alex grasped a large piece with part of the princess's crown on it. He only glanced at her and resumed trying to assemble the pieces.

The mom dropped off her child without Alex taking notice. Instead, he feverishly worked and kept attempting to join the girls' team. He found another side piece and shoved it toward the girl on his left. She glanced up at him long enough for their eyes to meet. Alex purposefully smiled and placed the piece in her palm.

"Thank you," she said.

Alex barely opened his mouth, when an olive-skinned girl sat down at the next table. Their eyes met, and he found himself starting. Milana could only offer a gesture that bordered on a smile, but her face looked worn and tired, like she hadn't gotten much sleep in days.

Standing up, he graced her with a warm smile and approached her as her friend. His heart sped up and his legs grew weary. He always knew he'd see her again. Milana always came back.

11:35

THE PLANE TAXIED ON the runway, as far away from the terminal as seemed possible. Rico sat next to Ben, chatted with a flight attendant, and then observed Ben's guarded face. Instead of speaking, Ben elected to stare out the window, but Rico had other plans.

"I guess it's over now," he said. "Maybe you should go back to tax fraud."

What a wise ass. Ben glared at him with the ugliest frown he could assemble. The plane turned around and stopped before Ben resumed his stare out the window. If all was right, why did misery confine him? Why did the world continue to careen out of control faster and faster until it all became a blur? Rico would perhaps have the answers, but Ben didn't want to talk about it.

Instead, he let his mind linger on Rose.

Rico nudged him and smiled. "Forget about it. Shut it out, because you got lots more to live."

"Your experiences shape who you are," Ben said flatly, without removing his stare from the window.

When the plane started to move again, Rico patted him on the thigh and nodded. "*Sí*, you got that right. The key is that you can't dwell on it. Fail to move forward and the plane will never get off the ground and you'll be left behind. Only when life has gone on without you will you stop and realize how much you missed."

"Zen advice," Ben said. "You know, you were always more than a driver."

"True," Rico admitted. "And you're more than a private eye."

The plane accelerated down the runway and lifted into the air. Ben stared out the window and watched the ocean and the shoreline drop below them. The flight would last maybe two hours, Ben guessed.

Without realizing it, Ben had fallen asleep. When the plane pulled to a stop near the terminal, he lifted his head, startled. Rico had risen to his feet and stood in front of the seat watching him. Ben nodded and slowly stood.

In silence, they found their way to the corridor, which rose slightly toward the gate. He rubbed his eyes as he reached the end of the hallway.

People crowded his perception on all sides. Rico punched him on the shoulder and pointed to a bank of chairs along the large window overlooking the runway. Rose smiled as he approached, but something didn't seem right with her. Rico drifted away from him, leaving Ben alone.

He quickened his pace as she stood. Her embrace brushed against him like a warm bed of flowers in the hot sun. Wrapping her arms around him, she allowed his heart to settle before talking. All Ben could do was stare into her eyes. Every moment seemed stolen from a page of eternity. His heart thawed and melted before her. In her eyes, the seeds of reconstruction blossomed, ensuring life anew if they nurtured it. Rose always exerted the effort, but Ben had become distant.

"You're home," she said, leaning in to kiss him.

Her lips were like velvet, cool and moist. She'd saved up all her energy for him, he thought. He placed his carryon on the floor next to his feet, attempted to smile, and let his heart guide him. With his eyes closed and his heart murmuring, he grasped her tighter, spun her away from the window, and buried his face in her shoulder.

The flight to Europe would be leaving in less than a half-hour. Ben glanced at the clock on the wall and grasped her hand before picking up his bag. Holding hands was still a foreign affair. The warmth bled into him through the hand and his heartrate picked up again.

They talked about life and what they missed on the flight.

When they reached Venice, Ben only had one thought. A picture existed in his head, and the more he shoved it away and tried to dismiss it as some ridiculous notion of love, the longer it lingered.

They held hands throughout the airport. Before checking into their hotel, he found a place where they rented gondolas. He slapped cash on the table and guided Rose into the vessel.

The canals of Venice teemed with dozens of boats. Ben and Rose navigated the waters and a found a narrow passage notched in a maze of old buildings. The sun glared overhead. Ben let the boat drift to a stop, took both of her hands in his, and gazed at her silently. A tear formed at the corner of his eye. Instead of suppressing it, he let it roll down his cheek. Rose grasped his hands tighter, spreading more warmth through Ben's veins. Her face transformed before his eyes, breaking down from complex examples of passive love and dismayed solitude into the roots. The longer she stared, the more familiar she became.

"Rose," he started softly. "It's been a long week. And I know I've been a pain in the ass about it. You know how you set your sights on one thing so much that everything else sort of goes away?"

"Like with your son," she said.

"No. With you, here. Now."

"Ben, I still can't get past what the Alligator Guy did. I couldn't go anywhere without him tailing me. Do you know how uncomfortable it made me?"

Ben lifted her hands and set them on her lap. Still holding them, he burrowed his heart into his expression, pushed closer to her and let the warmth and solace of a long kiss take hold.

"I know," he said, his lips just inches from her cheek. "It wasn't a hard decision. Alligator Dan is a creep, but he was the right man for the job."

"He was," she said. Tears swam in her eyes as she gripped his hands tighter. "But now, you are. The only choice I want to make is you. Alligator Guy did his job. He might have killed him. But I didn't want to find out."

"Allen?"

She nodded. Tears streamed down her cheeks and Ben again gathered her hands closer, placed them on his heart, and uttered a relieved sigh.

"At least you're safe."

"Thank you."

"And you," Ben said. He gazed into her eyes so closely that he could see his reflection. He bit his lip, pressed her hands against his heart and uttered the one sentence that made any sense.

"Rose Kierstien... will you marry me?"

Her eyes flooded with tears. She flung her arms around him, pressed her lips against his, and then pulled away. "Of course I will."

"I'll change," he promised.

"No," she said. "I love this Benjamin Carr. I can't imagine spending my life with anyone else. You are my dreams, my heart, my imagination, and my soul. My destiny. Forever."

Acknowledgements

If any of you have read my back catalog, you will no doubt recognize four of the principal characters in this book. Ben, Rico, Rose, and Allen were all central characters in *The Thousand Branches,* and prose in Rose's point of view in this novel references the original. While it is fun to examine the past and back stories of these characters, it is important to note that this and later books in this series are not sequels. You can read in any order you desire and still enjoy without confusion.

After *The Thousand Branches,* I knew at one point that I would reintroduce the characters. In fact, for some time, I had been considering a sequel to continue their stories. Instead, a new idea blossomed. I hope you enjoy it.

Passing out thanks to all parties involved in the production is one of the most enjoyable parts of the journey for me.

As usual, I would like to thank Jeanine Henning for her wonderful contribution of the stunning cover art. Her work is exceptional.

Elaine Morgan at Serenity Editing Services once again provided editing help. I would like to thank her for her attention to detail, her knowledge of formatting guidelines, and especially, her perseverance in checking the usage and spelling of the Spanish lines of the manuscript. I do not speak fluent Spanish; I only know pronunciation and some words and phrases. All authors make mistakes, and a great editor excels at eliminating them.

I would like to thank my wife, who has always found time to read and give unfiltered advice regarding the contents and flow of the story. I appreciate and love you, Kristy!

Last, but not least, my thanks go out to you, the beloved reader. Thank you for waiting and exploring this journey with me. Without you, it would all be for naught.

About the Author

BRAD MATHEWS BENDS GENRE rules by creating dynamic, unorthodox characters thrust into criminal investigations.

He is known to use abstract imagery to construct striking realities that build into suspenseful mystery tales.

Mathews is Certified in Plumbing design, and his extensive Building Information Modeling experience gives him a unique ability to detail mechanical and industrial settings in his novels.

Mathews resides in Boise, Idaho with his family.

www.ingramcontent.com/pod-product-compliance
Lightning Source LLC
LaVergne TN
LVHW040038080526
838202LV00045B/3393